# A MADNESS
# OF SUNSHINE

# NALINI
# SINGH

GOLLANCZ
LONDON

First published in Great Britain in 2019 by Gollancz
an imprint of The Orion Publishing Group Ltd
Carmelite House, 50 Victoria Embankment
London EC4Y 0DZ

An Hachette UK Company

1 3 5 7 9 10 8 6 4 2

A CIP catalogue record for this book is
available from the British Library.

ISBN (Trade Paperback) 978 1 473 22953 2
ISBN (eBook) 978 1 473 22955 6

Printed in Great Britain by Clays Ltd, Elcograf S.p.A.

www.nalinisingh.com
www.gollancz.co.uk

# ALSO BY NALINI SINGH

# THE FIRST FALL

Sunshine.
That's what she was.
Sunshine.
Bright. A thing of life. A thing that could burn.
And this heart, it beat only for her.
It could murder for her.
For love. For Sunshine.

# 1

She returned home two hundred and seventeen days after burying her husband while his pregnant mistress sobbed so hard that she made herself sick. Anahera had stood stone-faced, staring down at the gleaming mahogany coffin she'd chosen because that was what Edward would've wanted. Quiet elegance and money that didn't make itself obvious, that had been Edward's way. Appearances above everything.

His friends had looked at her with sympathetic eyes, believing her grief so great that she couldn't cry.

And all the while, Edward's mistress sobbed.

No one knew her.

Anahera hadn't explained who the woman was.

And she hadn't cried. Not then. Not since.

Now, she drove the dark green Jeep she'd bought sight unseen over the internet and arranged to have delivered to the airport that had been the last stop in her long plane trek from London.

Christchurch, New Zealand.

A land at the bottom of the world. So far south that she'd felt no surprise when their pilot pointed out a cargo plane being loaded with freight bound for an Antarctic research station.

How many hours had it been since she walked through the departure gate at Heathrow?

Thirty-six? Thirty-eight?

She'd lost count somewhere between yesterday and tomorrow. Between the gray drizzle of a city full of theaters and museums and the cold sunlight of a barely civilized land adrift in the ocean.

Edward had liked cities.

He and Anahera had never driven through such a primal and untamed landscape together, the trees born of ancient seeds, and the ferns huge and green and singing a song of homecoming.

*Tauti mai, hoki mai.*

And this moment a whisper from the end of her journey, she stood on a jagged cliff looking out over the crashing sea below as fog wove through the treetops, a light misty rain falling and dissipating before it ever got to her.

Dark gray water smashed against unforgiving black rock, sending up a frothy white spray that disappeared under the violence of the next crashing wave. The water went on endlessly, a tumultuous vastness that was nothing like the European beaches she'd visited with Edward. You couldn't swim in the water below, not unless you wanted to be swept out into the cold arms of the ocean, but its beauty spoke to Anahera's heart, made it ache.

She could watch it forever, might just do that once she reached the cabin. Josie told her it was still standing—and that no one had smashed in the windows.

Maybe it had been out of respect. Perhaps out of fear.

To some, the cabin was a place of ghosts.

To Josie, it was where she and Anahera had once sat on the porch and laughed, two nineteen-year-olds with their whole lives ahead of them. Her best friend from high school was the only person with whom Anahera had kept in touch after she left Golden Cove, and she'd told Josie not to bother worrying about keeping an eye on the place.

After all, Anahera was never going to come back.

Turning away from the cliff, she got into the Jeep and started it up.

Driving inland and away from the crashing sea—it was an illusion, the sea still there, just hidden by the trees—she drove the last ten minutes to the edge of forever. The sign startled her. Golden Cove hadn't had a sign when she'd left. Only an old gumboot on a fencepost that Nikau Martin had put there when they were eleven.

For some reason, the adults had never taken it off.

But it was gone now, and in its place stood a gleaming sign that said: HAERE MAI, with GOLDEN COVE lettered in swirling font below, and WELCOME below that. She went past, then stopped and looked back to see that, from this side, it said, HAERE RĀ, with GOLDEN COVE below, and under that, FAREWELL.

Shrugging off the disquiet of the unfamiliar after a long moment, she continued on down the otherwise empty road.

Her car hiccuped, then jerked.

"Don't you crap out on me now," she said, hitting the dashboard. But the Jeep was in no mood to listen to her. It spluttered and hiccuped again before going dead.

Managing to guide it to the side of the road, Anahera put it in park, then turned off the engine. Well, at least it wasn't a total disaster. From here, it would only take her about twenty minutes to walk into Golden Cove. She'd have to leave her two suitcases in the back or maybe not. They had wheels, didn't they? It just seemed appropriate that the angry girl who'd left this town in her dust would return dusty and travel worn.

Fate sure had a sense of humor.

A car engine sounded in the distance, growing increasingly louder. Before she'd left the stark emptiness of New Zealand's West Coast all those years ago, Anahera would've thought nothing of jumping out and flagging down that truck or car or whatever it was.

Despite her childhood and the chill darkness of her fourteenth summer, she'd grown up thinking of this entire wild landscape as safe, those who lived within it all people she knew. But the wider world had hammered it home that no one could be trusted. So she stayed inside her locked vehicle and watched a large SUV approach in her rearview mirror.

It was white, with a bull bar in the front. That wasn't unusual—what was unusual was the distinctive blue-and-yellow-check pattern along its sides, a pattern she could see because the SUV had come to a stop right alongside her, though it stayed far enough away that she could easily open her door should she need to.

The word POLICE was written in solid white letters against a large blue piece of the pattern. Since when, she wondered, did Golden Cove deserve any kind of a police presence? It was too small, the residents relying on the police station in the closest big town, Greymouth, to supply their needs, though "big" was a relative term on the West Coast. Last she'd heard, the population of the entire coast had been hovering around thirty-one thousand.

She cautiously lowered her window as the other driver lowered their passenger-side window so that the two of them could talk. A man. Thirty-something, with a hardness to his jaw and grooves carved into his face, as if he'd seen things he couldn't forget—and they hadn't been good things.

His hair was dark, his skin that light-brownish tone that made it difficult to tell if he was just tanned, or if he had ancestors on her side of the genetic tree. She couldn't see his eyes behind the opaque darkness of his sunglasses, but she imagined they'd be as hard as his jaw. "Everything all right?" he asked.

She noticed that he wasn't in uniform, but then, if he really was stationed in Golden Cove, it wasn't as if any of the locals would report him for breaching protocol. "Car trouble," she answered. "I can walk the rest of the way into town." She had no intention of getting into a vehicle with an unknown man on a deserted road surrounded by dark green native forest and not much else.

"Let me have a look at it." Pulling ahead of her car before she could answer, he got out and she saw immediately that he was a big man: wide shoulders; strong, long legs; equally strong arms. But everything about him was hard, as if he'd been smelted down until all softness was lost.

Gut tight, she raised her window a little farther, but he didn't come around to the door. Instead, he indicated that she should pop open her hood. Figuring she had nothing to lose, Anahera went ahead and did so.

As he disappeared behind it, she tried to imagine what it would be like to walk into the cabin after all this time. She couldn't. All she could see was her last glimpse of it, the floor scrubbed of blood and the ladder taken away to be crushed in a compactor.

The cop looked around the side of the hood. "Try it now."

She did so without hope and the engine caught. Not smiling at her shouted thanks, he unhooked and closed the hood before finally coming around to her window. "It doesn't look like anything major," he said, "but if you intend to drive through more of the West Coast, you should have a mechanic check it out."

It was good advice; these roads were exacting. It wasn't that they were in bad condition—for being in the middle of nowhere, the roads were just fine. But they were empty. Long stretches of nothing but wilderness and water; break down in one of those areas and there was no guarantee anyone would come along for hours. As for cell signals, the mountains played havoc with them.

"I'm going to the Cove," she told him. "Does Peter still work in the garage?" Maybe her old schoolmate had gone on to bigger and better things by now.

Raising an eyebrow, the cop nodded. "It's not tourist season. You here to do a retreat with Shane Hennessey?"

Josie had told Anahera about the famed Irish writer who'd relocated to Golden Cove. "No," Anahera said. "I'm coming home. Thank you again." She rolled up the window before he could ask any more questions.

But this man, he wasn't someone she could simply ignore. He knocked on the glass politely after taking off his sunglasses to reveal slate gray eyes as dark as the clouds gathering on the horizon.

When she lowered her window a fraction, he said, "I'll follow behind you, make sure you get in okay."

"Knock yourself out," she said, not certain why she was being so antagonistic to someone who'd helped her.

Maybe it was knowing she was driving back into the past.

She pulled out.

In the rearview mirror, she saw the cop take his time getting into his vehicle. Then she turned the corner and he was gone. But his SUV reappeared behind her soon enough, and then their party of two made its way into a town founded on a golden illusion.

The miners had thought they'd find gold here, find riches, find a future. Instead, they'd found nothing but a harsh and unforgiving landscape with water as treacherous as the rocks that crushed so many of them one after the other.

# 2

Will followed the unfamiliar vehicle through the heavily tree-shadowed road that led into Golden Cove. There was nowhere else to go from this point.

The town's self-appointed business council might have managed to get up a few signs, but come winter and even those signs wouldn't help those new to the area find the place Will had called home for the past three months. It wasn't surprising that he didn't recognize the dark-eyed woman with wavy black hair and striking cheekbones that pushed against skin of midbrown.

The skin was smooth but the eyes old.

Late twenties or very early thirties, he guessed, likely a child of Golden Cove who'd lit out of here the instant she was legal and who was returning to pay a visit to a parent or grandparent. You'd think with the town's younger residents almost universally restless, just itching to leave, the place would be a retirement village—but that was the strange thing with Golden Cove. It seemed to draw back its prodigals.

Peter Jacobs, the garage owner she'd mentioned, had spent six years working for a Formula One team and traveling the world before he landed back in the Cove. When asked why he'd given up his glamorous life in favor of running the family garage with his aging father and resentful younger brother, he just shrugged and said that a man got tired of Ferraris and wanted to return to the ocean.

Peter, however, had only been back for less than a year, and yet the woman with the car trouble had asked if Peter was "still" working in the garage, which meant she'd last been in Golden Cove at least seven years earlier.

Will's eyes narrowed: the woman and Peter might even be the same age or close to it. Could be they'd been schoolmates. And what, he asked himself, did it all matter? It wasn't as if he'd been dumped in Golden Cove to be a detective. He might hold the rank, but he'd been placed here as the community's sole policeman because he'd become a problem for the force— but was too decorated and senior an officer to simply fire. So instead, they'd put him out to pasture in Golden Cove and forgotten about him.

That was fine with Will. Prior to being offered this job, he'd been planning to quit. Since his plan after quitting had involved any remote job he could get his hands on, he'd thought why the hell not just bury himself in a sole-charge station that covered a sprawling geographic area but involved only a very small number of people?

There were far more trees in his patrol area than human residents.

Most of the folk in Golden Cove let him be, and the odd time that he did have to step in, it was usually to break up a bar fight or calm down a neighborhood dispute. Yesterday, he'd had to handcuff a drunk to a chair until the other man was sober enough to be dropped home.

Will didn't have a jail.

And so far, no Golden Cove problems had justified formal charges. Come summer, with tourists pouring in for various adventure activities thanks to the region's advertising campaign over the past couple of years, and he'd probably have more trouble. Which was also why the town now had a police officer. The regional tourism bodies had apparently gone apoplectic about a couple of tourists who'd gotten beaten up in Golden Cove after dark.

Bad for business to have visitors posting photos of black eyes and broken ribs instead of the bleak scenery, dangerous cliff climbs, or local cuisine.

So now Golden Cove had Will.

The first small home appeared on the right, complete with a white picket fence and hardy wildflowers in a neatly tended garden. Mrs. Keith sat on her rocker out front, her girth overflowing the white wood of it and her face a pale moon surrounded by a halo of teased black. Pink lipstick slashed across her mouth, her plump fingers bejeweled when she raised her hand in a wave.

Will didn't know if the curt woman in the Jeep waved back, but he raised his hand.

The next house was on the left, this one as ramshackle as Mrs. Keith's was immaculate. Peeling blue paint, a wheelless car rusting in the front yard, grass as high as his calves. On the front stoop sat a good-looking man with nut-brown skin, a cigarette in hand and his face tattooed with a full *tā moko* that might've been traditional, but that tended to make strangers wary. It didn't help that Nikau Martin consistently wore ripped black jeans, shitkickers, and T-shirts imprinted with the Hells Angels logo.

Right now, the other man's dark eyes were following the green Jeep.

Will paused in front of the rickety gate.

Nikau got up and sauntered over to jump the gate. Leaning his arms on the open window of Will's SUV, he said, "I never thought I'd see Anahera back in this town."

*Anahera.*

Will tasted the name, couldn't decide if it fit or not. His Māori was rusty, but he thought it might mean "angel." That suspicious woman with watchful eyes hadn't struck him as angelic. "You know her?"

"Went to school together." Nikau took a puff, turning his head to exhale so that the smoke wouldn't fill up Will's vehicle. "She peeled out of here at twenty-one. I remember, 'cause two months later, that's when I married Keira."

Well aware Nikau's ex-wife was a sore spot, Will said, "You know where she's been all this time?"

"London, I heard. Josie kept in touch with her."

Will had trouble putting Josie and Anahera together in the same image in his mind. The owner of the local café was as soft as Anahera was hard, as home and hearth as Anahera was dangerous winds and harsh rain. "Beer tonight?"

The man who dressed and acted like a hoodlum, and was probably more educated than anyone else in this town, nodded. "Around eight? I got a couple of city slickers coming in from their hotel in Greymouth—they want to go see the old gold-mining shacks."

"Don't lose them down a shaft." Waving good-bye as the other man laughed, Will carried on.

About a hundred meters after Nikau's place, the houses started coming closer together, some in good repair, some not so good, and one in the distance on a rise that lorded it over everyone else. At least on this side of the invisible dividing line.

Then came the town center.

It wasn't quite "blink and you'll miss it," not after the adventure tourism boom and the locals making the most of the adrenaline junkies who flooded in during the season. It had the police station, a small supermarket that sold groceries and other essentials as well as souvenirs, the pub that had probably been around since the first gold miner put his boots on the ground, a café, a dual-level B&B, a veterinary care center, a restaurant that opened up when the café closed, and the local doctor's examination room—which everyone referred to interchangeably as the surgery or the clinic.

At the far end of the town's main strip was a white-steepled church, an outdoor shop the last business prior to it. Across from the shop sat the fire station, the local tourism center facing it. It functioned as the base of operations for all the charters and tours that ran out of Golden Cove. The list of activities on offer was a long one. But, as the business council was eager to point out, Golden Cove had a "prominent place in the arts scene," too, courtesy of the artisan pottery boutique founded by a fifty-something local who'd made her name in Italy.

That was pretty much it.

There were a few other businesses run out of homes or garages, but this was Golden Cove's main street. The post was delivered regularly, but the town had no post office of its own—if you wanted to mail something, the supermarket had the ability to sell you stamps and packaging. The farming supplies store was in the next town over.

Right now, with the autumn chill heavy in the air and the waves too dangerous for even the most extreme surfers, the street boasted no beat-up tourist vans or muddy rental cars. The only new vehicle was the dark green Jeep. It was parked in front of the Golden Cove Café.

# 3

Anahera had seen the cop stop by Nikau's place. She should've stopped, too. She and Nik had been friends once—before distance and bitterness and loss changed them both in different ways. But she wasn't about to make Nikau Martin the first person to whom she said hello in Golden Cove.

Getting out of the Jeep in front of Josie's café, she shut her door and, taking a deep breath of the permanently salt-laced air, walked into the cheery warmth of a café that seemed out of place in this gray landscape full of cloud and mist.

"Ana!"

Face glowing, Josie threw her arms around Anahera almost before Anahera saw her coming. Her friend was shorter than her by a good six inches, but her height had never stopped the force of nature that was Josephine Wilson. No, it was Josephine Taufa now. Anahera had missed Josie's wedding for reasons too painful to think about, so she shoved them away and hugged the soft and curvy form of the best friend she'd ever had.

Josie's hard belly pushed into her stomach as Anahera held her close.

When they broke apart, Josie waved over a little boy who was sitting and coloring at one of the tables. "Niam's three already, can you believe it?" Her fingers in the child's thick black hair. "You know Anahera, Niam—you've seen me talking to her on the laptop."

The boy, his skin a warm brown that came from his Tongan father, smiled shyly at Anahera before running back to his coloring.

"Come, sit," Josie said, taking Anahera's hands and tugging gently. "The café's quiet today with the weather predicted to turn nasty, so we can have a catch-up."

Anahera let herself be led to a table near the window, in no hurry to go to the cabin. She had plenty of time to be alone with the memories, dark and brutal. "I brought you a gift," she told her friend as they took their seats. "It's in a suitcase, though."

"You're the gift, Ana." Josie's voice was as warm and gentle as always. "I'm so glad you're home."

*Home.*

Such a loaded word.

Josie glanced over her shoulder with a smile as Anahera's attention was caught by the arresting photographs mounted on the left wall of the café. "Miri, can you grab us a couple of cappuccinos? Decaf for me."

It was only then that Anahera realized her friend wasn't alone in the café. A slender long-legged girl, with a face so radiant that it stopped the heart and made Anahera suddenly, viscerally afraid for her, smiled back at Josie from behind the counter.

"Anything for you, Jo," the girl said, moving to the gleaming coffee-making apparatus with a dancer's grace. "*Kia ora*, Ana."

Anahera returned the greeting with a wave of her hand. It had been so many years since she'd been around people who said *kia ora* as easily as they said hello that the words stuck in her throat, rusty and old.

"You guys want cake, too?" Miri asked. "We've still got that carrot with cream cheese icing."

"Oh, twist our arms, why don't you." Josie laughed before turning back to Anahera. "Miri's been working for me for a while now. I mentioned it during our calls, remember? But six more weeks and she's off to the city lights of Wellington to take up an internship."

"You're Auntie Mattie's girl." It had taken Anahera's brain several seconds to make the connection between this striking creature and the skinny child named Miriama Hinewai Tutaia whom she'd known so many years ago and whom Josie had hired. As if time had slipped while she hadn't been watching.

"Auntie still has baby photos of you," Miriama warned, her eyes sparkling. "Don't worry, I told her it'd be bad form to frame them and stick them on the living room wall. Can't promise she won't pull them out if you visit, though."

Anahera laughed and the stab of fear rooted in a long-ago summer slipped away. Often, a person that genetically blessed felt no need to make the attempt at humor—or even civility. But maybe it was Miriama's very distinctiveness that had shaped her; the girl was a haunting beauty now, but that same bone structure had given her a markedly odd appearance as a child. As if parts of her were already adult sized, while others continued to grow.

"Who's the internship with?" Anahera asked, digging through fading memories for more than faint impressions of the child the nineteen-year-old had once been, but there wasn't much. Ten years' difference in age had been too big a divide for them to cross.

A smile so bright, it was as if the sun had come out. "A collective of professional travel photographers who want to support those wanting to get into the industry. I get to travel with them, learn from them."

"These are hers." Tone humming with pride, Josie pointed to the images on the café walls.

All featured Golden Cove residents caught in moments of laughter and joy. Nikau, the black curves of his *tā moko* defined with crystal clarity by the sun and his handsome face dipping a little as he grinned while thrusting a hand through his hair. Mrs. Keith throwing back her head and laughing so hard that you could almost hear the boom of sound. Josie, smile soft as she looked down at her baby bump, her hand curved under it.

"These are incredible." Anyone could do bleak West Coast landscapes— the landscape itself called for it, *posed* for it. But to get Nikau to grin like that when, from all Josie had told her, he'd changed in brittle, angry ways from the boy she'd once known, that took skill, and patience. Not only had Miriama managed the feat, she'd captured the moment in stunning color.

And it hadn't escaped Anahera's notice that Miriama had juxtaposed her subjects against backgrounds that posed unspoken questions about public and private faces, about the truth of happiness itself: torn pages and wadded-up paper strewn across a floor, a room crammed full of dolls, a lonely stretch of beach. "You have a gift."

"Thank you," Miriama said in open pleasure, as she brought over the two coffees. "My favorite is the one of Josie. It's pretty hard to outshine the ocean, but she did it like a pro."

"No need to butter me up." Josie scowled. "It's not as if you're going to ask for a raise."

Laughing, the young Māori woman with deep, dark eyes and black hair pulled back in a bun leaned down to hug her sun-kissed arms around Josie. "I love you, Jo. Sorry I'm being a disloyal brat and running off to the city."

"Just so long as you remember me when you're rich and famous," Josie said, patting the girl on the arm with sisterly affection.

"Always. Let me get you the cake." She brought over two generous slices. "Shall I walk the last piece over to our local tall, silent, and mysterious hunk?" A waggle of her eyebrows. "You know he has a weakness and he always pays."

Josie nodded. "The constabulary," she added after Miriama walked out.

"I think I met him." Anahera told Josie of her breakdown. "How long's the police presence been a thing?"

"Three months. His name's Will. Came from Christchurch."

"Christchurch?" That was the biggest city in the South Island. "What did he do to get banished to Golden Cove?"

Josie shrugged. "No idea—but I saw his name in the papers before that for solving some high-profile cases, so it must've been pretty bad." She turned slightly to call out to her boy. "Baby, do you want some cake?"

Engrossed in his coloring, Niam just shook his head.

"It's *so* good to have you back, Ana," Josie said afterward. "I've missed my best friend so much. It's finally back to how it should be."

Anahera smiled, but she knew that it was impossible for things to ever be the same. "It's good to be back," she said.

In truth, she'd had nowhere else to go, and here, at least she had Josie.

"Will you miss London?" Josie asked after swallowing a bite of cake.

"You had such a glamorous life, going to all those premieres and shows, and performing your music in those huge concert halls." Her face glowed. "I showed the articles to everyone. My friend, the star classical pianist."

Anahera took a bite of cake to give herself time to think of an answer that wouldn't shatter Josie's illusions. "Holy cow," she exclaimed in honest surprise. "This *cake*!"

"I know—amazing, right? Julia is a magician."

"Julia *Lee*? Didn't she become a lawyer?"

Josie set off on a welcome detour into the life of the other woman, but led back around to her question afterward. "You will, won't you? Miss London." In her eyes was another question she didn't ask—Anahera had said she didn't want to talk about Edward and Josie was good enough a friend to give her silence on that topic.

"It was nice while it lasted," Anahera said.

It *had* been nice until she'd realized her entire life was a lie, that, for six years, she'd been a prop in someone else's play. "The music . . . yes, that was wonderful." Even though it was now ashes inside her. "And I got to see the most amazing shows, meet so many incredibly talented people."

Anahera had used to joke that the theater was Edward's mistress, never imagining she had a flesh-and-blood rival. "But a girl can't live on premieres and concert halls when her *whānau* is back here." Anahera's husband was dead and so was her mother, which left Josie the only family she acknowledged.

Sometimes, it wasn't about blood ties.

If Josie had seen her at Edward's graveside, she'd have known that something was horrifically wrong, something more than Anahera's young and gifted playwright husband being dead.

The little bell over the door rang.

When Anahera looked over, it was to see Miriama walking in. She gave them a thumbs-up. "He took the cake and we're five dollars richer."

"She's beautiful," Anahera said quietly to Josie as the younger woman went to ring up the sale.

Josie caught the question in Anahera's statement. "Thankfully, she's managed to avoid the usual small-town traps—she'll be leaving Golden Cove before autumn falls into winter." A low murmur. "If she ever decides to come back, it'll be like you, on her own terms."

Anahera knew Josie's words didn't apply to Josie herself. Her friend was exactly where she'd told Anahera she wanted to be when they were only fourteen: married to Tom Taufa, mother to his babies, and owner of her own café.

"Hey, Jo, you mind if I bug out a little early?"

Josie nodded at Miriama. "Going for a run?"

"Need to stretch out the legs."

Anahera glanced at her watch after the girl left. "I better head out, too," she said. "I want to have some time at the cabin while it's still light."

Josie frowned. "Ana, I didn't think you were serious about staying out there, otherwise I'd have asked Tom to fix it up a bit. I made up my spare room for you."

Anahera's cold, hard heart threatened to crack. "I need to go there," was all she said.

# 4

Josie had made her a care package because, despite her hopes, she knew Anahera.

Anahera was putting the box of supplies into her Jeep when she felt a prickling at her nape; she glanced back and saw the cop watching her from outside his post. Keeping an eye on the stranger in town.

How could this city cop know that Golden Cove was branded into every cell in her body, that even when she'd slept in a soft bed in an expensive terraced house in London, while manicured grass grew in their shared city garden and designer gowns hung in her closet, she'd dreamed of this tiny town perched on the edge of an ocean so pitiless it had taken more souls than the devil?

Box stowed, she turned to hug Josie again, then got in the Jeep to drive toward that same pitiless ocean, and when she passed a narrow road that led inland, she deliberately didn't look its way.

There was nothing for her down there.

The old-growth forest on the edge of town closed in around her for five minutes before it began to thin out, let in flashes of the sea. But the cabin that stood on the far side of that growth, overlooking the sand below the cliffs, was shadowed by a huge rata tree. Sunlight only speared through on the brightest days, but that was all right. There was plenty of light on the beach once you made your way down the precariously narrow track.

Bringing the Jeep to a stop facing the side of the cabin, she just sat and stared for a long while, but nothing changed. There was no one there. No one would come out with a big smile and wave her in for a cup of tea. No one would invite her for a walk on the beach. And when Christmas came and the rata bloomed as scarlet as fresh blood, no one would sit with her under its shade.

She swallowed the lump in her throat, then made herself open the driver's-side door and get out. Leaving her stuff where it was, she crossed the short distance to the cabin and walked up the steps to the small porch. Leaves crunched underfoot and she saw a spider, legs furred and long, scuttle across the wood. Thick spiderwebs hung on the eaves, a thinner web around the doorknob.

Turning it, the mechanism stiff, she opened the door.

And walked into a thousand memories.

# 5

Will took a long drink of his beer, while beside him, Nikau nursed his. "She's something, isn't she?" the other man said.

Will didn't have to ask to know who Nikau was talking about; he'd learned quickly enough that there was only one woman in town who put that tone in a man's voice. "She's a little young for you, Nik." He looked over at where Miriama Hinewai Tutaia held court, her hair flowing past her waist and men buzzing around her like bees around a honeypot.

A woman that attractive to men didn't usually have many female friends, but Miriama did. They buzzed around her, too, wanting her attention, wanting her laughter. She handled their need with generous ease, giving just enough that no one felt left out, no one felt as if they weren't enough. And so that the black-haired man with thin wire-frame spectacles who had his arm possessively around her waist felt as if he mattered the most. "Dr. de Souza has also beaten you to the punch."

"You realize he's older than I am?"

"Only by a couple of years." Far too young a doctor to end up a general practitioner in a desolate West Coast town, but when Will had checked up on Dominic de Souza, he'd found no black marks, no problematic history. Seemed like the man was here for exactly the reason he'd said: in a big city, he'd have been the junior in a big practice, but in Golden Cove, he got to be his own boss.

"She'll get tired of him sooner or later," Nikau predicted. "A woman with that much *life* in her, she's not going to be happy with a podunk doctor. She'll want wilder and I've got it."

"Hate to break it to you, but the podunk doctor lives in a nice part of town and owns a flash European car. Have you seen the state of your place?"

Nikau shrugged. "If Miriama just wanted money, she'd have hooked up with one of the rich tourists who pass through here."

Will couldn't argue with that. Even in just three months, he'd seen more than one out-of-towner take a single look at Miriama and fall at her feet. Not all were young backpackers, either; Golden Cove also got the rich travelers who came for the pottery or to stay in the refurbished B&B, which had recently earned a place in a high-end travel guide as a "hidden gem."

"I hear she's leaving." That was the thing with this town—the way the gossip flowed, you'd think you knew everything. But there were secrets here, a thick tide of lava beneath the surface. Will felt them, and once, when he'd been a detective who dug and dug and dug, he'd have begun to poke around. But if he'd still been that man, he wouldn't be here, so the point was moot.

"Six weeks to go." Nikau took a sip of his beer. "Plenty of time."

Snorting, Will returned his gaze to the bottles behind the bar. There was no fancy lighting here, no glass shelves. It was dark wood and solid, the bottles lined up neat as soldiers. "She'll burn you up." Will was grateful he'd never felt a tug toward Miriama; she was too young, too shiny, too innocent.

Will had lost his innocence so long ago that he barely remembered the taste of it.

"Man likes being burned now and then." Nikau turned his attention back to the bar. "What about you? How long you gonna turn down the invitations coming your way?"

"Let's say I'm not in the mood." He wasn't in the mood for much, not even living.

"You still got a dick?"

"Last time I looked."

"Then you're in the mood. Go grab Miss Tierney of the big blue eyes and the big tits and heat up the sheets. She's been shooting you 'come to me, cowboy' looks since we sat down."

Will had nothing against the schoolteacher who worked in the next town over, but he had no desire to screw her, much less date her. It was like that part of him had switched off thirteen months ago. Will wasn't even sure he wanted it to switch back on.

Deciding to change the focus of the conversation, he said, "You ever going to tell me what you're doing in Golden Cove?" Will had run a background check on the other man the day after he took up the position of local cop—Nikau had looked like trouble and Will had wanted to know how bad it was.

What he'd discovered hadn't been anything like what he'd expected.

"Field research," was the mocking answer. "Talking of which"—he swung off the bar stool—"your dick might have taken a vacation, but mine hasn't." A slap of Will's shoulder. "Christine Tierney off-limits?"

"Only if she says so. I've got nothing to do with it." He raised his bottle. "Good luck." Throwing back the last of his beer, he put the bottle down on the stained and scarred wood of the bar and got up. "I'm going home."

Shaking his head at that, Nikau prowled off toward the group of women that held Christine Tierney. Despite the other man's question about Christine, Will wasn't sure who it was that Nikau had in his sights—and he wasn't sure Nik cared.

Having already confirmed that Nikau was planning to walk home, he said good-bye to a few others, then headed out. The night wind was cold, bracing, the salt water heavy in the air tonight. He strode toward the street that would lead him to the far eastern end of town.

He'd lived in the B&B for the first month, until he got sick of the landlord knowing his every move. So he'd rented a house that belonged to a couple who'd left Golden Cove but hadn't been able to find a buyer for their property. Not many people wanted to move to such a remote area on a permanent basis.

Spotting a group of teenagers loitering in front of the closed tourism center, he crossed the empty road to them. They immediately straightened. He caught the fading hint of tobacco smoke, decided to let it go. It was the harder stuff that was a real problem—and there was plenty of that floating around in town.

"I think it's time you went home," he said quietly. "I heard you guys have an exam tomorrow." The teenagers caught the bus to a high school an hour away, but that didn't mean the town didn't know the details of their studies.

The kids scuffed their shoes. "It's gonna be stupid basic," one of them muttered, but when Will met his eyes, the boy dropped his head.

"I'll walk you home," Will said, even though two of them lived out of his way.

The teens weren't exactly thrilled at the escort, but they were young enough not to give him lip. He knew Golden Cove wasn't a big city, that it was unlikely they'd get in trouble the way a city kid might—but then again, the most evil monsters often wore a familiar face. Could be he was walking them home to danger, but he knew the parents of all these kids: a couple were apathetic, uncaring of where their kids wandered, but the rest did their best on meager budgets.

Only once they'd all walked through their front doors did he continue on his way, his gaze drawn toward the trees that hid the ocean. He'd heard through the grapevine that the new face in town, Anahera Spencer-Ashby, formerly Anahera Rawiri, had moved into a clifftop cabin that had once belonged to her mother.

The place hadn't looked safe to him the last time he'd checked it out, so he'd made a few inquiries. The town was too small to have a mayor, but the leader of the business council had assured him the cabin was solidly built. "Though it'll be filthy," Evelyn Triskell had said with a shudder that threatened to dislodge the tight silver bun on top of her head. "Probably spiders everywhere. Anahera is braver than me."

Almost without thought, Will's feet turned toward the cabin. It was a long walk, but he had plenty of time—he didn't sleep much—and the night was crisp, the sky above studded with stars. He stopped halfway down the graveled drive to the cabin, able to see it clearly from his position. Light blazed from the window that faced the drive.

A body moved across the uncurtained window right then, the shape feminine.

She froze midmove, staring out at the darkness, as if she sensed him. He knew she couldn't see him out here in the blackness and he wondered who else might watch her. She needed to get curtains, he thought as she flicked off the light, putting them on an even footing.

Satisfied that she was safe for the night, he turned and left. The crashing thunder of the ocean was his only accompaniment as he walked, the rhythm a steady beat that was a dark pulse.

# 6

Anahera woke to the sound of tuis outside her window, the talkative birds chattering away at the crack of dawn, their song deeply familiar. She hadn't gotten much done yesterday, but she had cleaned out the bedroom that had always been hers in this small home—she couldn't bear to take the larger bedroom for her own.

That had always been her mother's.

The metal frame of her old bed had survived the years, but the sheets and bedding, mattress included, came courtesy of Josie and had been dropped off by her husband two hours after Anahera returned to the cabin. Except for his short beard, Tom Taufa was as Anahera remembered—big and husky and practical.

Josie had also sent a pillow and a little rug for beside the bed, plus plates, cups, and utensils. Anahera was very glad for her friend because the truth was that she hadn't thought this through. Her things were currently on a container ship somewhere in the North Atlantic. She'd brought a suitcase of clothes with her, as well as other odds and ends that had seemed important at the time, but she'd forgotten more than one necessary thing.

Obviously, her head was still not where it should be.

Pushing aside the memories, she lay in bed for ten minutes just listening to the birds, the crisp lemony scent of the sheets and comforter around her. It wasn't until her eyes began to burn that she realized she was waiting for her mother's soft knock on the door, and for Haeata to come in with a cup of coffee for her slugabed daughter. She'd sit on the bed, her silvery black hair in disarray from the walk on the beach she'd already taken, and her skin cold to the touch but her eyes warm and joyful.

Anahera swallowed hard and sat up, her gaze going to the window from where she'd felt someone watching her last night. "Curtains," she muttered to herself. There were no shops in town that sold homewares, but if Josie didn't have some old sheets that she could use then she'd drive out to the nearest town with a larger shopping district. She didn't know where the old curtains had gone. Maybe they'd rotted away until the kids who'd probably used this place as their clubhouse and hookup spot had finally pulled them off.

At least the kids hadn't graffitied either the inside or the outside.

She'd also, she thought after a quick shower, have to have new locks installed. And get a plumber out here to see if they could do something about the thin trickle of water that fell from the showerhead. That last should be simple enough—Tom was a plumber who worked all across the region, but last night he'd mentioned that with Josie so pregnant he was sticking close to town for now.

The one thing she didn't have to worry about was electricity—she'd remembered to call the electricity company from London. And since the lights had come on and her shower had been hot, the wires had apparently survived the years they'd lain unused, the cabin cold and dark.

Dressed in shorts and a large T-shirt, she set about brewing some coffee in the French press she'd brought with her from London; she'd picked up the coffee after landing. "I guess you know your priorities, Ana." She hadn't even packed the glass and metal object particularly well, but it had survived unscathed.

Given the haphazard way she'd packed, it was also pure luck that she had a mix of clothes. Enough to get by even with the reversal in the seasons. She'd boarded the plane on a rainy spring day, disembarked to the first bite of autumn.

Taking a steaming cup of coffee out onto the porch, she stood and watched the sun's rays paint the sky, the colors ruby red and deep orange and vivid pink with hints of golden cream.

There had never been a sunrise like this in London.

The crackle of car tires on gravel had her looking up her drive to see a small and beat-up old truck. It might've once been black, but was now more chips and cracks than anything. The face that hung out the open driver's-side window when the truck came to a stop beside her own car was unforgettable—but it was new, too.

He got out.

"Nikau," she said, walking down to join him on the grass that fronted the cabin. "Keeping early hours."

"I figured you'd have jet lag." Putting his hands on his hips, he gave her a sidelong glance. The *moko* he'd had done five years earlier was a thing of sweeping lines and curves that she was sure told a story of his *whakapapa*— his genealogy and place in the world. Nikau treasured *tikaka* Māori too much to have settled on the design lightly.

"So," he said, switching to a language she hadn't spoken since the day she walked out of this place, "you came back. I never figured you would."

Anahera returned her eyes to the horizon and to a sunrise that screamed "home" with the same angry beauty that it whispered of the dead. She didn't speak until the final echo had faded. "Last I heard"—she turned to face Nikau—"you were presenting on Māori culture at international academic conferences." The words came easier today, the language so much a part of her that even eight years of silence couldn't erase it.

"Yeah, well, shit happens." Nikau's face went hard as he glanced back and to the right, looking not at the drive but at something far beyond. "I guess Josie told you about me and Keira?"

"I was sorry to hear about the divorce." She'd always wondered what Nikau saw in Keira, but that he'd loved her wasn't in doubt. They'd been joined at the hip since they were seventeen: quiet, intense, and studious Nik with beautiful but somehow . . . empty Keira. She'd always seemed to echo others rather than being a whole person.

Nikau looked at her, his gaze strangely flat. "That's all you have to say?"

"I'm not sure what else you expect me to say." Anahera didn't have the emotional patience to read between the lines about another bad marriage. "I'm your friend. I'm sorry your marriage broke up. I know you loved her."

Nikau stared at her for another disturbing second before he blew out a breath and thrust a hand through his hair. "Shit, sorry. I guess Josie didn't pass on the dirt."

The answer to his bitterness lay in her own cold anger. "Did she cheat on you?"

"Worse. She hooked up with that asshole a year after our separation." A glance to the distant right again. "They got married fourteen months ago."

*That asshole*, when added to the direction of Nikau's vicious gaze, made the identity of Keira's new husband clear. "Daniel May?"

A hard nod.

They'd known one another all of their lives, Anahera and Josie, Keira and Daniel, Vincent and Nikau. There had been others—Tom, Peter, Christine—but those three had come and gone. It was the six of them who had been a constant, a tight-knit group that had snuck out at night to make bonfires on the beach and that had flowed back together each time the holidays rolled around and everyone was back in the Cove. It hadn't mattered that Daniel May and Vincent Baker were private-school kids who came from the two richest families in town, while Nikau and Anahera came from the poorest.

Then they'd grown up.

"That sucks, Nik." What else was there to say? Daniel had used his father's money and influence to "win" an international exchange scholarship for which Nikau had been far better qualified—and deserving. For Daniel, it had been another line to add to his CV later on in life. For a teenage Nikau, it had been the only way he could hope to travel internationally.

It was the kind of betrayal that could never be forgotten or forgiven. "What about Vincent?" she asked. "Did he turn into an asshole while I was away? I have him on my online friends list, but I haven't actually logged into my account in months."

A bark of laughter from Nikau, his coldness melting. "Nah," he said, "Vincent's still Vincent."

Which meant the handsome Baker scion was still living up to his family's expectations. "He looked happy in the last photos I saw of him—with his wife and the kids."

"Yeah, I think he actually is happy. Go figure, huh?" A shrug. "He should be the most messed up one of us with all the pressure his parents put on him."

Anahera nodded; she'd always felt sorry for Vincent—but he seemed to like the borders on his life, appeared to have thrived inside them. "They weren't the best parents, I guess, but he and his brother must miss them."

"Yeah, a fire gutted the old Baker place. No way for them to survive— I went to the funeral. Vin did a nice job of it."

Anahera would expect nothing less from Vincent. "Come on, I'll pour you some coffee." Nik had changed and so had she, but she found she was still comfortable with this angry man who'd once been a hopeful boy she'd known.

Nikau had settled down on a rickety chair he'd dragged from inside, Anahera passing him his coffee and bracing herself with her butt against the porch railing—after checking its sturdiness—when there was the sound of another car coming down the drive. "London has nothing on Golden Cove traffic."

She'd half expected a cheerful Josie in Tom's plumbing truck, but it was the police SUV that appeared in view a second later. The long-legged cop with the broad shoulders and the face that was too thin got out soon afterward.

"Will." Nikau raised his coffee cup. "You come to do a welfare check on our returnee?"

"Nik. Ms. Spencer-Ashby."

His words were a punch to the solar plexus. "Anahera is fine." Rawiri or Spencer-Ashby, she wanted to claim neither surname. "Would you like some coffee? I think I have another mug."

"Thanks, but I'll pass this time." Impossible to read those eyes, that grim face. "I did want to make sure you had a way of contacting help if you need it. I know there's no landline phone at this address."

Anahera wasn't certain if she was amused or not; it had been a long time since she'd answered to anyone. "I have a mobile phone, just like most of the universe."

No change in his expression. "You mind checking the signal for me?"

"And if I do?"

No smile. "Then I guess I'll be doing a welfare check on you every morning."

Nikau laughed at that, but his tone was serious when he met Anahera's eyes again. "Will's right, Ana. You should check. This place is in the middle of nowhere of the middle of nowhere."

Rolling her eyes, Anahera went inside and grabbed her phone. She brought up the home screen as she walked out . . . and cursed. At least the cop didn't say "I told you so." Instead, he said, "I suggest you move to a different provider." He named which one. "Their signal appears to reach even the far edges of Golden Cove."

"Upside is their plans are cheap," Nikau said. "I can lend you my phone until you switch."

Anahera waved aside the offer. "I'll be fine. I have nothing to steal and we all know petty burglary is at the top of the Golden Cove crime stats." Some folks stole out of boredom, others out of poverty.

"Crime isn't the only threat," the cop said. "If you have an accident, it's possible no one will find you for days."

Anahera could feel herself going white. Squeezing her hand around the phone, she stared at the cop. "You've done your job. Far as I know, cops aren't babysitters."

# 7

Will wondered what he'd said. Not only had Anahera iced up, but Nikau's face had gone hostile between one heartbeat and the next. Mentally tracing back the conversation, he realized it had been his statement about a possible domestic accident that had done it. Obviously, he'd stepped on a nerve. That was what happened when everyone in a small town knew something but no one talked about it: hapless outsiders put their foot in it.

"You're right," he said mildly. "I was a terrible babysitter. Used to let my neighbors' kids eat candy all night." He nodded at a stony-faced Anahera, then Nikau. "Have a good day."

He felt their eyes on him as he got into his vehicle, both dark, both impenetrable.

It was a good thing he'd never told himself that he understood Nikau; their friendship was a surface thing based on their liking for the same sport, a good run through the trees, and the odd beer. Will knew Nikau was pissed his ex had married rich-and-liked-people-to-know-it Daniel May, and that Nikau was in the Cove because of that same ex.

That was pretty much the extent of his personal knowledge of Nikau Martin.

Nik knew even less about Will.

As he backed down the drive, unable to turn with Nikau's truck parked where it was, he was again aware of both of them watching him leave.

Watching the outsider leave. He'd never had any illusions about that, either—in a place like this, a man stayed an outsider for decades, no matter how hard he tried.

Of course, Will wasn't exactly hankering to belong anywhere.

Which made him the perfect cop to send to Golden Cove.

# 8

Anahera drove to the garage after breakfast, her blood still cold. Peter, unsmiling as always, and just a *little* strange in a way it was difficult to define, said, "Hi, Ana," and got to work checking out her engine.

Nothing serious, was the conclusion. He changed a small part, told her the Jeep was a solid investment, then waved off the bill. "Next time won't be free."

"Thanks, Peter." Guilt nipped at her even as she said that. She'd never been able to make herself genuinely like Peter, though she'd tried; he was always nice and he'd never done anything to make her *dis*like him . . . but the tiny hairs on her nape stood up anytime she was alone with the lanky redhead. "Have a good day."

He nodded, standing unmoving in the garage entrance as she drove away. It felt as if his muddy green eyes tracked her until she turned onto the main strip. She spotted the cop's vehicle heading out of town, tried to guess who he was going to see. A number of Cove people lived way out in the wilderness, including a few who didn't much care for company. But she guessed that was his job—to show his face even in the shadows, make people know the law was around.

She wondered if it was working.

Parking the Jeep outside the café, she got out. But it was only Miriama she found inside. "Jo says her ankles are the size of tree stumps today," the girl informed Anahera, her smile sunny. "I told her to stay home and have some time to herself since Tom's taken the boyo with him on a job. With the weather so grizzly, it'll probably be quiet until the fishing boats come in later today."

Anahera had almost not noticed the change in the weather—the West Coast was often clear and bright even in winter, but for some reason of geography, the Cove collected what water there was in the atmosphere. The sky was stormy gray today, rain a dark mist that threatened to turn morning into evening. "Who's out fishing?"

"The usual crazy crew," Miriama said with a roll of her eyes, but those eyes were warm with affection. "Kev and Tamati and Boris."

"I know all those names except Boris."

"Backpacker who washed up here and decided to stay. A year now." Miriama shook her head. "He's from St. Petersburg. Decided he liked the quiet of the Cove better."

"If he's survived a winter already, maybe he'll make it."

"He keeps telling us he's Russian—'And Russians know winter. This is nothing.'" Dropping the thick Russian accent with a grin, she moved to her coffee machine. "What's your poison?"

"Straight black," Anahera said. "And I'll take a decaf cappuccino, too. Both to go."

Miriama made the drinks, then said, "Say hi to Jo for me." She drew a smiley face on the cup meant for Josie.

"Will do. Thanks, Miri." The Jeep had no cup holders, but thanks to the cardboard holder Miriama had provided, Anahera managed to make it to Josie's without spilling. Her friend's home was a small clapboard house painted a crisp white with a blue-green trim. Josie had planted native ferns around the sides, hardy flowering plants out front.

Going to the door, Anahera tested the knob and, as expected, it turned easily. "Locks exist for a reason!" she called out so Josie wouldn't get a fright when she walked in.

"You'd better have brought me a cappuccino!"

Anahera smiled and walked into the living room to find Josie sitting on a sofa, folding curtains of happy yellow with white daisies printed on them.

Her breath stuck in her chest. "Where—" She took a desperate sip of coffee to wet her bone-dry throat. "Where did you get those?"

"I saved them for you." Josie's smile was uncertain. "I'm sorry. Was that the wrong thing to do? I was worried they'd get moldy and damaged in the cabin after you left."

Heart thundering, Anahera put the coffees on the small wooden table in front of Josie. "I thought they were gone," she whispered, taking one of the crisply laundered and ironed curtains in her hands.

Josie touched her fingers to Anahera's shoulder. "Your mum spent so much time making these. I couldn't bear to have them just fade away."

A lump of rock in her throat, Anahera nodded. She'd left behind everything but the greenstone carving she wore on a thin braided cord under her black sweater, and the memories in her heart. She'd thought she was beyond the idea of needing objects to remember the woman she'd loved *so* much, and whose embrace she missed to this day, but these curtains sang to her in her mother's voice. "On that little sewing machine of hers."

"I still have that, too," Josie whispered. "You can have it back."

Anahera shook her head. "She would've wanted you to have it." That was why Anahera had given the machine to her best friend. "I can't sew. Not like her." Putting her hand on Josie's, she squeezed. "Thank you."

Josie's misty eyes scanned her face. "Are you going to see your dad?"

Steel in her spine, black ice in her heart. "No." She'd made her decision at twenty-one and that was how it'd stay.

"He's been sober for years."

"That's good. But it has nothing to do with me."

And then they sat there, awash in memories of a woman with Anahera's features but with silver in her hair and sadness in her eyes.

# INTERLUDE

She examined her face in the mirror, tried to see if it showed.

But no, she looked the same as always.

Frowning, she sat on the narrow single bed and leaned down to lace up her running shoes. They were good shoes, with stripes of orange down the sides. She loved running in them. Probably she shouldn't have accepted such an expensive gift, but her previous shoes had been falling apart to the point that she'd been considering running in bare feet.

Nothing worse than bad shoes, to her mind.

Getting up, she shut her bedroom door before moving down the hall-way as quietly as possible. But he heard. He always did. Wandering into the doorway of the living room, he scratched at the flaccid white of his belly and leered. "Going for a run?"

"Tell Auntie I'll be back in about an hour." She'd become expert at slipping past his grabbing hands and was at the front door before he could move his unwashed body anywhere near her. She couldn't understand how her aunt allowed him to touch her, but then, Auntie had always had hang-ups about her weight.

Men like him took advantage of that. And of Auntie's kindness.

She didn't stretch by the house as she'd done before he moved in. She walked a little ways to a patch of green in front of an abandoned property that was falling down around itself. As she did her stretches, she let her mind roam. Which way should she run today? Through the lush green of the old trees and native ferns? Along the main road out of town? It tended to be pretty quiet at this time of the year. The worst she'd get was a toot or two from locals who recognized her.

Or should she run along the cliffs above the beach? Maybe the beach itself?

It was the light that decided her, such a glorious clarity to it, the fog and mist having burned off during the day. She'd have it for at least two more hours and Auntie wouldn't worry if she was a little late getting home.

Route decided, she took off on a slow jog that built until she was flying over the landscape, her legs formed for this. Sometimes she thought about what it would be like to do this for a job, to become an athlete. However, then it wouldn't be pure joy anymore. And she loved this too much to diminish the experience.

She ran.

Seeing a standing form in the distance long after she'd hit her stride, she almost stumbled. Not many people in Golden Cove ran regularly and the ones that did tended to favor other routes. And this person was standing motionless, wasn't even in running or walking clothes. Her feet took her closer and closer, until she recognized that profile, those eyes, that mouth.

"Oh," she said, coming to a stop, startled and wondering if this was a sign. "I didn't expect to see you here."

# 9

Will was sitting at his kitchen table, staring at the letter he'd just received from the police commissioner, when his phone rang. He didn't hesitate to pick it up, the number one he recognized. "Matilda," he said, "do you need help?"

On meeting Matilda Tutaia, you'd never think she'd put up with a man raising his hands to her, but Will had been called to the house twice already, both times to kick out her unemployed boyfriend until he calmed the fuck down.

Too bad she always took the asshole back.

"It's Miriama." Matilda's voice was pitched noticeably higher than normal. "She went out for a run before dinner and she hasn't come back home even though she knew I was cooking her favorite tonight. She told Steve she'd only be gone an hour. It's been four."

Will was already on his feet. The most likely explanation was that Miriama had hooked up with friends and forgotten to call Matilda . . . but that didn't fit with the relationship he'd seen between the two women. Miriama was respectful toward her aunt. "Do you know which way she ran?" The young woman could've had an accident, might be lying on an isolated track waiting for someone to find her.

"I'm going to ask Steve."

"Wait, I'll do it when I get there." The asshole was scared of Will, wouldn't lie. "I'm on my way." Hanging up before Matilda could reply, he grabbed his keys.

He reached their house in under seven minutes. Matilda hovered on the front lawn, a woman with short dark hair and weight that had crept on over the years. Dressed in gray sweatpants and a large pink T-shirt printed with fund-raising information for a long-ago charity gala, she was scanning the street with desperate eyes. "I know Steve's got his problems," she said when Will reached her, "but he wouldn't hurt my Miri."

Will thought of how he'd caught Steve looking at Miriama more than once, a look that said he was weighing up his chances. But Matilda had blinders on when it came to her boyfriend. "I just want to make sure I get all the information I need," he said. "Have you called around to her friends?"

"First thing I did after trying her phone and getting that automatic 'out of range or turned off' message. I thought she must've gone in for a cuppa after her run and got carried away with the talking. She does that, you know. And people like her being around, so she's always being invited to visit."

"Who saw her last?"

"Tania, out toward the coastal road. Says Miriama waved to her as she ran by around a quarter to six. No one else saw her after that."

Will touched one hand to Matilda's shoulder. "Let's go talk to Steve."

Inside, Steve was where Will had expected him to be—on the dark brown armchair that was sagging in the middle and boasted cigarette burns on the arms; the man's eyes were on the television screen and he had a beer in his hand. He laughed at something onscreen, only to say, "Fuck off, you old bitch!" when Matilda moved to block his view.

"I'd rather you turn off the television," Will said.

Freezing at his voice, Steve looked up. "Hey, I never done nothing."

Since Steve appeared to have lost control of his limbs, Will reached over, picked up the remote, and switched off the television himself. "Now," he said to the other man, "tell me what happened."

Steve's Adam's apple bobbed. "Nothing happened! The girl went out for a run like she does all the time, and she was wearing her black running tights with the pink sides and that tight orange top, and those shoes she can't afford—when you find her, you should ask her how she bought those."

"Steve!" Matilda's voice was harder than Will had ever heard it. "I swear to God, if anything's happened to Miri and you know it, I'll kill you with my bare hands."

Steve's eyebrows drew together, the shadows under his eyes bruise-colored splotches against his pallid skin. "I was watching my shows until you got home at ten past six. It's not like I can run after her."

"What did she tell you before she left?" Will asked, because if Steve had been here at 6:10 and Tania Meikle had seen Miriama at 5:45, it was highly unlikely he was lying about not having done anything to Miriama. The man didn't drive and was about as fast as a snail with a limp. No way could he have made it to anywhere near the Meikle house.

"Just that she'd be back in an hour and that I was to tell Matilda." A sulky look at the woman he was supposed to love. "I did, didn't I? Just like your precious *Miri* ordered."

"Aside from the shoes and clothes you've described, was she wearing anything else? Jewelry?"

Steve scratched at his belly. "Nah, don't think so. Had her iPod that she wears strapped to her arm and her phone in that pocket thing built into the back of her tights."

"Purple stars," Matilda blurted out. "She put stickers of purple stars on the iPod, uses it with a set of black earbuds. And her shoes are black, too, with orange stripes." She rubbed her forehead. "I got her a new shell for her phone. Black with specks of silver."

Will returned his attention to Steve after noting down those distinctive details. "Did you look out to see where she went?"

"Nah, game was on. Couldn't be bothered."

Deciding he'd get nothing else useful from the man, Will turned his attention to Matilda and managed to get the exact model of Miriama's phone as well as the number. "I need you to write down who you've called and what they said. I'm going to drive out to Tania's and check the coastal road." If he'd had other officers, he could've stationed one with Matilda, but he was alone—and finding Miriama if she was injured was a priority.

Leaving Matilda scrambling for a pen and paper, he headed out to his

SUV but made two calls before he started the engine. The first was to Miriama. It got redirected immediately to the same message Matilda had heard, so either Miriama was in a dead zone, the phone battery was dead, or the phone had been destroyed.

His second call was to Nikau. "Nik, I need you to scramble the volunteer fire department and anyone else who can help in a search at night." It could be he was acting too soon, but Will's gut said otherwise. "Miriama didn't make it home after a run, might be lying hurt somewhere."

"Shit. I'll get them together."

"Gather everyone in front of the firehouse." The relatively large building with a single aging appliance was an easy central location, and it had enough space that the volunteers could all gather inside for instructions if the weather turned. "I'll be there after I chase down some information. I'll call if I catch a scent."

"You want me to rouse the bushmen?"

Will considered it. The generally unsociable folk who preferred to live deep in the wilderness that surrounded Golden Cove would be of invaluable help if Miriama had turned onto a forested track later on during her run. "Yes." He'd get cursed out soundly should this be a false alarm, but Will was willing to live with that.

"Call everyone," he said, and tried not to listen to the voice in the back of his head that whispered his response had nothing to do with Miriama, that he was attempting to fix a mistake seared in hot red flame.

The scars on his back felt suddenly stiff.

# 10

The porch light was on at the Meikle house, and when he got out of his vehicle, he heard loud music pouring through the upstairs windows. Probably courtesy of Tania Meikle's teenage sister. Tania herself opened the front door to his knock. The twenty-four-year-old carried a blond toddler on her hip, lines of worry marking her face. "You haven't found her?"

"No. Can you tell me what you saw?"

She tucked back a strand of pale brown hair. "Come in."

Walking inside because he figured she might want to sit, he tried to avoid stepping on the colored children's bricks scattered on the floor. "When's Gary back?" Tania's husband made his living on long-range fishing trawlers.

"A month. Can't wait." Tania tried to put her boy down, but he wailed at the idea and clung.

Snugging the red-faced toddler back to her hip, she rocked him out of the tears. "It wasn't much, you know? Just normal. Miri running by on those long legs of hers. I called out to her and she waved." A shaky smile that didn't reach the faded blue of her eyes. "I was thinking of sitting out there for a bit and asking her in for a visit in case she returned the same way, but the baby was fussy, so I brought him inside to play and forgot all about keeping an eye out."

The boy decided to wail again right then.

"Here, I'll take him." The voice was young and female. "He probably just wants to be walked around."

"Thanks, hon." Tania handed over the toddler to her teenage sister, a short girl with curly brown-blonde hair. "Alice, did you see Miriama today?" she asked as the teenager began to move around the room with her nephew in her arms.

"Yeah, when you yelled out to her." A roll of the eyes. "Totally interrupted my call with Lisa, but whatever."

"Were you upstairs in your room?" Will asked.

Making nonsensical noises at the baby, Alice nodded. "Yep."

"You had a better view than your sister. Did you see where Miriama went?"

Alice scrunched up her nose, making the baby giggle. "Down the coastal way. I watched for a little bit because she's pretty awesome to watch move. Like a dancer or something." Flushing at that, she shrugged. "Then Lisa started telling me about the total loser she has a crush on and I got distracted."

"Is it possible Miriama might've turned off the road onto one of the bush tracks?" What the locals casually called "the bush" was heavy old-growth forest, the interior dark green and difficult to navigate if you wandered off the rough dirt paths.

"Maybe, I guess," Alice answered. "But she was going pretty straight." A glance at Tania, youthful insouciance fading into shaky disquiet. "Tans? Did something happen to Miri?"

"I hope not." Tania stroked her sister's back. "I'm sorry we can't help more," she said to Will. "I'm so worried."

Taking his leave of the two sisters after asking Tania a few more questions focusing on what she knew of Miriama's favorite routes, Will drove slowly down the coastal road, scanning it on all sides as he went. He saw nothing and Miriama had been brightly dressed, would've stood out if she'd fallen—or even if a car had clipped her and she'd been thrown. But it was dark, no streetlights to penetrate the gloom. And if she'd headed down to the beach, then the only way to spot her would be on foot.

Jaw clenched, he turned around and made his way to the fire station, which someone had opened up. He was more than half hoping to arrive and find that the call-up of volunteers had unearthed Miriama—the news would've spread through the town like wildfire. If she'd been in anyone's kitchen or living room, she should've turned up. But he arrived to find the volunteers milling around with anxious looks on their faces.

"No sign of her?" he asked Nikau.

The other man shook his head. "I had everyone do a bit of calling around before they came here. Nothing. Couldn't get hold of Dominic de Souza—the message on his voice mail says he's been called out to one of the more remote farms and to contact emergency services if there's an urgent medical matter. He's probably out of cell range."

Will nodded. "From this point on, we assume Miriama is down and needs assistance."

He and Nikau both knew there could be a far more unsavory reason for Miriama's disappearance, but Will had to go with the most likely option first. Crime in Golden Cove was generally limited to domestic aggression, kids playing up, and a bit of petty thievery. Accidents, however, were more common, the rugged landscape intolerant of mistakes.

"Okay," he said to the gathered group, "listen up."

Waiting until they'd all turned to look at him and the murmuring had died down, he started with a detailed description of what Miriama had been wearing when she went missing. "Keep an eye out for any sign of her clothing, shoes, phone, or iPod. Report everything you find. We'll make the call as to what's relevant and what's not."

He saw a few people taking notes, but most would remember; like Will, they'd probably seen Miriama running in the same outfit multiple times. "I'm going to hand it over to Nikau to coordinate the search because he knows this area a hell of a lot better than I do." Will ran with the other man nearly every day, but he'd still only explored a small part of the wilderness that surrounded Golden Cove. "Before I do that, however," he said, "I want to make it clear you're to take safety precautions—we can't help Miriama if one of you gets injured as well."

It was a point he had to drive home because many of the volunteers were hard-living types used to toughing it. "The more time we have to waste rescuing one of you," he said, "the less time we have to help Miriama." He got a few nods, knew that peer pressure would do the rest. They'd look out for one another, make sure people didn't act stupid.

Nikau stepped forward. "What Will is too polite to say is don't be fucking assholes." His voice was harsh. "First up, we need someone to stay here and act as base command."

A female voice sounded from the back. "That'll be me."

Will immediately recognized Matilda's form moving through the crowd. "I'm too fat and slow to be any real help out there," she said bluntly after thrusting a piece of paper into Will's hand. "But I know how to run things like this. This isn't the first time one of us has gotten into trouble."

When Nikau didn't dispute Matilda's claim, Will realized once again that there was so much more he needed to know about Golden Cove. He'd never have thought that Matilda, gentle and with a tendency to fall for abusive men, had that kind of steel to her.

As he scanned down the written list of the people she'd called and what they'd said, Nikau parceled out the various areas, focusing the search in the direction Miriama had last been spotted. But, as there was a slight chance the young woman had decided to circle back and run on another route, he also sent a smaller number of volunteers in other directions. "Does everyone have flashlights and phones that will work through town?"

Nods all around.

"You're dressed for the weather?" Nikau asked, and though it might have seemed like an obvious question, Will knew why the other man was asking it—the weather around here could change in a single roll of thunder. If a volunteer did manage to injure themselves and got stuck out there in the dark, the rest of them needed to know that person wouldn't succumb to exposure.

That was also what was worrying him about Miriama; if she'd become disoriented as a result of an injury and wandered off into the landscape around them, she'd be vulnerable not only to any injuries she'd sustained, but also to the cold. She was only wearing running gear, had no jacket or anything else that might protect her from the elements.

He saw the same solemn realization on the faces of all those gathered around. It was quiet Vincent Baker, an unexpectedly decent guy for being born with a silver spoon in his mouth, who said, "We'll be careful." Expression drawn, he asked, "What should we do if we find her, and we're out of cell range? Signal can be patchy when the clouds move in."

"That's why I'm sending you out in pairs," Nikau said. "One of you stays with her, while the other one heads back until you either get a signal or you meet up with someone else who has a signal. At that point, pass on the message, then go back to your partner. I don't want anyone out there alone for a long period. Is that understood?"

Everyone nodded; Nikau might have a bit of a reputation in town, but no one would argue against his deep knowledge of the land in and around Golden Cove.

"Let's go," he said into the silence. "You get tired, you come back. No matter what, we all meet back here at dawn. If you need to leave earlier, tell Matilda so we don't waste time looking for you."

Matilda spoke up. "I'm going to do a roll call. If your name's not on this list, give it to me before you leave."

The teams began to disperse three minutes later.

Nikau had assigned himself and his partner one of the toughest and most treacherous trails. He hadn't assigned Will a search area—as they'd agreed on when Will first talked to him about how to handle such situations. Will needed to be open and available to respond to any possible sighting.

Nikau handed over a copy of the search assignments. "You going to see Ana?"

Will nodded. "If Miriama ran along the coastal route or went down to the beach, it's possible she might've spotted her."

Hands on his hips, Nikau nodded. "Look," he said, "sorry about this morning. Not your fault you didn't know." With that, he jogged off to join his partner in the truck they'd drive to the entrance of their particular track.

Obviously, Nikau was assuming that Will must've done some research, figured out what it was that had set off Anahera and Nikau that morning.

He was right.

Getting into his SUV, Will turned in the direction of Anahera's cabin just as Matilda came to stand at the entrance to the fire station, a strong woman who'd made some bad choices, but who knew how to love. Spotlit by the lights of the fire station behind her, she grew increasingly small in his rearview mirror as he drove away into the dark.

# 11

Flashlight beams cut through the pitch black on either side of the road, voices rising into the air as the searchers called out for Miriama. Will spotted several volunteers on the roadside itself, their task to check the ditches for evidence that Miriama might've been clipped by a car.

After that point, the world glowed red, lit by the taillights of the people who'd been assigned to the coastal area. All those Nikau had told to work the clifftop and the beach were either fishermen, ex-Navy, or people who lived along the coast. They respected the ocean while not being intimidated by it.

Will turned off to the left when he came to the graveled drive that led to Anahera's home. The others continued on straight, but he knew they'd be stopping within thirty seconds. That was as far as you could go in a vehicle; after that, the volunteers would have to search on foot, careful not to get too close to the cliff edge unless they wanted to use one of the narrow paths to scramble down to the beach.

That, too, would be a dangerous trip, but all these people had done it several times at least, probably in the last month. Dark and untamed and merciless though it was, this was their home.

His headlights spotlighted Anahera halfway up the drive. She was carrying an unlit flashlight, her body clad in jeans, boots, and a heavy outdoor jacket. Stopping his vehicle, he got out. She was the one who spoke first.

"What's happened? I figured something must have when I heard all the activity on the road. And don't say you told me so about the phone. I've already put in a request for a transfer."

Will didn't waste either of their time. "Miriama's missing. Last seen going for a run, and probably heading in this direction. Did you see any sign of her?"

Skin going tight over the fine bones of her face, Anahera shook her head. "I spent most of the afternoon inside, cleaning out the place. What time would she have passed by?" When he told her the estimated period, she shook her head. "I went for a walk to clear my head around then. I must've just missed her."

"Is it possible she might've run along the front of your property, along the cliffs?" It was technically private land, but no one in Golden Cove much bothered about things like that—the only people who seemed to were Daniel and Keira May with their mansion on the hill. Vincent Baker owned an equally large chunk of land, but he usually had no problem with hikers utilizing the walking trails that ran through his property.

"I noticed a strip of slow grass growth along the edge where I think people run," Anahera said. "Let's go have a look."

She jumped into his vehicle for the short drive back to her cabin. Getting out afterward, flashlights in hand and the lights of his running vehicle illuminating the darkness, they began to examine the area around the cabin. While he could see the path Anahera had mentioned, there was too little grass to tell if it had been recently crushed. He and Anahera checked regardless, all the way along, until they got to the point where a steep climb snaked down to the beach.

Farther on was a more dangerous stretch of clifftop they simply could not search in the darkness. The risk was too high. He and Anahera ran their flashlight beams over the area as well as they could regardless, but the grass was taller and hardier there and the lights not enough to penetrate the blackness. "We have to wait for dawn."

Anahera pressed her lips together but nodded.

Contacting the people who'd been assigned the first section of clifftop as part of their search radius, he told them that he and Anahera had checked it out and that they should focus on the rest of their assigned area.

"I'm going to go down to the beach," Anahera said after he hung up. "Can you climb down?"

Will just nodded. Golden Cove natives tended to assume he was a city slicker who didn't know his way around this land and he hadn't done much to disabuse them of the belief. "You should go first," he said. "I haven't used this path before."

"I didn't need your permission," Anahera responded, but the words held no heat. It was obvious her attention was on the search for Miriama. They made the climb down in silence, ending up on the farthest side of the beach search area.

Another fifty meters and the sand disappeared under a flow of water that turned into a whirlpool surrounded by rocks as black as obsidian and as jagged as broken glass. Everyone knew to keep their distance from the spot—there was simply no hope for anyone who fell into that water; they'd be smashed up against the rocks and sucked out to sea long before a witness could hope to summon help.

Growing up in the area as she had, Miriama would've been well aware of the danger, would have never run too close to it, or ventured near enough to the edge of the cliff to fall. Still, he and Anahera had to check. They swept their flashlight beams along the sand as they walked, looking for any sign of footprints. The tide was coming in, but it hadn't crept far up the beach—yet all they saw was a smooth ripple of sand.

No sign of man, no sign of anything but nature's fury.

Waves crashed in a black maelstrom only meters away, and then they were at the edge of the whirlpool, the white froth of it angry in the beam of their flashlights and the center a brutal black maw.

Turning in silence, they made their way back up the beach with just as much care, in the hope that they'd spot something, anything, that would lead to Miriama's whereabouts.

"I almost hope we don't find anything here," Anahera said into the silence stretched taut as a wire. "This is probably the most dangerous stretch of the beach."

"From comments she's made before when we spoke about running routes," Will said, "Miriama prefers the route along the other side of the cliffs." Decades of runners had created a well-worn path through there, and it looked out over the part of the beach where locals most often lit bonfires or picnicked. No one swam in the water, not given its ferocity—even the extreme surfers stuck to the next beach over—but it was still a hauntingly beautiful area in which to linger away a day.

"Good." Anahera didn't say anything else for the next ten minutes, the two of them intent on the search. "She have a boyfriend?" she asked when she did speak.

"Yes, Dominic de Souza, the town doctor." He told her what Nikau had shared about Dominic's whereabouts. "It's probably good he doesn't know, especially if he's on the road." The last thing they needed was for the young doctor to crash his car because he was rushing to get home.

"I asked," Anahera said, "because a lot of the men around here have resentments about how their lives have gone and they get drunk and take it out on the women."

Will wondered what to say—she had to know he would've done a background search. But at the same time, what right did he have to bring up her mother's death, or that it was Anahera who'd found Haeata Rawiri three days after her fatal fall?

"Let's hope I don't have to take the investigation in that direction," he said at last, because if he had to ask those questions, it meant that either they hadn't found Miriama . . . or they'd found her body.

# 12

Anahera walked down the beach with worry heavy in her gut and the taciturn cop by her side, the world quiet around them but for the pounding of the waves and, in the distance, the shouts of fellow searchers.

She and the cop called out, too, in the hope Miriama would answer. Maybe she'd fallen and broken her leg, or hit her head, and the shouts would rouse her. But they didn't rely only on that, both of them scrambling up and around any rocks that might hide a body. They even checked near large pieces of driftwood, on the faint chance that Miriama had fallen on the beach and the sand had brushed itself across her, camouflaging her injured body.

But they'd found nothing by the time they met up with the searchers walking toward them from the other end of the beach. "Anything?" Anahera asked before realizing who it was that she was facing. The darkness, the way his face had filled out, his thick white beard, it had all served to obscure his identity until she was nearly within touching distance.

Deliberately breaking eye contact with her father, she fixed it on the grizzled man who stood beside him: Matthew, one of the old-timers who'd been around so long that he was part of the foundations of Golden Cove.

Eyes crinkled at the corners and heavy lines carved into skin she knew to be a dark mahogany after years out in the sun, Matthew shook his head. "No sign of her," he said in that smoker's voice she remembered. "But we haven't got a signal down here, eh. Maybe one of the others found her."

Beside her, Anahera was aware of the cop taking out his phone and checking. He shook his head. "I have a signal and there's no word so far."

Everyone went silent.

"Reckon we should search the beach again," Matthew said. "It's bloody dark with the clouds so heavy, eh, maybe we missed something."

"The tide's coming in," was the rumbling contribution from the man who'd once been a violent and drunken part of Anahera's life.

The cop nodded. "Jason's right. But we have time to take another look behind the rocks and anywhere else where Miriama might've fallen if she stumbled on the cliffs."

Parting in silence, the two teams began their grim task. If Miriama *had* fallen from up on the cliffs, she'd be in bad shape, especially if she'd fallen onto the rocks. But, on the evidence of other accidents in the area, it *was* possible she'd survived the fall. They just had to find her in time.

Anahera clambered over rocks, almost slipped twice. The third time, strong hands gripped her at the waist and put her gently on the ground.

"Be careful," the cop said, his voice mild.

Anahera narrowed her eyes. She wanted to snap at him even though she knew he had nothing to do with this. He was an outsider. How could he possibly know the secrets that tied together the residents of this town? How could he hope to understand the wounds the man they'd just seen had hammered into her with his big fists and cruel words? How could he divine the chill in her blood as her mind tugged at a faint, disturbing thread of memory that had nothing to do with her parents?

He couldn't. She should cut him some slack. But he was the only one here, and she felt as if she'd explode if she didn't release some of the tension building and building and building inside her. "I've been climbing and falling off these rocks since I was three years old," she said. "I think I can handle myself."

He ran the beam of his flashlight over a hollow between two boulders, then went down on his knees to check underneath. "Actually," he said, "you've been away from Golden Cove for years. And you spent that time in a big city, so could be you should give yourself a little time to reacclimatize."

No anger in his tone, the words so even that he was either a psychopath who felt nothing—or he was a man who felt too much and was doing his damnedest to feel nothing.

Nikau had told her Will was a good guy after the cop left this morning. She'd also seen that for herself in his determined search for Miriama. Many outsiders would've shrugged and waited for morning to come, for Miriama to just turn up. Will had initiated a full-scale search. And at this instant, he was crawling his way under a bunch of rocks that formed a shallow cave, even as the sea waves inched closer.

She turned her flashlight beam on him, giving him as much light as possible.

"Nothing." Getting to his feet, he dusted off the sand from his jacket and swung his own beam out toward the ocean. "We have to go up."

Anahera wished she could argue with him, but he was right. Stay on the beach any longer and they risked being trapped. With the waves so violent, they probably wouldn't survive to morning even if they managed to climb onto the highest rocks. "Follow me." She led him to a path closer to their current position than the one by her cabin.

Despite what he'd said about her being away for years, some things didn't change; these rocks had been here for untold decades before she was born and would probably be here for untold decades after her death. The path was exactly where she'd remembered it being.

Anahera took care as she began to climb—going up was actually easier than coming down with this path, but all it would take was one slip and she'd be falling. There wasn't much to grab onto here, maybe a few grasses or jagged edges of mostly buried rock. She'd never thought about that as a child, had just assumed she was safe because her mother and father were watching.

At her weakest, she'd wished she could return to that carefree childhood when she hadn't known the truth, when she hadn't understood that her happy family was a mirage that would one day shimmer out of existence. Until she'd realized those years had been her mother's prison and that going back would be to put Haeata behind bars again.

Hearing a scrape behind her, she paused and glanced back. "You okay, cop?"

When he ran his flashlight beam behind him, she realized he was standing on the path looking down at the beach. "I'm making sure no one else is still on the beach."

Anahera hadn't thought to do that—she just expected the locals to not be stupid. But she should've remembered that people were people and emotions were running high. Joining him, she looked out for any other sources of light, but all the ones she spotted were of searchers climbing back up from the beach. "I don't see anything," she said. "You?"

He turned off his flashlight, then did a second careful scan. "No," he said, switching his flashlight back on before he turned cliffward again. "Let's keep going. I need to get a report from Matilda, see what areas have already been covered and what hasn't. The beach searchers can be reassigned."

Anahera moved quickly up the path, aware of the cop keeping up with her, his breathing even and his stride steady. Not a total townie, she thought with a corner of her mind. He'd done some climbing at least.

After reaching the top, the two of them made their way to his police vehicle and got in. They saw several others driving back into town when they turned onto the road, and by the time they arrived at the fire station, at least fifteen others had reported in.

"No one's had any news," Matilda told them, her voice firm, her fear held back with a strong hand.

Behind her was a whiteboard on which someone had written out a detailed description of Miriama's clothing, shoes, phone, and iPod. No mention of a watch or earrings and Anahera couldn't remember if the girl's ears had been pierced. But the other items were distinctive. Anahera took note.

"The ones doing the bush tracks are still out," Matilda continued, "but we haven't got anyone really searching the rest of the town. What if she got hit by a car or something like that?"

Anahera knew that was unlikely. *Someone* would've spotted Miriama if she'd been on or near a road, especially with search volunteers having come in from every corner of Golden Cove.

The cop didn't crush Matilda's hopes. "It won't do any harm for a volunteer to drive through the streets Miriama might've cut through," he said.

Vincent, who'd just returned and come to join them, put up his hand. "I can do it." His blond hair—like gilt when in the sunlight—was wind tousled and messier than it ever was in the publicity stills used for the family charity or his business interests. "My car's got those special high beams and they cut pretty well through the dark."

"I'll go with Vincent," his search partner said, her face seamed with life but her gaze alert. "Better to have two sets of eyes than one."

Anahera smiled tightly at Vincent as he moved past her, thinking that this wasn't how she'd wanted to run into her former schoolmate again, but Vincent didn't even seem to see her. Likely, he was already planning his route for maximum coverage. That was Vincent for you—he'd been the cleverest of them all. Always turned in the cleanest reports, had the most thoughtfully worked-out equations.

It was a wonder they'd all liked him as much as they had. But Vincent had a way about him—he was so quietly easygoing that he could fit into almost any environment and, as a friend, he was reliable. Back when they were eleven, before he was sent to boarding school, he'd once lent Anahera a copy of his completed math homework, after a night when she simply hadn't been able to concentrate because her parents were screaming at each other.

She'd gone out to sit on the beach in an effort to find focus, but it turned out she'd brought the screaming with her, her head full of violence. In the end, she'd settled in a spot on the cliffs from where she could watch the waves come in and stayed there till dawn. Maybe Miriama'd had one of those days, too; maybe she was just sitting somewhere, waiting for dawn to come.

"Let me have a look at that list of search areas," the cop said to Matilda. After scanning it, he began to hand out more assignments, covering little-used tracks and areas of the town that Nikau had marked as unassigned. "If I've given any of you an area you're unfamiliar with, speak up now. It's no good to Miriama if you're stumbling around."

Two groups spoke up, ended up swapping tasks.

"You're the only person without a partner except for me," he said to Anahera, then subtly angled his head in the direction of the doorway.

She went with him after catching the quick flick of his gaze toward where Matilda was speaking to another searcher. The cop wanted them out of earshot of the older woman. "What?" she said quietly once they'd moved.

"I have to make a call, then I'm going to check out that unofficial dumpsite outside of town. You happy to come along?"

Anahera's stomach clenched, but she nodded. "I'm surprised the dump's still there," she said after the two of them were back in his SUV. "I know when I left, the town busybodies were up in arms about it for the millionth time." As an adult, she could see their point; that particular area was an ugly blight on an otherwise striking landscape.

So, for that matter, was Nikau's house, which they passed on the way out of town. What the hell was he up to?

"It pisses off his ex's new husband," the cop said quietly, even though she hadn't spoken aloud. "The new husband owns four plots around Nik's place that he's trying to sell."

Anahera went motionless; she'd have to be careful around this man. She'd left her past behind in London and didn't intend for it to follow her here. That part of her life was done and would stay in the hole in which she'd buried it, the same hole that held Edward's lifeless body.

## 13

"Nikau did always know how to hold a grudge." Anahera had once accidentally kicked over his sandcastle when they were five or six. He hadn't forgiven her for two months.

"As for the dump," the cop added, "the business council hired a waste removal company to clean it up a few years back, but people apparently took that as an invitation to dump even more rubbish. Now the council's trying to get in touch with the owner of the land with the aim of buying it so the town can do something with it that'll stop the dumping for good."

Anahera shook her head. "Affordability aside, the land's too far out to be useful for any kind of a public building." Some Golden Cove residents might live deep in the darkness of the trees, but all essential services were centralized. It was the only way such a small and remote settlement could work.

"There's talk of establishing a greenhouse." The cop drove through the night with an unsmiling concentration that told her he missed nothing. "Area already has a few small organic growers who are starting to do well, and they've indicated an interest in possibly helping to finance the purchase."

The side of Anahera's face burned, as if she'd taken a brutal backhand to the cheek. When had that happened? Organic produce from Golden Cove? But the reality was, she'd been away a long time. Time didn't stand still even in the Cove. And Josie couldn't tell her everything. "Are they locals?" she asked. "The organic growers?"

"One of them is—Susan Perdue."

Anahera vaguely remembered Susan; born in a different generation, the other woman had already been a mother of two by the time Anahera left town. "Her kids must be teenagers by now."

"Fourteen and sixteen."

Spotting an unexpected light through the trees by the side of the road, Anahera leaned forward. "Isn't that the old Baxter place?"

"Shane Hennessey's father inherited it, but he wanted nothing to do with it. Shane's got it now."

"Right, I remember. Josie mentioned it when he first moved in."

Instead of driving past, the cop turned into the driveway of what Anahera remembered as a ramshackle property surrounded by out-of-control grass.

"Shane doesn't always answer his phone. Doesn't like to be interrupted when he's working."

Though the cop's voice held no judgment, Anahera detected what she thought was a note of cynicism underneath. Curious about the new owner, she stepped out of the vehicle after Will brought it to a stop. The old place had definitely been spruced up and was unexpectedly charming now, complete with white paint and leadlight windows instead of the broken and gaping holes of her childhood.

The house also featured a new porch stocked with a number of whitewashed rocking chairs. Nubile young women occupied two of those chairs.

"Oh, hello," one said in a cheerful way. "Shane's writing, so he can't see you right now. But we'd be happy to visit."

"Interrupt him," the cop said in such a flat tone that the cheerful girl blanched. "This is important."

The girls looked at one another at this departure from the script.

When neither made a move to enter the house, Will did so himself. Staying outside, Anahera took in the girls in their short shorts and flannel shirts. One was blonde and perky, the other dark eyed and sensuous with a stud in her eyebrow, but they both had the dewy-eyed look of creatures who hadn't yet had the shine rubbed off them. Nineteen, twenty at the most. "You're Shane's students?"

The blonde nodded, while the dark-eyed one gave Anahera an assessing look—as if checking out the competition. That one was tough and far more likely to survive life than the blonde bunny. Unless, of course, the bunny was fortunate enough to find someone who wanted to preserve her wide-eyed naïveté.

"We're so lucky." The bunny actually pressed her hands together in delight. "Shane is one of the most well-known novelists in the world and we get to have a residence with him." Joy sparking off every word. "My book's taking shape in ways I could've never imagined."

A thirty-something man followed Will out onto the porch before Anahera could respond. All messed-up black hair and stubble along his jaw, Shane Hennessey was the epitome of the suffering artist. He had soft full lips, flawless skin the color of cream, a height two or three inches under the cop's, and a build that said there was muscle beneath his ragged jeans and black shirt—a shirt he wore with the sleeves shoved carelessly up to his elbows. Only it wasn't careless. He was a man who knew he was good-looking and who took full advantage of it.

Edward had been like that, though it had taken her far too long to see the truth.

"I'm sorry, Will," the suffering artist said in an Irish accent so beautiful it couldn't be real, even as his eyes scanned Anahera then came back for a second look; obviously she'd fulfilled a list of basic prerequisites and deserved closer inspection. "I've been consumed by my characters since lunch—the girls can tell you. I wouldn't know if a flying pig went past, much less some local girl."

Anahera saw Will's face tense, his shoulders bunch. "Let's go," she said to him before he punched the pretentious asshole. "We have to check the other places."

A curt nod, but he wasn't done. "Did either of you see Miriama run past here today?" he asked the two groupies.

The girls shook their heads. Then they looked as one toward Shane Hennessey, as if waiting for him to tell them what to do next.

Anahera's skin prickled.

She was glad to get out of there. "Is it always like that?" she asked after they'd pulled out of the drive and were back on their way to the dump. "Him with a harem?"

"I have it on good authority that the people who win Shane's residencies are always young, female, and pretty. Such a strange coincidence."

Anahera snorted. "You have a gift for understatement, cop."

He didn't reply, the lights of his SUV cutting through the inky blackness in front of them as he slowed down just before the ragged dirt track that led to the cleared but never developed patch of land that had become a dumping ground.

The tourists never saw this part of Golden Cove, never glimpsed the slick black rubbish bags torn open by feral cats, never had any idea of the abandoned couches and—"Is that a refrigerator?" Fury punched through her. "Even the worst asshole knows to take off the doors before dumping a fridge."

Face grim, the cop brought his vehicle to a halt on the edge of the dump. "That wasn't here last time I did a patrol—which was yesterday, just before I saw you on the road. I've got tools in the back." Unsaid were the words that he'd take care of it before they left.

But first, they had to search for Miriama. That was when Anahera had a horrible thought. Heart thumping, she walked through the scattered debris to that fridge that hadn't been there yesterday and that had appeared right when a girl had gone missing.

"Wait," the cop said. "We need to preserve evidence if—" Leaving the rest of the chilling words unspoken, he grabbed a pair of thin rubber gloves from the kit he had in the back of the SUV.

Anahera's pulse thundered as he closed the distance to the fridge, images of Miriama's sunny smile playing across her mind. *Please, God, if you have any mercy at all, don't let her be there in the cold and the dark.* Around her, the dump emanated a sickly sweet smell that would usually turn her stomach, but at that instant, all she could see was the scratched white of that dented fridge.

"Keep the beam of your flashlight on the edge of the door." Again, the cop didn't say what they were both thinking: that if Miriama was in there, she was dead. She'd been gone too long and there wasn't much air inside one of those things.

# 14

Not reaching for the handle—saving any prints that might be there—the cop put his gloved hands carefully on the bottom edge of the door and managed to break the seal. Anahera's heart slammed like a bass drum as the door swung open . . .

To reveal emptiness.

Exhaling in a harsh rush, she bent down, her hands pressed against her knees. "Shit," she said. *"Shit."* It was sheer relief that made her muscles tremble, mixed in with a great big dose of adrenaline.

Rising, the cop opened the freezer compartment, and she wondered what he was looking for—it was hardly as if you could fit a woman inside there. An instant later, she realized you *could* fit a head or an arm or a foot and fuck, why was she thinking like that? Probably because she was with a cop who thought like that. And it made her wonder what he'd seen that he knew that such horror was possible.

"I'll detach the doors before we leave," he said when the freezer section proved thankfully empty except for an abandoned bag of peas. "We have to work the site in a grid. We'll start from the car and walk straight through a foot apart from each other, then back until we've covered the entire area."

Anahera followed him to the starting point and they began their methodical search. When his flashlight beam swung across the bleached white of bones, they both froze, but it turned out to be the carcass of a long-dead cat.

Its bones glinted in the flashlight beam, tiny and perfect.

They carried on. At least there hadn't been any blood. Anahera tried not to think of another time when she'd found a body. There had been blood then, old and congealed and drying blood. And other things.

Three days dead was a long time in summer.

"What are you expecting to find?" she asked when they turned to retrace their path.

"Nothing," he said. "A cop who expects things is a cop who misses what's right in front of him. But even if we don't find Miriama, if we locate some trace of her—a shoe, the iPod, a piece of fabric from her clothes—it would give us a direction and a place to concentrate the search."

Anahera nodded and they carried on, piece by piece by piece by piece. Three long hours later, they were at the SUV and had found nothing. Not saying a word, the cop went to the back of the vehicle and grabbed his tools. She trained light on the fridge so he could see what he was doing. It didn't take him long to dismantle the doors from the fridge so that no inquisitive kid or animal could get stuck inside.

That done, he trained the beam of his own flashlight on what turned out to be a serial number, snapping a photo of that with his phone.

Dawn was still four hours off when Will and Anahera arrived at the fire station. Nikau was the only one there. "I sent Mattie home," he said. "One of the other women went with her and knows to stay the night. That fuckwit she's hooked up with isn't exactly going to be any help."

Will nodded. "The search crews find anything?"

"No. I told everyone to go home, come back when it's light. No use going over and over the same areas in the dark."

"I've called in the situation," Will said, having taken care of that prior to heading for the dump. "We're not going to get any air support. They've got two missing children just outside Greymouth." An adult woman missing less than twenty-four hours couldn't compare to two children under ten who hadn't been seen since they left school the previous day. It didn't matter what Will's gut said about Miriama being in serious trouble.

"Daniel has a helicopter," Nikau bit out with a curl of his lip. "Maybe if you ask, his lordship will deign to help."

"Grab some shut-eye, Nik." Engaging the other man in a conversation that involved Daniel would never have a good outcome. "I'll need you at full capacity come morning."

Teeth gritted and blood in his eye, Nikau said a terse good night before leaving to walk home.

Anahera didn't speak until Nikau was out of earshot. "You're planning to talk to Daniel, aren't you?"

Glancing at his watch, the cop said, "Might as well wait till morning now. Probably have a better chance of getting his cooperation if I don't wake him up at two a.m."

"Daniel wasn't always an ass," Anahera felt obliged to say. "If Nik's your only source on him, well, they have a history . . ."

"No. I've had dealings with Mr. May myself." He left it at that, and she knew she'd get nothing if she attempted to dig deeper.

Hard gray eyes met hers. "I'll drop you home, but I need to detour to the station first and send through an information request to Miriama's cell phone provider."

"To check if her phone is still active?"

"Or when it was last active," Will said. "I assume you want to help with the search in the morning?"

"Of course." She wouldn't be able to breathe easy knowing Miriama was out there alone, likely hurt. "What will you be doing?"

"The same thing." The cop began to turn off the fire station's internal lighting. "And hope we find some small fragment of her. Because even in the dark, you can't miss an entire woman."

The last light went out.

# 15

Will drove up to the May estate twenty minutes before dawn, while the sky was steel gray brushed with smoke at the edges. He wanted to talk to Daniel before light broke over the horizon, so that if the other man agreed, they could get the chopper up in the air as quickly as possible.

If Daniel turned him down, Will had a few other strings he could tug, a few friends who'd step into the breach; the problem was, most of them didn't live near the coast. It'd take time for them to fly here, and every instinct he had told him time was critical. He didn't listen to the voice that said it was already too late.

Reaching the gate at the start of the long drive that led up to the house, he pushed the buzzer twice in a row. The male voice that came on was wide-awake and distinctly irritated. "No, this isn't a public road and no, you can't hike through."

"Mr. May," Will said before Daniel could hang up, "it's Detective Gallagher. I need to speak to you on an urgent matter."

A little to his surprise, the electronic gate began to draw back at once. He waited only until it had pulled back enough to allow his vehicle through.

Like all the properties in this area, the estate was surrounded by rich native ferns and ancient trees that blocked out the sunlight to form a lush green atmosphere reminiscent of a primeval rain forest. With dawn on the horizon, everything was soft and misty and colored in myriad tones of gray.

It was eerie, he supposed, but there was also a stark beauty to it as long as you knew that this landscape could kill you if you weren't careful.

The house that appeared out of the gray-shrouded green wasn't the showy monstrosity you might expect from a man who liked to flash his wealth, but then Daniel May hadn't built it; the house had been built by his parents, who'd both passed on a few years back within twelve months of each other. A graceful architectural creation constructed of glass and wood that had been polished to a honeyed shine, it rose just high enough above the treeline that, from the top of the house, you could see the ocean. Otherwise, it was designed to blend into the landscape.

The helicopter pad was set to the right of the property, some distance from the house itself. In between, there was a tennis court and a swimming pool. A guesthouse the size of an average family home sat to the left of the main house. None of these things on their own would've made Daniel a pariah in town; the Baker family had the same kind of wealth, though from a different source, and they were well liked. It wasn't money that divided Daniel from the others in Golden Cove, it was Daniel himself.

Parking his vehicle, Will got out. Daniel had already stepped out of the house and was walking toward him, a slender man of about six-two with shoulder-length brown hair tied back in a queue. His features were fine, his ethnicity difficult to pinpoint. According to the locals, Daniel's mother had been Korean, his father white—of English descent. May Senior had apparently been very proud that the family history could be traced all the way back to the first settlers in this region.

Despite the early hour, Daniel was dressed in crisp black pants and a raspberry pink shirt. The color should've looked ridiculous on a grown man, but somehow, Daniel pulled it off. "What's this about?" he asked, a frown between his brows and a steaming mug of coffee in one hand. "Does it have anything to do with all those flashlights I saw on the beach last night?"

Will didn't particularly like being talked to as if he was the hired help, but as he needed the man's assistance, he decided to keep it civil. "Miriama is missing."

"Missing?" Daniel took a sip of his coffee, not making any move to offer Will a cup. "Are you sure she hasn't just taken off to see the sights somewhere else? The girl's too beautiful to be happy stuck in a dead-end town."

"She went missing while out for a run." Will's temper had never been a hot thing of rage and fury . . . not until the night of the fire. It had cooled again in the aftermath, and he could handle Daniel's smug sense of superiority without losing control. "I came to ask if you'd help with an aerial search."

"I've got meetings out of town today. What about the police helicopters?"

"There's another ongoing case involving children." He'd checked in with his commander, been told the choppers would be going up again at first light, along with a massive army of search volunteers. Will could be frustrated with the allocation of resources while agreeing with them—the children had to be a priority.

"If you won't help, just say so. I'll have to call in private aerial teams from outside and they'll take time getting here."

He thought it was the word "outside" that did it—Daniel might turn up his nose at the town, snubbing all the social events to which he was invited and making it clear he didn't think most of the residents were fit to lick his boots, but he also considered himself the most important man in Golden Cove. It was *his* town; he couldn't stomach the idea of outsiders coming in and taking over.

That, of course, was part of his problem with Will. Daniel had expected Will to fall in line. His first month here, Will had accepted a dinner invitation from Daniel and his sulky-faced wife. In a place this small and remote, the local cop had to make an effort to build bonds no matter his own desire to keep a distance.

It had been toward the end of the night, as Daniel walked him to his vehicle, that the other man had made it clear he expected Will to keep him informed of everything that went on in Golden Cove. "You understand?" he'd said in that supercilious master-to-servant tone. "This is my town and

I like to keep my finger on the pulse. You'll find I'm a generous man to those who please me."

Will had simply said, "I'll pretend I didn't hear that," and left.

Two days later, he'd received a call from a friendly senior officer who'd told him to watch his back. Daniel, it turned out, had tried to get Will fired. "Just be careful," the older man had said. "May might live in Golden Cove, but he has connections everywhere."

Now the self-professed Lord of Golden Cove grimaced. "I'll take up the chopper." A pause before he added, "I'll need a spotter. Might as well be you if you're ready to go up."

Will looked at the horizon through the breaks in the trees, saw the first blazing edge of daybreak. "I'll call, inform the rest of the search party." While he did that, Daniel went back inside the house to tell his wife his plans and to inform his secretary that he'd be late.

"Nik," Will said when the call was answered, "I need you to run the entire ground operation for the time being. Go back over all the areas we did last night, search deeper where you can, and don't forget the dump and other outlying areas."

"No problem."

Will stared out at the trees backlit in orange flame by the rising sun. "And spread the word that I want to know if people saw anything even vaguely related yesterday afternoon." Will needed a starting point to begin the investigation—a piece of Miriama's clothing, a description of a stranger in town, a report of a local seen with Miriama, *something*.

"Where are you?"

"I'm going up with Daniel."

A taut silence, followed by, "I'll make sure the others know, so they can signal if they spot something on the ground that could do with a bird's-eye view."

"I'm not sure what the cellular reception will be like in the chopper," Will said, "but if you have a major discovery, get the people on the beach to all wave. It'll be easy to spot that with how low we'll be flying."

"You'll have a signal."

It was only after the other man hung up that Will wondered why Nikau was so certain about the cell signal. He knew damn well that Nik wouldn't have gone up with Daniel, and since Daniel was the only one who flew the sleek black machine . . .

*Right.*

It had to be Keira who'd contacted her ex-husband from the chopper. Either she'd done it at Daniel's behest, or she'd sneakily messaged Nikau while her husband was busy at the controls. Neither sounded particularly good for Nikau's already screwed-up head.

Daniel reappeared, having changed into jeans and a long-sleeved white shirt that was probably worth five times the monthly salary of most of the people in town. Neither one of them said a word as they headed to the chopper. Will had already grabbed the binoculars he kept in the SUV—in a place with terrain this rugged, it paid to have them handy.

Once inside the helicopter, he pulled on the headset that would allow him to talk to Daniel, then asked the other man to skim along the coastline first, before going inland and over the areas where Miriama was most likely to have run.

The sun's rays broke completely through the last of the mist as they rose into the air. Will glimpsed a small and curvy woman with blonde-streaked brown hair on the verandah of the estate house, her elegantly boned face lifted to watch the chopper and her hands gripping the railing. She was wearing a red negligee and, despite their distance from the house, the wind from the chopper blades pasted the silk and lace of it against her body, outlining a shape that had driven many a man to his knees.

Then the chopper was up and at an angle that made it impossible to see Keira May any longer. Dismissing Daniel's wife and Nikau's obsession, Will raised the binoculars to his eyes and began to scan the landscape. It looked even more unforgiving from up here. Serrated black rocks that thrust up from the sand in huge broken shards, foaming water that took no prisoners, and a wilderness so tangled and thick that it was difficult to see beneath the canopy.

Daniel went down low without prompting, low enough to give Will the best possible chance of spotting a woman lying injured below. The one thing in their favor was Miriama's bright choice of running gear.

"Did you try on the other side of the whirlpool?"

Will didn't look away from the trees below, intent on spotting even a hint of hot pink or orange. "What's on the other side of the whirlpool?"

"A kind of cave formed by the way the rocks fell there," the other man said, his voice echoing through the headphones. "We used to hang out in it as teenagers—it's safe at low tide."

Daniel angled the chopper back over a particularly dense patch of trees so Will could take a second look. "There's a running trail right above the cave that hardly anyone uses. It was totally overgrown the last time I over-flew it, but Miriama likes to run and she's good at it. Maybe she went there—it's definitely a more challenging track."

Will calculated how long Miriama would've had to run to get to that spot, knew it was far too long, but they had to check every possible option. Could be she'd been enjoying the run so much she'd gone far beyond her normal distance. "Let's go."

From above, the whirlpool looked like the mouth of hell, spilling and crashing and so dark that it felt as if its depths went on forever. Bones cold with the knowledge that if Miriama had fallen anywhere near the danger-ous spot, she was gone, Will continued to scan through the binoculars.

But if he hadn't known to look for the rock formation that formed a cave, he'd have missed it, it was so well camouflaged to match the neigh-boring rocks. A second later, he realized Daniel wasn't the only one who'd thought of the spot. A male body stood in front of the stone archway, one hand on the rock.

*Nikau.*

Though he looked up at the sound of the chopper, Nikau didn't wave. Instead, he ducked under the stone to disappear inside. "We should focus on the cliffs above," Will said to Daniel. "Nikau can check out the cave."

Fine lines bracketing his mouth, Daniel didn't argue for once. They skimmed along the top edge of the cliffs back to the other side of the whirl-pool and, while most of it was tangled growth that hadn't been disturbed for years, Will did spot what might've been a disturbance in one small section. Using his phone, he asked one of the nearby searchers to have a look.

"Definite signs someone stood or walked through here," the man confirmed. "But it's not churned up like if Miriama went over the edge." A small pause. "Almost as if a pig hunter maybe walked out of the trees behind me and came to stand here, look at the view."

"Okay, leave it as it is," Will said. "I want to have a look myself."

Hanging up, Will considered the cave again and frowned. That cave was exactly the kind of secretive and private spot teenagers loved. It should've passed from teenage group to teenage group in a town like this, but for whatever reason, it had been abandoned. Forgotten.

It made him wonder what secrets lay within, what secrets tied Daniel to Nikau, Nikau to Anahera.

# 16

Anahera trudged through the forested track beside Vincent, conscious of the sound of the chopper fading into the distance. Nikau had designated her and Vincent a search team after they were two of the earliest people to turn up at the fire station. Peter Jacobs had also turned up around the same time, but thankfully, Nikau had matched the garage owner with one of the more experienced hunters.

"You look bad, Vincent." Always his full name or Vin, never Vinnie; he simply wouldn't respond to anyone who tried to call him that. "Do you know Miriama well?"

"I love my coffee, you know that." A self-deprecating smile that didn't reach the arresting tawny shade of his eyes. "When I'm in Golden Cove and working from home, I see her pretty much every morning and every afternoon. She always has that smile. So bright. So much life to her."

Anahera thought again of the lovely young creature she'd met and felt a shivering chill within. The world had a way of crushing things that were beautiful and so bright that they glowed. "Is there any chance she might've just taken off?"

"Matilda says all her stuff is still in her room. Her wallet, her favorite jeans. She only took her phone and the iPod—just what she normally takes on a run."

Anahera had been afraid that would be the answer. She looked desperately into the trees, in the hope she might magically spot a flash of cheerful orange or brilliant pink. But there was only verdant green and healthy brown, the curling fern fronds delicately lit by the morning sunlight that speared through the canopy.

She'd missed this so much, this primeval landscape unlike any other place on Earth, but she knew the beauty around her could be deadly. There'd been more than one lost hiker over the years she'd lived in Golden Cove. The tourists came, saw the initially unthreatening lushness of the bush and didn't listen to warnings to be careful, to stick strictly to the marked paths.

They'd go off the track "just a little" to take a photograph or chase a native bird, and the next thing they knew, they'd be turned around and scared and unable to find their way back out through the dense growth. If the hikers had been smart and filed a plan with the town's tourism office, then a search would be mounted as soon as they didn't show up at the appointed time. But too many weren't smart.

By luck, most had stumbled out or been found by locals who lived wild.

At least three hadn't. All over the course of a single hot summer. And all young women from distant corners of the world.

Their bodies had also never been found—once this landscape took you, it held you close. In fact, the only evidence the first had even been in Golden Cove was a distinctive water bottle plastered with stickers from around the world. It had been found because of a search for another hiker who'd gone missing and who *had* filed a plan for her hike.

Only days later, a local hunter helping with the search had found a backpack half-buried in a stream; it was proved to belong to the second missing woman, the one whose failure to return from the bush had initiated the search.

At the time, the theory was the two must've become either injured or lost. A tragedy but these things happened in a country with such dense forests. The weather didn't help. Like today—it seemed so sunny, but according to the weather forecast, a storm was building over the ocean. It would turn dark and wet and cold in a few hours.

Anahera remembered hearing the news about the two missing women, but lost hikers were pretty standard in the region and she'd been a teenager awash in summer.

But the third missing hiker . . . that had ended the sunshine.

The gold identity bracelet found in their teenage hangout, the swarm of police, the beach flapping with crime scene tape, it had brought down the hammer on all their childhoods.

Shaking off the eerie memories she hadn't thought of in over a decade, Anahera glanced at Vincent. "Tell me about Miriama. I knew her as a girl—what's she like as a woman?"

"Hugely talented and with an even bigger heart," Vincent said in that restrained but intense way of his. "I've never seen her not smiling. She lives life like it should be lived—without limits, without trying to shove herself into a predefined box like so many other people. She's real, honest, beautiful in the deepest sense of the word."

Anahera wondered if Vincent was talking about himself and his perfect life with two picture-perfect children and a pedigreed woman who made the perfect partner on the charity circuit. It also seemed as if he was half in love with Miriama—but was that surprising? Miriama had the kind of glow that drew people.

Most of the men in town probably had crushes on her.

"I think we should head right," she said when they came to a fork in the path. According to the quick briefing Nik had given them, that track was rarely used—it was a little bit too uneven to allow for a smooth run—but according to Josie, Miriama had run competitively at high school. "The challenge might've appealed to her."

Vincent nodded and they went single file down the track. It was darker here, the canopy thicker, the bush more dense. It absorbed all sound yet made you feel as if the trees were whispering to one another, talking secrets that humans would never understand. Anahera's calves began to ache after a while, a subtle sign that she wasn't who she'd once been.

Jogging through the streets of her London neighborhood had in no way prepared her for the West Coast. It'd take her body time to remember that this land was in her blood. Which meant the cop had been right to tell her not to assume she could do everything she'd once done—and somehow, that pissed her off.

Poor cop, she thought. He was taking the brunt of all her anger, all her cold fury.

"She wouldn't have gone this deep," Vincent said from behind her, his voice certain. "It's too far for her to have been able to get back before dark and she's smart enough not to try to run these trails after sunset. The visibility just ends—you can't even see your hand in front of your face."

Bowing to his greater current knowledge, Anahera turned and they began to make their way back to the fork, from where they searched the left-hand track before going over an area others had already searched.

But lunchtime came and went, the helicopter landed, and still there was no sign of what had happened to a luminous, laughing girl named Miriama.

# 17

Will rubbed his face as he sat inside the hastily built police station; the place was just big enough for his desk and a filing cabinet. He'd told the searchers to stand down that afternoon, when it became obvious they'd covered every possible area that Miriama could've reached on foot. He'd gone over that suspicious part of the cliffs above the whirlpool, but like the searcher had said, while someone had walked there, there was no sign of anything untoward.

No drag marks, no blood, no clumps torn out in a desperate attempt to grab hold of safety. Nothing but indications of recent passage—the same in the trees behind it. He'd also walked the bush trail that opened up near that spot, but multiple teams of volunteers had already walked through it and there was nothing to see but tamped-down leaf litter.

Will also kept coming around to the fact that Miriama was too smart to have gone that close to the deadly edge above the whirlpool.

He'd known the searchers wouldn't follow his order to stand down, but he'd needed to give it so he'd have a better chance of talking his superiors into treating this as a serious incident.

"Sir," he said down the phone line. "We're now looking at either a drowning—which is unlikely, given how well she knew the area—or an abduction."

"Will, I've run this girl," his commander replied. "She has a history of running away from home."

*Fuck.*

Will had been hoping Miriama's past would slip under the radar. "That was when she was fifteen and her aunt had a boyfriend who took a little too much interest in her." It was Mrs. Keith who'd told him that, after the older woman flagged him down for a visit one day a couple of months ago.

Miriama had run by on the road while the two of them were chatting, and lifted a hand to wave, and Mrs. Keith had said, "Look at her. Like a flower just opening up. Good thing that no-good bastard didn't bruise her."

All Will'd had to do was look at her and she'd given him the full story. "Mattie, she's a sweet woman. A good friend. But she has the worst taste in men." A censorious shake of her head, her jowls trembling. "You'd think she'd have a little more sense after Miriama came to live with her as a wee thing—her mother was Mattie's sister, you know. Went up to the big smoke, made some wrong choices."

A look of true sadness, her eyes an incredibly beautiful blue in the fleshy roundness of her face. "Lovely girl, she was. Overdosed in a motel, poor little Miriama in there with her for more than two days before someone found them." Coughing, she'd taken a drink from the wineglass she kept on the table beside her. "There was no question but that Mattie would take her niece. She'd been trying to get Kahurangi—that was the sister—to send Miriama down here forever."

Another small sip of wine. "You know Mattie's first name is Atarangi," Mrs. Keith had added. "Her ma had a good friend called Matilda, and that's how she got that as a middle name. But you know how it goes with names. For whatever reason, everyone just started using Matilda. It's a shame really. Atarangi's such a pretty name."

Will had sat there on the porch and kept on listening, not because he was particularly interested in gossip or in Matilda's first name, but because he'd already come to understand that Mrs. Keith was lonely. According to Nikau, who sometimes went over to fix up her fence or clean the guttering, she used to walk into town two or three times a week, but she'd gotten too big to move far these days. She'd hired one of the local women to keep her house neat as a pin, and to help with her hair and makeup every morning, but, for the most part, she was confined to the porch where she watched life go by.

And perhaps to the bedroom where she might offer certain intimate services to truckers and forestry workers—or so went the rumors in town. If she did, it was none of Will's business. If it assuaged her loneliness and that of others, so be it. And if the whole thing was just a tale Mrs. Keith fostered to give her life a little excitement, it was a harmless one. Either way, she certainly didn't seem to mind. In fact, from the occasional subtle comment she'd dropped into her conversations with Will, she reveled in her notoriety.

"But," she'd said that day, "Mattie, good soul that she is, is as blind as a bat when it comes to men."

A huff of breath. "Well, you can see how it went. Miriama grew breasts and legs and the useless man Mattie kept around back then started trying to touch her. The girl ended up in Christchurch a few times, trying to get away from him, until poor Mattie finally realized what was happening and kicked him out. She never once took the bastard's side, that's one thing, and it's why Miriama never turned against her. She just can't pick the good ones."

"Be that as it may," Will's commander said in response to his clarification of Miriama's history, "it's a pattern. Can you say definitively that she didn't just hitch a ride out of town?"

Will's free hand curled on the pale wood of his desk. "She was in running gear. No money, no other clothes."

"You know as well as I do that those things can be easily circumvented if she has the right friends," the other man said. "Regardless, there's not much else we can do right now. You've already run a comprehensive ground and aerial search, and you said none of the locals have reported any suspicious activity or people?"

"Yes." He hated to admit it, but the other man was right—there was literally nothing the larger police branches could do that he, with Golden Cove's help, couldn't do himself. "I'm going to work it as a missing person, send out an updated alert." He'd already fired off a request to his fellow officers to be on the lookout for Miriama, and he'd tapped media contacts to get the story what attention he could.

"Now that your search has come up empty," his senior officer said, "I'll have our press team issue a formal media release using the photograph you sent. She's a beauty, so there's a good chance one of the major outlets will pick it up." No cynicism in the other man's voice, just pragmatism. "You might even get nationwide coverage because of this photographic scholarship she's meant to be taking up in a few weeks. If your girl's left the town, someone will report it in."

Hanging up soon afterward, Will considered his next step. Even if Miriama had been the victim of foul play rather than an accident, it didn't immediately follow that there was no hope of finding her alive. Her abductor could be holding her captive, might've incapacitated her so she couldn't try to escape or cry out for help.

Until Will had a body or other incontrovertible evidence of her death, he'd treat her as a missing person. And all missing person investigations began with those closest to the vanished.

He'd already spoken to Matilda and Steve. It was time he sat down properly with Dr. Dominic de Souza.

After sending Anahera and the others home in the early hours of the morning, Will had driven out to the main road and waited. Dominic de Souza's vehicle had appeared approximately twenty-five minutes later; by then, Will had spoken to the family who'd asked the young doctor to come out to their remote property and learned it was the mother who'd made the call—and that she'd done it just after the six o'clock news began on TV.

Approximately fifteen minutes after Tania Meikle saw Miriama run by.

So the doctor *did* have a small window of time where he could've done something to his girlfriend—except that Will had spoken on the phone to Mrs. Keith earlier in the night. She'd been adamant she'd seen Dominic's car drive by around 6:10, 6:12 at the latest. Which meant he must've left immediately after the call.

It further compressed his unaccounted-for time. It took a lot longer than a few minutes to subdue or hurt a strong young woman, dump or hide her body, then change clothes to obscure any blood evidence. That's after Dominic would've had to track her down. Usually, the boyfriend was the lead suspect, but Dominic's alibi appeared solid; he'd also broken down totally when Will told him the news.

Fear and shock could be faked, but Will was no first-year cadet. Dominic's response had been pure, naked emotion. The other man was devastated. He also had no marks or scratches on his arms or face—and Miriama would've fought.

"I don't know what to do," Dominic said when he opened the clinic door to Will, the brown of his irises startling against the bloodshot whites of his eyes and his jaw dark with stubble. "Nikau says I shouldn't be stumbling around out there, that I should sit here and think of anything Miri might've said that could help find her."

Will nodded, aware Dominic wasn't much of an outdoorsman, and with his head so screwed up right now, he'd be more liability than help. "Can we talk?"

"Yeah, sure." Looking lost, the doctor led him inside into the examination room. Will took a seat in the patient chair, let Dominic sink into the doctor's chair, in the hope the familiar surroundings would keep him calm.

The other man's white shirt was wrinkled, his black pants the same. It might've been the same outfit he'd been wearing when Will stopped him on the road in the early morning darkness, but it was hard to tell—Dominic wore the same thing every day to work, almost like a uniform. "When was the last time you saw Miriama?"

"Lunch yesterday." Dominic leaned forward to brace his forearms on his thighs, his skin holding a warm depth of color.

Evelyn Triskell had—unbidden—shared that Dominic's father was Indian, his mother Māori from one of the smaller North Island *iwi*. It was difficult to tell which culture held sway in Dominic; he was oddly colorless in his personality for a man who came from two such old and rich cultures.

"I went to the café," the doctor added, "and asked Josie if I could steal Miri for an hour. It wasn't so busy—it isn't this time of year—and Josie had just come in after having the morning off."

Will let Dominic ramble; at least the man was coherent this time around.

"Anyway, Josie said yes, even said it didn't matter if we were a little late back. She was kind of teasing us about not getting caught making out." He managed a shaky smile. "I'd prepared us a picnic basket with sandwiches and those tiny quiche things from the supermarket deli that Miri likes"—a sudden, harsh sob before he regained control of himself—"and we went to the eastern beach outlook with the little seat."

"Sounds like a nice date."

Dominic pushed up his glasses. "I never want her to regret being with me. I always want her to feel like she's the most wonderful thing in my life."

"How was her mood?"

"Good. Happy. She liked the picnic and she ate three of the quiches." Shoving his hands through the tangled black strands of his hair, he stared down at the hard-wearing beige carpet. "She was *so* happy, so bright. I kissed her and she was smiling and I felt like she was making me bright like her."

Will took in the other man's trembling frame and put a hand on his shoulder. "Dominic, you can't panic," he said, knowing he was asking the near impossible. "We don't know anything yet."

"Right." It was a wet sound. "Right. I have to keep telling myself that." Raising his head, he said, "I don't know what else I can tell you. I've been wracking my brain trying to figure out something that might help."

Will released Dominic's shoulder. "How about her upcoming move to Wellington to study? Have you two discussed it?"

"Sure. We've worked it out so she'll come home during the holidays, and I'll fly up to see her some weekends. We know it'll be hard, but we're serious about making it work." He swallowed. "I'm so proud of her for winning that internship."

"Were there any hard feelings about that? I know Kyle Baker was also on the short list." A bit of a town golden boy, Vincent's younger brother had been the favorite going in.

Dominic's face tightened. "That twat Kyle tried to make it seem like Miri got it because of her looks, but her talent outstrips his by a mile. And the judges were all outsiders—they weren't biased in favor of Kyle just because everyone thinks he's the great promise of this town, the shining star who can do no wrong."

Will had seen that particular bias in action; he'd caught Kyle and another nineteen-year-old tagging a building, both with spray cans in hand. The townspeople had blamed the other boy for leading Kyle astray, asked Will to be lenient so Kyle wouldn't end up with a record that might blight his future.

Will had given both young males a warning that there would be no second chance. Kyle had been remorseful, had even shut up his mate when the other boy went to mouth off. He definitely hadn't come across as entitled or a brat, but that could simply mean he knew how to work people in authority. Or it could be that Dominic disliked him for giving Miriama such stiff competition. "Anyone else ever make Miriama uncomfortable?"

Dominic stared down at the carpet with unmoving focus. "You know how men look at her. I got used to that—had to if I wanted to be with her, you know?—but I think it bothers her sometimes. Nikau Martin stares at her all the fucking time." A grimace. "He thinks he can get any woman he wants, but Miriama isn't interested. She isn't into anger or bitterness."

Will's mind flashed back to the other night in the pub and Nikau's unhidden—some might say predatory—interest. Dominic was also right about the effect Miriama had on most of the men in this town. It was possible she'd drawn the attention of the wrong man without realizing it. And small as Golden Cove was, she probably knew that man and wouldn't have felt any sense of danger if approached.

But there were other possibilities and he'd be a bad cop if he ignored them. No one had ever called him that, not even when his mistakes had led to two deaths. Will's policework had been stellar; it was his understanding of human nature that had let him down. This time around, he'd dig down to the bone and tear apart shields until he knew every secret in this town.

# 18

"Have you two recently had a fight?"

Dominic's head jerked up, shoulders knotting. "I'd *never* hurt her!"

"I'm not accusing you of anything," Will said. "I'm wondering if Miriama is the kind of woman who might've taken off to teach you a lesson."

Frown digging into his forehead, Dominic shook his head. "No," he said. "That's one of the things I love most about her—she's straight-up honest." He dropped his eyes to the carpet again, shoulders going limp. "I've never had to worry about lies with my Miri. If she's mad at me, she just tells me to go take a hike. She'd never just run away and make me worry. And she wouldn't make her aunt worry."

Looking up, Dominic exhaled and the air came out in a tremor. "She's tight with Josie at the café, too, and with Josie so close to her due date, Miri wouldn't want to cause her any kind of stress. She's even been talking about learning to knit so she can make socks for the baby."

All of that meshed with what Will knew of Miriama. "Is there anything else you think I should know? It doesn't matter if it's a minor detail."

"I've never felt so useless," the doctor said softly. "My parents are so proud of me for being so educated, but what use are my degrees now? I know nothing about how to search for someone in the bush. Nik and the others, they're out there looking for her and I'm sitting in here safe and warm and doing nothing to help."

"You're helping by speaking to me." Will was worried about Dominic's mental state. As far as he knew, Dominic de Souza had no other family in town. He'd only taken up the position as the town's GP a year earlier, after the previous doctor retired. "I have one more question."

Head still hanging low and his hair falling forward, the doctor took off his glasses and said, "What?" It was a soft, jagged, broken statement.

"How long have you and Miriama been going out?" Will tried to keep his tone bland, not wanting to trigger the other man's volatile emotions. "Was she going out with anyone else before you?"

"We had our three-month anniversary a week ago. I fell in love with her the first time I saw her, but it took me more than half a year to work up the guts to approach her—I mean, she was so young. I still can't believe she's only nineteen and a half now, she's so strong, knows exactly what she wants."

The other man put his glasses back on. "Six more months, I said to her at lunch. Then she'll be twenty and I won't feel like such a cradle-robber." Shoving his hands through his hair again, he got up and began to pace around the room. "She said no the first two times I asked her out, but I decided to try again a few months ago. When she said yes, I thought I was dreaming."

Stopping by his desk, he stared out the window. "I think she was going out with someone before me, but I don't know who. I'm pretty sure it was a man outside the Cove—she used to disappear for whole weekends and come back all smiley. But they must've broken up . . . And she finally saw me."

Will left the clinic soon afterward, stopping outside to make a call to Pastor Mark. "Dr. de Souza," he said, "could do with someone sitting with him."

As he'd expected, the elderly man was ready to help at once.

After making sure the pastor had a way to get to the clinic, Will drove to the fire station under a sky that had thickened with gray while he'd been with Dominic—what little sunlight that got through was weak. He found Matilda pouring mugs of hot coffee for the volunteers who'd come in for a break. One look at their faces and he knew the news wasn't good.

Matilda gave him a trembling smile when he stopped by the coffee station. "They haven't found anything," she said, and the words were hopeful.

Will understood why she was happy, but he couldn't agree with her. Especially not with rain forecast for this afternoon. If Miriama *was* lying hurt somewhere, the cold and wet could push her body dangerously close to fatal exposure.

Going to check the map someone had pinned to the wall next to the whiteboard, he ran his eyes over the areas marked with double *X*s, meaning they'd been searched twice. "Has anyone gone out here?" He directed the question at an experienced hunter who lived outside of town, tapping his finger on an area that wasn't anywhere near where Miriama had been seen, but that was a favorite hangout for the town's younger people.

There was a faint possibility that Miriama had met up with a friend and headed that way for a short period, only for something to go wrong. Bad enough that her friend hadn't reported it. He knew he was reaching, but they had to be sure.

The hunter looked at the spot Will had indicated, nodded. "Yeah, we should check it out. Might be she got drunk and is just sleeping it off there." He said the words loud enough to reach Matilda, and Will realized the heavily bearded male was trying to comfort the woman.

But after the volunteers got back in their vehicles and headed out toward their target locations, Matilda shook her head. "Miriama wouldn't do that. My girl doesn't drink that way—I always used to worry she'd get bored and be drawn into the drugs and drinking, like so many of the kids in this town, but Miriama, she's always had big dreams."

Taking a seat, her hands tight around a mug of coffee, Matilda kept on talking. "Half the time as a child, she had her head in the clouds, dreaming of all the places she wanted to see in the world. She even kept a little notebook full of pictures she'd cut out of old magazines—the Eiffel Tower, the pyramids, Uluru . . ."

Matilda's smile was fierce with belief, with hope. "I still have that notebook. I'm going to put it in her bag as a surprise when she leaves Golden

Cove for the internship. My girl has so much talent—it'll take her all over the world, to every one of those places in her little notebook."

Will sat down on a hard plastic chair beside Matilda. "I need to ask you some questions."

Wild eyes, a face going white under the brown of her skin.

"I don't know anything," he said at once. "But while Nik leads the search, I want to check other avenues. Just in case."

Matilda shoved her untouched mug of coffee into Will's hands. "I make good coffee."

He took a sip to keep things as normal as he could before he began to speak. "Here's the thing, Matilda," he said quietly. "Miriama is a beautiful young woman, and while we like to think of our country as a safe place in comparison to the rest of the world, we have our predators."

He'd been worried his plain speaking would further rattle Matilda, but she squared her shoulders and looked him straight in the eye. "You're taking this seriously," she said. "You're not treating her like a stupid nineteen-year-old who couldn't be bothered to tell her auntie she was taking off."

"That's not the girl I know." Will maintained the eye contact. "I know she ran away as a child, but she had her reasons."

Matilda's hands fisted in her lap. "My fault," she said. "But the sweet girl's never blamed me for it. She's always had such *aroha* in her heart."

"How friendly would Miriama be toward a stranger?" he asked, staying away from the topic of locals for now. "I've seen Cove residents pick up hitchhikers without thinking twice about it. And most people around here are used to helping tourists—would she?"

Matilda nodded slowly. "A normal tourist who came into the café or maybe stopped her on the main street," she said, "yes, Miriama would help."

Will nodded and took another drink to show Matilda he was listening, that he was present. He'd had to ask, but he wasn't truly concerned about the tourist angle; had any strangers been spotted in town, Will would've been told within an hour of Miriama's disappearance. The locals liked the money the tourists brought in, but they also never forgot that these were outsiders.

Mrs. Keith would've definitely noticed an unfamiliar vehicle. But, to be safe, he'd also check with the bus that came through Golden Cove twice a day, in case they'd dropped off a passenger in town. He wasn't expecting a positive answer. The bus stop was in the middle of town, right in front of the tourist center—a new face would've been noticed and welcomed, especially with everyone having been rumbling about how few tourists they'd had recently, with the weather so changeable.

"But," Matilda continued, "I don't think she would stop if an outsider pulled up next to her while she was running on the road, or if they flagged her down on the beach." She rubbed at her wet cheeks, her tears silent and slow. "You know when those three hikers disappeared, one after the other, everyone thought they'd just been dumb, walked into the bush expecting it to be like some gentle afternoon walk."

The latter was a continuing problem throughout the country—people saw the stunning landscape and wanted to explore it. What they didn't understand was that the beauty had teeth—you had to be ready to handle sudden cold and rain and hail, tracks without guardrails, and isolated areas where you might be the only human being for miles in every direction.

"That was what, fifteen years ago?" Will, a wet-behind-the-ears probationary constable at the time, had been pulled into the search effort as a result of his climbing and hiking experience in the region.

He could clearly remember the television spots about irresponsible campers and trekkers leading to huge search-and-rescue costs; it had been one of those things that became a minor media sensation because the political parties had weighed in with opposing views.

Lost in the noise had been the failure of the search effort. "They never found the missing hikers, did they?"

"They were all women." Matilda's voice was raspy.

Will's skin prickled, a ghost running her fingers across his nape.

# 19

"I never heard that it was considered anything but coincidence and bad decision-making."

"The police never said it out loud," Matilda replied. "Not in public anyway. But the man I was seeing at the time, he was a junior detective. Probably one of the few good men I've ever dated." A pause that hung in the air.

Regret, Will realized, had a taste. Poignant and acrid.

"Anyway," Matilda continued after a jerky inhale, "he let it slip that the cops weren't sure it was all accidental. Three women walked into the bush off Golden Cove over a single summer and never came out. They got especially worried after the dogs and the searchers and the hunters never even found one body. Not then. Not since."

If Matilda was right, the theory had been kept very quiet. Not one of his senior officers had ever mentioned the possibility of a human predator. Making a mental note to talk to the detectives involved, he said, "Did the investigators have a specific theory?"

Matilda nodded. "Maybe a serial rapist like they had up in Auckland around the same time, only he was killing the women after. But nothing else ever happened, no other woman ever disappeared the same way, and they figured it had just been an awful coincidence. I mean, it was high season for hikers back when it all happened, and we don't really have those kinds of killers here."

Will had always wondered if that was true, because it was equally possible that New Zealand *did* have serial killers, but that no bodies had ever been found. If you wanted to disappear bodies in a sparsely populated country covered in dense forests and jagged mountains, deep lakes and rivers fed by glacial melt, the landscape itself would be your coconspirator. "Did people in town wonder the same thing?"

"There were whispers," Matilda confirmed, "especially after they found that one girl's bracelet down on the beach where the kids used to go."

Instinct stirred. "The rock cave on the other side of the whirlpool?"

A nod. "Poor babies never went back there. But after the police found no blood or anything, people started saying the girl must've stumbled disoriented out of the bush and got herself drowned."

"You didn't agree?"

"I never forgot what my cop friend said and I always told Miriama how she should never, ever trust any man who came up to her while she was alone and away from other people." Swallowing hard, Matilda added one final line. "And those times she ran away to Christchurch, she got scared by men who tried to take advantage of her. Grown men coming after my sweet girl."

"She's approachable, but she isn't naïve about the world."

"Yes, you see what I'm saying. Just last month, my girl was telling me that she'd be fine up in the big city, that she wouldn't forget all the things I'd taught her about keeping herself safe."

Will asked a question Matilda wouldn't want to hear, but that had to be asked. "Would she be as wary if she ran into a man or woman she knew well?"

He saw the answer on Matilda's bleak face; like most of those who lived in a small town, Miriama would've assumed she could separate the good from the bad—and it was unlikely she'd have even considered that one of her neighbors might do her harm. But Golden Cove wasn't immune from the harsh reality that the perpetrators of violent person-to-person crimes were most often familiar with and to the victim.

When it came to sexual and other assault crimes against women, that percentage skewed even further. No one was more dangerous to a woman than a man who'd once professed to love her.

Will's hand fisted, nausea churning in his stomach. Forcing it down before the bile could burn his throat, he put down the coffee mug and met Matilda's apprehensive gaze. "Dominic told me he thinks Miriama was seeing someone from out of town before the two of them got together. Do you know who that was?"

"She *was* going out with someone, used to go to Christchurch to meet him"—deep grooves formed in Matilda's forehead—"but she just used to laugh when I asked her about him. She said she'd tell me everything once she was sure he wouldn't be breaking her heart."

Secrets were never good. Will had learned that over and over again.

"I was happy for her." Matilda's lips curved before fracturing. "The way she smiled . . . I thought she'd found a man she loved so much that she didn't want to jinx it by talking about it." She took the coffee Will had risen and poured for her. "But then she stopped going out of town and started up with Dr. de Souza . . . I'm happy about that, too. I mean, a girl could do a lot worse than a doctor."

Unvarnished emotion in her voice as she continued. "Just the other day, I was thinking my girl's life was made—she's going off to get the education she's always deserved, and things are real serious with Dr. de Souza. I know it probably means she'll end up living far away from here, because—young fella like him—he's not going to want to stay out here forever, is he? And my Miri's always wanted to fly."

Dark eyes ragged with pain lifting up to meet Will's. "Dr. de Souza asked me to sneak one of her cheap little dress rings to him. He wanted to make sure he got the size right."

"He's planning to ask Miriama to marry him?"

"I don't know if he plans to do it before she leaves for the city or if he's going to wait until after she comes back for her first break," Matilda said, "but he's mad in love with Miri."

"You aren't worried at how young she is to be thinking marriage?"

"Miriama's never been young in the head or the heart." Matilda's face twisted, but she managed to hold back a fresh wave of tears. "Maybe because of how small she was when her world turned so ugly. When I think of her in that motel room with Kahurangi . . ." This time, she couldn't stop the tears.

Wiping them off with the back of her hand, she took a restorative sip of coffee, then carried on. "Miri's always liked older men. Not old enough to be her father or anything, but men who are settled in life, solid as a kauri tree against the wind. Had the worst crushes on her teachers in school, but I brought her up better than to ever do anything about it."

Will had witnessed a much older man—midfifties or over—hit on Miriama. He'd later discovered that same man had once taught Miriama at high school. She was only nineteen and a half now. It wasn't a stretch to think that, student or not, certain men would've taken advantage of her given any indication of interest.

"Other boys and men she dated," Matilda said, "lot of them saw her as a trophy, like she was a pet, or a piece of pottery they'd bought from Sita's fancy store. But Dr. de Souza, he loves her. I know he'll treat her right."

Will wondered why Dominic hadn't mentioned his plans to propose— then again, why would the man think to do so when his girlfriend was missing? Dominic was probably praying she'd turn up alive and well so he could carry off his proposal exactly as he'd planned. "Did Miriama ever go out with anyone else in the Cove?"

"Not really." Matilda hugged the mug with tight hands. "She's seen how nasty it can get when people break up in a town this small. She got lucky and never had that with her first boyfriend. That was Te Ariki, Ngaio's boy. He and Miriama were together for two years, broke it off when they were both fifteen or sixteen. No hard feelings there."

Will knew one Te Ariki in Golden Cove. "He's the one who goes out on the big fishing trawlers?"

Matilda nodded. "You probably know him because he tends to get carried away when he comes off the boat and home with a paycheck in his pocket." An affectionate smile. "That's about as bad as he gets, Will. He gives most of his pay to his mother to feed the littlies, parties hard with the rest, then goes out and works even harder. He and Miri catch up for a drink every time he's in town."

Will thought back to his conversation with the doctor. "Does Dominic know about their relationship?"

"Miriama invited him along the last time she met Te Ariki." Matilda looked at Will. "I think Dr. de Souza was jealous before he saw them together, the way men are when they think an old lover is trying to horn his way back in. But there's nothing like that with Te Ariki."

Regardless of Matilda's take on things, Will made a note to follow up with the fisherman. It was possible that once Te Ariki realized how serious things were between Dominic and Miriama, he'd changed his mind about what he'd given up.

"Is there anything else you can think of, Matilda? Even things that you feel uncomfortable talking about? I need to know."

Matilda sighed. "You're wondering about Steve, but he really couldn't have hurt my girl—he was in the house when I got home just after six and he never left." A worn face staring at the chipped and scratched wall across from them. "I know he looks at her in a way he shouldn't, but Miriama's strong. She can defend herself if he loses his mind and tries anything."

Will found it truly difficult to understand Matilda. That she loved Miriama with every bone in her body was true. Also true was that she seemed incapable of removing the residential threat to her beloved niece.

In this case, however, Steve did appear to have an unassailable alibi. Strange blind spot or not, Matilda wouldn't lie for Steve when Miriama was missing. "Any secrets in the past?" he asked, his brain wanting to fill out the ephemeral outline of that mysterious former lover. "Anything that could've come back to haunt Miriama?"

Matilda didn't ask him why he was digging so deep for what was a missing person case that most probably involved an accident; she was the one who'd brought up the missing hikers. Some part of her knew things weren't looking good for the girl she'd raised as her own.

"She has been a little distracted lately," she said, "but you'd be, too, if you were moving to Wellington after growing up here. I think she's just getting her head in order. My girl is going to make something of herself. She's going to come home and then she's going to fly."

# 20

The last thing Will saw as he walked out of the fire station and into the cold chill of a day that was now utterly devoid of sunlight was Matilda crying quietly behind hands she'd raised up to her face. He nearly went back, but something about the way she sat, her body turned so that she was no longer facing the front, told him she wouldn't appreciate the company.

Her grief was private, her worry a lonely vigil.

And for all that Matilda was glad he was looking for her niece, Will remained an outsider. Quite unlike the dark-eyed woman who jumped out of the small black truck that had just come to a stop in front of the fire station.

Anahera wore the same knit cap he'd seen on her yesterday, a dark gray one that looked to be handmade. Below that was an olive green anorak. "Any news?" she asked as her search partner, a lanky youth who worked as a supermarket clerk alongside Matilda, came around the vehicle to join them.

Will shook his head. "You'd better mark off your search route." Waiting until the clerk had gone to do exactly that, he lowered his tone. "I think Matilda needs a shoulder to lean on." Steve hadn't made an appearance so far and Will wasn't expecting that to change. "Do you know her well enough?"

Anahera's eyes grew darker, a storm front crossing the horizon. "She used to be friends with my mother. I'll try, see if she'll let me comfort her. If not, I can call Josie and track down a friend she trusts."

Nodding, Will was about to head off to find out if Te Ariki was in town or out at sea, when Anahera stopped him with a hand on his forearm. "Why aren't you searching?" It wasn't an accusation but a question.

"Someone has to work the other angles," he said quietly and watched harsh comprehension dawn on her face.

Hand dropping off his forearm, she shifted both into the pockets of her anorak. "A few of the hunters brought in their dogs earlier, and Matilda was able to find some clothes Miriama had put into the laundry basket so the dogs had a fresh scent, but they all lose her partway along the coastal track."

Will's blood pounded in time with his pulse. "Did you search the beach and clifftop again?"

"Yes." Anahera's jaw worked. "Nothing, there's nothing. It's like she vanished into thin air." She tore the knit cap off her head, crushed it in her hand as her hair tumbled out to fall partway down her back. "Tell me if there's anything else I can do, anything that might help Miriama."

Will went to say this was police business and realized very quickly that he'd be throwing away a possible resource. "You're a local," he said. "And because you've been gone for years, no one will find it suspicious if you ask certain questions. I don't know what those questions are yet, but when I do, will you ask them for me?"

Anahera's eyes were unreadable. "Yes. Do you really think one of us hurt Miriama?"

"Everyone has hidden corners of their life, even the people we think we know inside out."

Breaking the eye contact, Anahera tugged her cap back on. "I'll keep my ears open. The other search teams are going to come in soon as the rain starts—we've already searched every possible area we can, most of them twice. It's getting to the point there's nowhere left to look. Everyone will want to theorize, talk, but it'll probably be more open if you're not there."

Will gave a curt nod. "I'll come by your cabin after dark to get an update. I won't be able to get away before then." Not only did he have to run down what flimsy leads he had about Miriama, he'd have to begin patrols the instant the rain hit. Every so often, the teenagers got stupid; he'd once caught a bunch of them heading down to a relatively safe patch of surf—safe, that is, on a calm clear day with adults watching and ready to help.

Things usually settled down after nightfall, when the addition of pitch darkness to cold and rain made it far less attractive to sneak about and get up to mischief. "Here's my number in case you need to touch base before then."

Anahera took his card, slid it into a pocket. "If anyone sees you and asks me about your visit, I'll tell them you're hounding me because I still haven't got myself on the right phone plan."

"It's not a joke." She'd be totally isolated out there should anything happen.

Anahera raised an eyebrow. "Which is why I *am* with the new provider now. But it'll make a good excuse." With that, she turned in the direction of the fire station.

Anahera took a deep breath on the doorstep of the fire station, struck harder than she'd thought she would be by the sight of Matilda sitting with her face buried in her hands, the comforting bulk of her body shaking with rough sobs.

Anahera remembered running up to hug that body as a child, her face squashed into the softness of Matilda's belly. Maybe she'd found such happiness in Matilda's arms because her own mother had been shaped the same, with wide hips and soft curves. And maybe it was for that same reason that she'd been unable to hug Matilda ever again after the day she walked into the cabin and found Haeata's broken body.

"Auntie," she said, using the same respectful tone she'd always used when it came to her mother's best friend. "It's Ana."

Moving a chair to face Matilda's, she reached out to place her hand on the sobbing woman's knee. "The whole town's doing everything it can." The Lees—Julia's parents and owners of the supermarket—would soon be bringing in sandwiches for the searchers, while two grandmothers had just walked in with towels for those who might get caught in the rain. "Will is, too. I ran into Tom during the search and he said Miriama's face is all over the news websites."

She'd been surprised by the cop's clear dedication—she'd expected him to be marking time, paying his dues for whatever infraction it was that had caused his superiors to bury him in the career black hole of Golden Cove. But he wasn't only doing his job, he was picking up and looking under every possible rock.

Matilda lifted her tear-ravaged face. "Ana," she whispered, as if becoming aware of her for the first time. "*Taku kōtiro*, Ana. Not so little anymore." Her smile was more a reflex action than anything like the huge beam of warmth Anahera remembered. "You've been gone a long time, girlie."

"I was in London." Of course Matilda knew that, but staying silent didn't seem like the right choice. "Miriama was all skinny legs and scraped knees when I left."

The smile gained a touch more depth. "You should've seen her at thirteen. How that girl used to moan about how she was so skinny. Couldn't put on weight even if she stuffed her face with doughnuts and chips."

"It obviously worked in the end."

A laugh that lit up Matilda's face. "Wasn't the junk food, eh. She gave up all that and started running—said if she looked like a runner anyway, she might as well be one." Rubbing away her tears, she sat up, and when she next spoke, it was in Māori. "I don't know if it was the power that came from the exercise, or if her body just kept on growing as it was always going to, but . . . You saw. My beautiful Miriama."

"She has a glow about her." A dazzling thing the cop clearly believed had attracted the wrong kind of attention, but it was equally obvious that Matilda didn't want to think about that—she wanted and needed to talk about her girl, about all the wonderful things Miriama had done and would do in the future.

Anahera listened with a patience that would've startled her mother. The young Ana hadn't been able to stay still; she'd wanted to achieve a million things at once, wanted to snatch at so many dreams. That innocently hopeful part of Anahera had somehow survived her father and the hellish battleground of their family home, but it hadn't survived a cold cabin and the woman she most loved in the world lying dead on the floor.

Anahera had married Edward partly because he'd caused a tiny spark to alight inside her, as if her hope was shrugging off the frost to come out of hibernation. Then he'd snuffed out that struggling light with a betrayal she'd never seen coming.

"The only thing I ever worry about with Miriama," Matilda said, "is that she wants so much. Not things like jewelry or cars. No, my girl wants *life*. Wants to see the world, wants to go to all the places she admires in the magazines."

"She won't forget you," Anahera reassured the older woman. "She'll come back to visit." Anahera sat there in silent testimony of her words, for Golden Cove didn't easily let go of its own.

"Ah, Ana, you don't understand." Matilda shook her head. "I was always scared that a man would charm her with big promises of making her dreams come true and she'd believe him and be left broken."

"She's too smart for that," Anahera said.

"Yes. And now she's with Dr. de Souza, so I can stop worrying." The older woman leaned forward to brush her fingers over Anahera's cheek. "I'm sorry about your husband. I hoped for so much for you, my little Ana who flew so very far from home."

And fell, Anahera thought. Fell and shattered while another woman wailed for the man who'd been Anahera's husband, a man who'd promised to love her and cherish her forever, a man who'd told her they'd have a small family of their own.

So many dreams. So many promises. So many lies.

Miriama had been smarter than Anahera.

## 21

Will was able to cross Te Ariki's name off his list within half an hour of leaving the fire station. The young man's uncle confirmed Te Ariki had been out on a fishing trawler since four days earlier.

He decided to talk to Miriama's rival for the scholarship next, wanting to clear that possibility before he moved on, but he had some trouble tracking down Kyle Baker, as Vincent's younger brother was out with a search team. When Will did finally find him, it was on the beach. Kyle was just standing there staring out at the crashing waves.

Will had long ago stopped wearing regulation police wear to work this remote town, favoring work boots and jeans paired with a shirt, over which he currently wore a waterproof jacket. He had no trouble clambering down one of the paths from the cliff.

Kyle didn't hear him until Will was nearly by his side. Jerking, he looked at Will with pale brown eyes identical to his brother's, but unlike Vincent's shining gold, Kyle's hair was a light brown threaded with blond. "I think the ocean's taken her," he said in a calm voice. "It does that. Just takes people. She'll never be found."

"You seem very sure."

Kyle smiled, as if Will had made a joke. "I didn't do anything to her," he said. "I didn't need to. I knew she'd fuck up her own life sooner or later."

So, Dominic de Souza had been right. Kyle Baker, it seemed, had more in common with Daniel May than his own brother—and he'd decided that it wasn't worth turning on the charm for Will. No doubt because Will hadn't let the graffiti incident just slide.

"You don't have a positive opinion of Miriama's intelligence?" he asked in the same even tone he'd used to date.

Kyle shrugged, his slightly overlong bangs sweeping across his forehead in a way that had the town's teenage girls swooning. "Look, no offense to Matilda, but she likes to date losers. I guess they're the only ones who'll go for a used-up old chick like her, but whatever." Another smile. "With that as an example, you really think Miriama was going to finish the placement and become a world-famous travel photographer like she wanted?"

*Was. Wanted.*

"You don't believe people can rise above their circumstances?"

"You kidding? Look at Anahera Rawiri. Everyone thought she'd made it, was living it up in London, but she's back with her tail between her legs, sleeping in the same crappy shed where her mother kicked the bucket."

Anger licked Will's spine. He suffocated it as fast as it had flared, depriving it of the oxygen it needed to grow. He'd almost beaten a man to death the last time he'd given in to the red haze of anger.

Will still didn't know if he'd done the right thing in allowing that monstrous bastard to live, but he couldn't go around killing every asshole he met—the world, unfortunately, was full of them. "How exactly did you think Miriama would mess up her life?"

"Hook up with some loser who beat her, get pregnant, and live in this town until she died." Kyle's smile never faded. "Looks like she proved me wrong by drowning while still a success."

"Let's talk about that success." The wind whipped at Will's hair. "You both applied for the internship, but she won it."

No flicker in the smile, but Kyle's voice turned ice-cold. "The board that decided it fell for her tits and ass."

"Must've pissed you off." Money was one thing, but being invited into an industry fraternity quite another—Kyle couldn't buy his way into the environment that had warmly embraced Miriama. "Seeing someone like Miriama be welcomed by people you view as your peers."

"I knew I'd get there," Kyle said. "I have the drive and the staying power." Another smile, this one lighting up his eyes. "I also know how to make people want to be around me." It was like watching a switch being turned on. Kyle was suddenly the town's golden boy again, all politeness and down-to-earth personality. "Even you'd like me if I wanted you to like me."

It was too bad you couldn't arrest people for being psychopaths. Because many psychopaths ended up never committing a single crime, instead becoming successes in fields that rewarded a lack of empathy. Maybe Kyle would head in that direction.

And maybe he'd already killed.

"Did Miriama like you?" He deliberately used the past tense to feed into Kyle's mentality.

Kyle sneered, switching off the charisma as easily as he'd switched it on. "I didn't need to lower myself to a piece of trash. I've got much better meat gagging for it."

He was pushing it now, Will thought, using deliberately crude language in an effort to provoke Will. Why? What would that get him? Was it possible the nineteen-year-old wanted a reason to complain to Will's superiors?

Given Will's history, such a complaint could lead to his suspension or removal.

And without Will here to keep it active, Miriama's case would slowly slip off official radar, just another woman who'd taken off for a more adventurous life. It wouldn't be malicious and it wasn't that his fellow cops were bad at their jobs, but they didn't know Miriama, hadn't seen the light in her expression when she spoke of her upcoming internship.

The last time Will talked to her had been when she'd brought him a piece of carrot cake, which felt like a lifetime ago. He'd told her she'd make him fat. She'd laughingly said it wasn't a possibility, not with all the "long, angry walks" he took on the beach. "We have to make sure you don't waste away, even if you are a cop."

He hadn't known until then that anyone had spotted him striding down the beach during the early morning hours before true dawn. She'd probably seen him from along the clifftop running route, a long-legged young woman who dreamed big and who was well on the way to achieving those dreams despite a bleak start in life.

"Anything else you want to tell me?" he asked the young psychopath in front of him.

"Just to stop wasting your time. It's not like you have the budget."

"Thank you for the advice," Will said with deliberate mildness.

Kyle's face tightened a fraction before he turned to stare back out at the water.

"By the way, Kyle." He waited until Vincent's brother turned toward him before he finished what he had to say. "Perhaps you should talk to Anahera about her failures."

Walking away before Kyle could ask him any questions on the topic, Will allowed himself a faint smile. It faded in the next wave of wind, the sand gritty in his teeth . . . and the ghost of a three-year-old boy whispering in his ear.

# 22

The rain began to pound down around four that afternoon. It still took an hour for everyone to return to the fire station, the toughest of the tough staying out till the last possible moment. Despite having been gone for eight years, Anahera recognized pretty much everyone from before she left.

The only exceptions were three outsiders who'd moved in during her time away. Strangely enough for a self-absorbed and pretentious ass, Shane Hennessey had joined in the search, pairing up with a local who knew the area like the back of his hand. The soulful, moody-eyed novelist straight out of a gothic drama was drenched to the skin when he came in.

Anahera passed him a mug of hot coffee, having become Matilda's assistant in the task. The other woman had rallied and was once again making coffee and ensuring everyone logged their searches on the map Nikau had put up.

"Thank you," Shane said with a smile, Ireland rolling through his words so thickly that Anahera could almost see the velvet green hills. "It's pissing down, isn't it? But that's the rage of the wild for you."

"You don't strike me as the outdoors type."

"I grew up walking over some green hills of me own."

If he laid on the Irish any thicker, she'd be drowning in shamrocks. But Anahera played along. "Do you know Miriama?"

His smile deepened to reveal dimples in both cheeks. "I'm guessing you mean in the biblical sense." Dancing eyes. "She's too clever for me, alas. Not that I didn't try to rob that particular cradle."

Amused despite herself, Anahera was about to tell him to grab a towel when Shane shoved back his dripping hair again and said, "She knows what and who she wants, does Miri. And it isn't a washed-out novelist drinking himself to a slow death on some excellent whiskey."

"The doctor, you mean?"

Shane lifted one shoulder in a move that could mean anything. "Doc's only been around for a year. Pretty girl like that, I don't think she was sleeping alone before he came along."

"Shane!"

Looking up at the sound of his name, Shane said, "I'll be off, then. Seems you're too smart for me, too."

"Wait." Anahera put a hand on the rain-soaked sleeve of his jacket. "Do you know who she was dating before the doctor?"

"No, but she had a watch with a platinum band that she started wearing a couple of months after she turned eighteen." He absently tapped his wrist. "Most people took it for a pretty fake with colored stones, but I was born in the 'right circles,' as my sainted mother used to say—that watch is real and those stones are pink and blue diamonds."

As Shane went to join the group that had hailed him, Anahera thought about what might lead a man to give a woman such an expensive gift . . . and was hit by the memory of the diamond pendant Edward had given his mistress two months before he simply dropped in the street and never again moved.

The insurance documents for the pendant had been in his desk drawer, a drawer she'd had to empty after his death. He'd also bought the other woman a car around the same time, and begun to pay the rental on her home. The mistress had said it had all been done out of love. Maybe it had been, but Anahera wasn't so sure it was for his mistress that Edward's heart had beat.

Miriama, though . . . she was as bright as a star. A shining creature who could make a man fall so deep that he'd lay treasures at her feet.

"The watch?" Matilda frowned when Anahera asked after the item of jewelry Shane had mentioned. "Yes, I remember it. She told me she picked it up at a market, but I knew it was a gift from that man she dated before settling with Dr. de Souza, the one she used to go to Christchurch to see."

"Does Miriama still have it?" It should be simple enough to confirm if Shane was right about its value.

"I haven't seen her wearing it lately." Matilda poured another mug of strong black coffee. "But I don't think she would've got rid of it. She loves that pretty thing, used to wear it all the time before she and the doctor became a couple."

Not wearing one lover's gift while with another? It was a sensitive thing to do. "Do you think you could look for it for me?" Anahera asked. "I want to show it to the cop, in case it helps him track down the Christchurch man."

Matilda's jaw firmed. "My girl wouldn't just have gone off with him and left me to worry." The words were censorious. "But I'll look for you, Ana. You make sure you give it back for when Miriama's home again."

"I will." Anahera picked up the fresh tray of coffees, drifted back into the crowd to make sure everyone had a mug. And she listened as she'd told Will she'd do.

Most people were despondent.

"I even went off-track," one of the gray-bearded locals was saying. "Did the parts I knew you buggers might not be able to. Didn't find no sign of her."

Kyle Baker, his hair wet, murmured, "Do you think the water took her?" He directed the soft, worried question at Nikau.

Anahera was surprised. Not by the question—everyone was wondering if the sea had taken Miriama, if she'd slipped and fallen in the wrong place and been swept out without a trace. No, what surprised her was Kyle's deferential tone.

Last time she'd seen Kyle Baker, he'd been a boy of eleven, but he'd been a boy well aware of his "station in life," as one of Edward's more pompous friends had used to say. A private-school boarder during the week, he'd come home to Golden Cove for the weekends. Where he'd made sure the local children knew he had the best of everything—the best music player, the best shoes, the best education.

Anahera had thought him an obnoxious prat.

From what she could recall, Nikau had shared her opinion. Today, however, he gave the younger male a tight smile. "Miriama's too respectful of the ocean to get so close to the water."

"Yeah, yeah, she is," Kyle said, his relief open.

Eight years was a long time. Maybe Kyle had grown out of his prat nature.

"What about those hikers from back when we were kids?" Tom said, his beard glittering with droplets of rainwater and his callused fingers closing gratefully over the last mug on Anahera's tray. "Josie was saying last night how it was strange, so many women going missing in the bush near here."

"I've heard the stories," Kyle said. "It was three women, right?"

Nikau nodded. "Pretty young women." Unspoken were the words "just like Miriama."

After drinking down half the mug of coffee, Tom said, "We should tell the cop."

"I'm pretty sure Will already knows." Dark clouds rumbled across Nikau's face. "You realize what it would mean if Miriama's disappearance is connected to the missing women?"

Puzzled expressions all around.

Anahera, unblinded by fresh bonds and able to look at things as an insider who'd turned outsider for a while, said, "It would have to be one of us. A stranger who came back fifteen years apart would've been noticed—and there are no strangers in town."

Tom, Kyle—everyone but Nik—all stared at her before Tom swore under his breath.

"This has nothing to do with those lost hikers." Vincent's voice. He'd come to stand beside his taller younger brother. "Golden Cove has its problems, but a serial murderer?" A hard shake of his head. "Even the police back then said it was just bad luck and coincidence." His tone was calm, practical. "We're not kids making up scary stories now, and Miriama is alive, probably hurt. I, for one, am going to keep looking."

Several heads nodded at his firm statement, but Anahera caught the bitter truth in too many eyes—most people thought Miriama was gone, never to be found.

As she began to move on, Kyle stepped out of the group and toward her. "It feels weird to say this now"—an uncomfortable teenage shrug—"but welcome back to the Cove, Ana."

"Thank you, Kyle." Leaving him with a small smile, she headed back to the table that held the large coffee urn.

A slender woman stood nearby: blonde, with lovely green eyes, she had the kind of face and bearing that shouted private schooling and wealth. Or maybe it was her waterproof jacket. Though that, in itself, wasn't unusual in this crowd. All the old-timers as well as many of the younger crew had brought along waterproof gear when they saw the clouds on the horizon.

What made the blonde stand out was that her waterproof gear likely cost something like five times—no, that was being conservative—it was probably more like ten times the price of what everyone else was wearing.

She also wore a black knit cap, which had survived being soaked through, so she'd been smart enough to pull the hood of her jacket over it while outside. Her facial bones were the kind that would age beautifully. But she wasn't beautiful, this woman. She was . . . elegant. That was when it clicked, the woman's identity.

Jemima Baker, Vincent's wife.

Anahera had seen her in the photos Vincent had posted on his social media page. In those photos, however, Jemima was always dressed to the nines and out at some charity gala or other black-tie event. Her hair was usually a sleek blonde sheet, glossy and without a strand out of place, her makeup flawless.

In the last image Anahera could remember seeing, the other woman had worn a black sheath dress, a string of pearls around her neck. In her hand had been a little clutch with the double *C* logo that defined Chanel.

No wonder Anahera hadn't immediately recognized her; today, despite her expensive gear, Jemima Baker stood as damp and bedraggled as everyone else. On her feet were worn-in hiking boots suitable for this climate and area, and the backs of her hands bore fresh scratches, as if she'd pushed through the dense growth looking for Miriama.

Shame pricked Anahera—she, along with all their friends, had just assumed that Vincent had married Jemima because she fit the mold of what his parents would've wanted for him: an educated, lovely woman who'd be the perfect hostess, but who was also smart and intelligent enough to rise with him as he climbed the political ladder. The timing of the marriage— a bare year after the elder Bakers' deaths—had only cemented that general opinion.

None of them had ever considered that Vincent might've fallen for his wife because she had a heart as down-to-earth as his own. Seeing Jemima as she stood looking at the search map with worry carved into her features, Anahera resolved to do better, to get to know this woman her friend had married. "Here." She handed Jemima a mug of freshly poured coffee. "You look like you could use this."

Jemima's fingers brushed hers as she took the mug. They were like ice. "I hope Miriama isn't out in this," the other woman said in a soft tone that wouldn't reach Matilda. "It's getting cold out there. Really cold."

"Which section were you in?" Anahera asked, and was surprised when Jemima mentioned a location quite distant from Vincent's. As if reading her surprise, Jemima said, "I arrived a little after Vincent—I wanted to make sure the children were settled."

Anahera kept forgetting Vincent was now a father. "I'm Anahera, by the way." She held out her hand. "The one who's been in London for a while."

Jemima's face softened as they shook hands, her grip firm but not crushing. "I was so sorry to hear about your husband."

Anahera still didn't know what to do when people offered their sympathies about Edward; it wasn't as if she could open her mouth and say, "I'm not sure I'm grieving for the bastard. You see, I found out he was a lying, cheating piece of scum two hours after I stood trembling over his body in the morgue."

His lips had been blue, his face so waxy he hadn't looked real. A mannequin shaped like Edward, that's what her brain had kept trying to tell her. Just a mannequin. Not real. Nothing to do with her.

One hundred and twenty-seven minutes later, forty-nine minutes after news of Edward's death hit the media, she'd opened the door of their home to a sobbing stranger who'd collapsed into her arms with a wail of grief.

# 23

Anahera's tight smile seemed to satisfy Jemima.

The other woman sipped at her coffee, then said, "Not the kind of homecoming you would've wished for."

"No." She'd expected and been prepared for old memories and older anger, but not this. "I remember Miriama as a young girl, but I've only met her twice as an adult."

Jemima's eyelids lowered, her hands cupping her mug as she took a deeper drink. When she looked up again, her gaze was softer yet oddly difficult to read. A woman, Anahera thought, who was used to putting on a mask that didn't look like a mask. Necessary for someone who wanted to stand next to the man who would be prime minister.

"I'm afraid I've never really gotten to know her," Vincent's wife admitted. "She's so much younger. Just that age gap where we don't really have anything in common, you know? I feel so old saying that."

"It's funny, isn't it?" Anahera said, liking the self-deprecating woman under the polish and spin. "There's such a difference between nineteen and twenty-nine. Ten short years but a lifetime apart."

"It's even worse between nineteen and thirty-one." Jemima's smile was quick, bright. "I married a younger man," she whispered.

"Sorry, you fail the scandalous test. Unless you were sixteen and Vincent was fourteen when you met, and I know that didn't happen."

Jemima's smile deepened, reaching the sea green of her eyes. "After this is all over"—the smile rubbed away, her gaze going to the map before meeting Anahera's again—"and I mean when it's settled in a good way, with the best news, I hope you'll come up to the house for a coffee or to have lunch."

Anahera hesitated; she hadn't come to Golden Cove to make friends. She'd come here to lose herself in the shadows.

In front of her, Jemima's expression began to grow distant and Anahera knew suddenly that the other woman was used to rebuffs from Vincent's friends—or perhaps it was from all of the locals. She certainly didn't seem the kind of person others would shut out, but on the other hand, she was wealthy and lovely and an outsider; just because she'd married one of their own didn't mean she would've been welcomed with open arms. Still, it was odd, given how well Vincent was liked.

"I'd like to," she found herself saying. "I may not be the best company, though—I'm not sure I'm at the point where I can socialize."

Jemima's expression fell. "Oh, God, I'm stupid. I should've realized." She touched her fingers hesitantly to Anahera's hand. "Whenever you're ready, the invitation is open. Here"—she dug around in a jacket pocket, found what she was looking for—"this has all my contact details."

Anahera took the crumpled card, slipped it safely away. "Thank you." She could detect nothing false in Jemima, which made the fact that she seemed to have been braced for rejection even less understandable.

Jemima spoke again, both slender hands back around her mug. "I love this part of the country, but Vincent and I are away so often that I haven't had a chance to really nest here, if you know what I mean?"

"Yes, I do." She'd loved Edward, and so she'd tried to love London, too. Just as she'd tried not to miss the water that crashed so hard against the rocks that it sent up a white spray, the grit of sand between her toes, and the green, the endless dark green that could never be tamed.

All things she'd wanted to escape as a girl.

All things she'd ached for desperately when surrounded by red double-decker buses and stately museums, designer shops and theaters that glittered, the civility of it threaded by a constant buzz of humanity.

"You and Vincent have two kids, right?" she said. "I'm sorry, I forgot their names."

This time, Jemima's smile lit up her entire face. "Jasper and Chloe. My little cheeky monsters. One's four and the other's three. They're with their nanny now, a wonderful older lady who used to look after Vincent when he was young."

That there was one reason Jemima might've had trouble fitting into Golden Cove. Women here generally didn't get the opportunity to have nannies or to fly around the country and the world. Sometimes, even the nicest people could give in to the green-eyed monster of jealousy. Especially when Jemima had married one of the few bachelors in town who offered a ticket out of poverty or a humdrum small-town experience.

"Jemima." Vincent's hand on his wife's lower back, his face worn. "Do you want to get back? Kyle's about to leave so you can catch a ride with him again. I might stay a little longer."

Jemima nodded. "The kids will be missing me." Leaning in, she kissed Vincent on the cheek, the fingers of one hand rising to touch his jaw. "Don't stay out too long, okay? You've done everything you can. No one could ask for more."

As Vincent and Jemima walked away after Jemima said a warm good-bye, Anahera wondered if Vincent saw Golden Cove as his responsibility. It wasn't out of the realm of possibility—the Bakers had always been big on public service. While Golden Cove didn't have a mayor, if it did, it was probably a Baker who would've filled that role. And now Vincent was beating himself up because Miriama had disappeared on his watch.

"Trust Vincent to take this on his shoulders," she said to Nikau when he came to join her.

The man who'd once been her friend, and who she thought might still be, stared after the departing couple. "Vincent always seems so straightforward, doesn't he?" He folded his arms, his shirt a checked blue; he'd hung up his wet outdoor jacket by the door.

"Do you have any reason to think he isn't?"

Nikau shrugged. "He never talks about her, you know—the wife, I mean. But all the times I've met her, she seems nice enough. A little posh, but you expect that with someone Vincent would hook up with. He never brings her to any of the town events, either. It's weird when you think about the parties and things he takes her to all across the country."

Someone hailed Nikau just then and he walked off to talk to a grizzled older man with blue prison tattoos across his knuckles. His words, however, stuck with Anahera. Jemima didn't seem the type of person who thought she was too good to attend Golden Cove events. Perhaps her absence was a case of jealousy of another kind. For Vincent, Golden Cove was his home. Maybe he couldn't share it even with the woman he loved.

And Anahera was making up answers out of thin air. For all she knew, Jemima could keep up the appearance of enjoying small-town life for a short period, but had no particular desire to become part of the fabric of Golden Cove.

Every couple had their secrets and their polite lies.

# 24

After leaving Kyle, Will had gone back to talk to Steve. He'd wanted to squeeze Matilda's live-in boyfriend while Matilda wasn't around. Men like Steve had a way of posturing and lying in front of the female sex, as if the behavior would prove their status as an alpha male.

But Steve stuck to his story—and he wasn't smart enough to lie that well. Those of Steve's type, when they killed, weren't clever about it. They were violent and brutal and caught up in the heat of the moment. Had the searchers found Miriama's body beaten and strangled somewhere nearby, Will would've come down hard on Steve as a primary suspect, but with Miriama missing and Steve simply not having had the time to get to her, he had to accept that the other man was telling the truth.

"She wasn't ever going to let me touch her," Steve muttered sourly, just as Will's phone vibrated with a message.

"Who? Matilda?" Will had remained standing while Steve sat in the dark brown couch that swallowed him up. The other man was wearing a greasy and sweat-stained white tank, gray chest hairs sticking out from over the top of it, while he'd pomaded back his scraggly once-blond hair as if he was reliving the seventies.

"Matilda, too," was the answer. "I wasn't gonna force her precious Miriama or nothing," Steve added piously, "but I'm a man. I had to try my chances in case she had an itch she felt like scratching."

Will fought the urge to kick Steve in the balls. The image of the asshole crumpled whimpering on the floor was a particularly compelling one. But he checked his phone instead, giving Steve more time to stew.

The message was short and to the point and it made his blood pound:

Shane Hennessey says Miriama used to wear an expensive platinum and diamond watch. Most people thought it was a fake. Matilda's agreed to look for it for us.–Ana

"Miriama said no when you tried it on with her?" Will nudged after sliding away his phone, using his well-worn technique of keeping his voice mild and emotionless. As if he was only slightly interested in the answer. The reason it was a well-worn technique was that it worked. Suspects and bystanders alike read what they wanted to hear in his voice.

Today, Steve nodded his head like a bobblehead doll. "I know you're doing the whole search thing so the morons in this hick town will like you, but don't waste your time. Miriama's a sharp operator who can look after herself. Like that watch she has. I used to work with jewelry before, recognize quality."

Will interpreted that to mean Steve had stolen or fenced jewelry at some point in time. "What's so interesting about her watch?"

"It's seriously fancy, that's what." Steve's piggy little eyes glinted. "Worth at least twenty grand."

Will pinned the other man to the spot with his gaze. "That's a whole lot of motive, wouldn't you say?" In a town like Golden Cove, twenty thousand dollars might as well be twenty million dollars.

Two hot red flags flaring on his cheeks, Steve lifted his hands and waved. "Hey, hey, don't you go trying to pin anything on me. Watch's still in her room—come, I'll show you."

Following the other man down the short and narrow hallway, Will put a hand on Steve's shoulder and held him back from entering the room when they arrived. "You stay here." There was no reason to think Miriama's room was a crime scene, but he still didn't want Steve inside. "Where does she keep the watch?"

"That little drawer to the left. It's under a pile of panties."

When Will just stared at him, Steve licked his lips and Will could almost hear him thinking of an excuse for pawing through Miriama's underwear drawer.

"She asked me to get her a pair once, when she forgot to take it into the shower," was what he came up with.

Deciding the obvious lie didn't deserve a response, Will retrieved the watch after tugging on a pair of disposable gloves from his jacket pocket. Instinct and experience told him Steve was right—this was no well-made fake. He put the glittering object that was more jewelry than timepiece in an evidence bag he'd pulled from another pocket, then wrote out a receipt and placed it on the dresser, beneath a glass trinket box. He'd make sure Matilda knew he'd picked up the watch, just in case Steve decided to be a vindictive shit and not mention it.

As he was in the room already, he took a quick look around. He didn't want to invade Miriama's privacy, but at this stage, it was looking more and more likely that she wasn't okay; Will needed to know anything and everything that might help him find her.

The room held a bed, a built-in closet, a small desk, and an old computer. Prints of Miriama's photographs were pinned to the walls, but he saw no camera equipment. The latter didn't surprise him; Miriama had once mentioned that Josie let her use part of the back room of the café as an office. Not only could she work in peace there after the café closed, she probably didn't have to worry about Steve selling off equipment she'd worked hard to buy.

He turned to spear the man to the spot with his eyes again. "Fingerprints don't rub off as easily as people think," he said. "Am I going to find yours all over this room?"

Flushing hot red under the pasty white of his skin, Steve folded his arms and bristled. "What're you trying to say?" When Will just held the eye contact, the other man dropped his arms and looked left, then right, then down at his feet, then back up again. "I just wanted to look at her things, okay." His hands fisted by his sides. "I'm at home a lot. I get bored."

"Does she have another hiding place?" Instinct told him the watch had been shoved in the underwear drawer quickly, maybe because Miriama had been looking at it, only to be interrupted. It couldn't be the permanent spot. Not with Steve in the house.

The other man didn't try any bullshit this time. "Behind the bed," he said, pointing his finger at the single bed with its metal frame. It was neatly made up with a soft pink flannel sheet and matching pillowcase; a dark blue blanket lay folded at the bottom. "There's a board on the floor that comes up. She hides her diary and stuff in there. The watch's usually in there, too."

"How many times have you read that diary?"

Steve's lip curled. "I don't need to read her diary. Probably the same crap women always write—feelings and shit." A snort accompanied by a scratch of his protruding belly. "Only thing I'm interested in is between her—" Cutting himself off when he finally looked at Will's face, Steve began to back away. "Look," he said, "I don't read too good. I just wanted to look at her stuff. I didn't touch that diary."

Waiting until the other man had backed himself all the way into the living room, Will shut the bedroom door before retrieving the single item beneath the floorboard: an old tin box heavy enough to hold a diary. As a hiding space, it was a good one. If Steve hadn't been unemployed and at home so much—and likely a former thief—he probably wouldn't have put together the sounds of the bed being moved with a hiding spot.

Will's eyes moved to the computer; he wondered if Miriama had hidden her secrets a second way.

Deciding to talk to Matilda then and there, he made a call to the fire station.

"Take whatever you need," she told him when he explained where he was and what he was doing. "But you take good care of it."

"I will," Will promised, and booted up the computer. "Do you know where Miriama keeps her old diaries?"

"She cuts out all the pages, then goes deep into the bush to bury those pages. Says it's about saying good-bye to the past and living for the future."

Will thought of the pages rotting away in the silent dark, an act of hope for the future turned into a somber omen. "I've got another question— what was the name of the man who molested Miriama as a teenager?" He was far more dangerous to the young woman than Steve.

"Fidel Cox." Matilda's voice quivered with rage. "That *pokokōhua* did a runner, cops never found him. You think he came back to hurt my Miri?"

"I don't know, but I'm going to check it out."

"Just find my girl, Will. Just find Miriama."

Will didn't make any promises; he'd learned his lesson about making promises and he'd learned hard. Never again would he tell a victim that everything would be all right. Because, too many times, the monsters won.

# 25

Will had one more thing to do before he left Matilda's home. "I want you to remember something, Steve," he said to the man in the sagging armchair. "Matilda might let you push her around, but I won't look the other way. I see her with a single bruise, I'm coming after you."

Steve postured, all raised shoulders and lifted chin. "A man's got a right to do what he wants with his own woman in his own home."

"You just remember what I said anytime you get the urge to hurt Matilda." Will knew his eyes had gone flat in that way one of his partners had once said made him look like a psychopath. Will wasn't always so certain he wasn't a psychopath—psychopaths didn't have feelings and his had burned down to ashes thirteen months ago.

Steve glared at him, but Will was satisfied Matilda would be safe from abuse, at least until Steve forgot his fear. Will wouldn't have dealt with the situation the same way had it been a different man—some mean bastards would've hurt Matilda out of pure spite at being ordered not to, but Steve was both a coward and just smart enough to know that Will was too big a predator to challenge.

Walking out into the rain, the tin box and watch protected under the high-visibility police-issue jacket he'd changed into after the weather turned, Will put both items on the passenger seat of his vehicle, then ran around to get into the driver's seat.

He made a call on his way back into town, asking Tom Taufa to meet him at the café. The other man was waiting when he got there. "I was at the fire station," he said as he let Will into the café's back room. "That's Miri's corner there."

A much newer computer sat on a spacious desk, along with several cameras.

Metal jangled as Tom took a key off his key ring. "I have to get back to Josie—she's not doing so good. Stay as long as you like, keep the key in case you want to look at stuff again." He dug in his pocket. "I asked Josie about the computer after you called and she said there's a password." Handing over the piece of paper on which he'd scribbled the mix of numbers and letters, he said, "Josie knows it because technically the computer is the café's, for accounts and things, but she mostly got it for Miri to use."

"Thanks, Tom." Will was already turning back to the computer as Tom left, but he didn't expect to find anything private, not when Miriama knew Josie also used this computer. Still, he had a quick look. The only emails on it related to the café.

Miriama must have an email account—if nothing else, she'd have needed one to apply for the internship—but chances were high it was a web account she nearly always used from her phone. He'd found no emails on her home computer either, and her browser history and bookmarks hadn't included any webmail sites. The same proved true here.

Given Miriama's age, her reliance on her phone for communication was unsurprising.

Photo editing software made up the bulk of what was on this computer. Will checked Miriama's current projects, then slotted in the memory cards from her cameras, but nothing jumped out. Shot after shot taken in pursuit of her signature portraits, plus several finalized images—including one of a bare-chested Dominic in bed, his smile intimate, and a stunning one of Pastor Mark sitting stoop-shouldered on a church bench, but none of it told him how to find her.

He took the memory cards regardless, and made a mental note to dig deeper later. Right now, he had another priority: he needed to follow up on Fidel Cox. Locking up the café, he returned to the police station.

The system spat out the correct case file after a single inquiry.

According to the notes of the officer who'd driven in to record Matilda's complaint on behalf of Miriama, the police had sent Fidel's photo out across the country and received exactly zero tips in response. Fidel was an experienced hunter, so everyone figured he'd "gone bush" until the heat died down.

It had probably not helped the search that Fidel Cox was one of the most nondescript individuals Will had ever seen. His mug shot, taken in the aftermath of a drunken brawl a year before his molestation of Miriama, showed a man with pale brown skin, black hair, and brown eyes. He was neither big nor small, neither tall nor short. He had no distinguishing marks, no tattoos, no scars. No feature on his face that stood out.

Fidel Cox was a man who could blend in anywhere. If he hadn't wanted to slink off into the wild, all he would've had to do was change his name and grow a beard or shave his head. Either would've dramatically altered his looks.

Was it possible he'd come through Golden Cove and been missed?

Will had already made a short call to the tourism center on the way back from Matilda's, been told that aside from the Japanese couple Nikau had taken to see the gold-mining shacks, Golden Cove hadn't had *any* visitors in the previous five days. As far as the center was aware, there were no hikers on the local trails, either. Still . . .

He picked up the phone and called the tourism center again. It was Glenda Anderson who answered this time, not her part-time student assistant. The fifty-something woman with bright pink hair and a penchant for stilettos was a legend in the town after her years dancing in the cabaret show of a cruise liner.

"Have they found that poor child?" she asked, clearly recognizing Will's number. "My heart's just sick about it. She is such a sweetie. Always saves me a piece of that cheesecake I love."

Will's eyes went to the trash bin where he'd thrown the takeout container in which Miriama had brought him his carrot cake. "No," he said. "But I'm hoping you can help me with something."

"Anything for you, you handsome young man." The flirtatious statement lacked its usual spark, more rote than anything. "Shall I get on to the computer?"

"Yes." First, Will repeated the same questions he'd asked the assistant, in case the youth had missed something. When that all failed to pan out, he moved on. "Do you have any records of a male tourist going onto the trails over the past six months?" A very long window, but per Matilda's words to the responding officer, Fidel Cox had been intimately familiar with this area and with living wild.

"Well now," Glenda said to the accompaniment of the click-clack of her keyboard, "that'll be a long list since it covers four months of the tourist season. Shall I email it to you?"

"Yes." Will stared at Fidel's mug shot again, thought about how the man was a chameleon. "Can you also email through their identification?" The tourism center made it a point to request some form of photo ID that could be copied and kept on file just in case things went wrong and searchers had to be provided with an image.

Will didn't think Fidel Cox would've given them any real identification or that he'd have even checked in with Glenda and her people—odds were, if Fidel had come back into Golden Cove, he'd slipped into the bush miles from the town itself. But Will would be careless in his duties if he didn't clear this particular avenue of investigation. And not all criminals were smart. Any number had been caught because of stupid errors.

Two hours later, he'd gone through every single one of the names and ID photos and come up with nothing. If Fidel Cox had returned to the area, he'd done so in a way that wouldn't be noticed. None of the other hikers appeared suspicious: every single one had provided either a passport or driver's license as ID and a quick search on various data banks—or via social media profiles—told him none had lied.

Not ready to give up yet, Will called a colleague of his who worked in the crimes against children area. "Hamish," he said when the phone was picked up on the other end. "I need a favor."

"You never call, you never write, and now you want a favor," the lawyer said in his usual dry tone. "This keeps going on and I might get suspicious that you're just using me."

"We have a use-use relationship."

"True." The sound of creaking, as if Hamish was tilting back his chair as he so often did while he sat in his office. "But you used to buy me a beer now and then before you went full hermit-mode."

"Put it on my tab." Will wondered when he'd be . . . equalized enough to go back into the world he'd once not only inhabited but owned with a casual expectation that he could control it. He had the feeling the answer was never.

"Maybe I'll come visit you in that West Coast town of yours," Hamish threatened. "I looked it up—the wife thinks it might make for a nice romantic getaway when the weather's a bit less pissy. On the flip side, my middle-aged body isn't keen on going hiking or participating in the various dangerous activities on offer. Can you fish there?"

"There's a spot on the rocks that's probably safe enough if you wear a life jacket and hook yourself onto the cliffs with anchor ropes."

Snorting, Hamish said, "What can I do for you, my good friend who I never see?"

"I'm trying to trace a man named Fidel Cox. He was never prosecuted, but he was implicated in a crime against a child." Hamish was a walking encyclopedia when it came to men and women who might target innocence. "I'm going to email you his photo. It's five years old, so keep that in mind."

A short pause, while Hamish waited for the photo to download on his end. "Got it," he said. "I'll run it through my private database. I've also got this fancy software that'll age Mr. Cox. Said software is from sources who shall not be named because they might be providers of illegal knockoffs—but tell anyone and I'll deny it. It'll take a while. I'll call you back, whatever the result."

"Thanks, Hamish." Before hanging up, Will found himself saying, "You should come to Golden Cove this summer. I'll borrow a boat and we'll go fishing and have that beer."

"You're on," was the enthusiastic response. "I should probably mention that I hate fish. You'll have to eat them all."

Hanging up afterward, Will stared at the windows awash with rain. He'd made an effort to sound normal for Hamish, but the man who'd once grabbed an after-work beer with the lawyer was long gone. This Will . . . This Will wasn't so sure who he was anymore. But he knew how to do his job.

He turned back to his desk, and ran a deeper search on all the tourists whose names Glenda had forwarded. All came back clean. Most had been international visitors who'd long ago returned to their countries of origin; the small group of New Zealanders had no criminal records among them.

He then began to make his way through the stack of memory cards he'd taken from the café.

It was only when he looked up after going through all of them that he realized it was dark outside. Going to the doorway, he pulled it open and looked over to the fire station, the rain hitting his face as it slanted in under the eaves.

No lights. No vehicles parked out front.

Hardly a surprise—the rain was crashing down. He took care of a few other matters, then made sure his phone was fully charged and shrugged back into his high-viz jacket for the drive to Anahera's.

This rain was made to cause emergencies and he needed to be ready to respond. Most Golden Cove residents would call him rather than the official emergency line. At the last minute, he went back and picked up the watch and tin. The station did have a safe, but he wasn't comfortable leaving the items here before he'd had a chance to examine them.

He put the memory cards not in the main safe but in the hidden gun safe; there was nothing suspicious on them, but it was Miriama's work and deserved to be protected.

Once in his car, his hair damp again and his jacket gleaming with transparent droplets, he drove past the clinic to make sure Dominic de Souza wasn't still just sitting inside, shocked and lost. Seeing the place was dark, he swung by the two-bedroom house the doctor rented from Daniel May. It wasn't far from the surgery.

The single light in the kitchen showcased Dominic at the table, head slumped on his arms. Will frowned. The other man didn't look in good shape. He was about to get out and knock on the door, make sure depression wasn't getting the best of Dominic, when another person moved into the frame.

It was the pastor. The gray-haired man was holding a mug of something, and a plate of what looked like toast. He put both in front of Dominic, then placed his wrinkled hand on the doctor's shoulder and squeezed. When Dominic raised his head at last, the older man sat down next to him, seemed to be talking intently. After a while, the doctor nodded and picked up a piece of toast to take a small bite.

Satisfied Dominic was under careful watch, Will turned his vehicle toward Anahera's place. He thought about picking up something for dinner and taking it along with him, but it looked like everyone had shut up shop early because of the weather. Well, he had half a loaf of bread in his fridge at home. He and Dominic would be having the same meal tonight.

As he drove through the dark and deserted streets, he could see the May estate in the distance—lit up against the night. He wondered if Daniel had returned home from his meetings or if it was Keira up there alone. Just then, he glimpsed red taillights through the trees, as if a car was climbing up toward the estate. Someone from Golden Cove? Or had Daniel come into town to attend the gathering at the fire station, and was now driving home to his wife?

No way to tell from here, the rain diminishing even the limited visibility he normally had of the road up to the estate.

The tourism center, he was happy to see, was also shut up. Glenda lived literally behind it, but he swung around anyway to make sure she was safe. She came to the window and waved when his headlights cut across her front window, well used to his patrols by now. Will flashed his headlights at her in a silent response, carried on. He had to check up on a number of others, elderly and vulnerable individuals who might've been forgotten in the tidal wave of worry over Miriama.

All of them proved to be snug inside their homes.

As he drove on, he tried not to think of Miriama out in the cold and wet. He was thinking he should go by Mrs. Keith's, too, when he got a call. The signal was patchy, but he recognized Evelyn Triskell's voice: ". . . Vincent . . . his car."

# 26

"Evelyn, where are you?"

It took him two minutes of conversation through crackling static to work out that Evelyn was somewhere on the road out of town. Telling her to stay put, he did a U-turn and headed that way. A car went past him in the opposite direction around the halfway point, but they passed on the turn and he couldn't see much of the make and model through the heavy rain. It had been small, though, not a truck or an SUV.

It was another ten minutes later that he caught the blurred rear lights of a car on the side of the road—and it wasn't Evelyn's old Mini. It was Vincent's silver Mercedes, a car the other man usually only drove for short trips and never in this kind of weather.

Bringing his vehicle to a stop beside the crippled sedan and turning on his hazard lights as well as the blue and red flashers atop the roof and in his front grille, Will got out. Vincent's car had smashed into the ditch, the front crumpled in. Not enough to have crushed the driver, but enough that the car would need a tow. More worried about Vincent than the car, Will blinked the rain out of his eyes and wrenched open the driver's-side door.

Vincent looked at him, a streak of blood down one side of his forehead and a faint smile on his lips. "This is the last thing you need, isn't it, Will?"

"Where's Evelyn?" Will yelled to be heard over the pounding rain that thundered on his head and dripped in rivulets down his face. The extremely low visibility made it difficult to see any markings on the road right in front of him, much less farther down the road; Evelyn's smaller vehicle could be lying broken ten meters up and he'd never spot it.

"Evelyn?" Vincent stared blankly at him for a second before shaking his head. "I sent her home. She was driving back in after running one of the hunters home, and she saw I'd spun off the road. Insisted on stopping to call you."

Will knew the chairwoman of the Golden Cove Business Council; a bulldog had nothing on her. "How could you possibly have convinced Evelyn to go home?" At least that explained the car Will had seen heading into town—it had been the size of Evelyn's compact.

"Wayne."

Will should've thought of that himself—Evelyn's husband was in a wheelchair as a result of a stroke, and while he had good mobility around the home, he still relied on Evelyn for a lot. He was older than her by fifteen years at least and far more frail.

If Will had realized Evelyn wasn't home, he'd have checked on Wayne during his patrol. The Triskells lived on his street and he often lent them a hand if they needed physical help with something. Half the time, the request was a thin excuse for Evelyn to attempt to pump Will for scandalous details about her fellow Covers.

"How seriously are you hurt?" He'd automatically grabbed a flashlight as he left his vehicle, now focused it on Vincent's head wound.

Blue and red flickered against the night around them, the police lights incongruously like neon flashes in a bar.

"It doesn't look too bad from here." Will could see a little blood along Vincent's hairline, but there was no sign of a gash.

"It's fine." Vincent raised his hand to his forehead. "I'll probably have a headache tomorrow, but that's about it."

"We still need to get you in front of a doctor," Will began.

"Dominic de Souza isn't in any condition to help anyone." Vincent's tone was tight. "And I don't think you're going to be driving me out of Golden Cove for treatment. We'll be in more danger from the weather than I am from this shallow cut."

The other man was right. With Dr. de Souza crushed by Miriama's disappearance, and the town cut off by the heavy rain and rising winds, Vincent would have to wait until tomorrow to get any medical care. That was, if the rain let up. "Come on," Will said, "I'll run you home. Grab your stuff."

Vincent didn't seem to be in any hurry, but Will had things to do. And as far as he could tell from Vincent's speech and general mental responsiveness, it wasn't the head injury that was slowing him down; Vincent just seemed oddly unmotivated. When the other man made no move to get the sports bag he had in the backseat, a bag most likely filled with outdoor gear he'd used during the search, Will opened the back door and grabbed it himself.

Returning to the sedan after dumping the bag in his SUV, he turned off the car's lights, then took the keys out of the ignition before leaning down to look into the other man's face. "Look," he said, his patience at an end, "you want to sit out here all night, fine. But I can't sit with you and I can't leave you here. So get off your ass. There are a lot of other people who might need me tonight."

Vincent blinked, as if becoming aware of his situation for the first time. Swearing under his breath, he got out into the rain. "Will the car be safe here?" he asked, blinking water away from his eyes. "I mean for people on the road."

Will had been thinking the same thing himself; he had accident alert beacons with him, but they'd be washed or blown away in this weather. And calling Peter at the garage to tow this would just put another man at risk from the worsening weather. "How's your back?"

"I haven't got whiplash, nothing like that. The car slid very gracefully into the ditch." Vincent raised his fingers to the cut on his head. "This is from me leaving a metal business-card case on the dash. It flew up during the slide."

Trusting the other man's analysis of his own injuries since he gave every appearance of being fully lucid, Will handed the keys back. "Put the car into neutral. Let's see if we can push it farther into the ditch so it's not half hanging on the side of the road."

The heavens seemed to open up even more as the two of them attempted the maneuver. The one good thing was that the rain made the land slippery. Peter Jacobs's younger and far more hotheaded brother would probably bitch about the work involved in towing the sedan back out of the ditch, but they got it safely off the road and into the depression. No one should hit it unless they themselves went off the road.

Drenched to the skin and with fingers like ice, the two of them finally got into the police vehicle. Vincent reached into the backseat for his sports bag, pulled out a towel. He offered it to Will. "This is the least you deserve after coming out to get me."

"No, that's fine. Dry your forehead so we can check that cut. Head wounds aren't something to just shrug off." His headlights cut fleetingly across the wreck of Vincent's Mercedes as he did a U-turn; the Baker property was situated relatively close to town, off a long drive. "What the hell were you doing out here anyway?" Vincent's car had been pointed *away* from Golden Cove and his home.

"Just driving." Vincent's words were muffled by the towel, came out sounding oddly thick. "Trying to get my head on straight. Trying to understand how something like this could happen in Golden Cove."

Will shot the other man a look, but Vincent's head was conveniently covered by the towel. So he waited to ask his next question—it took a while, as if Vincent was deliberately attempting to wait him out. But the other man couldn't keep on rubbing his hair forever without it becoming a noticeable point on its own.

When he did finally lower the towel to push back the rain-dark strands of his golden hair, Will made him check his wound in the mirror on the back of the passenger-seat sunshade. Only after Vincent confirmed it was shallow, with no sign of bruising, did he say, "Do you know Miriama well?"

"She's the kind of person everybody knows. You can't miss Miri."

"That doesn't answer the question."

The other man sighed. "I like her," he said at last. "She makes me think about being young and hopeful and going after your dreams." A wistfulness that made it pretty obvious Vincent harbored a crush on Miriama.

"You ever say any of that to her?" He chanced a quick glance at Vincent, to see him staring out the window, his classically handsome profile shadowed by the darkness outside.

"I'm just a foolish married man who likes talking to a pretty girl, Will." Vincent's voice wasn't aggressive but sad. "She's so beautiful and so full of life. The idea that I might never again walk into the café and see her smile is a nightmare."

Will had put his eyes back on the road a split second after his glance—he couldn't afford to be distracted in this kind of weather. It frustrated him not to be able to see Vincent's face, gauge his reactions. "Be honest with me," he said. "Lies won't help Miriama."

"What do you want to know?"

"Did it ever go beyond talk with you and her?"

"No. I wouldn't do that to my wife." A long inhale followed by an even longer exhale. "I love my wife. But Miriama has something inside her that I lost a long time ago and it makes me happy to flirt with her a little and fantasize. I'd never shame my family by crossing that line."

Had anyone asked Will a week ago about Vincent Baker, he would've said that Vincent was one of the most straight-up men in town, honest to a fault despite his political ambitions. He was no longer so sure of that belief. There'd been so much *want* in Vincent's voice when he spoke of Miriama, so much . . . Greed wasn't the right word. It was softer than that. A desire almost to cherish.

But, as Vincent had pointed out, he was a married man with two young children. And Miriama wasn't the right kind of woman to be the wife of a future prime minister—she was too wild to accept the strictures of a political life, too much a free spirit. Still, that kind of thing had never stopped a wealthy man from making a less-than-honorable offer to a beautiful younger woman. Was it possible Vincent had approached Miriama, been rebuffed, and decided to take what she didn't want to give?

The only problem was that scenario didn't fit with what Will knew of Vincent—but he wasn't about to rule out anyone or anything at this point. As soon as the weather cleared, he planned to go into Christchurch to talk to jewelers about Miriama's watch. Someone had given it to her—and maybe, just maybe, it hadn't been an out-of-towner.

Vincent had that kind of money. So did Daniel May.

And Christchurch was where Miriama had traveled to meet her mystery lover. It was possible she'd had a hand in designing the watch.

"I'm going to make a stop," he said to Vincent. "I need to check on Mrs. Keith." She was older, might be in bed if he waited till after he'd dropped Vincent off.

The other man said nothing in response to Will's statement.

Pulling up beside the small white-painted house minutes later, Will jumped out and ran up the steps. He couldn't see any lights, but he knocked nonetheless. Then he waited. He knew how long it took Mrs. Keith to get to the door.

A light finally came on several minutes later; the door cracked open two minutes after that. "I knew it would be you." A smile that made her wrinkles fold in on themselves, her makeup yet in place. "I'm all fine and snug in my house. And if it hasn't fallen down in the past forty years, it's not going to fall down tonight, either."

"Do you have everything you need?" Will knew the people in Golden Cove were self-reliant, but Mrs. Keith wasn't in the best health. "Emergency supplies just in case?"

"Why are you asking this old dog if she knows all the tricks?" It was a chiding question. "I'm fine, honey." She patted at the bouffant perfection of her hair, the color a pure, impossible black. "You get yourself to your own house before you catch a chill."

Will waited until Mrs. Keith had shut her door and locked it before he ran back down to the flashing red and blue of his vehicle.

Not long afterward, he turned into the long drive that led up to the Baker homestead. The electronic gate was wide open despite the stormy darkness, probably because Vincent's family was waiting for him to come home.

Will glanced at Vincent halfway up the drive. "I don't want you driving until you've got clearance from a doctor. Make sure you show me that clearance before you get behind the wheel." Stopping the car before they reached the house, he pulled out a Breathalyzer he had in a small case behind his seat. "You know what to do."

Vincent didn't argue.

"Reading's clean." Will hadn't really expected anything else. He'd never seen Vincent drunk—the other man only ever had one beer when he came to the pub.

"I just slid on the road," Vincent repeated as Will drove the rest of the way up the drive. "Misjudged how slick it was." It almost sounded like he was practicing what he was going to say to his wife.

Pushing open the passenger-side door once the SUV had come to a standstill, Vincent looked over at Will. "Thank you. For doing everything you can to find her. She deserves that." He shut the door on those words and walked up to his front door, in which a lovely blonde woman stood silhouetted by golden light.

## 27

Will wished he could see clearly through the rain that crashed against his windscreen—he'd be very curious to see the look on Jemima Baker's face. Because if something had gone on between Miriama and Vincent at any point, the wife had to know. That was something Will had learned on one of his first cases as a detective—the wife almost always knew.

The only problem was, in a town as small as Golden Cove, the town also always knew—and not a single person had pointed Will in the direction of Vincent Baker. Right now, Vincent remained a "foolish married man" with a crush on a young woman who'd always flown free, in contrast to Vincent's own mapped-out life.

As for the other wealthy man in town capable of affording that watch, he'd already proved willing to indulge in an affair with another man's wife. Not many people knew that. Will only did because he'd driven a drunk Nikau home once, and the other man had angrily blurted out the truth.

It turned out that Nikau and Keira had still been living together in Wellington and trying to work on their troubled marriage when Daniel entered the picture. "While I was speaking at a conference in Paris," Nikau had said, "that motherfucker was sleeping with my *wife* and selling her on a life I could never give her. I came back home to find her wearing a necklace she told me she'd bought on special from a local shop, and I was stupid enough to believe her."

It wasn't a stretch to imagine Daniel giving another woman jewelry as part of a new affair.

But though Daniel and Vincent made convenient targets, Will couldn't afford tunnel vision. Miriama could as easily have met a rich tourist. There was also the slim chance that someone in town had more money than Will realized. Shane Hennessey, for one. The novelist had a habit of saying he worked for "love, not money," but he'd had enough cash to tidy up the old Baxter place. Then there was the residency he offered. According to the listing on the creative sites, it came with room and board and a stipend.

Will would do nothing to narrow the focus of his inquiry yet.

He'd switched on the heat when he and Vincent got into the SUV, but he wasn't appreciably warmer or drier by the time he turned the vehicle around and headed down the drive. The gate began to close behind him straight after he passed, so someone at the house had been watching the feed from the discreet security camera trained on the gate.

It was a fairly unusual thing in Golden Cove, that gate, but Will could understand Jemima's need to keep her and Vincent's kids from running out onto the main road. They'd have to get down a long drive to do so, but kids had fast little legs and could easily tumble out, and on these quiet roads, people didn't always think to watch their speed.

The Bakers certainly didn't begrudge anyone who wanted to walk the trails that cut through their sprawling property, only asked that any walkers or hikers remain outside the wire fences that marked the family's residential area.

The trees were opaque shadows around him as he drove through the road unlit by anything except his headlights. The wind howled beyond, bending the trees as the rain began to batter the landscape in slashing punches.

Golden Cove seemed even more deserted when he went through this time. Only the police station glowed with anything but basic night lighting—Will had left the station lights blazing and the door unlocked so that if anyone got caught outside, they could stumble out of the rain and into shelter. He wasn't worried about damage. The safe was empty, the filing cabinet was locked—and didn't contain sensitive documents anyway—and his computer was hardly cutting-edge.

As for the gun safe, it was heavy duty and concealed under his desk. Will was qualified to handle both a Taser and a gun, but he had neither of those at the moment. His Taser had acted up the last time he'd checked it, so he'd sent it in for repair or replacement. As for the gun, the paperwork was still going through—or that was what he'd been told when he inquired.

Will had a feeling his superiors weren't sure he could be trusted with a deadly weapon. He didn't know why. A gun had nothing to do with why he was in Golden Cove. He'd beaten that murderous bastard's face to a bloody pulp with his bare hands.

Those hands tightened on the steering wheel.

The upper windows of the bed-and-breakfast blurred gold in the rain as he passed by. The place had only three guests right now, all seasoned hikers who came regularly enough to Golden Cove that they were honorary locals. Will had run them anyway, found nothing. All three had been helping with the search.

He looked in his rearview mirror out of habit to make sure there was nothing problematic in town as he left, was surprised not to see any lights in the supermarket. Usually, the Lees left on their bright green sign if nothing else. Could be Shan and Pat had decided to switch to backup generators to make sure their fresh goods didn't spoil should the power go out tonight. He'd talk with them tomorrow, find out how it had gone.

For now, he drove on through a Golden Cove that was silent and cold and dark.

It got even colder and darker once he hit the far edge of town and left behind what few lights were burning. He drove with care, his eyes on alert for a patch of pink or orange. He didn't even realize he was doing it until his headlights flashed on something and he stopped the vehicle . . . To see it was only the silver underside of a wind-tossed candy bar wrapper.

It blew away with the next gust.

Putting the car back into gear, he carried on and made the turn into Anahera's drive.

His SUV rumbled along the gravel, pulling up to a stop next to her Jeep. She'd left on the porch light, and he was grateful for it as he got out and jogged toward the cabin. He'd locked the watch and tin safely inside a special compartment he'd built himself in back of his vehicle, hidden beneath the well for the spare tire. He'd also made sure the sirens would go off if anyone tried to get into the vehicle—and they were loud enough to penetrate even this weather.

The door opened before he reached the porch. "I heard your car," Anahera said as his boots hit the wood. "You're drenched."

"Accident on the road out of town," he said, shaking himself off as well as he could.

"Everyone okay?"

"Yeah." He wiped his face. "I should leave my jacket out on the porch. I'll dribble all over your place otherwise."

"The wind will rip it away and down to the water." Anahera waved him inside. "There's a little area here where you can hang it up. My grandmother didn't like mess, had this put in when my grandfather built the cabin."

Will saw what she meant when he stepped inside. The cabin had what might be called a mudroom in some places. Except it wasn't that big. It was more like a shallow pre-entrance. On the left side was a board with hooks. Anahera's anorak hung on one. On the other side was a large shoebox bench seat with a pair of boots already underneath.

Will undid his jacket and hung it on a hook beside Anahera's anorak, the orange color and white high-visibility stripes bold next to the olive green. Then, taking a seat on top of the bench seat, he bent down to unlace his boots and get them off his feet. He chucked his soaked socks beside his boots, having placed the boots under the seat. By then, Anahera was back with a thick yellow towel.

"Thanks." He began to dry his sopping wet hair.

"You can thank Josie. She's the one who supplied me with extra towels—sometimes, I think that woman sees the future."

Will still couldn't see how Anahera and Josie's friendship had endured— Josie might have a business, but the café wasn't her focus. She was the kind of woman who made a packed lunch for her husband and who doted on her son; she'd been known to shut the café if her son's school needed a parent volunteer and she didn't have staff to manage the café while she was gone. She'd no doubt bestow the same maternal attention on the child she was currently carrying.

For Josie, her life was complete. She felt no need to ever leave this small town.

Anahera couldn't be more different. Not only had she left Golden Cove to carve out a life so unique that many here would never understand it, she had a hardness to her that Josie would never have. Anahera, Will thought, knew more about the dark side of human nature than her friend could even imagine.

"I'll be sure to thank her," he said after rubbing his hair to some semblance of dryness. "I don't suppose you have a heater out here?"

Arms folded over the thick cable knit of her chocolate brown sweater, Anahera leaned against the edge of the doorway into the cabin proper. "Townie. Soft as they come."

"That's me. Can't do anything without my fluffy slippers and cup of tea."

Anahera laughed as she walked into the cabin, the sound unexpectedly husky. When he followed, still using the towel in a vain effort to dab himself dry, he found the place warm and snug. A fire crackled in the fireplace, a pile of logs stacked to one side of it. "Did you get the chimney cleaned?"

"Are you always this way?" Anahera asked. "Annoying?"

"It's my job. And if you burn down this place, I'm the one that's going to have to do the paperwork."

"Thanks for the vote of confidence. And yes, the chimney's fine. My mother taught me how to take care of that myself."

Will looked around the room, taking in the cleanly swept surfaces, the old wooden table that stood neatly in one corner, two rickety chairs tucked in underneath. There was no bed, which meant there had to be more to this place than met the eye. "You have another room?"

Anahera used her thumb to point over her shoulder. "Facilities down that way," she said, misunderstanding the reason for his question. "I don't have anything for you to change into."

"I'll dry out." To make that go faster, he took off the gray shirt he was wearing over a white T-shirt and, dragging one of the chairs close to the fireplace, hung the shirt on the back. While his jeans would no doubt remain heavily damp until he made it home, his lightweight tee should dry quickly enough.

Deciding he needed to wash his hands, he walked down the small hallway hidden behind the kitchen area and found himself facing the partially closed door to another room. Prior to that and on the right were the toilet and shower. On the left was the open door to an empty room that had probably been Anahera's mother's bedroom.

He was more interested in the other bedroom. It boasted a bed, from what he could see, and not much else. And Anahera isn't a suspect, he reminded himself when his brain began to scan automatically for signs of trouble. He supposed that, technically, she was as viable a suspect as anyone in Golden Cove, but she had no motive that he could see. She'd returned only days earlier and he was beginning to get the feeling that whatever had happened to Miriama, it had to do with the town—and with secrets.

# 28

Stepping into the bathroom, he washed off the traces of black grit that had sunk into the lifelines on his palms, probably while pushing Vincent's sedan off the road.

When he examined his face in the cracked mirror above the sink afterward, the man who looked back at him had a haggard edge to him, dark stubble having appeared on his jaw and his cheeks still a little sunken. "You'll never be a poster boy, Will."

The scent of coffee was warm in the air when he returned to the living room.

"Have you eaten?" Anahera asked from where she stood at the compact kitchen counter that ran along the back wall.

Will shook his head. "I'll grab toast when I get back home. We should talk over what you heard tonight at the volunteer meeting." Will didn't know Anahera, but he'd run her the day she arrived; it was only prudent to find out if the town's new resident had a record. The last time a prodigal had returned to Golden Cove, he'd turned out to be a drug dealer who hadn't quite left his old life behind.

He'd abandoned his plans to set up shop in town after Will made it clear he'd do everything in his power to throw the other man in prison.

Anahera, by contrast, had no criminal record.

What she did have was a glittering career as a classical musician. Yet there was no sign of music in this room. Not even a small radio.

Of course, it was obvious most of Anahera's belongings hadn't yet arrived. She'd also have taken everything important with her when she said good-bye to the Cove; no point leaving it here to be stolen, vandalized, or impacted by the elements.

"You can have some of this pasta," she said, stirring in the sauce. "The sauce is from a packet, but it's hot and it'll fill you up. And I won't have to eat leftovers for three days in a row. I'm so used to cooking for—" She cut herself off with the suddenness of a woman who'd slammed up hard against an emotional wall.

Will didn't need her to finish her sentence. He knew she'd buried her husband seven months ago. "Thanks," he said, as if he hadn't noticed her abrupt silence. "I never say no to pasta."

"I'm having a glass of red with it." She lifted a plain drinking glass filled about a third of the way up. "I'd offer you the same in my incredibly elegant stemware, but I'm thinking that you're probably still on duty."

"Not officially." Will moved to lean his hip against the counter on the other side of the portable gas stovetop she was using to cook the pasta. A lot of the locals owned one of those; most used them for camping or hunting trips. Probably a good idea for Anahera to stick to that until she could have all the wiring in the cabin checked out.

"But," he added, "in a place like this, where I'm the only police officer around, I'm never really off duty." Will liked it that way. It gave him less time to think, less time to relive the past, less time to apologize to the small ghost who never seemed to hear him.

Anahera took a sip of her wine before saying, "I made coffee, too. Mugs on your right."

Taking hold of a thick green mug from the grouping of four mismatched ones on the counter, Will picked up the old-fashioned and heavy metal teakettle she'd used to keep the coffee hot. "Something like this," he said, lifting up the teakettle, "it'd probably set you back two hundred dollars in one of the designer stores in the big cities."

Anahera laughed, the emotion reaching the darkness of her eyes.

"You're right. But that particular kettle has been in my family for the past fifty years or so."

"They don't make them like they used to." Will put the kettle back down on the large wooden coaster beside the stovetop—that coaster looked like an offcut from a plank, but it did the job.

"Is your electricity from a generator?"

Anahera shook her head. "My mother had the lines put in when she was living here." Her smile faded. "I asked the electricity company to turn the lights back on and everything seems to work. But I'm not chancing using the stove or oven yet."

She'd lifted the pot of pasta and taken it to the table before he realized her intent. "Come on, let's eat."

Will picked up the wine bottle and his mug of coffee, then walked over to join her. After putting both on the table, he went and removed his sodden shirt from the back of the chair, leaving the garment spread out on the floor in front of the fire.

As he moved the chair back to the table, Anahera picked up a loaf of French bread from the counter. "Courtesy of Josie again." The smile was in her voice. "She says she didn't sell it at the café today, had Tom pass it to me at the volunteer meeting. I think she's afraid I'll starve myself out of grief if she doesn't make sure I'm fed."

Tearing the long loaf in half, she placed one half on the cutting board she'd put on the table beside the pot of pasta, then broke the other half into quarters. She took one quarter and bit into it, as if in silent repudiation of her friend's assessment.

Will had seen grief manifested a hundred different ways: in the movies, they liked to show people weeping and wailing or going numb and collapsing. But the truth wasn't always so simple. Some people got angry.

Like Anahera.


The cop ate quietly, Anahera thought. Methodically. As if it was a task that had to be completed, as if the taste of the food meant nothing to him.

Anahera might've been insulted except that she knew she was a good cook even when limited to packet sauce and the basic spices she'd picked up at the Lees' supermarket.

However, she had the feeling she could've put a cordon bleu meal in front of the cop and he'd have eaten it the same way. This wasn't a man who took time to enjoy the small pleasures of life.

Had he been born like that, or had life changed him, made him into this?

If she had to guess, she'd say the latter. No one was born without the capacity for joy in the soul. Life leached it out of them, drop by drop.

Lifting up her glass, she took a deliberate sip of the wine. The smell of alcohol used to make her throw up, but she'd refused to be held hostage to the past and to her father's addictions. So she'd taught herself to enjoy it as it was meant to be enjoyed—in small doses.

Edward had helped; he'd introduced her to a whole new world of fine wines and decadent cocktails. Before that, all she'd known was the cheap plonk you could get down at the local supermarket. But no matter how good the wine, Anahera had never felt the desire to overindulge. To do so would be to spit on her mother's ashes and that was the one thing Anahera would never do.

"This is really good." Will's voice was steady, his eyes watchful.

Anahera was near-certain he was trying to make the kind of conversation he thought he should make. "You eat like it's fuel," she said, her tolerance for bullshit at an all-time low. "Are you sure you even tasted it?"

The face that looked back at her wasn't expressionless as much as opaque. Controlled. Probably a good skill to cultivate when you were in a line of work that involved interrogating suspects. "I tasted it," he said evenly.

But Anahera was no longer thinking about the food. "Am I a suspect?" It wasn't something she'd considered, given how recently she'd returned to Golden Cove, but by that same token, Will didn't know her, had no reason to rule her out. "Is that why you asked me to watch people and report back? So you could compare my report with someone else's and see if I lied?"

He held her gaze with the flinty, unforgiving gray of his. His eyes reminded her of the ocean on a perfectly still day before a storm—it might appear calm, but turbulent currents dragged underneath. "You have a good imagination," he said mildly.

Anahera narrowed her eyes. "Don't try that tone of voice on me." It came out cold, flat. "I was married to a man who grew up in the British public-school system." It had taken her time to get her head around that—that what the English called public schools were actually exclusive private schools. "If you want to play the unemotional-tone game, I can do it as well as you." She demonstrated with her last sentence, saw his eyes wrinkle slightly at the corners in response.

He took his time answering. "Kyle Baker is of the opinion that you ran back to Golden Cove with your tail between your legs because you couldn't hack life in the outside world."

That, Anahera hadn't been expecting. Eyebrows drawing together, she did what he'd done and took a drink before answering. "He was very respectful at the meeting this afternoon," she said. "Even made a special effort to welcome me back to Golden Cove." Anahera thought back, recalling his apparent discomfort with the situation, the way he'd shrugged and moved his feet.

"Kyle is a little psychopath." This time the flatness of the words was hard, the edge of a blade. "It took me this long to see it and I've had experience with the personality type. He does a very good job of covering it up with charm, and with his perfect, shining golden boy act."

Putting down her wine, Anahera leaned forward with her arms braced on the table her mother had found on the side of the road and polished back up by hand. "You sound sure."

Chewing and swallowing a bite of bread he'd just torn off with his teeth, Will said, "He's decided I'm not worth cultivating—I think it gives him a perverse thrill to expose himself to me. He knows no one will believe me if I speak against him."

Anahera had known Vincent her whole life, which meant she'd known Kyle peripherally since his birth. The rare times she'd ever thought about him, she'd just dismissed him as a spoiled brat, but she did remember Vincent telling her that Kyle was the perfect son—Vincent's parents had often held up their younger-by-ten-years second child as an example to Vincent. But there were other things.

"Back when I was thirteen, fourteen—so Kyle would've been only three or four at the time—Vincent told me and Keira that his brother threw a huge tantrum if he didn't also get lots of gifts on Vincent's birthday." At the time, they'd rolled their eyes and told Vincent his brother was just being a baby.

The only reason Anahera even remembered the conversation was because Keira had suddenly said, "I had a brother. He died when he was three, before I was born. His name was Keir." Her black hair pushed back by the sea winds, she'd stared out at the water, this girl who even then had struck Anahera as a blank slate just floating through life. "Keir and Keira. My parents think I have his soul, that I came back from the dead."

Her words had made Anahera's skin pebble with goose bumps.

Will's voice fractured the unsettling memory of the other woman's confession. "Kyle's gotten better at hiding his need to be the best, to be fawned over and adored and treated as better than anyone else, but it's still there under the surface. Be extremely careful around him—and if you ever end up alone with him, change that as fast as possible."

Slate gray eyes locking with her own. "Anyone who lies as well as Kyle and with such a total lack of remorse could be smiling at you one second and shoving a butcher knife into your spine the next. And he'd never lose the smile."

# 29

A chill creeping over her despite the fire in the hearth, Anahera pushed aside her half-eaten bowl of pasta. "Do you think he hurt Miriama?"

Will tapped the fingers of one hand on the wood of the table. "According to Kyle, he has no reason to hurt Miriama. He thinks she'll end up messing up her own life and humiliating herself by crawling back to Golden Cove."

It was odd. Though Anahera had only met Will recently and had, technically, known Kyle far longer, she believed Will. There was something about the cop that said he didn't play games, tell lies.

Of course, her instincts weren't exactly the best.

She'd trusted Edward all those years, especially after they'd suffered a devastating loss and he'd been nothing but loving. She'd believed him when he'd said they'd make it through, that it didn't matter as long as they had each other.

Such a good liar, her dead husband.

Anahera had never suspected he was having an affair, had always accepted his words as the truth when he said he had to stay late at the office or go out of town for work.

No, she couldn't trust her instincts; she needed a second opinion on Will. On Kyle.

She'd talk to Josie, get her friend's take on things. Though, if Kyle did wear a mask, perhaps it had taken an outsider to see beneath it. Anahera would watch him more closely, see if she could spot any cracks in his personality or actions.

"You don't have to believe me about Kyle," Will said, proving he was a damn good cop. "Just be careful. And try not to cross him if you can—he's the kind of man who'll hold on to that insult, or perceived insult, and get his revenge when no one is looking."

A cold feather of sensation along Anahera's spine. "Noted."

"Can I ask you a question?"

When she just looked at him, he said, "Why did you come back? Your fans are begging for a new album and your record company has said publicly that they'll back you whenever you're ready."

"You did your homework."

He didn't back off at her terse response. "You were offered residencies at prestigious schools of music, asked to consider another tour, and yet you came back. Why, when you'd made it out? Isn't that what you wanted?"

Anahera laughed, the sound as bitter as the tears she hadn't shed for Edward. "I think we're both old enough to know that sometimes, what we think we want isn't what we want at all." She'd run from Golden Cove full of dreams and fueled by anger. She'd come back to it a disillusioned woman who knew that some ghosts couldn't be outrun and some nightmares followed you forever.

"I did my homework, too," she said, turning the tables on this man who had a way of making her face things she didn't want to face. "You're pretty famous for a cop."

"I never wanted to be famous." Curt words, a flat tone.

Anahera knew she shouldn't push it, that some darkness a man was permitted to have, permitted to keep secret, but he'd started this and she was in no mood to cut him any slack. "Most cops don't have a big shiny medal pinned to their chest by the leader of the country. Most cops don't face off against a violent drug addict holding five children as hostages and manage to take down the addict without loss of life. You're a goddamn national hero. So what're you doing in Golden Cove?"

A storm in his eyes. "Don't believe everything you hear in the media."

Silence.

"There's another thing," she said into the heavy weight of it. "Miriama's currently the center of attention of the entire town. How would that fit in with Kyle's pathology, if he is a psychopath?"

Will leaned forward, bracing his arms on the table in an echo of her position. He nodded slowly. "That's a good point. Kyle really doesn't like being anything but the center of attention. If he did this, he miscalculated how many people care about her—maybe in his mind, she'd just be forgotten, shrugged off."

Shadows grim across his face. "The only way Kyle can take back the spotlight is if he's the one to find Miriama. If he did something to her, even if it started out as a cruel prank, it's gone too far. He can't find her alive now and still get away with it."

"Jesus." Anahera shoved a hand through her hair and, instead of reaching for the wine, got up and poured herself a mug of coffee. Bringing over the teakettle, she topped up Will's mug as well, then put the teakettle on the table between them and retook her seat. "Are we seriously considering the possibility that Miriama is dead?"

"No. Until I see a body, she's alive. Hurt, perhaps badly, but not dead." He leaned back in his seat. "And Kyle's not the only person I have on my radar."

When he didn't say anything further, Anahera raised both eyebrows. "You're not going to go all 'this is confidential police business' on me now, are you?"

"You're a stranger I barely know," he replied in the mild tone she'd warned him against using on her.

This time, she thought it was deliberate, meant to irritate.

Leaning back in her own chair, she took a sip of coffee before responding in a tone exactly as mild. "Shall I tell you what I heard this afternoon?" Then, as he listened, she went through her list of points. Of how most people had talked about continuing the search, but how she had the feeling everyone thought Miriama was gone. "Kyle said something about her maybe having been taken by the sea. He posed it as a question, kind of hesitant, unsure."

"That's what he said to me, too—only he wasn't uncertain or hesitant." Will placed his mug on the table. "Interesting, isn't it?"

The chill yet in her blood, Anahera blew out a quiet breath. "'Interesting' isn't the word I'd use."

"Did anyone mention the three hikers who disappeared fifteen years ago?"

Anahera frowned. "Yes—Tom brought it up, thought we should let you know." She had to push past her continued dislike of sharing information about her friends to say that. "Nikau figured you must already have the details." She held Will's eyes. "Kyle would've been way too young back then."

"I'm not sure if Kyle has ever gotten his hands really dirty, though I think he's fully capable of it," was the quietly controlled response. "But we can't allow him to twist the focus onto himself—he probably said half the things he said to me today for exactly that reason. To manipulate the spotlight."

"I also met Vincent's wife." Anahera replayed those moments inside her mind. "Doesn't reflect well on me, but I didn't expect to see her there. I'd just filed her in the 'rich ladies who do lunch and attend fancy charity events' category."

"Why did you have that impression?" Will asked softly, the mildness in his voice replaced by humming interest. "Have you ever met her before?"

Anahera shook her head. "I couldn't make it to their wedding—that was when the big volcano erupted and grounded flights." Even though the wedding hadn't been held in the Cove, she'd been ambivalent about coming back, not yet far enough from the past to return to it.

"I remember. You didn't see Jemima Baker at Josie's wedding?"

Of course he'd assume she'd have returned for her best friend's wedding. "No, my wedding bad luck continued with Josie. I had an accident, ended up on bed rest for a while." The lie was so easy to tell now. At first, Anahera hadn't been able to bear talking about how she'd bled out her dreams on the unforgiving cold of an Italian marble floor, then later, she hadn't been able to bear the pity. So she'd just kept on with the lie and Edward had never disputed her choice.

He'd just gone and gotten what he wanted from another woman.

*Four years.*

That's what the wailing woman had said.

She and Edward had been together for four years.

"So if you'd never met Jemima, why did you have that impression of her?" Will prompted again. "Think carefully."

Frowning, Anahera tried to track back through the years. "Before today, the only things I knew about Jemima came from others."

"Josie?"

"She said once that Jemima didn't seem interested in attending town events. Nothing malicious, just a passing observation during a phone call." Anahera had used to curl up in a window seat during Josie's calls, her view of the street below, but her heart in a misty, green land far from London.

Josie's voice had been a song of home. And a memory of pain.

"She and Tom had just bought their own place and the renovations pretty much consumed her life—we'd talk about paint, about wallpaper, about rugs, even about the best tapware for the kitchen." Anahera's lips curved. "A family of her own and Tom, that's all Josie's ever wanted."

"Is that what shaped your perception of Jemima?"

"No. Like I said, Josie was cheerfully obsessed with Tom and their new home—they'd only been married a couple of months then." Less than a year later, Josie's obsession had switched to her first pregnancy.

It had been raining the day she woke Anahera up with the news, her joy incandescent. Anahera had been alone, Edward on one of his business trips—even with all his success as a playwright, he'd continued to put in time at the family firm. The devoted son. Upright and steadfast. That day, Anahera had lain in her bed watching the rain create trails down the windows, and she'd listened to her friend bubble on about the new life growing in her womb.

Afterward, she'd gone to the bathroom and thrown up until her throat was raw.

"Josie and Tom got married less than a year after Vincent and Jemima."

One a large society wedding, the other a cozy local affair, yet Vincent and Josie had shared many guests. Josie had been ecstatic when Vincent chartered a plane to fly his Golden Cove friends up to Auckland for his fancy do.

"I think if Josie hadn't been so involved in planning her own wedding when Jemima first came to Golden Cove, she'd probably have made an effort to draw her out, take the initiative in starting a friendship." That was how Anahera and Josie had first become friends. Josie had literally run over to Anahera while Anahera was in the supermarket with her mother, and taken her hand.

They'd been three years old at the time.

"When Josie mentioned Jemima being standoffish," Anahera continued, "I figured maybe Jemima didn't feel comfortable coming into town because everyone was friends with Vincent and they all knew one another. I felt that way in London for a while."

Marrying Edward had meant integrating into a tight-knit public-school community. Most had been nice people—though their definition of comfort was Anahera's definition of total luxury—but she'd never forgotten they were Edward's friends first, hers a distant second.

Will continued to watch her. "When did that sympathy change? When did you start to think of her as a, what, 'lady of the manor' type?"

Taking another sip of her coffee, Anahera let the deep, rich flavor seep into her tongue as she wound back time. "I think," she said slowly, "it was the pictures Vincent posted. There never seemed to be any . . . normal ones. You know, just hanging out in jeans and tees, throwing a ball around with the kids, or having a sunburned nose at the beach. I've only ever seen photos of her in formal gowns or evening dresses."

"Always?" Will pushed. "Not even in hiking gear? She's a keen tramper."

Chewing on the inside of her lip, Anahera tried to think of a single nonglamorous image of Jemima, and couldn't.

Surely that couldn't be right.

She put down her coffee and went into the bedroom, to return with her old laptop. Opening it up, she used her phone to create a hot spot, then logged into her social media account and clicked her way to Vincent's.

# 30

There it was, the evidence showcased in glittering dresses and sparkling diamonds. All of them with Jemima perfectly posed and made up. The ideal woman to hang on a man's arm and act as his hostess, or to stand supportively behind her politician husband, but one with no real personal drive outside of her defined role in life.

An intelligent doll.

"I can't believe I never consciously noticed this before." In her defense, she'd had no real reason to ever think about Jemima. If the other woman did cross her mind, it had been as an adjunct of Vincent.

Having come to stand at her side, one hand on the back of her chair, Will reached out to tap an image. "Vincent puts up normal photos of himself. Could be he's just one of those men who likes to show off a beautiful wife."

The heat of Will's body brushed against her. For a furious instant, she wanted to tell him to get back, wanted to *push* him away. She had no need for men in her life. Her aloneness had been brutally earned, was craved.

Gritting her teeth, she wrenched the betraying impulse under control and forced her attention to the photos: Vincent playing with his kids, coming home from a bike ride through the countryside, and that infamous one of him caked in mud after a charity soccer match that had taken place on a rain-soaked field.

He looked real, human.

"You didn't connect with Jemima online?" Will asked.

"I really only joined to keep up with close friends." Pausing, she thought about it. "Though, I am friends with Keira, but she sent me the request and I just accepted it." The girl who'd once told her about her dead brother had been Nikau's wife at the time. "I don't know if Jemima even has a profile. Vincent hasn't tagged her in any of these photos."

She did a search to make sure. "No profile. At least nothing that comes up."

Will released the back of her chair, rose to his full height. "Doesn't that strike you as strange? She's a woman with a certain public image to maintain. I'd think she'd want control over that."

"Let's try something else." Opening up a tab on her browser, Anahera put Jemima Baker's name into the search engine.

The results came up quickly.

At the very top was a site that showcased the charities Jemima supported. Each charity had a separate page with details about its work and instructions on how to donate. The images of Jemima were airbrushed and touched up, her makeup flawless. No photos of her laughing or interacting with the staff at the charities, not even a stereotypical shot of her doling out soup to the homeless.

"Odd she's not milking her charity work more for political gain," Anahera murmured, "but she might just be a private person who prefers the world have a particular impression of her." Anahera herself was the queen of masks and illusions.

"Look at the name of the company that designed the website." Will pointed out the tiny script at the bottom of the first page that linked back to a company under Vincent's umbrella. "It's almost as if that's all he sees her as—the perfect, beautiful wife. Not a fully rounded woman."

Anahera turned in her seat so that she was facing Will. "What brought on this line of questioning?"

Walking over to retake his own seat, Will picked up his coffee to take a drink before answering. "The news will be all over town tomorrow anyway," he began. "That accident I mentioned? The reason I was drenched?"

Anahera nodded.

"Vincent drove his car into a ditch."

"My God. Is he—"

"He's fine. A cut on the head, but it doesn't look serious. He told me he skidded because of the rain, but I don't think that's true. I think he was distracted and not paying attention."

Anahera sucked in a breath, a sudden knot in her gut. "At the fire station, he was adamant that the search continue. He seems very passionate about finding Miriama alive."

"'Passionate' is the appropriate word." Will shoved back his hair with one hand. "He's admitted to having a crush on Miriama. You know him better than I do—do you think he'd cheat on his wife?"

She did know Vincent. He was one of her oldest friends. And this cop was asking her to betray him.

Getting up, she went to check the fire. It crackled and sparked in direct contrast to the heavy drumming of rain on the cabin's tin roof, the howling wind held barely at bay. "As a child," she found herself saying after getting up from her crouch, "I always loved storms. The sounds, the smell of ozone in the air, how my mother would sleep over with me so I wouldn't be scared."

Anahera stared down at the orange-red glow of the flames. "I wasn't scared, but I never told her because I liked it so much when she stayed with me." Her mother's body had been a warm bulk, one that meant love and affection and safety.

"I used to like storms, too—before I became a cop," Will said from his seat at the table. "You'd be surprised how stupid people get during this kind of weather. Worst is when cabin fever sets in."

"Do people hurt each other more?" Her father had punched her mother so often that Anahera had seen no difference during storms.

"Yes. And it's mostly people who know each other and say they love one another."

The words fell in between them like unexploded grenades. She saw realization dawn in his eyes a second later. He immediately shook his head. "That wasn't a dig. Every cop I know hates domestic violence callouts. They have a tendency to go bad very quickly."

Anahera turned her attention back to the fire, to the flames and the heat and the warmth that couldn't reach the ice in her heart. "No need to tiptoe around the truth," she said. "My father did beat my mother. Badly. Everyone in Golden Cove knows that."

It was impossible to hide bruises when they went three deep.

"Nikau and Josie tell me he's turned over a new leaf, goes to AA meetings every month. But that doesn't change the past, does it? It doesn't disappear my mother's black eyes and broken bones and splintered spirit. It doesn't bring her back."

Anahera didn't believe in forgiveness, not for that crime. Whether or not Jason Rawiri had physically pushed her off that ladder, sociable Haeata had only lived in this cabin far from her friends because she owned nothing else. Jason had taken it all, every cent she'd ever earned. Only Anahera's grandparents' cabin remained. A safe place for Haeata to move with her daughter, but not one she could've sold for any real gain. As it was, even with Anahera contributing through part-time jobs, they'd barely managed the outgoings.

If Haeata had had the money to rent in town, a neighbor would've noticed she wasn't around outside pottering away. Someone would've checked on her.

And Anahera's mother wouldn't have bled to death cold and alone.

"I can't answer your question about Vincent's loyalty to his wife," she said into the heavy silence. "The boy I knew was the straightest arrow in our group. But those pictures he puts up of Jemima, like she's a shiny trophy and not a real person . . . that's not the Vincent I know."

Her mind kept gnawing on the whole thing. What if it wasn't just bragging about a trophy or showing off? What if he wanted to shape his wife's image to keep others at a distance from her?

Why would he do that? Consciously isolate Jemima?

The cold in Anahera's bones turned as brittle as her mother's too-often-fractured left arm. "You don't think he might be hurting her?"

"I've never seen any indications of that." Will rose to join her by the fire. "But people are good at hiding the bruises. A woman in Jemima's position, with such a strong public profile, would probably work extra hard to make sure no one found out."

"My mother wasn't wealthy or well-known like Jemima, but she was still ashamed to admit that her husband beat her." Even though everyone already knew. "She couldn't bear it that others would think her weak." Never understanding the shame wasn't hers but his. "The psychological damage can be as debilitating as the physical."

Will nodded. "And Jemima probably hasn't got anyone to turn to in this country."

It was only then Anahera remembered that Vincent had met his wife in South Africa. "She doesn't have an accent."

"I always thought that was a political move meant to help Vincent." Will braced his forearm on the mantel. "Losing the accent and trying to sound like a local."

The more Anahera thought about what they were considering, the heavier the stone in her gut. "Vincent's been my friend for a long time and I've never *once* seen him be violent—to anyone. He's the one who always broke up the schoolyard fights." Jemima could well be a willing coconspirator in her glamorous public image. "Maybe the glamour is to help build up her profile so she'll have media clout when Vincent launches his campaign." It was a more realistic possibility than educated and connected Jemima having nowhere to turn. "The world likes following the lives of beautiful people. And glamorous political wives get a lot of airtime."

"No one really knows much about the situation inside the Baker house," was the disturbing answer. "Vincent and Jemima invite people up for dinner now and then. I got an invite the month I moved in—but all I saw was the flawless veneer. The smiling hostess, the good-humored host, the perfect, well-behaved children who didn't throw a tantrum or fidget when paraded out to meet a stranger."

Putting both hands against the rough-hewn wood of the mantel, Anahera stared at the flames as the wind threatened to tear off the roof. "I have an open invitation from Jemima to visit. I'm going to take her up on it."

She needed answers, needed to find out if there was something terrible going on in Vincent's house.

Because if there was and Anahera looked away, she'd never forgive herself.

"If nothing else, I want to let her know she has a friend in Golden Cove. She must know my family history by now." Anahera had never before consciously used that history, but if it would help a woman trapped in a violent home, then she didn't think her mother would mind. Haeata had been one of the most generous people she'd ever known.

"That's a good idea," Will said. "She'd never trust me the way she might trust you." Moving away from the fire, he began to pace across her small cabin, the floorboards creaking beneath his bare feet.

Anahera turned and found herself watching those feet, big and slightly pale as they walked back and forth, back and forth. "Miriama is very young for Vincent," she said, going back to his question about cheating. "But . . . Jemima *is* the perfect wife. The kind of wife Vincent's parents always wanted for him. We didn't email much, but when he invited me to their wedding, he mentioned that she was the daughter of family friends."

Will paused in midstep. "A modern-day arranged marriage?"

"That was my feeling." Anahera couldn't shake the sense of disloyalty, but she also couldn't let this go now that Will had planted the seed in her head. It didn't matter who it was, if someone was making another person's life hell while putting on an act of loving and cherishing that person, then Anahera would do everything in her power to change that.

Thunder boomed at that moment, lightning flashing beyond the windows.

Walking to the front door, she opened it. The cold swept in, but it wasn't a blast, the wind and the rain both slanting in from the opposite direction for now. It allowed her to stand in the doorway and watch the storm rage above the ocean, a cauldron of bruise-colored clouds and black fire.

She was aware of Will coming up behind her, a large solid presence, and suddenly her body, which had been in deep freeze for seven months, decided to wake up. It liked the smell of this cop, liked the look of him, liked those moody eyes and the way he was hunting so hard for a girl many in his position would've forgotten.

"Do you have any other clues? Anything to go on?" she asked, shoving back the part of her that wanted to turn to him and say, "Let's go to bed." The mindless physical act would offer a little relief to her body, but her anger and her grief would all still be there in the morning.

"I located the watch," he said. "It's too unique to have come from an ordinary shop."

"International, you think?"

"We start here first. I'm planning to go to Christchurch, show it around the high-end and custom jewelers, see if anyone recognizes it."

"How about sending them a photograph? Wouldn't that speed things up?"

"I want to see their faces—it's an expensive enough piece that the jeweler might feel the need to be protective of the client's privacy."

Staring out at the huge waves slamming into shore, Anahera said, "You really shouldn't be driving in this."

A single wire-taut moment, their breaths in time, before Will stepped back. "It's a very short drive." He went to the fire and picked up his still-wet shirt, pulling it on with a grimace.

Once back out in the entranceway, he sat down on the shoebox and began to tug on his boots. He shoved his wet socks into a pocket of his jacket when he pulled the jacket on. Zipping it up, he flipped the hood over his head, then paused on the edge of the porch. "Stay safe, Anahera. And if you hear anything, you'll let me know?"

Anahera met those gray eyes that hid so much. "As long as you return the favor. I'm not going to betray my friends if I don't know why I'm doing it."

The cop's answer was indirect. "You probably have things you want to get from the big stores in Christchurch. If you want a ride there, come by the station around ten tomorrow morning—storm should be well over by then." He was gone a second later, lost in the rain mere footsteps from the house.

Anahera didn't realize she was holding her breath until his headlights came on. The twin beams swung toward the ocean before she was faced with red taillights blurred by rain into smudges. Moments later, they began to fade into the distance, the cop heading back to the town he'd vowed to protect and serve.

Long after he'd left, Anahera stood in the doorway of the home where she'd found her mother's lifeless body, and stared out to the sea that may have taken a hopeful young life.

# 31

Will watched Anahera's cabin be swallowed up by the storm and had to fight the urge to stop his vehicle and turn around, go back. He wondered what she'd do, if they could recapture that one fragmentary instant that could've ended the night a whole other way.

He shook his head.

No, going down that route was not an option; Anahera might've been away from Golden Cove for eight years, but her loyalties were openly divided. Putting either one of them in that position would further mess up an already messy situation. But at least now he knew—his body wasn't dead. Because it had definitely reacted to Anahera with her prickliness and her anger and her presence that was as untamed as this landscape.

Will wasn't sure how he felt about that. He'd been quite comfortable being half-alive. He didn't want to come back to full life. Especially not when a young woman was missing, he had a budding psychopath in his town, and the one man everyone thought a good guy might be beating his beautiful wife.

He drove at a snail's pace. He was confident of his driving ability, but he wasn't so confident of anyone else who might have decided to venture out into the night. The world was an ugly maelstrom beyond the windscreen, the trees and native ferns hidden by a gloom that suffocated all life.

Finally pulling up to a stop in his drive, under the carport, he got out. At least he wouldn't get much wetter. The carport was connected to the house on one side, though the wind and rain continued to howl in from the three open sides.

Going to the back of the SUV, he removed the items he'd hidden in the secure space beneath the spare tire well, then locked up and moved in the direction of the door into the house. Unlike most of the people in Golden Cove, he always locked his door, so it took him an extra couple of seconds to get in.

Just as he was about to step inside, his mind on a hot shower and dry clothes, he got that crawling sensation on the back of the neck that said someone was watching him. But when he looked out into the blackness, he saw nothing. The storm was too violent, the rain coming down in slashing sheets.

Will stood there unafraid, staring down whoever it was that thought they could intimidate the small-town cop. Maybe he was going mad, the dead little boy who followed him around ready to take his due. But Will didn't think so—someone stood out there in the rain, watching him, wondering what he knew.

Will was glad he'd put the watch and tin in a thick yellow plastic shopping bag earlier that night—his only aim back then had been to give the evidence a little extra protection from the rain. But now, even if the person watching had managed to spot his actions despite the terrible visibility, they had no way of knowing what it was he had inside the bag.

The crawling sensation faded at last.

Not entering the house until at least five more minutes had passed, he locked the door behind himself, then checked the lounge, kitchen, and spare bedroom. It didn't take long—the place was no mansion, though, judging from their style choices, the owners had clearly considered it their castle.

The two old-fashioned rifles mounted crisscross above the mantel had been lovingly polished and dust free when Will moved in. The first thing he'd done was to pull them off and check their status. As they'd been properly decommissioned and were now nothing but decorative, he'd put them back in place. Neither had he moved the overstuffed sofa upholstered in bright orange and black stripes. It wasn't as if he ever sat in the lounge.

The rest of the house cleared, he took the evidence with him into his bedroom. He was probably acting paranoid for a cop in a small town, but he'd been a cop in a much bigger town, and he knew that homes weren't always safe.

Homes were where people let down their guards and invited the monsters in.

Which was why he locked his bedroom door, too, before checking to ensure his windows were locked. He wasn't worried about himself—but he needed to take a hot shower, and he didn't want the evidence stolen in the interim.

After stripping with quick motions, he left the bathroom door open as he stepped into the shower just long enough to warm up from the inside out. The fire at Anahera's had done a good job of chasing out the chill, but the damp shirt he'd put back on, while distracted by a moment that shouldn't have happened, had undone that during the drive here. Stepping out of the shower only a couple of minutes later, he looked out at his bedroom to confirm nothing had been disturbed.

No sign of an intruder.

A fast rubdown to dry himself before he pulled on a pair of faded jeans and a gray sweatshirt, then he took the evidence and a pair of disposable gloves with him into the kitchen. There, he made himself a cup of decaffeinated coffee—any more caffeine and he'd probably be wired all night.

Sitting down at his small kitchen table with a notepad, pen, and the mug of coffee on one side, he put on the gloves before emptying the plastic shopping bag. Leaving the watch in its evidence bag for now, he retrieved the tin box and looked at the rusted lock. It definitely needed a key. But Will didn't have time to waste waiting on a locksmith and he had Matilda's permission to open it. No court in the world would throw out any evidence he uncovered as a result.

First, however, he found his camera and took photos of everything. A small ruler from the junk drawer acted as a scale marker.

He'd continue to document as he went.

Next, he decided to grab his toolbox and see what he could do with the lock. It didn't take much to break it. Putting it aside, where he'd eventually place it into an evidence bag, he carefully opened the lid. Then, though he wanted to immediately pick up the book on the top, he grabbed the camera instead and took several photographs of the contents.

Only once he'd documented everything in situ did he pick up the bronze-colored book he'd seen, the word *Journal* written in curly gold writing across the front. Someone had also pasted small heart stickers around the edges of the word.

Will ran his thumb over one of the stickers.

It was such a girly thing for a young woman as beautiful and as experienced at handling men as Miriama appeared to be; some part of her, Will realized, was still a girl. Dreaming of hearts and flowers.

Jaw hard, he checked the first page, then the last one in which she'd written something. A glance at the dates confirmed this was Miriama's most recent journal. It appeared to span a year, beginning about six months after Miriama would've turned eighteen. From the amount of pages filled, it was clear she hadn't journaled every day.

He went back to the first entry. It was a short one:

> *Hello, new journal. We're going to have some wonderful*
> *adventures together. I feel it in my bones. Love, Miriama.*

She hadn't made another entry for a week. That entry was a chatty one that talked about working in Josie's café and her application for the internship.

> *. . . I know I probably won't get it. Kyle's also applying, and*
> *everyone loves him. Sometimes I wonder why they can't see*
> *through him. Is it just that beautiful face? Are people really so*
> *taken in by looks? Why can't they see that he manipulates*
> *everyone around him? Anyway, I'm going to try. I hope it*
> *doesn't mess everything up.*

The next three entries were all about the internship and how difficult it was to get through to the interview stage. After that began a week of entries one after the other.

> *He gave me a watch today. It's the most beautiful thing I've ever owned in my entire life. I couldn't believe it when he opened the box and showed it to me—it sparkled in the sunlight, rainbows coming off it. When I stared at him and said, "Are those diamonds?" he just smiled and slipped it onto my wrist.*
>
> *"Only diamonds for a diamond," he said in that sweet way he has of talking. "Do you think you'll be able to wear it?"*
>
> *Of course I'm going to wear it, but I knew what he was asking. "No one will think it's real," I told him. "I'll tell them I picked it up at a flea market while I was in Christchurch."*
>
> *I keep on admiring that watch. It's so pretty. He makes me feel so pretty, so loved and wanted. I asked him if I could get an engraving on the back of the watch with our initials, but he told me I shouldn't, that there was too much risk the wrong person would see it. I know he's right, that I shouldn't ask for things I can't have, but I love him so much.*

Will made a note of the date of that entry on the notepad. It would make it easier to ask the watchmakers and jewelers to search their sales records if he at least knew the date by which the watch had already been sold.

That done, he read through until he found the next entry of interest.

> *We had the most amazing day yesterday, spent it all with each other. The only bad thing was that we couldn't go out because he might've been recognized. It's a big city, but it's still not such a big city when you compare it to all the other cities in the world.*

*Even I might've seen someone I knew.*

*He says one day, he'll take me to faraway places like London and New York and Paris. He says no one will know who we are there, that we can laugh and hold hands on the street and dance under the stars.*

*I have this knot in my belly when I imagine that, all hot and needing and wanting. I know this is wrong. I know Auntie would be so disappointed in me for coveting another woman's husband, but how can I help it when he's so wonderful? Surely, God wouldn't have put him in my path if I was meant to stay away from him?*

*Each time we're together, I'm torn. I love him like he's another part of me, but I also go to church with Auntie and I promise not to commit a sin. And yet I sin with him with every kiss, every touch.*

The next time she'd written about her lover, it was in a fast flowing hand, as if she'd been jotting things down quickly:

*I told him today that I wouldn't see him anymore. Last night, I had a dream and I dreamed that God was so angry with me. Surely, it's a sign. God himself is talking to me.*

There was a smudge on the last line, a droplet of liquid having fallen onto the page and melted the ink.

The next relevant entry was only a week later and longer, more detailed:

*I have no willpower around him.*

*He came to see me as soon as he could, and he held me and he said, "You know I can't breathe without you. You're my air."*

*I tried to tell him about sin and about following God's commandments, but he said, "How can this be a sin? We love each other. Our love is honest. You've done nothing wrong."*

*Then he pressed his forehead to my own and he cupped*
*my face and he said, "I'm the one who's the sinner, Miriama,*
*not you. I fully accept that. I'm the liar. But I've never lied*
*to you."*

*I believe him.*

*I love him.*

*And this sin is what we have.*

The next two months of sporadic entries were mundane, technical jottings about her photography, funny comments that made Will want to smile, and only the occasional note that she was seeing "him" that weekend, or that "he'd" messaged her "the sweetest thing."

But the next entry that focused specifically on her relationship—dated six months ago—had a bleaker tone:

*I love him too much to walk away, but I'm starting to think*
*about where this will lead. He tells me I'm young, that I have*
*the time to wait, and for him, I won't be selfish. I can wait. But*
*today Auntie was talking about a girl she knew who'd been*
*taken in by an older man. He never married her, not like he*
*promised.*

*And I wonder if that's going to happen to me.*

*But then I look at the watch that he gave me, a watch that's*
*worth thousands and thousands of dollars, and how can I not*
*believe him? He picked this out personally, risked everyone*
*finding out about us.*

*Surely that means something, surely that means he's*
*committed to me.*

*But I still worry. And I'm sad. Especially when I see Josie*
*and her husband walking down the street, their hands linked*
*and their little boy walking between them. I can never walk*
*like that with him. Not for a long, long time.*

Will turned the page to read the final entry for that week.

*He's asked me to meet him again. I will, of course I will. When I'm with him, nothing else matters. I think I need to trust him a while longer and see where this goes. After all, we've made it this long.*

*If anyone had known, they'd have said we wouldn't even make it a month. But we've made it for ten now, and we'll make it another month and another and another and another. We'll make it until he's free, until he can be mine.*

# 32

Will put down the journal and thought about what he'd just read, making a few more notes on his notepad. Miriama's married lover had been wealthy and, for some reason, couldn't divorce his wife to be with Miriama. Maybe he'd been stringing Miriama along, as she'd feared, or maybe it had been because he had ambitions that wouldn't allow for a scandal, especially one that called his image as a family man into question.

Again, he told himself not to focus on Vincent. The other man's crush had probably been exactly that—because Vincent would have to be one hell of a liar to have pulled off an illicit affair under the town's nose.

And Daniel still fit all of the parameters; throw in his history with Keira and he fit them even better. Then there was the fact that nothing Miriama had written so far told him whether or not her lover had been an outsider or a local.

He refreshed his coffee before he turned the page into the world of a girl so beautiful and so full of life that she'd glowed like sunshine. As the entries continued—closer together now—she never once mentioned the name of her lover, as if keeping their secret was so ingrained that she didn't dare utter the truth even in her private journal. Though the secrecy seemed to weigh increasingly heavily on her.

*I wanted to shout his name to the heavens today. It was such a*
*sunny, clear, blue-sky day and I wanted to swing myself around*

*and around in a circle and shout out how much I loved him,*
*but even though I was alone on the beach, under the old cabin*
*where Ana used to live with her ma before she went away to*
*London, I didn't do it.*

*I'm so used to keeping his name secret that I sometimes*
*wonder if I remember it. And then I wonder if he remembers*
*mine. Or do I only exist for him behind the closed doors of hotel*
*suites where no one knows us, and I check in under my own*
*name and he just comes up to my room, no record of his*
*presence.*

*When I use my credit card to pay for the room, I always*
*think about the money he gives me to make sure I can clear the*
*payment. Always cash. No trail. I don't exist anywhere in his*
*actual life. He only exists in mine in the pages of this journal—*
*and even here, he doesn't have a name.*

*Can a relationship survive without names? Without an*
*identity?*

Will frowned, realizing he'd made certain unconscious judgments
about Miriama. He'd thought her pretty and talented and sweet. But he'd
never realized she thought so deeply, saw so clearly—for one, she'd seen
Kyle's real face when the young man had fooled everyone else.

Eyes gritty, he glanced at the time that glowed on his microwave
and knew he should go to bed. But he couldn't put down the journal. It
might not give him a name, but Miriama may well have dropped other
clues. And he wanted to know two things in particular. Deciding there was
no way he could read through the entire journal tonight, he flipped
forward.

There. Three months and two weeks ago.

*I've ended it. This time, forever. I have a life to live and that*
*life needs to be out in the open, under the sunlight. I need a*
*partner by my side, not a ghost no one knows, no one sees.*

Two weeks after that came the second entry Will was hunting.

*Dominic asked me out again today. This time, I said yes. He's
gorgeous in that nerdy, cute way, and he looks at me like I'm a
goddess. He also has ambitions just like I do.*

*He told me he knows I don't want to be stuck in Golden
Cove forever. He doesn't, either. He has a three-year plan. After
he completes his contract here, he'll have enough experience to
get work in a larger town, from which he'll eventually move to
a city practice.*

*And after that, he says he'll look for international
opportunities.*

*I'm going to try.*

*Dominic is perfect.*

Something about that entry struck Will as "off," but maybe it was just
the idea of Miriama making a list and ticking boxes. She'd called Dominic
gorgeous, but the words she'd written about the doctor had been without
passion, holding none of the terrified joy that infused her entries about her
previous lover. Maybe that was a good thing—the girl was smart enough
to know she was on the rebound.

Will flipped to the very last entry in the journal. Along the way, he
caught sight of an entry that had his shoulders bunching.

*I've become so good at keeping secrets. Until I can't even write
some things here, in a place no one else will ever look. It scares
me sometimes, who I've become because of him.*

The final entry was dated four days before her disappearance.

*I think Dominic's getting ready to ask me to marry him. Auntie
keeps smiling at me in a secretive way and he went out of town
the other day, then blushed bright red when I asked him where*

*he'd been. He never lies to me, so I didn't push it, but I think
he went to pick up a ring.*

*I don't love him like he loves me and I feel guilty about that
sometimes, but I do love him. He's so happy when he's with
me—what I can give him, it's enough. And what he can give
me, it's what I need. I don't want to be alone. I've never really
liked being alone. Marriage will be a good thing. It's what I
want. I'll say yes.*

Closing the journal, Will stared at the wall across from him. Covered
by yellowed wallpaper dotted with tiny brown flowers, it was honestly the
ugliest wall he'd ever seen, and that included the one in his grandmother's
house that featured giant blue roses. He'd loved his gran, missed her when
she passed, but that wallpaper . . .

Will glanced back down at the final entry. Tight timeline or not, he'd
been chewing over Dominic de Souza as a possible suspect in the back of
his mind—lovers were always at the top of the list. But if Miriama had
decided to say yes to his proposal, then rejection as a motive was off the
table. Dominic clearly knew he was punching above his weight when it
came to Miriama—she was the kind of woman who'd inspire envy in other
men, and Will had the sense Dominic enjoyed that.

He could see no reason for the doctor to have harmed Miriama when
she was about to give him everything he ever wanted.

Which took Will back to the lover Miriama *had* rejected.

Reading between the lines, that man had been very possessive of
Miriama—he was also wealthy and likely not used to being told no.

Thunder rumbled again, a massive boom of sound.

It didn't look like it now, but according to the weather report, this
storm would clear by morning. If that held true, he'd make the trip to
Christchurch and get started on the jewelers and watchmakers; first, however, he'd run a wide patrol through Golden Cove and surrounding areas,
make sure everyone had come through the storm okay. The volunteer
search teams would no doubt go out again, but Will was grimly certain

that if Miriama had been anywhere where she could be found, she would've already been found.

Setting aside the journal for now, he decided to look quickly through the rest of the items in the tin. He found mostly what he'd expected: ticket stubs from a show in Auckland, a curling photograph of a stunning woman who might've been Miriama with twenty more years on her, a Valentine's Day card that had the words *To my love* and *Always, I'm yours* written within and was signed only with *xoxo*.

The flotsam of Miriama's life—flotsam she'd kept as reminders of moments that had meant something to her. He'd have been disappointed not to find a photograph of her lover if he hadn't already read her journal and known how carefully she kept that secret. If she *did* have an image of the man, it was most probably on her phone.

Or, he realized, it could be out in the open in a way that'd raise no eyebrows—one of her photographic portraits. He'd seen images of Vincent, Daniel, other men both known and unknown in her files. He'd look at those portraits again, but with Miriama skilled at bringing out emotion in all her subjects, he wasn't expecting a sudden epiphany.

The Valentine's Day card might be useful in providing a handwriting sample to compare against the lover's, but that would come after he'd tracked down a solid suspect.

Will picked up and looked at the snapshot of the woman again. This had to be Miriama's mother—the resemblance was striking except for one thing: the older woman's face displayed none of Miriama's sunny joy in life. Her eyes were jaded despite the smile that curved her lips, her face set in lines that hinted at petulance.

When he flipped the photograph over to look at the back, he found a note in the same large and generously looped handwriting as in the journal:

*Ma just before she found out she was pregnant.*

It struck him as an odd thing for Miriama to have put on the back of the picture; most people would've used another marker for their mother's life. Will had the bleak feeling Miriama had grown up knowing her existence had forever changed her mother's. Matilda would never say a hurtful thing to a little girl. Which meant the message—and the rejection—had come directly from Miriama's mother.

What did that do to a child?

Did it leave holes in the soul?

A hunger to be wanted, to be loved?

Just the kind of vulnerability a smart, selfish man might exploit.

Putting down the photograph, Will finished looking through the other items in the tin box. Nothing that immediately jumped out, though the two ticket stubs from an exclusive stage show were interesting—dated months before Miriama began seeing Dominic, they must've cost in the hundreds.

He'd follow up, but he knew the chances of tracing Miriama's lover through the tickets was unlikely. If the unknown male had stuck true to form, the tickets had been purchased either in cash or in person or—more probably—by Miriama after her lover gave her the cash to cover the credit card repayment.

Will's hand fisted.

An affair was one thing, but for this man to protect himself with such caution, even using Miriama as a shield, it spoke of an intense and manipulative self-interest. Miriama had been right to fear that her lover would never fulfill his promises to her. And she'd been smart to break away.

But had she stayed smart?

Love could make people do stupid things.

Sometimes, that stupidity led to death. And to screams Will had never heard, but that haunted him each time he closed his eyes. As long as he lived, he wouldn't understand why a loving mother would pick up the phone and invite a monster to visit. Daniella Hart had been safe. Her little boy had been safe.

But she'd picked up the phone.

So no, Will didn't trust that Miriama had stayed smart.

# 33

Anahera walked into Josie's café just after nine thirty the next morning, the world sunlit around her, knowing she'd see this through to the bitter end. Something bad had happened and was continuing to happen in Golden Cove and Anahera wasn't about to ignore it. People did that too often. Just ignored things because those things were uncomfortable or awkward, and in the end, all they had left were broken pieces and blood.

She forced a smile onto her face as Josie bustled around the side of the counter. "Shouldn't you be sitting down?"

White lines bracketing her mouth, Josie used both hands to cradle her bump. "I can't sit still," she said. "I'm so worried about Miri. Working in the café, making sure the fire station is supplied with tea bags and milk and sugar and whatever else they need, it gives me a way to be in the thick of things, get any news as it comes in. The idea of sitting at home and just waiting . . ."

Anahera nodded. "I'm sorry, Josie. I know you two are close."

Her best friend smiled tightly before walking over to fuss with a table centerpiece—a tiny glass bottle that held a couple of freshly picked daisies. "We're too far apart in age and interests to be friends like me and you," she said. "I like to think of myself as her older sister, someone she can come to for advice."

Not particularly liking herself for pumping her friend for information, Anahera nonetheless knew she had to take advantage of this opportunity.

If Miriama had confided in her, Josie could well know things no one else did. "Did she tell you anything that could explain her disappearance?"

Josie stopped fussing with the table decoration and went around to the coffee machine. "Cappuccino, right?" She began to make one without waiting for an answer. "I've been digging through my memories since she went missing." The high sound of steam, of milk being frothed. "But the thing is, even though I like to think of myself as her older sister, I'm not sure Miriama thinks of herself as my younger sister."

Taking a seat near the counter, Anahera shrugged off her anorak. "Why? Did she say something?"

Josie didn't reply until she'd finished making the cappuccino. Bringing it out with an ease that made it clear she'd done the same a thousand times, she placed the drink in front of Anahera, then took the seat across from her. "No, it's just . . ." Her friend pushed both hands through the fine strands of her hair, the light brown intermingled with a glint or two of silver. "I feel like I'm gossiping about her behind her back."

"You can't think like that." Anahera got up to grab the chocolate shaker to dust the fine granules over the froth of her coffee, more to give Josie space than because she wanted it. "Not if what you know might be helpful in finding her."

Swallowing hard as Anahera retook her seat, Josie stared at the wood grain of the smoothly planed table. "I heard her on the phone a few times," her best friend said at last. "She had that look on her face—the same look you had on your face that weekend I came to stay with you up in Auckland. It was right after you'd met Edward, and you were glowing and giggly and happy."

Anahera could barely remember that version of herself. "That can't be an unusual thing for a girl as beautiful as Miriama," was all she said.

"You'd think so, wouldn't you?" Josie said. "But—and this is before Dominic—Miri's never really dated as much as you might assume. She has big dreams and she's determined to make them happen. She did go out on the odd date, don't get me wrong, but it was a year and a bit ago that she got that look on her face and I knew it was serious."

Anahera just nodded, the fingers of one hand around her coffee cup.

"I sort of teased her about it," Josie continued, tracing the wood grain with a fingertip. "Like I did you about Edward. Nothing pointed or mean. Just kind of saying how she was looking happy and when was I going to meet the lucky guy."

Leaning forward, Anahera took one of Josie's hands in her own. "You're ice-cold," she said with a frown, and began to rub Josie's hand between her own to warm it up. "Do you want me to get your shawl?" She could see it draped over the chair behind the counter.

But Josie shook her head. "The cold is from inside," she whispered. "It's from fear of what might've happened to Miri."

"Just tell me if you change your mind." Anahera didn't stop attempting to warm Josie up. "How did Miriama react to your teasing?"

"She—" Josie paused, bit her lower lip. "Her reaction was odd . . . hurtful." Hazel eyes held Anahera's. "My response feels so immature now, but back then, I was badly wounded by what she did."

"Was she angry with you?"

"No. She lied to me." Josie's voice shook. "Laughed and said that I was mistaken, that she'd been talking to a friend. I knew she hadn't been, knew that tone in her voice was for a lover, not a friend."

"Did she ever admit the truth?"

"About a month later—she came up to me out of the blue and said she was sorry for having lied to me, but that she couldn't talk about the person she was dating. She said he was inappropriate and that she wasn't ready for anyone to know about the relationship." Josie extended her other hand toward Anahera. "Since you're doing such a good job."

Laughing at this small glimpse of the content, happy Josie she knew, Anahera switched her warming-up attentions to her friend's neglected hand. "When she said 'inappropriate,' did you have any idea what she meant?"

A shake of the head. "I nudged her about it, asked if there was anything I could do, even cautioned her against getting involved with a man who might not be good for her, but she just hugged me and said she loved me for caring."

Josie sank her teeth into her lower lip. "Then she told me not to worry, that her guy wasn't abusive or a drug dealer or anything bad like that, only someone it might take her aunt a little bit to warm up to, so she was going slow with it."

It wasn't much to go on. Inappropriate could mean all kinds of things—the lover could've been significantly older, for example. "Did you two ever talk about it again?"

"I accidentally walked in on another phone call a few months later. She was out back having a break, but I needed her to come in because a tourist bus had turned up early and I knew we were about to be slammed. I pushed open the back door and heard her say, 'We are sinners.'"

Josie's face turned stark. "She hung up as soon as she saw me and we didn't talk about it then, but at the end of the rush, she looked at me and said, 'Will you still be my friend when you find out what I've done?'" Her fingers tightened on Anahera's. "It was so sad, the way she said it. I told her nothing could break our friendship and then, because I thought she needed a laugh, I said the only caveat was if she attempted to seduce Tom. Then all bets were off."

"Unless Tom has had a personality transplant, I don't think you ever have to worry about him straying." Even Anahera, with her dim view of men, couldn't fault Tom's loyalty or love. He'd do anything for Josie, including hauling over supplies for her crazy friend who lived in a cabin on the edge of town—he'd also checked Anahera's plumbing while he was there.

Tom Taufa was one of the good guys.

"That's why it was so funny, the idea of him being seduced." Releasing Anahera's hand, Josie resettled herself on the chair. "But Miri's face went kind of still and odd, and she said, 'You never have to worry about that, Josie,' and then she left to deliver a coffee to Glenda at the tourist center, and we never talked about it again."

Anahera sat back in her seat. "A married man?"

"That's what I thought, too," Josie said with a sigh. "I really didn't want to believe it—I take marriage vows dead seriously. But I love Miriama. I decided my job was to support her. And I wasn't about to blame her when she wasn't the one who was breaking vows." Her voice was harder on the next words. "If I ever find the man who convinced her to break her faith, however, I'll have a few things to say to him. She was tormented at committing a sin."

The small bell above the door tinkled.

Anahera turned to see Dominic de Souza; she recognized him only because Matilda had shown her a photo of Miriama with "her doctor boyfriend." There'd been so much pride in Matilda at that instant, her tear-swollen eyes momentarily suffused with happiness.

There was nothing of happiness in Dominic de Souza.

Grief had ravaged his face, creating new grooves in his skin, and his hair was as wild as his eyes behind the clear lenses of his glasses, but he had on a fresh white shirt over a pair of black pants. "I've got patients to see," he said without a greeting. "I'm the only doctor in town."

Pushing herself up by using the table as a brace, Josie walked over to take Dominic's hands. "I'll make you your usual," she said softly. "If you need anything else, you just call from the clinic."

Anahera rose and began to put on her anorak while Josie went around to make the coffee. The doctor just stood there, his face more than a little vacant. Anahera didn't know if he should be treating patients today, but maybe being in the surgery would wake him up. And, unfortunately, he was right: he *was* the only medical help around unless you were prepared to drive fifty minutes to an hour south—and that was assuming clear roads with no slips from the storm.

In a local emergency, Dominic de Souza was the only choice.

"Are you sure you'll be okay treating patients?" she asked, careful to keep her voice nonjudgmental.

Blinking, he turned to stare at her. Intelligence sparked in the pale bloodshot brown of his eyes, his shoulders squaring. "I'm a good doctor," he bit out.

Anahera couldn't fault him for his edgy reaction to a complete stranger questioning his competence. She'd probably lose her shit, too, were their positions reversed. Looking back over her shoulder, she said, "Josie, I've put the money for my cappuccino on the table." She left before her friend could tell her to take her money with her—the way Josie looked after everyone, it was a wonder she was turning any kind of a profit.

Having walked into town, Anahera began to head toward the police station.

When a gleaming black sports car crawled up along the otherwise empty street littered with fallen leaves, dirty candy wrappers, and other storm-borne debris, Anahera noticed it without paying it much mind. Not until it pulled to a stop a few meters ahead of her and the driver shut off the engine.

The door opened seconds later, a familiar man getting out.

# 34

Daniel May came straight toward her. "I thought that was you, Ana."

"Daniel." Anahera stopped, her hands in the pockets of the anorak. "How much is that car worth?" She recognized the make—Edward had owned a sedan because he was far too sensible to drive around London in a car worth the same as a house, but he'd always lusted after fast cars that were all about speed and elegance.

Before everything had gone wrong and they'd broken so deep the fracture could never be patched, Anahera used to tell him he should buy one on his fortieth birthday and to hell with anyone who thought he was having a midlife crisis. Instead, he'd gone out and gotten himself a mistress. "It's a Lamborghini, isn't it? Did you get it the same time you grew a ponytail?"

A bright white smile from the man who'd once been a boy on whom she'd had a crush. She'd been thirteen at the time, Daniel fifteen.

"Nice to know you aren't going to give me the cold shoulder." His sunglasses hid eyes she remembered as being unusually dark, but his tone was open enough—and cuttingly bitter. "I'm getting sick of it from everyone else."

Anahera shrugged. "I guess people figure friends aren't supposed to poach from friends."

Expression cooling, Daniel slid his own hands into the pockets of his dark gray suit pants. His shirt was a vivid aqua, his watch a Patek Philippe

Anahera vaguely recognized from a catalog the highly respected watch company had sent to Edward.

The watch was probably worth more than the Lamborghini.

It wasn't a surprise that Daniel enjoyed fine watches. But it was something to note.

"It takes two to tango," he said in response to her sally. "And Nikau wasn't exactly interested in dancing with his wife. He was too puffed up with his own importance, always away at a conference or in 'office hours' with nineteen-year-olds who thought he was a god. Not my fault if she decided to seek greener pastures."

"That's why I'm talking to you." Anahera wondered if Daniel still drew. He'd once given her a pen drawing of a kea, showing the rabble-rousing native parrot in the midst of one of its favorite activities: destroying the rubber seal around a car's window.

She could see no signs of that whimsical boy in this sharply dressed man.

"Like you said," she added, "the entire mess involved three people, not just you." She didn't think Nikau had cheated on his wife as Daniel was implying; Nikau had always been obsessed with Keira, far too obsessed to play outside the marriage bed.

But, unlike Nikau, she wasn't about to turn Daniel into a black-hearted villain who'd lured Keira away. Whatever strange emptiness she had inside her, Keira was no one's puppet. "Not that you're exactly an innocent party, Dan. You made the decision to be with Keira while she was still married to another man." Separated wasn't the same as divorced. "You had to know what was coming."

"Trust you to cut right to the heart of it." Daniel's wry smile struck her with a bolt of memory, a reminder of his charm when they'd been teenagers.

Anahera had not only been hopelessly gawky back then, she'd dressed in hand-me-downs and cheap fabrics that her mother made into shorts and dresses. She could never hope to compete with the glossy private-school girls Daniel had favored. But the rich, pretty, popular boy had still spoken to her and they'd still played together on the beach.

Once, he'd even paid for her movie ticket so she could see the superhero movie everyone was talking about. He'd also come into the cabin and eaten jam sandwiches together with her for lunch, never once commenting on the poverty in which Anahera and her mother existed.

Daniel might be arrogant, but he'd never been an ass to Anahera personally.

"I was sorry to hear about your husband." It seemed a sincere statement. "You were never meant for a town this small, Ana. I was glad for you when you got out."

That was the Daniel who'd challenged her to barefoot races on the beach and who'd bought her a movie ticket. But there had always been another Daniel that she'd sensed even as a girl, well before he'd manipulated his way into the scholarship meant for Nikau: that ruthless Daniel who would do anything to get what he wanted.

"What're you doing in town?" She couldn't respond to the condolence today, not without betraying the icy, hard anger that lived in her.

"Just want to grab a coffee from Josie." He slid off his sunglasses to reveal eyes as dark as she remembered—like chips of black granite. "I'm driving to Greymouth—have a meeting with a developer."

"Don't you have a helicopter for that?"

"Why have a gorgeous fucking machine like the Lambo if I never drive it?" His smile didn't reach those opaque eyes. "Has there been any other news on the missing girl?"

Anahera shook her head. "Do you know her well?"

It was Daniel's turn to shrug. "Like I know most people in this town."

Considering the watch on his wrist, Anahera decided to chance another comment. "I only really knew her when she was small."

"She sold me Girl Guide cookies once," Daniel said suddenly. "Came to our door dressed in that uniform they wear. I guess she must've been about seven or eight. I was nineteen and home for the holidays."

He slid his sunglasses back on. "I bought a whole bunch of cookies off her, and she smiled this great big smile at me, and I thought: The world's going to crush you." No smile now, just ruthless cold. "That's what it does to fragile, beautiful things."

He moved past her the next second.

Anahera watched after him until he disappeared into the warmth of Josie's café; that had been a distinctly odd story to share, but it could be just Daniel playing games. He'd had a way of doing that even as a boy, of manipulating people for his own enjoyment—or sometimes for no reason at all.

Anahera had always thought he hadn't tried it on her as a child because she was so far beneath him in terms of power and wealth or even family. She could never do anything to hurt or to help him. So he'd put down the knife, stopped the power plays.

Looked like that no longer applied.

# 35

Will hadn't been sure Anahera would turn up this morning, so when she pushed open the door to the station, he turned from the filing cabinet with a quiet inhale. He was struck once again by how contained she was; he wondered if anyone, even Josie, truly knew her. Maybe Nikau had an idea—the two seemed close, but if they'd ever had a romantic relationship they'd left it behind long ago.

The entire time that Will had known Nikau, the other man had been obsessed with his ex-wife: Keira seemed to be the only woman Nik noticed—and *had* noticed for years. Though Will couldn't forget that night in the bar and the way Nikau had talked about Miriama.

Will had to be careful not to let his friendship with Nikau cloud his judgment. Because Nik fit all the parameters of someone Miriama would've trusted even if she'd run into him in an isolated spot—he was a local who knew her aunt and was considered a good man, a man who'd step in and help if you needed it.

Will had once spotted Nikau slipping a twenty into the hand of an elderly woman who'd been struggling after the death of her husband.

Nikau also spent considerable time hiking the various trails around Golden Cove, both for work and for pleasure, so Miriama wouldn't have found it unusual to see him along her route. She'd probably run into him multiple times over the two years since he'd moved back to the Cove.

All of that was why Will had quietly checked the search map to make sure Nikau alone had never searched a particular area.

His relief at seeing multiple initials on all squares bearing Nik's own initials had been an easing of muscles he hadn't realized were knotted. The map didn't totally clear Nik, however. If he'd hurt Miriama, the ocean would've been the natural dumping ground for a man who knew this landscape so intimately.

"Done your rounds?" Anahera asked, her wavy hair down around a face that gave nothing away and that had the hard edge of knocks taken and survived.

"Yes, no major damage." He'd started on the cusp of dawn, been out for four hours. "I had to return Julia Lee's dog—Cupcake the bulldog took shelter in Christine Tierney's house, after apparently managing to dig his way out from under Julia's fence and becoming caught in the storm. And I righted a trampoline over at Tania Meikle's, but that was the extent of the excitement."

No smile on Anahera's face. Her expression was difficult to read, but he could guess that she remained conflicted about working with Will behind her friends' backs.

"So," she said, "we're ready to go?"

"You sure you want to be seen getting into my vehicle?"

"Twenty seconds before I walked in here, I ran into Evelyn, made sure to mention that I needed to get some supplies from Christchurch and was catching a lift with you because my car was playing up." She shoved her hands into the pockets of her anorak. "That's one thing I don't miss about living in a small town—having everyone's nose in my business."

Grabbing his navy jacket but not putting it on over the finely pinstriped gray of his shirt, Will stepped outside the station, Anahera preceding him out. He locked up before leading her to his SUV. It wasn't until they were inside and he'd thrown his jacket on the backseat that he said, "But you did miss some things about it?" Pulling away from the curb, he made automatic note of the cars on the street, the people on the sidewalks.

"You've seen the best of us in this hunt for Miriama," Anahera said softly. "Rich or poor, wild or civilized, asshole or saint, when bad things happen, we come together."

Will thought about that. And then he thought about the dark side of such closeness. "In a town this small," he said, "there's a tendency to imagine that you know everything about your neighbors. But everyone has secrets."

Anahera's laugh was cynical. "Is that your way of telling me you dug deeper into my sordid family history? You won't exactly find any surprises."

"No. But I did run a background check on you the day after you came into town. I had to see if you'd brought trouble with you."

"What did you find?"

Will concentrated on the road in front of them, the trees that shadowed it so thickly canopied that they nearly shut out the sun. "That you had a reason to leave," he said as they passed the spot where Peter Jacobs and his brother were in the midst of towing Vincent's crashed Mercedes.

Will didn't stop; he'd already been out here just before he returned to the station.

"I was sorry to read about the circumstances of your mother's death." Just because they both knew he had the information didn't mean the words didn't need to be spoken.

"Everyone was sorry." Flat tone, her eyes fixed on the windscreen. "Just like everyone was sorry when my father hit her every night. Just like everyone was sorry when they glimpsed her bruises. And everyone was *so* sorry when she was found dead in the cabin they couldn't be bothered to visit. But no one did anything to the man who caused it all."

Will had read the case files, knew what she was talking about—and it wasn't just the abuse. "There's no reason to think your mother's death was anything but an accident. Her injuries were consistent with a fall from a ladder." That ladder had been found next to her, as had a smashed photo frame.

An empty picture hook on the wall had stood silent witness.

"I've done my reading, too." Harsher words now. "So I know that cops and forensics people can't always distinguish between a fall and someone pushing you off so that you fall and break bones, crack your skull."

Will couldn't argue with her; he'd witnessed a number of high-profile cases where the question of whether a fall had been accidental or not had never been answered. "Why didn't your mother ever press charges against your father?" The lack of any such report had meant the outside investigators had no reason to consider foul play.

Anahera's head swung toward him. "Are you saying it was my mother's fault?"

"No." Will kept his tone even by sheer strength of will. "Abuse is the abuser's fault." It was what he'd always believed, what had led him to promise a little boy named Alfie that he'd be safe, that the monster wouldn't get to him. "I just don't understand her choice." As he hadn't understood the fatal choice made by Alfie Hart's mother.

"From everything I read in the file, your mother was a strong woman." Haeata Rawiri had run her own small dressmaking business throughout the marriage, was spoken of as a valued member of the community. Yet she'd stayed with her violent husband. And she hadn't reported his violence. Not even when her husband hit their child.

Will's hands squeezed the steering wheel.

Anahera didn't reply.

Eventually, Will turned on the radio and the two of them moved through the lonely, beautiful landscape while listening to the cohosts bantering with one another about a rock star who had an addiction to rehab.

He'd long ago given up on getting an answer when she said, "He saved her once." Her voice was cold, distant. "My mother was born into an abusive family and my father came along on his motorbike and whisked her away to a life of adventure and exploration. The first three years, she always told me, were wonderful. She was free and she wasn't afraid and he was her Prince Charming."

"What changed?"

"My father likes to blame everything on losing his job when the big factory out Greymouth way shut down." Her tone made it clear what she thought of that excuse. "That's what my mother used to say as well—that he lost his manhood when he couldn't support his family and we had to rely on her income and on welfare." She snorted. "All pure bullshit. What kind of manhood is it to pound on your wife and child?"

Will's mind blazed with the image of a burning house, flames licking up to the roof and the heat so violent it scalded. "That's not manhood," he said as the scarred skin on his back seemed to tighten. "That's weakness."

Anahera went silent again, and the two of them drove on through empty roads surrounded by trees and tangled undergrowth, past a glacier-fed river that glittered arctic blue, and in the shadow of mountains that had stood for thousands of years, their peaks capped with snow.

They stopped for coffee midway, but neither one of them was hungry for lunch.

Traffic began to pick up during the second half of their journey, but it was free-flowing, no breakdowns or delays. They'd made excellent time—just over three hours, forty-five minutes—and all too soon were in the heart of civilization and it felt like a bright flashlight shining into the face after the smudged light of Golden Cove.

Too many cars, too many people, too many noises—from the construction site on the corner to the teenager banging out a rhythm on an outdoor drum set to the driver gesticulating angrily at another.

"Do you have anything else to do in the city?"

Anahera stirred. "I need to pick up a new laptop. I ordered it online and they're holding it for me. I didn't want to risk it coming via courier."

"Let's pick that up last. Otherwise, you'd have to carry it around or risk leaving it in the vehicle." He was too pragmatic to imagine that this being a police vehicle would stop thieves from breaking in—some people lived to cross boundaries, the thrill of the act as important as what they might get.

"That works for me. How many jewelers will we be visiting?"

"I've got a list of ten." He stopped at a red light. "That doesn't include the more mass-market jewelers. We'll head there if we strike out at the specialist jewelers and watchmakers—even if they didn't make or import it, they might know who did." New Zealand was a small country and the jewelers were in a niche industry.

"You sound pretty sure about it being a specialist piece."

"I woke before dawn this morning. No use doing the patrol in the dark, so I spent the time online, trying to find watches similar to the one gifted to Miriama. Zero results. My gut says it was custom-made and the ten places I have on my list all do custom jobs."

"It's possible it was purchased internationally."

"I found a tiny *koru* design in the platinum of the band—on the underside, where it locks into the right side of the watch face." Inspired by the curl of a fern frond, it was a distinctly New Zealand symbol, one that signified new life and creation, growth and change. "That doesn't rule out an overseas watchmaker, but it lessens the chances."

He maneuvered around a large roadwork truck. "If the trail does run cold, I'll do what you've suggested and upload the image to the web, see if someone recognizes the design or workmanship." But first, he'd search closer to home. Miriama's lover would—at the time—have had no reason to think anyone would come looking for the origin of the piece.

The lover had also come across as highly possessive and controlling in the journal entries. A man like that would probably want to direct the design process, possibly even supply his own gemstones. Far easier to do that with a local. "Our first stop is a boutique in the city. According to a friend of mine who works in high-end thefts, the boutique's known for its discretion as well as the high caliber of its work. You okay to wait on something to eat till after this stop?"

"I'm not the one who's been up since before daybreak."

"I'll fill up at lunch."

Managing to find a parking space only about five minutes away—a miracle in a city lined with orange cones and construction vehicles—he got out and the two of them began the short walk to the boutique. The midday sunshine was crisp against their faces, the city buzzing with life, but scars from the earthquake that had devastated it years earlier remained impossible to avoid.

Beside him, Anahera took care not to step on a hairline crack in the pavement that had escaped repair, and he wondered what it must have been like for her to be so far from her friends when news of the quake first broke. "There." He nodded toward a discreet little shop tucked in between an electronic goods store and a designer clothing boutique. "That's our first stop."

# 36

The jeweler didn't boast a security guard, but Will spotted two video cameras and an automatic metal grille that could be slammed down at a moment's notice. He'd bet the window glass was bulletproof and that the staff all had access to silent alarms under the counters. He also wouldn't be surprised if some of the items on display were beautiful fakes, with the real gems kept in locked safes and only brought out for serious buyers.

Pulling open the heavy door, he walked into the air-conditioned inner sanctum behind Anahera. The woman who looked up from the other side of the pristine glass counter was an expertly groomed brunette in a maroon dress that hugged her body without being too tight. "Hello," she said with a warmly professional smile. "How may I help you today?"

Clearly, the clerk had been trained to never judge a customer based on appearance. It was good advice, given what Will knew of the multimillionaires who lived in the region. One had a habit of walking around town in flip-flops, while another drove a twenty-year-old junker and dressed like the eighties had never gone out of style.

"Good afternoon." He showed her his police ID. "I'm working a missing person case and I'm hoping to track down the origin of a piece of jewelry."

The woman's professional facade fractured. "Oh, goodness." Wide green eyes. "Of course, I'll be happy to help, but our master jeweler's probably the one you should talk to."

"Does he come into the shop?"

"Not normally," the clerk said, "but you're in luck today. He's here this morning to personally accept a delivery. If you'll excuse me, I'll go fetch him."

Instead of leaving the sales area, the clerk went to the back of the room and picked up a phone, speaking quietly into it before returning to her previous post.

A small man who might've once been blond, but whose hair had faded to ash gray, bustled out from the back soon afterward. "Detective," he said, holding out a sinewy hand. "Ava said you were looking to identify a piece of jewelry?" His eyes held a question, but it wasn't about the jewelry—his attention was on Anahera.

"I'm sorry for staring," he said when she raised an eyebrow, "but I could swear I've seen you before."

"I get that a lot."

The jeweler began to turn back to Will . . . halted midmove. "You create the most extraordinary music—your gift is truly angelic," he said in a hushed tone. "I'm deeply honored to have you in my store."

Anahera went still. "Thank you."

"I was very sorry to hear of the passing of your husband."

Shoulders stiff, Anahera gave the man a tight smile before turning to look at some of the jewels on display. Will, meanwhile, took charge of the meeting. Removing the watch from his pocket, he took it out of the evidence bag to show it to the jeweler. "Is this one of your pieces?"

The man shook his head at once. "No, I do watches in partnership with a trained watchmaker, but this isn't my style. Too flashy. That said, the craftsmanship is exquisite—nothing mass-market. Not even an elite mass-market line. This is definitely custom."

The clerk, who'd come to hover near her boss, craned her neck to look at the watch. "I don't recall seeing anything like this before—the design, I mean," she said. "And Dad and I know most of the other jewelers in the country who do custom work."

Her boss—her father—frowned. "Ava's right. It's very unique, especially that sunburst design with the diamonds. Some of my competitors do have new jewelers on staff—it might've come from one of them."

Will didn't sense deceit in either of these two; if anything, they seemed eager to help. Putting the watch back in the evidence bag, he said, "Would you recommend I speak to any other jewelers or watchmakers in particular?"

Together, father and daughter came up with a list of seven, all of whom were already on his list. "Thank you."

Anahera walked out with him without saying anything further to either the jeweler or the clerk, though she did incline her head toward them in a silent good-bye.

"Why release your music under the name Angel?" Will asked once they were on the sidewalk.

Anahera rolled her eyes and her shoulders, as if shrugging off the stiffness. "Record company's idea. They did a search on the meaning of my name, decided the stage name would be great for promotion. You know, the 'plays like an angel' shtick."

"Is it true that you're self-taught?"

"I used to sneak into the church and practice on their piano." A faint smile. "When Pastor Mark came out to the cabin the day I got back to Golden Cove, he told me I could come play on the church piano anytime I wanted."

"I hear they tune it once every ten years, so you might be in luck."

Anahera laughed, and for a moment, they were just a man and a woman taking a walk in the sunshine.

A minute later, she stopped by a food truck selling fresh-made wraps. "Yes?"

Will nodded and they were soon eating their lunch as they walked to the next stop. "What's it like being a famous musician?"

"Famous pianist," Anahera corrected. "We're nowhere near as well-known as pop stars. I have no idea how he recognized me." She took a bite of her wrap, waited until she'd swallowed before continuing. "I only ever did a few shows and the photo they used on the cover of the last album is all darkness and broken shadows."

Much like the music on that album. "You planning to get a piano in the cabin?" He finished his wrap. "Must be hard for a pianist to be in a place where you can't practice your passion."

A skateboarder whizzed down the sidewalk on the other side of the street, expertly dodging the orange cones that marked out a construction zone. He stumbled to a stop when his cap flew off and he had to run back to retrieve it, but a few seconds later he was off again. "Do you remember ever being that young?" Anahera asked, her eyes following the boy until he disappeared down the street. "Having no responsibilities, no real worries."

"I had a cop for a father and for a mother." Will threw both their wrappers into a trash can after holding out his hand for Anahera's. "I grew up waiting for them to come home. Later, when I realized how dangerous their jobs could actually be, I was always half-afraid to answer the door in case the news was bad."

Anahera looked at him, her head angled and her eyes incisive. "Yet you became a cop."

"I guess you can't fight destiny. We are who we are."

"Isn't that a little fatalistic?" A sharp question.

"Don't you believe that we're shaped by our experiences?"

"If I believed that," Anahera said, "I would've never escaped Golden Cove. I'd be like Matilda, giving my trust to the wrong man over and over again."

Even as Anahera spoke those words, she knew she was being a hypocrite. Maybe she hadn't fallen for a physically abusive man like her father, or like the users Matilda dated, but she'd fallen for a liar, hadn't she? Wasn't that a kind of abuse, too? Making a woman fall in love with you, then smashing an anvil into her already broken heart.

"This is our second stop." Will opened the door of what looked to be nothing but a vestibule and his next words held the cool caution of a cop. "Better if I go up first here."

Anahera followed to find herself facing a narrow flight of steps, the kind that usually led to dingy apartments or fading internet cafés. But these steps were not only well lit, with the wood polished to a shine, there was also tasteful artwork on the walls—including a reproduction of one of Monet's water lily paintings.

At the top was a heavyset Asian male dressed in a black suit; he stood with his feet braced apart, one hand loosely clasped over the wrist of the other, and his face expressionless. The only thing missing was a neon sign with the word SECURITY on it. Will had clearly already spoken to him, because he said nothing as she walked in through the door Will was holding open for her. She could see it was much heavier than the one below and reinforced with metal.

Beyond was the hushed quiet of an upscale jeweler's. Anahera knew immediately that this wasn't a place for casual browsers. You made an appointment during opening hours, or, if you were important enough, they'd accommodate your schedule—or bring the jewels directly to you.

Not surprisingly, there was no friendly smile from the clerk this time. Instead, he gave them a supercilious sneer down his blade of a nose before scanning his gaze up then down both their bodies. "I'm afraid we're not open to the public," he said in a voice that matched the look on his face. "I do apologize if the security guard gave you a different impression." Not an ounce of sincerity in those words.

Anahera wondered what he'd say if she told him she could afford the things in here. He'd probably call her a liar without saying a word. For some reason, that made her want to laugh . . . and then she remembered the jewels Edward had bought her during their marriage. Anniversary gifts. A glittering bauble for each year.

She'd left them all in a safety-deposit box in London.

Will didn't react to the clerk's condescending manner except to take out his ID and say, "I need to talk to someone about identifying a piece of jewelry." His tone was so even and unruffled that it was deadly.

The clerk visibly paled. "Of course, Detective," he said and picked up a nearby phone to murmur into it.

Another man walked out from the back seconds later, followed by a woman. Of East Asian descent, they were as identical as it was possible for two people of different genders to be—the same sleek hair, the same wide but fine bone structure, the same color suits. Charcoal, not black. Both paired with crisp white shirts.

"I'm Shannon Chen and this is my brother Aaron Chen," the woman said, holding out a hand toward Will.

Not just siblings. *Twins.* Anahera would bet every cent she had on that.

Releasing Will's hand after the introductions between them were over, Shannon Chen reached out for Anahera's.

Anahera accepted the handshake, intrigued by this woman with the dark and brilliant eyes and her silent brother. "Anahera," she said without adding anything further.

"Detective, Anahera," Shannon Chen said, "if you'd please come into the back to our private sitting room. We have an international client and her family arriving in ten minutes and I'd rather they not see us being questioned by the police."

"No problem," Will said. "We'll follow you."

A faint smile on the other woman's face before she and her brother led them back into the private sitting area—though no one made any move to actually sit.

Instinct telling her that Shannon Chen liked the look of Will, Anahera lingered in the hallway outside the actual room. She made a point of looking at the abstract painting on the wall, the pigment carved in austerely straight lines, but her ear was tuned in to the conversation happening within.

# 37

"I'm attempting to track down the maker or seller of this watch," she heard Will say. "I'd appreciate it if you didn't attempt to lie to me. This is a serious missing person investigation and if I find out that you withheld information, I won't hesitate to charge you. It doesn't matter if you have friends in high places—they'll drop you like a hot potato if it turns out our missing person was the victim of foul play."

His voice was matter-of-fact rather than threatening.

"Our customers are used to privacy," Shannon Chen replied, "but we don't use that as a shield. The nature of our business means we've previously been targeted by thieves—I'd much rather you and your fellow officers not think of us as criminals." The words were crisp and professional, even a little sharp, but Anahera noticed Shannon Chen had chosen her words with care. She hadn't said that they weren't criminals, only that they preferred not to be thought of as criminals.

A subtle distinction and maybe no distinction at all, but it was interesting.

"As for this watch . . ." A pause. "I don't recognize it and I know all of the pieces we've ever made or traded. Aaron?"

Another long pause, as if the watch was being examined. "No," said a deep male voice that was oddly soft. "The style is too delicate for one of mine. I prefer harder edges. Shannon's wearing one of my designs."

Anahera had noticed Shannon's watch when they shook hands. It was more blocky than she might've expected on such a slender wrist, but it suited Shannon Chen. There was a sense of power to her and to the watch both; it was likely her brother had made the watch specifically for her. Anahera had seen far more delicate pieces in the showroom.

Will had clearly noted the same. "It's not worth putting your entire business in jeopardy to protect one client," he said in that mild tone he could turn lethal. "Think carefully before you answer my question. Is this one of yours?"

"I don't have to think, Detective. This isn't one of ours." Shannon's tone had cooled from professional to glacial. "However, I recognize the workmanship. I'll write down the address for you."

Voices drifted in from the showroom, the language Korean from what Anahera could make out. The clerk answered in the same language, though he was clearly not ethnically Korean. She'd pegged him as more likely to be Indonesian. "Good service," she said quietly to Shannon after turning to see Will sliding the watch back into the evidence bag. "How many languages does he speak?"

"Five at last count." The other woman smiled at her, the act unexpected. "You don't sell jewels that start in the six figures without offering service of the highest caliber. Now"—she shifted her attention back to Will—"if you don't mind, Aaron will show you the back way out while I go and greet our clients."

"Thank you for the help."

Shannon Chen headed to the doorway. "Come by sometime when you're not in the mood to interrogate and we'll have lunch." She'd already passed Anahera, her perfume a subtle, elegant, and expensive musk, when she paused suddenly and glanced back. "I knew I remembered that face. Your husband bought your engagement ring from us when we were based in Auckland, showed me a photo of you." Her eyes dropped to Anahera's left hand, but she was too professional to mention the lack of either a wedding band or that tastefully extravagant engagement ring.

Despite the courtesy, Anahera barely made it down the chipped concrete of the back steps without screaming. "It's like Edward's ghost is following me around today," she said the instant she was alone with Will in the delivery bay behind the building.

She shoved her hands into the pockets of her anorak, fisting them to white-knuckled tightness. "And how creepy is it that the brother doesn't speak until the sister tells him to?"

"Twins can be that way. It's like they each take on certain duties. With the Chens, Shannon is the talker and the leader while Aaron takes care of everything in the back—and is probably the only person Shannon truly trusts."

Sudden dark heat burned at the backs of Anahera's eyes. She looked desperately toward the light at the end of the small street, needing a way out. She couldn't break down, not here, not now, not with this cop with his hard eyes and his body that made hers threaten to wake.

"I'm going to get the car," Will said, stepping ahead. "No point in you walking back, too. Wait by the parking sign on the street and I'll pick you up."

Always a cop.

Seeing too much.

If he'd pushed, she'd have pushed back harder, her rage a smashing wave.

But he was giving her room, was taking the first steps to the busy street beyond.

"I miscarried twins." The words she'd never once spoken shoved out of her throat. "I was far enough along that I had the bump, that the doctors could tell me I was carrying twins. But I waited to tell the people at home." Some London friends had known, but those friends lived in a different world than the people of Golden Cove. "I wanted to surprise Josie and Nikau and the others with a great big six-month bump. And then I never told anyone at all."

Shifting on his heel to return to her, Will looked at her not with sympathy, not with pity, but with an understanding as desolate as it was angry. "It never fucking stops hurting, does it?"

Jesus, God, someone finally *got* it. "I keep waiting for it to stop, but no, it never does." And on days like today, when she'd come up against a pair of twins, the wound dug its way in and twisted.

What would her twins have grown up to be like? Would they have been like Shannon and Aaron Chen, two people so in sync that they each had a specific role in the relationship and in the world? Or would her twins have been so different from each other that it was difficult to even tell that they were siblings? Anahera would never know. "Did you lose a child?"

"He wasn't mine, but I lost him anyway." Voice rough and fingers curled viciously into his palms, Will nudged his head toward the street. "Let's go. The address Shannon gave me is on the outskirts of town. We may as well pick up your laptop before we leave."

Walking out with him and into the chaos of life, Anahera blinked against the influx of noise. "You're certain Shannon gave you the right person?"

He handed over a piece of paper. On it was written an address; below that the words: *The koru paired with the minuscule ruby embedded in the back is her trademark.*

# 38

"This is it." Will brought the SUV to a stop on a leafy suburban street, outside a white villa fronted by a manicured lawn and the bare limbs of dormant roses. "Your laptop should be safe enough to leave. This is an exclusive area, no street crime to speak of."

"Did you already have this place on your list?"

"Yes. We were going to hit it last."

Anahera glanced at the other side of the street, her eyes on a new build that had been made to match the style of the older homes. A few more years, Will judged, a little more age on the plantings around it, and it would lose that unpolished new shine, begin to truly blend in.

"It doesn't look like the jeweler advertises." Anahera turned back to the villa. "How did you find out about her?"

"I'm a detective."

A hint of a smile on her face. "Touché."

Will wasn't expecting the smile, or how beautiful she was when the light hit her eyes. Getting out of the vehicle without replying because he had no idea what the fuck to do with his response to her, he met her by the villa's small white gate. Her smile was gone, her face back to its usual difficult-to-read state, and her hands stuffed into the pockets of her anorak.

Going through the gate and up the drive lined by those roses that appeared dead, he knocked on the front door. The woman who opened it was sixty and well preserved, her skin a smooth, unblemished white as a result of a liberal dusting of powder and her eyes an acute blue, her silkily white hair pulled back in an elegant knot. She wore a string of small pearls against a long-sleeved knee-length dress in a dark navy wool. "Yes?"

"Siobhan Genovese?" Will held up his identification.

The woman took his ID, scrutinized it carefully. "If you wouldn't mind," she said, "I'll ask you to wait here while I verify that you are who you say you are." She shut the door in their faces without waiting for an answer.

"Not the trusting type." Anahera's tone was bone-dry.

"If she has the kind of gems I suspect she has in there, that she even opened her door is surprising. As is the fact she doesn't have a security grille. On the other hand, not many people know she exists."

One minute, two, before the door opened again.

"Thank you for waiting," Siobhan Genovese said. "Please do come in, Detective Gallagher." A questioning glance at Anahera. "I assume you can vouch for this young woman?"

"Yes."

Apparently satisfied with that, Siobhan Genovese led them into a beautifully appointed living room, the colors shades of blue and gray. It was the kind of tasteful and quietly wealthy arrangement with which Anahera had become intimately familiar in Edward's London home and in the homes of his friends.

To be fair to her gifted liar of a husband, he'd told her she could redecorate as she liked, but Anahera had hesitated over even the heavy damask curtains she'd hated.

God, she'd been so young.

So conscious of her poverty-stricken past and lack of knowledge about the moneyed world in which she found herself, a lone Māori girl far from a thundering turbulent sea that sang a song of home and of grief both.

"Please sit," Siobhan said, taking a seat of her own in a lush gray armchair with curved edges of a dark gold that bore the patina of age. "How may I help you?"

Will told her why they were there before handing over the watch. "I know this is one of yours," he said quietly in that way he had, so that you felt as if you were the entire focus of his attention. "What I need from you is the name of the buyer."

Siobhan Genovese examined the watch with care, running her fingertips over the glittering hardness of the blue stones that edged the face, then flipping it over and brushing her thumb across the tiny ruby embedded in the back. "Very few people recognize my signature," she said as the much larger ruby on her right ring finger shone bright as fresh blood. "I handmake all of my pieces, which means there aren't many around for people to compare."

Will shook his head, the action gentle. "My sources are mine, but I will tell you that you do stunning work."

Frost in her responding words. "Part of the reason I'm still in business despite my astronomical prices and slow production rate is that I value my clients' privacy."

Taking the watch back, Will said, "A young woman is missing." He held those searing blue eyes. "Someone you know gave her this watch. You need to tell me the identity of that person."

"If I ask you to get a warrant?" was the soft rejoinder that held a steely will.

"I'll do it—but such things have a way of going public. I'll need to list your address and why I'm seeking the warrant."

"That could be counted as a threat, Detective." Siobhan crossed one leg over the other.

Watch now safely stored in the inner pocket of his jacket, Will leaned forward with his forearms braced on his thighs. "I have no desire to play a game of one-upmanship, but I'm looking for a young woman who doesn't deserve to be gone. If you get in the way of that, I won't hesitate to take whatever steps are necessary, no matter how messy."

Siobhan's expression didn't change. "You realize most of my business is by word of mouth?"

"I'm sure you've earned more than enough by now to buffer you against any momentary dip—we both know that, as good as you are, the clients will come back even if it gets out that you shared one of their names with the police."

An amused smile from the older woman. "People always want the best." Her eyes went to Anahera. "And who is she?"

"Her identity doesn't matter to you. Give me a name, Ms. Genovese." There was something so unbending in his tone that Anahera's back muscles tightened.

This man, she realized, could be ruthless.

Siobhan didn't seem to have come to the same realization. "William Gallagher," she murmured, "why do I know that name?"

"I was accused of beating a suspect." No change in Will's tone or expression. "There was an inquiry."

"Ah." Siobhan gave a small nod. "The fallen hero. Yes, I remember."

Anahera had no idea what the two were talking about—whatever the inquiry had been, it hadn't appeared as one of the top hits when she typed Will's name into a search engine. She'd read only about his heroism.

"And do you have the support of your superiors for this investigation?" Siobhan asked, reaching to the small table beside her to pick up a tiny porcelain cup that seemed to hold tea. She didn't offer any to either Anahera or Will. "I have people I can call, ask."

"You might not have noticed," Will said, "but the police department doesn't like having inquiries. Especially not corruption inquiries dealing with wealthy and connected people who might've gotten away with murder."

The slightest tinkle of porcelain on porcelain. "Murder?" Siobhan put aside her tea. "You didn't say anything about murder."

"How many young women do you know who've disappeared mysteriously while going about their everyday lives, and then have been found alive?"

His words hit Anahera in the gut. She knew he was right; part of her had always known the most likely outcome, but she'd hoped. And she continued to hope. Maybe Miriama was being kept captive. A horrific thing to wish, but at least it would mean she was alive, that they could rescue her.

"I see." Siobhan placed her hands very carefully on the wool of her dress. "Well, I will likely lose a rather significant client because of this, but murder is where I draw the line."

Then she told them the name of the man who'd commissioned the watch.

# 39

"What will you do?" Anahera asked Will an hour later, after they finally broke free of the gridlock caused by a three-car accident. No fatalities, thankfully, but the tow trucks had taken their time getting there and hauling the wrecks off the road.

Now, they drove through the autumnal darkness. It had fallen with quicksilver speed, a black curtain sweeping across the world. With the lack of light had come a call from Nikau confirming the day's searchers had found no signs of Miriama.

"Talk to him again," Will answered, "try to get the truth."

Anahera shoved her fingers through her hair, her heart a drum in her chest that hadn't stopped thudding since Siobhan Genovese's revelation. "Vincent's always been such a straight arrow." With a wife who didn't have a single friend in town and whose online presence was doll-like perfection.

Her stomach churned.

"I'm more likely to get the truth from him if I can talk to him alone." Will took a corner, his headlights flashing off the reflective barriers. "I'll see if I can convince him to meet me tonight, but if not, it'll be tomorrow."

"I won't say anything." Anahera might be loyal, but she'd never again be foolishly trusting and blind. "Some of us used to wonder if Vincent felt trapped by his parents' expectations, but he always did such a good job of appearing happy that we bought it."

Will increased his speed to pass a tanker rumbling along the road.

"Everyone has secrets," he repeated after completing the maneuver. "It's often the people who look like they have no secrets at all who turn out to have the biggest ones."

Anahera's mind returned to Siobhan Genovese's elegant living room and to the conversation she hadn't fully understood. "Tell me about the inquiry," she found herself saying, the hushed darkness of the night enveloping them in a cocoon where questions could be asked and secrets revealed.

Will's hands tightened on the steering wheel to the point that his bones pushed white against his skin. "I was in charge of keeping a woman and a three-year-old child safe in the buildup to the woman giving testimony against a man." His words were clipped, a cop giving a report. Nothing but the facts.

"He was her husband and the father of her child, but he also happened to be a serial rapist who got careless—his wife began to notice the washing machine running in the middle of the night, after her husband got home 'from work,' saw rope, gloves, and duct tape in his car, and lined up his absences with the violent rapes in the area."

He passed another tanker, this one festooned with lights that turned it into a traveling star. "When she questioned him about it, he punched her five times, knocking out three front teeth, then kicked her in the stomach and left the house. She took her son and came to the station with blood on her shirt. I was the detective on the case. I told them they'd be safe. I was wrong. Daniella and Alfie are buried in a private family cemetery on a vineyard in Marlborough."

So many things not said, so many truths buried in the details. "Their killer's the one you were accused of beating?"

"I did beat him."

"Did your superiors cover it up?" She wouldn't blame them if they had—because sometimes, the law didn't work; sometimes, lines had to be crossed.

"No. He refused to testify." Will's smile was grim. "Apparently, he found God two months into his time on remand, right as the inquiry began. He called me, said he deserved what I'd done to him and he not only wouldn't be cooperating with the inquiry, he was recanting his statement about police brutality and blaming his injuries on a bar fight earlier that night. I told him I didn't need the fucking favor."

Will's jaw worked. "I was ready to walk into the inquiry and say I did it. Only reason I hadn't already done that was because the prosecution team on the rapes was worried it'd bring my credibility into question, give the defense a way to attack my work on the case."

He released a harsh exhale. "In the end, I never had to talk to the inquiry board. My superior officer got the entire thing dismissed for lack of evidence. The official letter came this week, closed the book on the whole thing.

"No one much argued with the decision—turns out rapists who carve up their elderly victims, then murder three-year-old boys aren't popular with anyone. Even the media barely reported on it. Nobody asked me what it felt like to know I owed my continued career to a murdering rapist."

She got it, saw why he was in Golden Cove. "Alcohol? Drugs?"

"I almost beat up another asshole, then another. My partners had to hold me back. You can work out the rest."

Anahera had the niggling feeling she was forgetting to ask something important, but the shape of it stayed frustratingly out of her reach. And since she understood about nightmares and about not wanting to look back, she took Will's lead and dropped the subject. "I think Siobhan would've made a good murderer."

Will's fingers eased on the black of the steering wheel. "Most people wouldn't think so."

"That's exactly why she'd be a good one. She's cold, ruthless, but she looks the part of the rich old lady. No one would ever suspect her." Pausing, she looked out at the blackness beyond; they were well out of civilization and in the heart of an unforgiving landscape that offered no second chances. "Have you looked into her dating or marital history?" She returned her attention to the cop who told no lies but didn't tell her everything all the same. "Any suspicious disappearances or deaths?"

Will's grin was a sudden thing; it changed his whole face. "Never married, self-made woman. Tough as granite."

"And with a strange sense of morality," Anahera said. "She balked at murder, but a suspicious disappearance didn't even register on her radar."

A smoky ballad poured out of the radio as the night grew darker around them, the singer's voice husky and soulful.

Anahera's skin rippled with a sudden cold. "This was the song we danced to at our wedding." Will didn't care about her and Edward and maybe that was why she could tell him. "I wore a long white dress that I used all my savings to buy and he wore a tuxedo. We got married in a small hotel ballroom decorated like a winter wonderland, with thirty of Edward's family and friends who'd flown over, and my closest friends, in attendance." She'd had no family by then, no one she acknowledged anyway. "And we danced to this song."

It had been a fairy tale come to life, one against which Anahera's battered and scarred spirit had no defense. "Have you ever been married?"

"Came close once, but then Alfie and Daniella were murdered, and I wasn't quite right in the head for a while. She couldn't handle it. I don't blame her for that. She didn't sign up for a messed-up cop who was placed on administrative leave while the inquiry ran its course."

"What happened to in sickness and in health?"

"We hadn't taken any vows yet. And we all have our breaking points."

"Yes."

"What's yours?"

But Anahera shook her head. "Enough confessions in the dark, cop. You keep my secrets and I'll keep yours—but let's not pretend that we're anything but two broken people who happened to run into each other." There was nothing else, no strong foundation on which to build.

"No," Will said, his eyes on the dark beyond the windshield. "But I'm still going to ask if you want me to come in tonight."

Anahera hadn't yet decided on an answer by the time he brought the SUV to a stop in front of her cabin. Then the high beams of his headlights picked up the figure slumped on the porch, and the question was moot.

Getting out, they ran over to find a chilled Nikau drunk off his ass and slurring his words. "Saw her today," he mumbled as Will hauled him into the cabin and Anahera got to work starting the fire. "Wearing emeralds. Guess *pounamu* wasn't enough for her."

He kept on rambling about his ex-wife while Anahera got the fire going and Will wrestled the mostly empty bottle of whiskey from his hand. Giving the bottle to Anahera, Will told her to get rid of what alcohol remained. Anahera had no compunction in pouring it down the sink. If Nikau had wanted to save his expensive whiskey, he shouldn't have come drinking on her porch.

"Just leave him in front of the fire," she said to Will. "It won't be the first time he's slept on a floor, but I do have a spare pillow for his head." She went into her bedroom and found it—another little gift courtesy of Josie.

Taking it to the fire, she placed it under Nik's head, then covered him using a throw she'd had on one of the chairs. When he mumbled again, she sat down beside him and began to brush her hand over his hair.

Sitting down in a chair across from her, Will just watched. A patient wolf, she found herself thinking. Not a dog, because he'd never come to anyone on command. But a man who was a hunter, and who could be dangerous if he slipped the tight leash he kept on himself.

The next time she looked over, she found him staring into the flames. It gave her a chance to examine him without being watched in turn. He was all craggy lines carved into his skin, experience woven into his bones, and pain stamped onto his features. Life had been hard on him, but he was still moving, and he was still working, and he was still fighting for those who couldn't fight for themselves.

Suddenly, Anahera didn't care that Nikau was here. She wanted to steal some of the cop's fire, that smoldering heat that kept him going, that dark anger deep inside him that called to her own fury. But leaving Nik wasn't an option—he might throw up in his sleep, end up choking to death.

Frustrated, she got up and went to the cop. His eyes turned to take her in. He didn't stop her when she shoved her hands into his hair and tugged back his head as she bent down and took a kiss as harsh as it was needy. He accepted her demand, his hands coming to settle at her hips and his body heat sinking through her clothing to scald her flesh.

Beside them, the fire crackled . . . and Nikau moaned.

Wrenching back from Will, Anahera looked over her shoulder to see that her friend was asleep but restless. "Consider this an IOU," she said to the cop with the fogbound eyes. "Come for dinner tomorrow night."

# 40

Will knew he shouldn't be getting in deeper with Anahera, but he also knew he'd return to her cabin tomorrow. Tonight, as he sat in his kitchen again while a new band of heavy cloud blotted out the stars outside, it was time to read more of Miriama's journal.

Finding out the identity of her lover was no longer the reason why. He had Vincent's name, would talk to the other man tomorrow. Even as that thought passed through his head, Will second-guessed his choice.

What if Miriama was alive?

What if, by delaying until morning, he cost her that life?

Decision made as soon as those questions formed in his head, he got up and, popping the journal into a plastic bag, slid it into the inner pocket of his outdoor jacket, then went out to the SUV.

He didn't call Vincent until he was nearly at the other man's home. Then, he just said, "I need you to come down the drive. We have to talk about Miriama."

The smallest pause before Vincent's reply. "I'll be there."

The lights of his vehicle cut through the pitch-blackness about three minutes later. Will flashed his own lights from where he'd parked a little off the drive.

"Thank you for not coming up to the house," Vincent said, after they'd both gotten out to stand between the cars—under a sky so dark that a few more feet of distance and they wouldn't have been able to make out each other's faces. "I told Jemima I was heading out to have a quick drink with you, said you sounded down about the lack of progress on the disappearance."

Will didn't care what lies Vincent had told his wife; he was already well aware the man was a better liar than any of them had ever expected. "I know you had an affair with Miriama."

Smart enough to read the situation, Vincent didn't feign shock. "She was the most honest thing in my entire life," he murmured. "If I'd known who she'd grow up to be to me, I would've never married Jemima." He dropped his gaze to the ground. "Back then, I thought it was time to get the right kind of wife, create the right kind of family, begin building the profile that would help me advance in politics."

When he looked up, his eyes shimmered with wetness. "That's what I've always done—the *right thing*, or the right thing as mandated by whoever it is that decides the rules. In my case, that happened to be my parents."

A mocking smile. "They wanted the perfect son and I was happy to give them one. It was easy when I had no other passion in my life—not like Anahera with her music or Nikau with his academics, or even Daniel with his lust for money. Following my parents' script gave me direction."

"How did it start with Miriama?" Will took nothing Vincent said at face value. The other man's tears could be window dressing, his anguish perfectly pitched to arouse Will's sympathies. It was also equally possible that Vincent *had* been deeply in love with Miriama and unable to stand her rejection.

Vincent blew out a shuddering breath. "It began the first time I saw her after she went from being a girl to a woman." Gritty words. "It took me two months to build up the courage to speak to her about anything but how I liked my coffee, even longer before I dared kiss her. I was terrified the entire time that she'd slap my face and tell me I was reaching above myself, but my beautiful Miriama never did that. She loved me as much as I loved her."

"What about Dominic de Souza?" Will had deliberately thrown in the question cold, with no buildup; he wanted to see Vincent's unvarnished reaction.

He wasn't disappointed.

Hands fisting, Vincent spun on his heel to stalk down the narrow space between the two cars and all the way to the tree line. He stood staring out into the pitch dark for at least two long minutes after Will joined him before he spoke. "He's not good enough for her. He's promised her a life of travel and adventure. But what his small mind conceives as travel and adventure will bore her within the space of a year."

"Did you offer better?"

Vincent turned, his face haggard. "I should have. But, heaven help me, I didn't." Legs crumpling, he fell to his knees. "I should've said to hell with political aspirations and the perfect 'family man' image and just divorced Jemima. Only then . . . I would've had Miriama, but I would've lost the chance to watch my children grow up. My wife would've fought tooth and nail for sole custody and it wouldn't have taken much for her to prove that she's always been the main parent."

Dropping his head into his hands, Vincent choked back a sob. "But dear God," he said afterward, his voice rough, "much as I love my children, not breaking up my marriage so I was free to be with Miriama is the biggest regret of my life. If anything's happened to her, if I've wasted my one chance at true happiness, I'll never forgive myself."

It was a believable performance, but conversely, Will had once believed that Vincent was a happily married man with a wife he appreciated, even if they didn't appear to share a passionate love. Today, however, he'd heard a disturbing offhandedness in Vincent's voice when he spoke of Jemima, as if she was no more than an unwanted piece of furniture.

Which opened up a whole other can of worms. "Does Jemima know?"

Vincent wiped away his tears and struggled to his feet. "No, of course not."

He had the confidence of philandering men everywhere, and just like them, he was probably wrong. Though, when you factored in how well Vincent had insulated his family from the locals, it *was* possible that Jemima had no idea. But if she had worked out the truth . . .

"I'll need to speak to Jemima at some point," Will said.

Vincent's face turned to flint. "You'll have to get through my lawyers first."

"That's how much you love Miriama?" Will asked softly. "Enough to block me from talking to someone who might know what's happened to her?"

"Miriama left me. She chose Dominic de Souza." The words were like ice. "She'll still choose him when she comes back. I'm not going to lose my wife, too."

There it was, the rage. Deep and black and violent. The kind of rage that came from passionate love. "Do you know where Miriama is, Vincent?"

"Go to hell, you bastard."

Will didn't stop the other man when he got into his car and sped off down the drive, away from the house. Right now, he had nothing with which to further push Vincent.

That didn't mean he was about to give up.

Starting his own vehicle after a short delay but not turning on his headlights, he followed Vincent. As it was, the covert surveillance ended up a bust: Vincent parked in front of the pub.

Going around to the back of the local drinking hole, Will managed to get hold of the manager, a great bearded man who was a well-known hunter and who'd spent hours searching for Miriama. When Will asked him to keep an eye on Vincent and to let him know if the other man said or did anything out of the ordinary, the manager stared at him with hard eyes.

But his response wasn't the stonewalling Will had expected, wasn't the town protecting one of their own against an outsider. "I saw the way he looked at her," the other man said, twisting a tea towel in his nicked and scarred hands. "Also saw the way she looked back. Miri's too good for the likes of him and I'm glad the girl was smart enough to see that. Using her, that's what he was doing."

"Did you know," Will said, "or did you suspect only?"

"Didn't know for sure. Was hoping I was wrong." He slapped the tea towel over his shoulder, his black T-shirt branded with the fading emblem of a metal band. "Her thing with the doctor? That's got a real future—he's a townie but he respects little Miri enough to want her to be his wife."

"So his plan to propose is open knowledge?"

A faint smile. "Mattie isn't too good at keeping happy secrets. She whispered it around when the doctor asked her to sneak away one of Miri's rings so that he could have the engagement ring made the right size." Smile fading, he folded his arms over muscle gone to hard fat. "I'll keep an eye on the rich boy, don't worry."

"Don't do anything," Will warned. "He's not the only one I'm looking at."

"When you know for certain, you sure as hell better drive whoever it is out of here before I get my hands on them. But Vincent's safe for now."

The journal sat heavy against Will's heart as he drove off after that exchange.

He knew he wouldn't be getting any sleep tonight.

Before he returned home, however, he'd do a sweep of the town, make sure no trouble lurked in the shadows.

Though the air was clear of the scent of rain, the cloud-heavy sky held no stars, no moon, and it felt to Will as if the entire town was suffocating under a blanket of darkness. Miriama's disappearance had stained Golden Cove's heart. Nothing would scrub away that stain until they found her or discovered what had happened to her.

Spotting a huddle on one particular corner, he came to a stop by the curb and rolled down his window.

# 41

"You should all be at home," he said to the teenagers loitering outside the closed fire station.

Kyle Baker flicked off some ash from his cigarette. "We were just discussing Miriama. Thinking about what else we could do, where we could search." Insolence in his eyes but pious worry in his tone. Kyle was putting on a show for his fans, and, interestingly, many of those fans were younger than him.

"That's a good thing," Will said, "but, if anything happens to any of you, it'll make a bad situation even worse." He wasn't surprised to see a number of faces familiar to him from the other night—in a place this small, "hanging out" was a popular nighttime activity for the underage crowd. "The town can't afford to squander its resources right now. I need you to follow the rules so I don't have to worry about that and can focus on finding Miriama."

One of the girls bit down on her lower lip. "Sorry," she said softly. "It's just that we're so worried about Miriama and Kyle said maybe we could meet up and come up with some ideas."

Kyle shot the girl a narrow-eyed look that she didn't notice but Will did. He made sure his own eyes caught Kyle's on the return journey, the message in them clear: *anything* happened to that girl and Will would come for Kyle.

Shrugging her off as unimportant, Kyle took another drag of his cigarette. "You're absolutely right." He slid back into his golden boy persona without missing a beat. "We'll all go home. But we want to join in the search tomorrow."

"The search has been suspended." When he'd spoken to—then sober—Nikau on the drive back to Golden Cove, he'd agreed with the other man's call that there was nothing and nowhere left to search.

"Do you think she's dead?" Kyle asked, eyes devoid of empathy mocking Will.

"For Matilda's sake, and the sake of everyone else who loves Miriama, I hope not."

His words made several of the teenage girls tear up, the boys nearest them taking the opportunity to put their arms around the girls' shoulders. "Claire, Mika," he said, "hop in. I'll give you a lift home." The sisters lived the farthest away. "Kyle, I know I can trust you to see the others home safely."

The nineteen-year-old stilled, realizing too late that he'd been led into a trap. "Of course," he said at last and Will knew he'd keep his word. Kyle Baker might be a psychopath, but he was a psychopath who liked being the top dog in teenage circles in town.

Nodding good-bye to the other kids, Will turned his SUV in the direction of Claire and Mika's home. They were quiet on the ride but thanked him when he dropped them off. Will, however, wasn't done. He spent the next ten minutes getting in touch with the adults in charge of the other teenagers and alerting them their kids should be home within the next quarter hour.

Not all the adults who answered the phones were sober.

After hanging up, he swung by the two homes where a missing child might not immediately be noticed or reported. Catching sight of a teenager's lanky form through the open window of one, and spotting the other sitting safely on the back stoop of her home sneaking a cigarette, Will continued on his way. He felt no surprise when a low-slung car with its headlights off fell in behind him as he turned into his own street.

Kyle Baker didn't like being told no.

Halting the police vehicle in the middle of the otherwise empty road without warning, Will got out and pointed a flashlight directly at the driver's seat of the car sitting on his bumper. Kyle jerked up a hand to block the glare before backing up and screeching into a U-turn to head back the way he'd come.

The rest of Will's drive home was unremarkable.

Once inside, he made himself a cup of coffee, then opened Miriama's journal. This time, he read sequentially, his focus no longer on discovering the identity of her lover.

Many entries were simple descriptions of her day, or of something she'd seen that had caused her to pull out her camera, but she'd also filled the pages with dreams. Of travel, of passionate love, of creating a better life for her children than she'd had herself.

> *I love Auntie, but I've always missed having a mother. A proper one. One who'd take me shopping for my school shoes, and teach me how to cook and put on makeup.*
>
> *Auntie did a lot of that, and I'd never disrespect her by saying how much I wanted my mother—except without the drugs and the men—but it's a hole inside me, that need. I can't ever have a real mother, but I can be one. I'm going to have babies and I'm going to do all those things with them. Not just yet, not before I'm ready and strong enough to take care of a child, but one day.*

It was months later that she mentioned the topic again—after her breakup with Vincent, and soon after she'd begun to see Dominic.

> *I asked Dominic if he wants children. It's a scary question so early into a relationship, but it's important to me. I can't be with a man who doesn't want to build a family.*
>
> *He said yes. His face glowed because I was talking about our future. I asked him if he'd be okay with it if we had four*

*kids—he looked a little petrified by the number, but he said that if that was what I wanted, then he'd figure out how to look after four little ankle biters.*

*I can see it, see how much I'll love him one day. Not the way I love the man I shouldn't, but in the way of a dear friend. Dominic will never hurt me, never treat my dreams as anything other than important.*

*We'll create a family, and we'll be happy.*

Dominic turned up again several pages—and a couple of weeks—later.

*Dominic made me a picnic today. I asked him how he had the time—I know he's busy at the clinic. He admitted that he'd asked Auntie to help him, and it was so cute, the way he blushed.*

*The other day, I wrote that I'd never love Dominic the way I do someone who'll never be mine, but when he does things like this, when he treats me so wonderfully . . . I think my feelings for him will grow and grow. I'm so glad to know that. I never want to hurt Dominic. I'm going to be the best wife. I'm going to make him so happy.*

*And I'm going to leave this town. Leave the man for whom I broke God's commandments. Leave the memories of his smile and his kisses and his promises. I'm going to fly free and I'm not going to look back.*

# 42

Anahera spent hours thinking while Nikau snored in his drunken sleep.

Sometime in the midst of it, she took out the card that Jemima had given her and sent the other woman a quick email asking if Jemima was free for coffee midmorning the next day.

The answer was waiting for her when she woke:

> Ten o'clock will be perfect. Vincent has to fly to Auckland on company business and our nanny has the week off, so the children and I will be alone all day. Vincent won't get back till after nine tonight.

Anahera found it worrying that the other woman had so deliberately pointed out that her husband wouldn't be around, but that might just be her suspicious mind at play.

After kicking out a badly hungover Nikau—though she did have mercy enough to give him coffee first—she looked at the work emails she'd been ignoring for weeks. All about her music, music that she'd played for hours and hours and *hours* the day she saw Edward's body, so pale and motionless. Like a wax mannequin of the man she'd loved.

She hadn't played since.

Anahera glanced down at her hands, flexed them. And decided to take Pastor Mark up on his offer.

The church door was open as always, the pews empty and the interior cold. Exposed timbers arched above her head, while the floor beneath her feet was worn down by the passage of thousands of feet over tens of years. No fancy stained glass for this church on the edge of nowhere, but the quiet within was as profound as in the greatest cathedrals in Europe.

Sitting down at the old piano, she lifted the lid . . . and put her fingers to the keys.

It was the sound of tears that brought her back to earth. Letting the notes fade, she looked at the pews to see that she had an audience of three. The pastor, Evelyn Triskell, and a man with a sea-battered face she thought might be the uncle of Tania Meikle's husband. "Thank you for getting the piano tuned." She knew it must've been done for her.

"Ana, dear, what a gift you've given us in return." Pastor Mark patted Evelyn's shoulder.

Sniffing, the older woman looked at Anahera with red-rimmed blue eyes. "You play with such sadness. It breaks my heart."

What could Anahera say? In this house of God where anger seemed a sin and forgiveness was cherished. "I played my first-ever nocturne on these same keys." She ran her fingers across them, the touch featherlight.

The man who might've been related to the Meikles said, "Will you play more?"

So she did.

Her hands ached by the time she left for the Baker estate, and the sun had banished any lingering clouds, the sky a crisp blue. Jemima had messaged her to say she'd leave the gate open. As a result, Anahera didn't have to stop at the foot of the drive. The landscape looked far different in bright sunlight than it did in the moody gray that so often swathed the area.

Sunshine glimmered and glinted on the dewdrops that had survived the morning sun, and speared through the green of the leaves to turn them translucent, and she could hear the distinctive song of the tuis with their white ruffle at the throat and iridescent black feathers.

Sometimes, Anahera could imagine no more beautiful place in the world.

Other times, she wondered why she'd come back to a place she'd always wanted to escape. Maybe it had never been about the place at all.

She'd seen him in town as she drove through, the man who called himself her father. He'd seen her, too, had paused on the sidewalk, as if expecting her to stop.

Anahera hadn't stopped, would never stop for that man.

It was only as she was about to reach the top of the Baker drive that she realized while Vincent was gone, Kyle might well be home. If that turned out to be true, hopefully Jemima would either usher him out or he'd stick to a distant end of the house.

A second later, she saw Kyle pull out of the top of the drive in what looked like a Ferrari, the color a lustrous obsidian. Sending her a brilliant smile, he raised his hand in a wave as he headed down while she headed up. Anahera raised hers back, keeping things friendly. If he was a psychopath as Will suspected—and the cop had good instincts—it'd do well not to let Kyle see that she wasn't taken in by his act.

Parking, she got out and had just begun to walk up the two shallow front steps when the door opened from the inside. Jemima stood smiling on the doorstep. "Oh, you're here." A delighted brightness to her, a hint of surprise.

Because Anahera had kept her word?

"Thanks for having me," Anahera said with a smile of her own, "but I'm starting to feel a little underdressed." Jemima was wearing a white dress with little red flowers on the fabric, the bodice nipped in at the waist and the calf-length skirt flaring out below. Her hair was blow-dried to perfection, shone under the sunlight.

Vincent's wife laughed. "Oh, don't mind me," said the woman no one seemed to truly know. "I used to dress up even as a little girl. I don't get much of a chance to do it when in the Cove. I hope you don't mind."

"As long as you don't mind that I'm wearing jeans and a shirt." She hadn't bothered to put on her anorak after leaving the church; the sun took some of the bite out of the air.

"You look beautiful." Jemima's face glowed. "Come in."

When Anahera walked into the living room, it was to see two cherubic children playing on the rug in front of the crackling fireplace. "I always get cold," Jemima said. "The whole house is heated, of course, but nothing beats a fire, don't you agree?"

"Mama!" The boy held out his arms.

Not hesitating, Jemima went over and picked him up for a cuddle. Not to be outdone, his younger sister asked for the same.

"They're so competitive at this age," Jemima said afterward, "but they do play well together. We should be able to talk without too many interruptions." She showed Anahera to a comfortable seating area in front of wide windows that looked out over the dramatic untamed landscape beyond.

Anahera didn't immediately sit. "Damn, that's magnificent." It came out as a long exhale.

There were no pathways in this part of the bush, no trails for hikers to follow. If you went into the dense growth so thick it turned the world quiet and dark, you did so on your own steam, knowing the wild could swallow you whole.

Jemima came to stand beside her, her perfume a delicate floral note in the air. "It is beautiful, isn't it?" she said softly.

Anahera turned to look at the other woman's unsmiling profile. "It must get lonely, though," she said. "I used to feel that way in London, a country girl lost in the big city."

"It's not so much the country—I grew up in a large game reserve. It's that . . ." She wrapped her arms around herself, her hands cupping her elbows. "Everyone knows each other already and they don't seem to want to know me." A glance at Anahera out of the corner of her eye.

"Small towns," Anahera said. "They have their good points and bad points."

Releasing her arms to her sides, Jemima nodded. "We've witnessed the good over the past few days, don't you think? People coming together to search for Miriama."

"The bad, unfortunately, is the insular nature and the gossip."

They both moved naturally back to the seating area, with Jemima taking the armchair that would allow her to keep an eye on her children while they spoke. On the small table in between them was a fine china tea set and a plate of small, beautifully iced cakes. "It's not actually tea," Jemima whispered with a grin that seemed far more real than any other expression Anahera had seen on her face. "It's coffee. I hope you don't mind."

That was the second time the other woman had used those words: *I hope you don't mind.* A nervous habit? Or had someone trained her to be uncertain by being constantly irritated or annoyed at her actions?

It was equally possible Anahera was letting her own past color her reading of Jemima Baker.

"Are you kidding?" she said, determined to get to the truth. "I live on coffee."

Jemima laughed and poured the rich, dark liquid into both cups. "Cream? Sugar?"

"I'll do it." Anahera reached for the sugar bowl as she spoke. "We're friends—or at least I hope we'll become friends. Friends don't stand on ceremony."

Sea green eyes filled with light. "I'm so glad you're back, Anahera." Her hand flew to her mouth almost before the last word was out. "I'm so sorry. That was incredibly thoughtless of me."

Anahera shook her head. "It's all right. I've had time to accept my husband's death." Accept his perfidy and his generosity and his betrayal and the love he'd once had for her. Maybe one of these days, she'd even stop being so angry at him—not for the affair, but for dying and leaving her with no target for her grief, her rage.

"Vincent and I saw one of the shows he wrote when it did a run on Broadway," Jemima said softly. "The one about Jane Austen's life, with those amazing costumes and that strange, fascinating timeline."

"That was always Edward's favorite." He'd been so happy when it won award after award, such a kid about showing off the statuettes to anyone who came around.

Old affection stirred in her chest, waking from a long sleep. "We flew over to see its Broadway debut, and the whole time, he sat there grinning while holding my hand." It seemed a memory of two distant strangers. "We traveled constantly in the first year of our marriage. You and Vincent do a lot of travel, too, don't you?"

"We used to do a lot more." Jemima held her teacup of coffee on her knee. "But since the children, I prefer to stay in one place for longer periods and Vincent doesn't seem to mind traveling alone when needed."

The Anahera who'd sat next to her grinning husband in that darkened theater wouldn't have caught the bitterness hidden beneath the unexceptional words. But to the Anahera who'd helped her husband's distraught mistress from his graveside, the acrid taste was as familiar as the knot of anger and resentment and grief in her own chest.

Jemima knew.

# 43

The question was if she knew only that Vincent had been unfaithful, or if she had the name of the woman who'd become a silent third party in their marriage.

Anahera liked Jemima, but Miriama also had a call on her loyalty.

And the time for lies and rumors was over.

"You can tell me to shove off and mind my own business if I'm crossing a line," she said, "but I get the feeling you aren't happy in your marriage."

Jemima's face closed over. "That's a very personal thing to say."

"Comes from experience."

Jemima froze in the act of stirring more cream into her coffee. Looking up after several long seconds, she searched Anahera's face. "Do you usually tell strangers?"

Anahera felt her lips twist. "I haven't told anyone. I only found out after my husband died and she turned up at my front door."

China rattled against china as Jemima nearly dropped both cup and saucer. Putting them down, she stared at Anahera with horrified eyes. "I am *so* sorry." Her next words trembled, white lines bracketing her mouth. "My God, why couldn't she have waited?"

"She loved him, too." Anahera had never blamed the woman—it was Edward who'd been married, Edward who'd broken vows, Edward who'd made his lover promises of forever. "She couldn't stop crying."

Smoothing back her flawless hair with an unsteady hand, Jemima looked over at her two small children. "Let's go onto the balcony. It's so lovely out."

Only once they were outside, the sliding door mostly shut behind them, did the other woman say, "I haven't told anyone, either." A rough whisper. "No one suspects. We have such a perfect life."

Anahera leaned her forearms against the wooden railing, drinking in the landscape as she inhaled the crisp air. "Is it a woman connected to his business?" She had to know if Vincent's wife had identified a stunning nineteen-and-a-half-year-old girl as his lover.

"I don't know." Jemima's fingers clenched tight around the railing. "I thought about hiring a private investigator to follow Vincent, but then I'd actually know and have to do something about it." Releasing a shuddering breath, she said, "Right now, I can pretend that it's all in my imagination. And we can keep on living this perfect life."

Anahera turned her gaze from the view to the elegant lines of Jemima's face. "You love him." It was written in every tormented inch of her. Whatever Vincent's reasons for marrying her, Jemima had done it out of love.

"From the moment I first met him," Jemima whispered. "I always knew he didn't feel the same way about me, but I thought it would grow. And we were doing okay, were building a strong friendship around our shared determination to get Vincent to the top of the political ladder, and then . . ."

Jemima looked back through the sliding door, making sure her children remained involved in their game and out of earshot. "Then he found a woman who made him feel alive in a way I've never managed."

"That doesn't give him the right to hurt you."

"The thing is"—Jemima dropped her head—"even if he came to me today and confessed each and every detail, I'd tell him I'd be willing to look the other way as long as he came back to me. That's how pathetic I am, that's how much I love him."

Anahera closed a hand over the other woman's, squeezed, but part of her couldn't help but think that a wife who was willing to put up with that much from her husband might not take it well if she believed her husband's affair had a chance of becoming real—of coming out of the shadows to disrupt her perfect life. Maybe Vincent had slipped up, or maybe Jemima *had* hired that private investigator.

Was it possible Vincent had tried to win Miriama back by offering marriage?

"Are you worried that Vincent's considering divorce?" Anahera pushed off the railing, angling her body to face Jemima. "And again, you can tell me to shove it if that's going too far."

"I think you might be the first real friend I've made since I walked down the aisle." A tendril of golden hair whispered against her cheek. "I don't want to lie to you. The truth is, I used to worry about divorce, but he's never once mentioned it as a possibility. I keep hoping it's just a madness that'll pass and then I'll have my husband back." Words raw with hope.

Jemima truly seemed to believe the affair was ongoing.

So either Vincent had already found someone else . . . or he remained obsessed with Miriama despite their breakup.

## 44

Will fought the urge to slam his fist down on the steering wheel. He'd spoken to everybody he could, run down every possible lead, even quietly checked the whereabouts of a number of different men at the time of Miriama's disappearance—men who'd looked at her as Nikau had looked at her—and still he had nothing.

Nikau himself, it turned out, had been hanging in the garage with Peter Jacobs. Peter Jacobs, who had no record, but who'd been a "person of interest" in an American rape investigation. Will had discovered that piece of well-buried background earlier today, his blood running cold, but Jacobs's alibi was solid.

Evelyn Triskell, of all people, had confirmed that she'd walked in on Peter and Nikau "stinking up" the garage with "awful cheap cigars." She'd been certain of the date and time because she'd come in to have an oil check before she and Wayne left to see a movie in a neighboring town. She'd even had the ticket stubs to confirm the timing.

Another dead end.

The same as the information that had finally come in from Miriama's cell phone carrier: her phone had last pinged off towers that placed her in Golden Cove—near the time of her disappearance.

Will's superiors had more than once pointed out that his strongest trait was also his worst weakness: Sometimes, Will, they'd said, you have to give up. Sometimes you can't save people.

He knew that, had lived the cruel truth as he fought to get inside the blazing funeral pyre of a "safe house" that held a bright-eyed little boy and his mother. But still he couldn't stop himself, still he couldn't give up.

Miriama deserved better than that. Golden Cove deserved better than that.

Because he'd also been chasing down the rumors about the three missing hikers from fifteen years ago. Everyone had a theory about what may have happened to the young women. Will had even received an anonymous tip in the form of a note shoved under the station door while he was out. A note full of vague innuendo and speculation. No one had facts.

He'd sent off a query to check the allegations in the note, but right now he wanted to talk to Matthew Teka. The man had been around a long time. If anyone knew the secrets of this town, it'd be Matthew. Which was why Will was driving to the man's cabin out in the bush.

The hunter called out a hearty *"Tēnā koe!"* and invited him in for a cup of "gumboot tea." While it brewed, he regaled Will with a story about the tahr bull he'd been tracking recently. "Sly bugger. I could almost see him laughing as he scrambled up a mountainside like he had crampons on his feet." He checked the tea he had going on the stove in a heavy teakettle even older than Anahera's. "You ever tasted their meat? Bloody good *kai*."

"Can't say I have." Though, having grown up in the south, he was familiar with the goat-like animals. Endangered elsewhere in the world, the introduced species was considered a pest in New Zealand.

"I'll get you a steak after I bag this bull." Matthew picked up the kettle and began to pour.

"You supply one of the wild-game restaurants?"

"Yeah, but don't worry about paying city prices. Your feed's on me—I always keep aside a bit of meat."

*"Kia ora*, Matthew."

Putting a dented tin cup in front of Will after waving off his thanks, Matthew took a seat at the wooden table—not across from Will, but to the right, next to the window. "So, you want to talk about the lost hikers."

Will drank down a third of the hot, strong tea heavy with sugar and dark with caffeine. "Anything you can tell me?"

"Those girls didn't just disappear," Matthew said bluntly while rolling up tobacco into a thin cigarette. "I tramped through that part of the bush day in and day out, and didn't see no sign of the girls until I found that water bottle."

He finished sealing his roll-up, but didn't light it. "Piri found the pack that belonged to the second *wahine* later—in the same spot where I stopped for a breather the day before. I got eyes in my *upoko*. I would've noticed a pack. Got put there after."

"Did you tell this to the original investigators?"

"Sure." A shrug. "But most of the city cops, they think we're *pōraki, nē*." He circled a finger by his temple. "Living out here in the bush."

Unfortunately, Will couldn't disagree with Matthew's take. Hell, if he hadn't been assigned to Golden Cove, if he hadn't gotten to know these people, he might've been the same. The brain shied away from the sanity of making a home out here in this primeval wildness. "Did the locals have any suspicions at the time about who it might've been?"

"People did look at each other funny after they found the bracelet of the third girl, but it was just fear, eh. We didn't have anyone acting like a perv or anything."

In a town this small, someone inevitably ended up a scapegoat. That Golden Cove hadn't fixated on a single individual told him exactly how difficult the case must've been for the cops who'd investigated it. A water bottle, a pack, an identity bracelet. No remains. Not even a single bone fragment.

"What about you?" he asked. "You ever wonder about someone?"

Finally lighting his roll-up, Matthew politely puffed toward the open window rather than Will's face. "Interesting question, that."

Instincts prickling, Will just waited.

"You're a good listener." Matthew gave an approving nod from behind a plume of smoke. "Would've made a great enemy interrogator."

Will wasn't the least surprised to learn the other man was a veteran. He got that haunted look in his eyes sometimes that Will had seen in the eyes of others who'd come back from war. "It used to drive my mother nuts," he said. "For the first few years of my life she worried I was mute."

Laughing uproariously at that, the older man slapped at his knee. *"Ka mau te wehi!"* When he finally calmed down, he said, "You'll think I've lost my mind alone out here."

Will held his gaze. "I've learned things during this investigation that make me question everyone in the Cove, so whoever you name, I'm not going to be surprised."

The name Matthew spoke made the hairs rise on the back of Will's neck. "Why? I need to know why you suspected him."

Matthew took a while to think about that, smoking his roll-up halfway down before he said, "Just . . . too perfect, eh." Another thoughtful puff. "A man—he was a boy back then—who never makes mistakes has got to have a madness trapped inside. And, there was the *punua kurī*."

"A puppy?"

Matthew nodded, then went silent.

"I didn't grow up here, Matthew," Will prodded. "What about the puppy?"

After taking a last puff, Matthew crushed his roll-up in the ashtray balanced on the window ledge. "Kid's father gave him one for his ninth birthday, I think it was. Maybe it was eight, or maybe it was ten, eh? *Tamariki* all look the same to me."

The hunter coughed, his chest sounding clogged up. "Then one day, I see him running out of the bush near their place, saying his puppy had run away. He was crying, all red-faced and scared." Another hacking cough. "I knew that pup wouldn't survive out there all alone and I had Ripper with me—good hunting dog, never used to get distracted. I figured he could track down the *punua kurī* quick enough."

Will had the feeling he was about to hear something that wouldn't ever leave his memory. "Did Ripper live up to his reputation?"

"Yeah, he found the puppy, what was left of it. Someone had bashed its brains in using a rock."

Matthew looked at Will with sharp, dark eyes. "I couldn't believe a boy that young could've done that, eh, so I just buried the puppy and told myself to forget it. But, I kept seeing that pup with its brains bashed out every time I closed my eyes. So next time I saw Trevor Baker down at the pub, I told him maybe he shouldn't give his boy another puppy."

"What did he say?"

"Nothing, but that boy never again got a *kurī*."

As Matthew got up to pour himself a cup of tea, Will worked out the logistics in his head. "Vincent would've only been fourteen at the time the hikers went missing."

"He got his growth early, that boy." Matthew topped up Will's tea. "Was as big as a man by that age. As big as he is now."

Which wasn't huge by any estimation, Will thought, but it was plenty big enough to overpower a woman of average size. He'd looked up the files on the missing hikers, knew they'd been small boned and ranged from five-one to five-four in height, their weights on the lower end of the scale. A strong fourteen-year-old boy could have taken each one.

Especially if he came at them with a rock from behind.

One blow to disorient, the other to incapacitate. And more to smash in their skulls just like the lost puppy's.

"'Course, Vincent wasn't the only strong boy in the Cove that summer," Matthew added without warning. "Back when he was younger, after I told him I couldn't find the pup, he started crying harder and said another boy in town must've stolen the *punua kurī*, that he was jealous of Vincent's gift."

"He ever name the other boy?"

"I never asked." Matthew drank some of his tea, then put down the mug and began to roll another cigarette. "Needed a beer after what I'd seen, just wanted to get down to the pub."

"You think it's possible another child was involved?"

The hunter took his time answering. "Rich, good-looking boy with all the nice toys living in a flash house? *Ae*, another boy might see that and get a hot head." Sealing the roll-up closed, he said, "No way to hide a stolen pup in Golden Cove."

This time, every single tiny hair on Will's body rose up. What kind of a child would bash in a helpless puppy's brains rather than allow another boy to possess it?

# 45

Will drove back into Golden Cove as night was falling, not sure what he was going to do with the information, or even if he believed all of it—because Matthew didn't only smoke tobacco. Will had smelled weed on him more than once, but since there was no indication the hunter was cultivating or selling . . . and because of those haunted eyes, he'd let sleeping dogs lie.

If a man wanted to self-medicate to escape the nightmares, who the fuck was Will to stop him?

He might not have made the same call as a shiny young cop, but now he knew that a man could be broken. Sometimes, oblivion was a gift.

But if Matthew's information *was* right, Will had to follow it up all the way to the horrific end. A teenage boy who'd murdered three women and gotten away with it wouldn't have stopped. No, he'd just have gotten smarter, slyer. And maybe stopped hunting on home ground.

Jesus Christ, how many bodies were buried in the bush?

He pulled into the supermarket lot on the heels of that thought, ran in to grab a six-pack of beer from the chiller, though he was unlikely to have more than a single one. The town was too unsettled for him to be incapacitated. Whether he even had one would depend on whether or not Anahera was in the mood to let him stay the night.

"Any news?" Shan Lee asked him at the checkout, the man's face smooth and without wrinkles but his eyes worn.

"No. Nothing." He paid, picked up the beer. "Your daughter's a smart woman, Shan, and she knows to be careful."

"Never thought I'd have to worry about those things here."

No, neither had Will.

The front door to Anahera's cabin was open when he went up to the porch, and he could hear rock music within. "Anahera," he called out.

When she didn't answer, he stepped in, looked around, his shoulders tight and his abdomen clenched. A pot sat bubbling on the makeshift stove, while half-chopped vegetables lay on the cutting board. Listening harder, he heard the sound of water running nearby.

Anahera appeared from around the corner seconds later. "Had to go wash off some dirt. A sparrow slammed into the window and when I went to see if it was okay, I managed to stumble into muck." She made a face. "Didn't want to wash in the sink, not when I'm cooking."

Will wasn't listening—he was too focused on the fact that she was wearing only a towel, hitched around her breasts. Yellow and short, it made her skin glow. "You left the door open." The words shoved out.

"You did message to say you were on the road out of town," she pointed out. "Can you watch the stove?" Turning on her heel, she walked off toward her bedroom. "I was in the middle of changing."

Will wasn't sure he took a breath until he heard the click of her bedroom door closing. "Fuck."

The woman packed a punch.

Closing the front door, he kicked off his boots before heading in and putting the beer in her small fridge—it appeared secondhand, was probably a loaner from Josie and Tom. When he looked at the pot, he thought she might be making stew. Whatever it was, it smelled damn good. After making sure it wasn't going to bubble over, he turned to the cutting board. A wash of his hands, then he finished chopping up the vegetables on the board.

He'd just put down the knife when she walked back into the room, having changed into a slinky black dress with long sleeves that hit her midthigh and exposed her shoulders. Her only accessory was a greenstone pendant worn on a braided black cord. Her feet were bare, her hair down.

Not saying a word, Will went to the fire and stoked it up to a blaze.

Anahera laughed, the sound big and husky. "Does that mean you like the dress?"

Shrugging off the shirt he wore on top of a white T-shirt, Will hung it on the back of a chair. "That's not a dress that inspires a simple like." It was too punch-in-the-gut sexy for that.

Anahera didn't answer until she'd scraped the vegetables into the stew pot. "It will taste good," she said. "I know not everyone's a fan of stew, but you'll have to trust me on this."

"Oh," Will said, "I didn't realize you were talking about the food."

Another laugh. "I didn't know you could flirt, cop."

Neither had Will. It had been an age since he'd done it, since he'd wanted to do it. "Should I have a beer?" he asked.

She took one of the beers from the fridge and, pulling back the tab to open the can, placed it on the counter. "You could pour me a glass of wine."

Spotting the bottle of red she'd opened the other night, Will did as asked. Then he leaned back against the wall and watched her move around the kitchen. It was a small space and she filled it to overflowing, her energy intense.

He took a swallow of his beer, ran his eyes over the elegant curves of her body. She caught him at it. "Somehow, cop, I don't think your mind is on food."

"I am thinking of eating something."

Anahera turned off the stove. "Food's done." She prowled over to him until her breasts touched his chest, her bare feet against his. When she tilted up her head, it was with unhidden challenge in her eyes.

Will slid his free hand behind her neck, under the dark heaviness of her hair, and massaged. "You like the taste of beer?"

"I don't mind it."

Keeping his hand where it was, he leaned down to kiss her. She rose up into the kiss, no passive receiver but an active participant. If his mouth tasted like beer, hers was rich red wine and something deeper, more potent, intrinsically Anahera.

He knew already she'd never be an easy woman to be with—if tonight

wasn't the only night they were to spend together. Anahera was complicated and strong and apt to be difficult at times. Of course, Will wasn't
exactly easy himself.

Sinking deeper into the kiss, he fisted his hand in her hair but drew
back before it could go any further. "How about a bed?" He leaned around
her to put his beer on the counter.

"It's a single," she warned.

Will looked to the fireplace. "Hold that thought."

Leaving her with an amused look on her face, he went into the bedroom
and hauled off the mattress to put it in front of the fireplace. She padded
across to him as he was throwing the sheet over it. He'd just finished tuck-
ing it in when she reached back and undid the zipper on her dress. "Protection's in the bedside drawer," she said as the dress slid down her body, the
firelight flickering over her proudly naked form.

"I got us covered." Pulling the foil packets from his jeans pocket and
throwing them down beside the mattress, he put his hands on this woman
who made him remember he was alive.

Anahera felt as if she was coming out of a long winter. That winter hadn't
begun with Edward's death; it had started in the years prior, when they'd
slowly become strangers to one another.

Will's hands, rough and large, were as different from Edward's as she
was from the girl who'd once run wild on the beach below the cliffs. Sinking into the sensations, she pushed up his T-shirt until he tore it off, then
ran her own hands over the hard ridges and hollows of his chest and around
to his back.

The ridges there were unexpected, the skin coarse.

"Burns," he said, breaking the kiss. "They bother you?"

Anahera devoured his mouth in response. A few scars didn't bother her.
Not when her nerves crackled with an electric heat. All she wanted was to
feel more and more and more. Like a prisoner who'd been starved, she
wanted to gorge.

The firelight pulsed against Will's body as he rose to strip off the rest of his clothing, and she had the best view in the house. When he came down over her, she picked up one of the flat packets beside the mattress and slapped it to his chest. "Put it on. We can do the foreplay later."

She wanted him inside her, wanted to feel sexually alive from the inside out.

Rising up onto his knees, he sheathed himself. "Ready?"

"Since you arrived." Her words seemed to pitch him over the edge, this controlled man who burned against her.

The next few moments weren't controlled at all, the two of them coming together in a storm of need and lust and hunger.

Racing heartbeats.

Demanding hands.

A guttural grunt from Will.

A short scream from Anahera.

Harsh breaths.

# 46

"I haven't screamed for a long time," Anahera said long minutes later. It might've been a cold crash into reality except that Will had his arm around her shoulders, and she was lying with her head against his chest. Anahera wasn't sure how she felt about the intimacy—sex was easy, it was the rest that complicated things.

Will stroked his hand down her spine. "I haven't been with anyone for over a year."

"High standards?" she said with a self-mocking smile.

"Nightmares."

"Those nightmares have anything to do with the burns on your back?"

"Same case that led to the inquiry." He ran his hand down her spine again. "You've got some scars of your own." The words didn't demand.

Maybe that was why she gave him an answer . . . of sorts. "It shouldn't be such a big scar, but it was an emergency and there were complications."

Will didn't ask the obvious probing question, but he raised his free hand to brush her hair from her face. The gesture was oddly tender and it struck her with terror.

Sitting up, she reached for her dress, tugged it on over her head. "Zip me up?" She swept her hair to one side.

Will did as asked, then let her use the bathroom before he did so himself. He'd taken his clothes with him, came out fully dressed. "Should I drag the mattress back to the bed?"

Anahera knew what he was asking. "I don't have an answer for you yet." She'd had no intention of tonight being anything other than a physical release, but Will wasn't a simple man. He was the kind of man who got under a woman's skin and made her *feel*. Made her come awake on the inside—along with memories of the sterile cold of an operating theater, memories so painful that she didn't talk about them even with her best friend.

Will said nothing, just set the table before coming back for the pot of stew she'd reheated and was stirring.

Pot on the table, he took her hand and tugged her to a chair. "Stop running, Anahera." A press of his lips to her temple before he took his own seat. "I can tell you from experience that the demons eventually catch up with you, no matter what you do."

"Sometimes, we need to run, need to give ourselves time to heal enough to fight the demons."

"Do you think all wounds can be healed?"

Anahera laughed, the sound more than a little ragged. "You're a damn good cop, Will." The wound inside her would never heal.

Will looked at her with far too much insight, but didn't say anything further. It was Anahera who finally spoke ten minutes later, after they'd served themselves and were eating. "Hysterectomy," she said without attempting to soften the blow. "I guess that answers your question."

"My burns were second degree. But that doesn't answer your question, does it?"

She stared at him, at this man who was forcing her to confront the past, and she wondered . . . "Why the sudden desire to know my past? Am I still on your suspect list?"

"No." He closed his fingers around his beer but didn't drink.

"Then what's with the questions?"

"Because I want to get to know you." Those gray eyes, so difficult to penetrate. "The sex, I could've had if I'd wanted it. I'm no prize, but there aren't that many single men around for competition."

Anahera wondered if he truly believed that, if he truly didn't understand the magnetism of his intensity and quiet competence. It kindled a compulsion to unravel him, see beneath that disciplined control. Ironically, one of the things Anahera had loved most about Edward was that he was an open book—and look how well that turned out. At least Will was upfront about his secrets.

"I feel so special." She took a sip of wine. "What sets me apart from the herd?"

He didn't flinch at her sharp tone, didn't set his jaw or look away. "You're unapologetically you," he said. "Complex, difficult, gifted." The slightest upward tug of his lips, the faintest whisper of a smile. "I'm a cop. We love solving mysteries."

"The only mysteries about me are sordid," Anahera said, suddenly tired of pretending. "They involve a cheating husband, a pregnant mistress, and a case of deep-vein thrombosis that led to a fatal pulmonary embolism." Such an unfair way for healthy and fit Edward to die, such a senseless waste. "Mystery solved."

"No, that's just a splinter of you." Will held the dangerously intense eye contact. "You're a creature of mystery and you always will be. I'll never solve you."

Anahera didn't know why, but she said, "Leave the mattress by the fire."

As she lay down on the mattress next to Will later that night, she knew this was nothing like what she'd had with Edward. That had been a bright, hopeful thing with butterfly wings. She was harder now, her wings torn off to be replaced by scar tissue.

Will was the same.

What would come of that? What *could* come of that?

Will's arm crept around her waist, hugging her to the heat and muscle of him. But Anahera's eyes stared out into the darkness sketched in shadows by the firelight, her ghosts loud tonight.

———

She woke to the sound of movement. Her eyelashes lifted, her body heavy with the kind of sleep she hadn't had for a long, long time. Still drowsy, she watched Will put on his clothes and boots, and wondered if he'd sneak out of the house, doing his version of a walk of shame.

But, of course, that wasn't Will. She saw him grab a small notebook she'd left on the counter, begin to write a note.

"Will."

Abandoning the note, he came to crouch by the mattress. Brushing her hair off her face with one hand, he said, "I have to go. A local found something not far from the rubbish dump. The call just came in."

Anahera had a vague memory of hearing an annoying buzzing.

Sitting up, she let his hand drop away, her attention fixed on his face. It gave her nothing. "What do you mean they found something? Is it Miriama?"

"I hope not." Hard lines bracketing his mouth. "Because that area was heavily searched. I asked Nikau to send extra teams out there."

Anahera sucked in a breath. "That means if it is her, somebody deliberately returned to put her there." She had to say it out loud to get the horror of it straight in her mind. "I'll come with you."

Will shook his head. "You'd just have to sit in the car. I can't take a civilian into a possible crime scene." He rose along with her. "I'll call you the instant I know anything."

Frustration gnawed at Anahera, but she didn't argue. This might be a small town, the rules not as hard and fast, but Will was a cop, a good one. And Anahera wasn't about to mess up a future trial by being where she shouldn't be; evidence mattered, blood splatter mattered. "I'll keep my phone with me."

Walking him to the door, she thought about if she should kiss him good-bye, but what they'd done in the night wasn't quite settling in the pale dark before dawn.

"I'll call you," Will repeated before heading out across the porch. He was halfway down the steps when he turned and came back. Closing one hand around the side of her face, he pressed his lips to hers.

Embers low in her belly ignited, but this was no long burn. Will drew back almost at once and jogged over to get into the police SUV. She watched him reverse into the mist, her lips burning from his kiss and her face bearing the imprint of his palm.

# 47

Will's radio crackled as he drove away from a woman for whom he'd never planned. Despite not having any staff who might contact him, he wasn't surprised by the static. Something about the area did funny things to his radio every now and then. One of the old bushmen had been with Will during a previous static burst; he'd immediately made the sign of the cross.

"Ghost," he'd muttered. "Never figured one would want to haunt a cop car."

Will wasn't afraid of ghosts. It was the real-life monsters walking around that terrified him. Not for the first time, he thought about Vincent Baker and how his mask of grief had slipped when Will mentioned speaking to his wife, how quickly Miriama had changed from his true love to an object he'd used and discarded.

Then there was Kyle Baker.

Both hiding in plain sight. But where Kyle's ego led him to flip off authority, Vincent had played the part of a trustworthy friend and neighbor his entire adult life. He'd never let the mask slip in public. Which, to Will's mind, made Vincent the more dangerous of the two brothers.

And Will had nothing on either Baker.

What he did have—courtesy of an email that had come through last night after dinner—was a disturbing report about Tom Taufa: Assault on a girlfriend when he was thirteen and spending the summer with his grandparents in Tonga. Bad enough to have left the girl with a broken nose.

All of which Will only knew because of that scribbled anonymous note telling him to "look into Tom Taufa's record in Tonga." He'd followed it up to cross it off the list, never expecting his contact to confirm the allegations.

*Boy was never officially charged,* the other officer had written. *Families sorted it out between themselves. Felt sorry for Tom because his father had been in and out of prison since he was a baby, and his mother had mental health problems.*

*But the villagers have long memories, and it was a big, shameful thing for his grandparents. They say he's been making it up to them since—and the girl involved has forgiven him. Apparently, he even helped pay for her wedding.*

Tom hadn't had a single brush with the law since then, so maybe the shock of what he'd done, accompanied by witnessing his grandparents' shame, had put him on the straight and narrow. Or maybe Tom Taufa had become a plumber because no one noticed plumbers or thought it strange if they saw a trade van parked on the street.

Tom had also been a poor kid with dysfunctional parents to Vincent's rich boy cocooned in the heart of a successful family.

Not the kind of boy who'd be gifted a puppy by his father.

Will's hands flexed on the steering wheel as he drove through the eerily silent town. Even Josie's café was cold and dark—he was used to seeing a light in there in the early morning hours, as Josie and Miriama got to work on the day's baking. Julia Lee provided the cakes, but the breads, pies, and other products were all made in-house. Every so often, when he had an extremely early start, he'd knock on the door and the women would open up to make him a coffee to take on the road.

The weather didn't help the sense of gloom that clung to Golden Cove.

The clouds had returned with a vengeance; they hung black and heavy, just waiting to thunder down with rain. He always had a couple of tarps in the back of the SUV, along with some tent poles, in case he had to protect a crime scene from rain, but even as he turned into the road that led to the dump, he was hoping there was nothing to protect, nothing to see.

The idea of Miriama forever gone, all that light, all that talent snuffed out, it seemed hellishly wrong. But hellishly wrong things did happen. Sometimes, they happened to small boys, and sometimes, they happened to beautiful young women just about to spread their wings.

Parking his vehicle in the same spot he had when he'd come out here with Anahera, he grabbed a flashlight, then ran across the dump to the spot where the informant had told him he'd be waiting. "Shane!" he called out from a short distance away, after spotting the writer sitting on what looked to be an upturned plastic crate.

The other man jerked up his head, the dark curls of his hair tumbling across his forehead. "You actually came," he said, getting to his feet and thrusting that hair back with a shaking hand. "I'd almost convinced myself I'd hallucinated the entire nightmare."

Taking in the other man's stark white features and dilated irises, Will said, "You don't have to come with me. Just tell me where you found it."

Shuddering, Shane sank back down on his makeshift seat. "That way"—he pointed—"about fifty feet in. Follow the path."

Will had a lot of questions for Shane, chief among them, what the hell he was doing here at this time of the morning—it wasn't even five thirty—but first, he had to see what the other man had found.

Heading in the direction Shane had indicated, he followed the pathway of beaten-down grass that looked to have seen several pairs of booted feet relatively recently.

Shane's find was impossible to miss.

Bones, bleached so white they glowed under the beam of the flashlight. A full skeleton.

Nothing appeared to be missing. Not the smallest finger or toe bone. And while Will was no forensic anthropologist, he had eyes. The leg bones weren't anywhere near long enough for a woman of Miriama's height.

# 48

Will had kept his promise to Anahera. He'd called.

Just long enough to say, "It's not Miriama."

The full horror of his words had only penetrated after he hung up. Because Will hadn't said there was no body. Just that it wasn't Miriama's. Which meant someone else was dead.

The first thing Anahera did was call Josie.

*Please answer. Please answer.*

Her relief when her friend said a cheery, "Hello, Ana. Are you keeping baker's hours now?" threatened to crumple her to her knees.

Wrenching it together, she somehow managed to sound normal in her reply. "You prepping for the café at home?"

"Yes, Tom doesn't want me in there alone right now." A pause. "I don't want to go anyway. It feels awful knowing Miri won't walk in the door yawning and demanding a coffee before we get to work."

"I'm sorry, Josie. I know you miss her."

"So much." Josie bit back a sob. "Even Tom misses her and you know him—he likes things settled and orderly and Miri's never been that way. She puts smiley faces on his coffee or bags him up chocolate cake when he came in to grab a muffin."

Anahera felt a stab of suspicion, shook it away at once. Tom Taufa was as in love with Josie as it was possible for a man to be with a woman; the idea of him cheating on his wife . . . no, it didn't fit.

But she'd thought Vincent a man of honor, too. "Do they know each other well?" she asked and hated herself for mistrusting a man who'd done nothing to deserve it.

"Well, he's her cousin—in a long, roundabout way. Used to babysit her way back when. I think he still sees her as that small girl." A smile in her next words. "Now and then, when we see her dressed up to party, he shakes his head and mutters about her short hems. Honestly, he can be a fuddy-duddy, but I adore him."

A man who noticed the length of a woman's dress might just be a pro-tective older cousin—or a jealous one. *No.* Anahera fisted her hand. She couldn't allow this situation to poison her ability to trust. Tom was a stick-in-the-mud tradesman who didn't enjoy change. He'd do nothing to frac-ture his life with Josie. "I'm in awe of how you've managed to keep him in the dark about your own wild ways, *Josephine.*"

Josie giggled at the pointed use of her full name. "Shh. Josephine the Bad Girl shed her skin and became Josie the Good Girl the day I realized Tom had grown up into a big, beautiful creature I wanted to kiss."

"Yes, I remember your sudden fondness for church." Josie had made Anahera go week after week.

Laughing, Josie said, "Faith, keeping his promises to God, that's always been important to Tom." Her voice softened. "I knew from the first that Tom Taufa would never break any vows he made to me."

A sharp, beeping sound.

"Oh, I have to go! That's the oven timer."

Hanging up, Anahera wondered what a man of such deep faith would think of a young woman who was partner to the sin of adultery. "No," she said again, this time with conviction. She'd known Tom his entire life and had *never* seen him be violent.

This whole situation was just getting to her.

She consciously put aside the dark thoughts and got herself ready for the day—and as soon as the clock ticked over to seven, she called Nikau. "I wanted to make sure you weren't passed out drunk."

"I'm making hot dogs for breakfast," Nik replied. "Want one?"

"No, thanks, I'll stick with cereal." That done, she called Jemima, exhaling quietly when the other woman answered.

"Anahera, I'm so glad you called."

"Is everything all right?" Anahera went to stand in the open doorway, watch dull morning light creep over a turbulent ocean. "You sound different."

Jemima laughed. "I'm happy," she said. "Vincent came home last night with the most gorgeous diamond necklace for me *and* a huge bunch of red roses. I don't know what's gotten into him, but it's like I have my husband back again. He's the way he was when we were first dating."

Anahera's hand clenched on the phone, a bad feeling in the pit of her stomach. "I'm very happy for you," she said, while her mind tried to make sense of Vincent's abrupt burst of affection. "Are you both going to be in town for a while?"

"Yes. Vincent doesn't need me to accompany him to any cocktail functions. He's also going to fly in and out when he does have meetings. Doesn't want to be away from me." The poised and elegant woman sounded like a teenager in love for the first time, a giggly excitement to her.

After Anahera hung up, she stared at the sea. Was it possible that Will's interrogation of him had brought it home to Vincent just how much he had to lose? He'd smothered Jemima in love in the aftermath. Edward had been like that at times, so suddenly loving. In his case, Anahera thought it must've been as a result of guilt.

With Vincent, could it be a combination of guilt and fear of losing his family?

It made sense. But Anahera wasn't inside the Baker marriage, could only guess—and hope for Jemima's sake that Vincent wasn't setting her up for an even worse fall. Because it could be that he'd shrugged off Miriama's loss and turned his attention to another conquest. It sounded cold, but it was also cold to ignore and isolate your wife while stringing along a gifted young woman full of dreams.

She called a few others on the pretext of catching up, but no one had worry in their voice for anyone but Miriama. Whatever Will had found, *whoever* Will had found, it wasn't a person who'd already been missed. It might, she suddenly realized, not be anything suspicious at all—one of the locals who lived rough could've had an accident. Sad, but not a thing of horror.

Despite that realization, she felt too restless to stay inside the cabin. She needed air, needed the salt, the sand. Pulling on a lightweight jacket, she slipped her phone into a zippered pocket. It was cold out, the sky heavy, but Anahera didn't want to be too comfortable. She wanted to feel the chill on her face, wanted to experience the wind cutting across her skin, wanted to be brilliantly, painfully alive.

She closed the door behind herself but didn't bother to lock it—though, surprisingly, the old lock on the door still worked. Whoever had picked it after Anahera left Golden Cove hadn't damaged the mechanism. Josie had even dug up a copy of the key.

While Anahera used it at night, when she slept, she couldn't see the point otherwise. She'd hidden her laptops, old and new, under a hiding spot beneath the floorboards, and there was nothing else for anyone to take. Anahera wasn't naïve; she knew people stole even in a small town. But she also knew that if the clouds broke, someone might stumble out of the bush seeking shelter.

She was halfway down the porch steps when she paused.

What if the person who'd taken Miriama hadn't done it because she was Miriama? What if he'd done it because she was a beautiful young woman?

Anahera didn't consider herself beautiful by any measure. Neither was she tall and lissome like Miriama, but she *was* a woman. And some predators weren't that picky. Frowning, she went back inside the cabin and brought out a blanket to leave on the chair outside. She added a bottle of water and several energy bars.

Then she locked the door and pocketed the key.

The winds were hard but not vicious today, and she scrambled her way down to the beach without too much trouble, though she did have to keep her eyes on the path the entire way down. A single slip and she would've gone tumbling.

Anahera did not want her headstone to read "Death by Stupidity."

When she reached the beach at last, her heart was racing and her breath coming in hot puffs. Drawing in the salt-laced air, she looked up at the sound of chopper blades. Daniel, no doubt, being an arrogant ass flying in such portentous weather. Her guess seemed borne out when the chopper swept around to face her.

As if he was saying hello.

Anahera waved up at him. Yes, he could be an egotistical bastard, but it wasn't looking like he'd had anything to do with Miriama in life or in death.

The chopper turned back around, the waves frothing under the wind created by its blades, and then it was gone, sweeping across the water. She wondered where he was going that he was crossing the water rather than heading inland. Most likely, he was taking the scenic route and would swing back inland soon enough.

Shrugging off the encounter, she began to walk down the beach. The waves were big today, huge smashing things that pounded hard onto the sand. It looked like they'd been in a mean mood the previous night as well; she could see mounds of waterborne debris deposited on the wet gray sand. Long streamers of seaweed; sea glass polished and rubbed until it was as smooth as stone, no edges to it; broken and battered shells along with the odd one in perfect condition.

Anahera picked up a couple of pieces of particularly lovely sea glass. She'd collected it as a child and as a young woman, lining them up along the window where the sunlight would hit them. She'd thrown away her collection after her mother's death, but today, she found beauty in watching even the cloudy morning light spear through the glass.

It was as she was putting a third piece into a pocket that she spotted a huge hunk of seaweed up ahead. It almost looked like the seaweed had wrapped itself around a tree trunk or perhaps the carcass of a dolphin or small whale.

Anahera walked over, curious but careful. The seaweed sat close to the far edge of the ocean. A single freak wave and it would be pulled back in—and so would Anahera if she got too close. The seaweed fronds gleamed wet and dark, splayed out across the sand like fleshy fingers. The closer Anahera got to the hunk, the less she felt like exploring it, but she couldn't stop her feet from moving forward. There was something about the shape of it, the way it curved. And the color. Not just green.

Pink.

Orange.

Anahera didn't realize she was running until she'd reached the seaweed that wasn't wrapped around anything as prosaic as wood or a whale bone. Her breath painful in her throat, she began to drag the seaweed as far as she could up the sand. She had to make sure it didn't get sucked back out to sea.

A massive wave crashed ashore, licking dangerously at her feet. Anahera braced her legs, somehow just managing to keep hold of the seaweed and its chilling cargo. Then she pulled, pulled, *pulled*.

Collapsing on dry sand well clear of the water, her knees sinking into the fine grit of it, she forced herself to look at the seaweed again . . . forced herself to acknowledge that it wasn't seaweed she'd hauled up the beach but a body. A body that was discolored and so badly damaged as to be unrecognizable, but that wore an orange top and black leggings with pink side stripes.

Miriama's shoes were gone, but she still wore her socks.

For some reason, that single detail was enough to crush Anahera's lungs and drive a scream from her body.

# 49

Will had barely finished organizing for a forensic team to come out to Golden Cove for the skeletal remains when he got the call from Anahera.

"I found her," she said in a toneless voice. "The sea brought her back in."

Will shuddered, bracing his palm against a tree trunk, the bleached bones of the skeleton in his line of sight. He'd done nothing to disturb the scene, but he'd ventured back to the car to grab his camera, then taken as many high-resolution images as he could, well aware that when it came to the actual investigation, he'd be relegated to the bench.

As far as his superiors were concerned, he was a burned-out cop with his best years behind him. No one would trust him to be in charge of a case like this. Will wasn't about to let that stop him. Not having access to the bones shouldn't matter as long as he could access the report to do with the probable height, age, and ethnicity of the victim in life.

He didn't think the forensic team would find any other physical clues.

Whoever had left the bones, whoever had *arranged* the bones, had done it with clinical care.

It was a taunt, that skeleton. And since Will was the only cop in town, the person raking up old horrors, it was difficult to believe the taunt wasn't aimed at him. But that was no longer important. "Are you sure?" he asked Anahera.

"Yes." Her voice almost swept away by the wind, she added, "I'm watching over her. When can you get here?"

Will stared at the skeleton. He couldn't leave it, not until another officer got to Golden Cove. The chance of someone disturbing the site was too great. "I need you to keep on watching over her," he said, his hand fisting by his side. "I've got someone else here who I can't leave."

"Just tell me this—is it someone I know?"

The news would be out soon enough and Anahera wasn't a woman who spilled secrets. "Skeletal remains," he told her. "I can't risk anyone moving the bones."

"Skeletal . . ." Another harsh wind, ripping away her words.

But Will had heard the last word she'd said: *hiker.* It was the same thing he'd thought the instant he'd seen the bones. It could well be one of the three women who'd disappeared fifteen years ago and never been found.

He called the district commander again.

It took an excruciating two hours for the first forensic team to arrive. Will had spoken with Anahera several times, both of them caught in their separate hells and unable to move. He'd considered sending someone else out there—there wouldn't be a crime scene to contaminate, not if Miriama had come out of the sea—but Anahera had said no.

"Miri shouldn't be seen like this," she'd said. "She deserves for us to take care of her."

As he'd expected, the forensic crew was accompanied by two detectives. "Will." The older one of the two couldn't quite meet his gaze, the wrinkles in his brown skin deeper than the last time Will had spoken to him but his body in excellent shape. "I'm afraid we've been assigned the case."

"Robert." Will shook his hand. "Keep me in the loop, won't you? I've picked up more than a bit of knowledge about this town that might be helpful." He wasn't used to justifying his need for information, but he needed his fellow detective's cooperation if he was to have access to the reports.

Openly relieved at Will's lack of rancor, Robert immediately agreed to copy him in on any results. "I hear you've got a second scene?" he said with a raised eyebrow.

Will nodded. "I'm heading out to keep it under surveillance until the second forensic team arrives." He'd argued hard for the first team to go to Miriama's body, aware it was decomposing quickly with every second that passed, but those in charge had overruled him. In their view, while she'd died more recently, the body of a drowning victim wasn't going to hold anywhere near the forensic evidence that might be discovered on a skeleton that had been laid out for someone to find.

In their minds, it was tragic accident versus pathological murder.

"This Shane Hennessey fella." Robert shot a look over at where Shane still sat on the crate, his head cradled in his hands. "He a likely?"

"My gut says no—he threw up halfway into the wait." Shane had been desperate to get out, go home, but Will hadn't been able to let him leave.

"Yeah," Robert murmured, "whoever laid out these bones had to have ice for blood. Jesus, the bones are lined up as if he used a ruler."

"Shane's a novelist, says he walks this trail in the early morning when he wants to think." Will wanted to pass on the information, then leave, get to Anahera. "No indications of any violent tendencies and no record in either New Zealand or Ireland." That information Will had discovered during his initial run on all possible suspects in the Cove. "Shane's mentored a number of young female writers, but they're all accounted for." He'd spent the wait making calls, confirming that. "My take—he's just the unlucky bastard who found the bones."

The two detectives exchanged a look, but Will didn't much care what they thought of his instincts. They'd come to the same conclusion after a couple of minutes with Shane—the man remained green around the gills. "Look, unless you need something else right now, I have to get to the second site."

"Yeah, we'd better go examine the skeleton. I'll let you know what the bone specialists say."

As Will drove away from the site, he saw curious locals beginning to slow down their battered trucks and rusty sedans as they passed the dump—they'd probably come to abandon rubbish, been startled by the forensic van and multiple police vehicles. Just wait until the second team arrived. Golden Cove was about to become a circus.

He shut his mind to all of it as he drove, thinking about what Shane had found, what Anahera had found. Coincidence? Yes. No one could manipulate the sea. But he'd have to look at the body first to confirm. It'd all depend on how long Miriama had been in the water. Because if you knew the sea really well—as so many of the men and women in this area did—it might be possible to drop a body in at a particular point with a fairly good expectation of it being washed up on the beach.

Will should've gone straight to the beach, straight to relieve Anahera's lonely vigil, but he knew how fast information could travel in the Cove. And he knew Matilda would've heard about the sudden appearance of police vehicles at the dump site.

So he went to her home. She was waiting for him wrapped up in a faded gray polar fleece robe, her face strangely motionless. "Did you find her?" she demanded. "Did you find my baby?"

"We found her."

She keened and collapsed onto the floor before he could tell her anything else.

Going down beside her, Will did what he could, but it wasn't enough. He was grateful to see one of her neighbors—Raewyn Clark—running over, her blonde hair a mass of frizzy curls; Raewyn's flinty expression told him she'd guessed exactly what terrible news he'd brought. "I'll take care of her." The heavily tattooed former gang member went down beside Matilda, put her arms around the broken woman. "You know she'd want you out there, looking after our Miri. Don't let the outsiders treat her as nothing."

Will rose, got back into the SUV.

It felt as if it took him forever to get to the water, and all the while, the clouds grew blacker and heavier overhead. Scrambling down the pathway after reaching the edge of the cliff, he ran toward Anahera's seated form. She didn't get up, just waited for him to come, a silent sentinel with dark hair knotted by the wind and eyes struck by grief. "She shouldn't be dead," were her first words to him. "No one as alive as Miriama was should be dead."

Crashing down onto his knees beside her, he took her into his arms. She resisted, stiff and unbending, but he didn't let go, and at last, she allowed herself to wrap her own arms around him and hold on tight. There were no tears, but he hadn't expected any. Anahera was used to holding her pain within.

If and when she chose to share it, it would be on her terms.

When they separated, he did what he didn't want to do: he went and looked at Miriama's body. One glance and he knew that she'd been in the water a considerable time. Odds were, since the day she disappeared. The condition of the body eliminated the possibility she'd been thrown in recently with the hope she'd wash up close to when the skeleton was discovered. That didn't mean the same person wasn't responsible for both crimes.

One new. One old.

Taking out the slim but powerful digital camera he'd slipped into his pocket before Robert's arrival, he began to snap. Anahera watched in unmoving quiet. It was only when they heard the sound of a police vehicle getting closer, the siren carrying on the air, that she got up. "I'll show them the way down. Give me the camera's memory card."

He slipped it into her hand, replacing it with an empty one he had tucked into the case, then put the camera back in his jacket pocket. If anyone thought to ask if he'd taken photos, he'd hand over the camera.

But when his colleagues finally arrived, all of them ill-prepared for the sand and the waves and the wind, Anahera wasn't with them. And he was faced with a surprise. It appeared he was still in charge of Miriama's case.

"I've been sent to assist you." Short and solid, with a cap of fair hair and wearing a standard dark blue body-armor vest over a light blue uniform shirt, Kim Turnbull was someone Will had worked with on a prior case. "Everybody wants in on the skeleton you found, what with it being all serial killer like, so the junior gets the drowning." She seemed to realize what she'd implied a second after the words left her mouth.

Going bright red under the freckled paleness of her skin, she said, "Sorry, sir. I didn't mean—"

Will waved off the apology, too damn glad to be insulted. Being officially in charge of Miriama's case gave him a far better chance of getting her justice. He wouldn't have to rely on others to access the necessary reports and he could openly interview people of interest.

As for the skeleton so cruelly laid out on the edge of a dump, it had kept for a long time, and the men in charge of that victim weren't incompetent—though they'd be handicapped by their lack of knowledge about this town and its secrets. Oh, people would talk to Robert and the others, but whether they'd tell them anything useful was another question.

Once Will had put Miriama's ghost to rest, he'd find a way to do the same for that lost woman's ghost. Because he had not a single doubt that it was a woman's skeleton Shane had found. The way it had been displayed, the way it had been *discarded*, that was a thing too many men had done to too many women across time.

Waving across the new forensic team, he was startled to see Dr. Ankita Roshan with them. "I expected Robert to keep you captive!" he yelled out to the forensic pathologist over the rising wind.

"Told him I can't do much with bones!"

Today collided with yesterday. Because Ankita had called in a forensic anthropologist in the aftermath of the fire, too. The smallest person in the house, the smallest body, hadn't survived with enough flesh on his bones for a viable autopsy.

In the now, the painfully thin forty-something pathologist shook his hand. "Let's get to the remains before the skies open up."

There wasn't anything she could tell him that he hadn't already guessed. "You'll have to wait for the autopsy for more," she said.

"Ankita." Will crouched down beside her. "Can you prioritize Miriama?" He lowered his voice. "Everyone's writing this off as a drowning, but I knew her. She was too smart and athletic to stumble off a cliff or go running along the beach too close to the waves." He'd had to push to convince the coroner to order a full forensic postmortem, rather than a less invasive evaluation.

"You don't have to justify the request to me, Will." Having already bagged Miriama's hands, Ankita began to zip up the body bag. "You've always had stellar instincts—I'll start as soon as I get her back to Christ-church."

"I owe you one."

A thin-lipped smile. "If all the cops who owed me one actually paid up, I'd be a millionaire." Sharp words, but her dark brown eyes were kind. "I'll take care of your girl."

He helped load Miriama's body onto a stretcher. The remainder of the scene investigation went rapidly. The team took photographs, even packed up the seaweed, but though they sieved through the sand below the body, there was nothing else to find.

The wind had already wiped away the drag marks Anahera had created when she pulled the body to safety. It was as if Miriama hadn't been there at all, as if this had been a black dream that was about to fade.

# 50

William helped carry Miriama's body up the narrow cliff pathway, the young woman with a dancer's grace having become heavy in death. The cutting wind scraped sand across his skin, and he was grateful for the solid grip offered by his boots. Several of the others slipped, but no one fell and they got Miriama safely into the hearse that would take her to the forensic mortuary in Christchurch. A subdued gray with a sleek modern shape that didn't shout its purpose, the hearse should hopefully slip out of Golden Cove without attracting attention.

Kim puffed up the track a couple of minutes after Ankita left with Miriama.

He told her to hold the fort at the station, handle any calls that came for him, and note the names of locals who popped in to see him. Most would be hoping to get information on what was happening, but one or two might have information to share. "Make sure you let them know that I'll be back either later today or tomorrow morning, and that I'll speak to them then. Anything urgent, call me."

Kim nodded, assiduously writing down his instructions in a little notepad.

Leaving her to help the forensic team pack up their gear, he made his way to Anahera's cabin—and found the front door locked. *Good.*

He knocked, had to wait a couple of minutes before she opened the door. And she didn't do that until she'd confirmed who it was. She was wrapped in a towel, her hair dripping wet. Washing away the touch of death, Will thought, trying to wash away the grief.

Reaching into the pocket of the jacket hanging to her left, she handed over his memory card. "Someone needs to tell Matilda."

"She knows we found Miriama." Will would never forget the raw sound of her keening wail. "I'm on my way there to tell her what we have so far." Little though it was. "Will you come with me? I left her with Raewyn Clark, but I know she has young kids she'll have to get back to as soon as her boyfriend leaves for work." She might've already been forced to do so.

"Give me one minute. I'll follow you in my Jeep."

Anahera was true to her word, returning to him dressed in jeans and a dark green sweater under her anorak, her heavily damp hair pulled back into a ponytail and her feet stuffed into sneakers.

In her eyes, he saw as much rage as grief.

They arrived at Matilda's to find a furious Matilda sitting on her living room couch, her hands closed around a cold mug of tea and Raewyn seated beside her. The neighbor rose when she saw Will. "Mattie—"

"You go, sweetie." Even in her rage, Matilda found the kindness to give the other woman a gentle pat on the hand. "I know Hem's boss is a *pokokōhua*. He'd better get himself to work."

"How dare they?" Matilda said the instant the door closed behind Raewyn. "How dare they throw my baby away in the dump?"

Will spoke before she could say anything else. "We didn't find Miriama at the dump. We found her on the beach."

She just stared at him. "On the beach? Then . . . the police cars by the dump . . ."

"Something else. Miriama was in the sea."

Matilda's eyes flicked to Anahera. "Ana?"

"It's true," Anahera confirmed softly, going to kneel beside the older woman. "I found her. I made sure Miriama was safe until Will could get there."

"I want to see her."

Anahera shook her head. "No, Auntie. Remember her as she was. Remember her laughing."

Matilda's shoulders began to shake, her tea slopping out of the mug. Taking the mug, Anahera put it carefully aside, then enfolded the older woman in her arms. As Matilda sobbed, Anahera met Will's gaze. Her own gaze was dry, but that made her rage and sorrow no less furious.

Waiting until the crashing wave of Matilda's grief had passed and before a new wave could hit, Will said, "I know you'll want to go to her so she isn't alone." To sit with their dead, ensure they had loved ones nearby, it was a deeply rooted part of Matilda's culture. "The liaison officer will be here soon and he'll organize everything for you."

Will could've offered to take her, but not only was she exhausted by grief, it'd be better for her if she arrived after the autopsy was complete; she could sit in a room near Miriama without being confronted by the ugly reality of what had been done to the young woman she'd raised. More, she shouldn't be making the heartbreaking journey without a support system. "You have friends, family who can come with you?"

Matilda nodded jerkily. "You make sure your people treat my baby well until I reach her."

"They will." Ankita was a woman who respected her patients, for all that they'd already taken their last breath. "And I'll get justice for Miriama. I promise you that, Matilda. No one will forget your girl." It was the first time he'd made a promise since the day of the fire that had ended Alfie Hart's short life. And it tore the scars inside him wide open.

# 51

The next notification was even harder.

Dr. Dominic de Souza refused to believe Will.

"No. It's not her."

"Dominic—"

"*No!*" The other man came at Will, punching and shoving while Will tried to keep him contained without doing harm.

"It's not her! It's not my Miriama!" His glasses flew off in the struggle, to land on the beige carpet without a sound. "It's not!"

Eventually his words began to tremble, began to turn into questions that pleaded for Will to give the right answer. "It's not her? It's not Miriama?"

"I'm sorry, Dominic."

The young doctor collapsed into his arms. "She was so beautiful. So lovely. I thought she'd be mine forever."


Nikau responded quickly to Will's call asking him to stay with Dominic.

"Thanks, Nik. I appreciate this."

The other man shook his head. "No need. This is fucked up. You mind if I get the doc drunk?"

Looking at where Dominic sat blank-faced in his clinic chair, mindlessly straightening the bent arm of his glasses, Will said, "He could probably use a drink or five." Then maybe he'd sleep, forget for a minute.

Tomorrow was soon enough to face the truth.

Dominic wasn't the only one who slowed him down. The team dealing with the skeletal remains needed to talk to him about any missing person cases in the region. Will could've brushed them off, but he knew Miriama's autopsy would take time. There was no point in him riding Ankita's tail.

He met Robert and the others at the dump. The forensic and police teams were only partially into their painstaking search of the area. Will would bet his badge that there was nothing to find, that the skeleton had been left in this location because it was a way to further dehumanize the victim and cause exactly the kind of pain he'd seen in Matilda when she'd thought someone had thrown Miriama's body in the dump.

"Thanks for this, Will." Robert took out his notebook, his lanky partner beside him. "Look, to be blunt, we need your help. We don't understand the area or the politics of this town—and I don't want to waste time running down information you probably have in your head."

Will could tell the other man was uneasy about asking, when Will had been pulled off the case, but Will had no desire to play games. "Here's what I know."

The older cop tapped his pen against his notebook when Will finished telling him about the missing hikers. "Residents really believe they might've had a serial killer running around?"

"It's not too big of a stretch," Will said. "Not when you take into account the physical similarities between the three women." He'd brought his laptop and now opened it up, pulling up the file on the three women who'd gone missing over the course of a single hot summer.

Their ethnicities were different, but all of them had skin of light brown, their hair dark, their bones fine, and their height on the shorter side of average. But it was their smiles that tied them together—there was a primal vitality about the women.

All three were vividly alive.

Robert's younger partner whistled. "Jesus, I see what you mean. Why wasn't this picked up on before?"

"I don't know that it wasn't—it's just not in the official files," Will said.

"I tried to get in touch with the detective in charge, but he died of a heart attack a few years ago, and the team that worked with him could—or would—only give me what's already on record." Wherever Matilda's junior detective had picked up his intel, no one was willing to discuss it now.

"How extensive was the search?" Robert frowned. "I'm remembering the cases now, but I'm fuzzy on the details."

"It went for weeks—and began after the second missing hiker."

"Not the first?"

"She didn't file her route anywhere." Never knowing how easy it was to walk into the bush and never return. "No one knew she was heading to Golden Cove." A number of the editorials that had come out in the aftermath of that summer had been flat-out cruel, blaming the women for a lack of preparation.

"And the third?"

"Reported as missing by her family, but again, with no filed route, there was no reason to connect her to the Cove." It was a small place in a country full of wilderness. "Then the media began a series on women who'd gone missing and never been found."

"Right." Robert snapped his oddly slender fingers, fingers more suited to a pianist than a cop. "I remember my commander at the time being pleased at the exposure. She was hoping it'd bring closure to some cold cases."

"It did—an elderly couple came forward to say they'd given the third woman a lift to Golden Cove, while a bus driver remembered the first one getting off at a trailhead just outside the Cove." It wasn't an official stop, but most of the drivers didn't mind a quick stop so hikers could jump off.

He brought up the paltry list of recovered belongings: the pack, the water bottle unique enough to be identified as belonging to the first missing woman, and finally, the identity bracelet found at the "cave" on the beach. "The bracelet was discovered two days after the end of the first official search, which focused on the bush trails." Will had his own thoughts about the timing, but no proof.

"With the terrain and the lack of any evidence of foul play," he said, "the disappearances were eventually ruled accidental. Most people thought the women got lost or stumbled into a crevasse or down into the sea. The detective in charge kept making notes in the files after the official acciden-tal death finding, so it's safe to say he had his suspicions, but he was never able to link another missing woman to the town."

Robert's next question was predictable; he'd been staring at the map of Golden Cove on which Will had marked the recovered items. "How far to where the water bottle was found?"

"Only about a twenty-minute walk from here." Will looked over at where Shane had made his chilling discovery. "The relevant track loops around to eventually join the one on which the remains were located." The murderer amusing himself with a little game of memory. "It's overgrown but was walked by volunteers during the search for Miriama Tutaia, so it should be passable." Nikau hadn't said anything overt, but he'd made sure the search covered all areas related to the lost hikers. "You want to see it now?"

Robert nodded. "I'll pull a couple of the SOCOs off the dump—that's going to take forever. They might as well walk ahead of us and collect any evidence our boy left behind."

Will was too experienced a cop not to sense the older man's skepticism beneath his outwardly cooperative response. Robert was wondering if Will wasn't stretching the truth to make himself more relevant to the case. But skeptical or not, he was doing Will the courtesy of listening, because once upon a time, Will had been a hotshot cop with an instinct for running down predators.

The hotshot was gone, but it turned out his instincts had survived the fire.

Soon as everyone was ready, Will took them to the start of the track and had the forensic people walk ahead about a foot, one on either side of the trail. Tree ferns, their bodies lush and dark and their leaves a silvery light green, grew thick around them, along with taller, more ancient trees that blotted out the cloudy light.

Moss hung from branches and he saw a perfect spiderweb strung be-tween two ferns.

In the shady and cool dark, the freshly trampled undergrowth cushioned their footsteps, creating an eerie silence that Will broke. "The water bottle wasn't found on the track itself, but about ten feet to the left, just lying on the ground."

"Like it fell from her pack and she didn't notice?"

Will nodded at the younger detective's question. "Or like she dropped it while disoriented after being injured."

This particular track, with its hidden rocks and slight but steady incline, was hard going despite the inroads made by the searchers. He could hear Robert huffing behind him, but the other man kept on going. It was his partner who whispered, "Are we seriously planning to follow the crazy cop deeper and deeper into the bush?"

Will didn't allow the question to distract him; he kept an eye on everything around them, just in case the killer had made a mistake this time. "That's where the water bottle was found." He pointed out a jutting rock barely visible through the tangled army of tree ferns. "Her family requested and was granted permission to place a memorial plaque against the rock just above where the bottle was found."

Stepping off the path, he led the other two detectives to the spot. Such a lonely, quiet place, he thought, looking down at the moss-brushed engraving to a "beloved daughter and cherished child." He wasn't a man for prayer, but he hoped she'd been hit from behind, that she'd died without fear and with the sound of songbirds in her ears.

"Imagine having only this to remember your kid." Robert's hand rose reflexively to his jacket pocket, where Will knew he kept snapshots of his wife and son. "Maybe we can give them something to bury at last."

Will took his colleagues back to the path in silence, and they carried on walking.

But there was nothing to find. He could feel Robert and his partner glancing at one another, caught the edges of a furiously whispered conversation. The two scene-of-crime officers, however, kept on moving ahead, their white coveralls making them appear ghosts against the dark green of this quiet and whispering place.

Robert coughed. "We should head back."

"It'll be easier to go this way." Will had never walked this track, but before leaving Nikau with Dominic, he'd asked Nik to confirm his understanding of how this track connected to the one Shane Hennessey had taken that morning.

"Are you sure?" the younger detective asked in an overloud tone. "No offense, but I don't plan to end up worm food in the fucking bush."

"Just follow the track back." Will had his mind on the mental map. "I'm going to check out something."

Neither man turned around; they were probably afraid he'd lost it and would wander off into the wild unless contained.

The SOCOs stayed silent, but fell back so that they were walking pretty much alongside Will.

Five minutes later, he stopped. "There's your crime scene."

The two detectives moved past the rest of them, the younger one saying, "Well, fuck!"

"Shit, Will"—Robert took a stick of gum from his pocket—"there's a goddamn plaque commemorating the spot where the water bottle was found." He crumpled up the gum wrapper.

"Yes, anyone could've chosen the location to lead you on a wild-goose chase," Will said, but he didn't believe it.

The killer had returned to the location of his past glory.

# 52

Will made a quick stop to call Anahera after he was out of sight of the police presence at the dump site. "Be very careful," he told her. "You're a couple of inches too tall, but otherwise, you fit the same profile as the missing hikers." It had been her laugh last night—he'd seen it then, the vital wildness of spirit evident in those other women.

Even with that, it had taken him until the conversation with Robert to realize the dangerous similarity. He didn't think of Anahera as petite—she had too big a presence. But in a purely physical sense, she was only five-six and weighed less than she should. She also had the right skin tone and hair color. "I know you're tough," he added, "but this guy is a psychopath."

"Don't worry, cop," she said. "I'm staying with Matilda, helping her with whatever she needs—right now, that's making sure the *iwi* liaison officer knows what's important to her. She kicked Steve out a couple of days ago, so he's not an issue."

Exhaling silently, Will leaned his head back against the headrest. "As far as I know, no one else in town matches the profile." Most fell outside the height or weight range. The ones that didn't either had significant tattoos, smoked, or had short hair, traits not shared by any of the three hikers.

"If you think of someone," he told Anahera, "pass on the warning." Will didn't much care if he got disciplined for sharing unauthorized information with civilians; if it kept a woman alive, he'd wear the punishment.

"Matilda knows everybody. I'll get her talking, find out who we need to warn—she'll feel better if she thinks she's doing something to help."

"I'm driving to Christchurch." To the forensic mortuary where Miriama had been taken. "I need to find out what Miriama has to tell us."

Her response was . . . unexpected. "You be careful, too. It looks like the rain is finally going to come down."

"I will," he said before hanging up.

It had been a long time since anyone cared what happened to him. He wasn't sure quite what to do with it, but it didn't feel like a burden or a cage. Anahera, he knew, would never seek to hold on. She might invite him in, but the choice to enter or not would be his.

He pulled out just as the rain began to hit his windscreen, had gone only a few meters when Tom Taufa's plumbing van appeared heading in the opposite direction, into Golden Cove. The bearded man raised a hand to him in greeting as they drove by one another.

Will considered what he'd learned of Tom's past and made a quick call to Kim. "Keep a quiet eye on Tom Taufa, the plumber. He should be stopping at the café within the next five minutes." Tom always did when passing through the Cove's main street.

"You want me to head on over there and strike up a conversation?"

"Yes." Kim had the ability to talk to anyone and, underneath her stolid exterior, was good at picking up nonvocal cues. "Bring up the find at the dump, gauge his reaction."

"Person of interest?"

"I don't know." It was the timeline that bothered him—one long-ago summer, Tom had experienced shame and humiliation because of a young woman. The next summer, three young women disappeared. "Call me if he sets off any alarm bells for you."

"I'm on it."

Hanging up, Will began the nearly four-hour drive toward the hopeless scent of a beautiful young woman's death.

# 53

Anahera sat watching the rain from the covered back stoop of Matilda's house, occasional droplets bouncing off the walls to collide against her skin. She'd finally gotten a worn-out Matilda to rest by telling her it was no use her rushing to go to Miriama if she collapsed when she got there. Which left Anahera free to think about the past, and a horror that had marked Golden Cove without anyone ever admitting to the darkness beneath the sunshine.

She remembered that summer, remembered the clear sunlight and the heat that had built in fine sky-blue layers.

Their group, they'd all been down on the beach as often as not. Josie, Anahera, Vincent, Daniel, Nikau, and Keira. Tom and Christine and Peter had floated in and out, but the six of them had been the core.

"You lot are as thick as thieves," Anahera's mother used to say with a laugh. They'd been close enough to venture into the water even when it wasn't quite safe, when it was an adventure on the edge between safety and danger. Close enough to build bonfires on the beach after dark.

Close enough to make out under the stars.

Her lips curved. She'd almost forgotten playing truth or dare and being dared to kiss a blushing Vincent. She'd taken the dare, and he'd gone red to the very tips of his ears. Daniel had teased him endlessly about it, but back then, there'd been no malice to the teasing, all of the laughing words and shared memories weaving the threads of their friendship ever tighter.

There'd been no malice in any of them. They'd just been teenagers growing into adulthood, coltish and full of dreams. It felt awful to think it now, but even the discovery of the water bottle and the possibility of a lost hiker—then two—hadn't really changed things.

Yes, they'd talked about it and those with experience in the bush had helped with the search, but it had seemed like a distant thing. Not only were the two women strangers, they were adults. In their mid to late twenties, from what Anahera remembered. She and the others hadn't identified with either one, never worried about themselves, not seeing anything of their youth in those two adult faces.

Then Tom and Josie, sneaking into the cave to make out, had found the bracelet.

Their group had disbanded naturally and inevitably in the aftermath—Daniel and Vincent off to their private schools; Josie attached at the hip to Tom, her official boyfriend by summer's end; Anahera so desperate to get out of Golden Cove that she'd begun to study as hard as Nikau always had, while spending every spare moment on the piano; Keira flying back to Auckland because the school terms were her mother's, the summers her father's; and Nikau, writing letters to Keira alongside intricate essays for school that won him awards and scholarships and pride.

Peter . . . Anahera frowned. She couldn't remember what Peter had been doing. Probably because she'd kept her distance from him even then, but she had a vague memory of Christine's fists bunching and her face going hot and hard when Peter's name was mentioned, so it was possible the two of them had hooked up over the summer and it had come to a bad end.

Looking back, that had been the last summer they'd all been together and all been friends. After that, it had splintered piece by piece, so slowly that Anahera hadn't truly noticed at the time.

Her phone rang in her hand.

Seeing that it was Josie, she answered it. Her friend had heard about the find out by the dump. It wasn't surprising that she didn't know about Miriama. People had been focused on the dump by the time the second forensic crew came in, would've assumed it was all connected.

No one in the Cove expected so much death in the space of a single day.

"They're saying Shane Hennessey found a skeleton," Josie said. "Did Will tell you anything?"

So, it had already gotten around that Will's SUV had gone out toward her cabin last night and not returned till morning.

That was the town Anahera remembered, the town that had suffocated her, the town where there were no secrets—and far too many hidden things. "Not about that," she said. "There's something else, though, Josie, but you can't share it." She knew her best friend loved gossip, loved the very things about Golden Cove that had threatened to stifle Anahera's spirit. She also knew that Josie would never betray her.

"You know me, Ana," her friend said. "I never tell your secrets."

Veiled in between those words was a secret Anahera had shared with Josie fifteen years ago. That same hazy summer. A secret only the two of them now knew because Anahera's mother was dead, and with her, the name of the man she'd loved while a married woman.

Haeata had let it slip one night while she was drunk—such a rare thing that Anahera couldn't remember any other time she'd seen her mother with a drink in her hand—and she'd said enough that Anahera had hoped her father wasn't her father. Such a false dream that had been; the mirror showed her too many echoes of the brute her mother had married.

"I know," she said to her best friend. "You've never let me down."

"I'll never forget how you held my hand when we sneaked off on the bus to buy"—her voice dropped—"you-know-what."

Anahera felt a fleeting smile cross her face at the memory of that secret trip out of town to get condoms when Josie decided to sleep with Tom. It had always been Josie who'd set the milestones in her relationship. Tom might be big and strong, but he was putty in Josie's hands and always had been. "Here's the thing," Anahera began. "The remains might have something to do with the missing hikers back when we were kids."

"Good lord. Imagine that, she's been lying out there all this time."

Anahera knew what Josie wasn't yet ready to see. She'd thought back to the map pinned up inside the fire station, realized searchers had combed through that area while looking for Miriama. And the idea of no one passing through there in more than a decade simply didn't hold water. It was too close to the dump, too near a favorite trail used by hunters.

The remains had been placed there for an unlucky walker to find.

And how strange that all of the summer kids were back in Golden Cove when it happened. Anahera, Nikau, Vincent, Josie and Tom, Daniel and Keira. Even Christine and Peter. They'd all, but for Josie and Tom, traveled the world, seen cities that had been ancient before the first rock was broken in Golden Cove, and yet here they were, back home as the ghosts of the past began to rise.

"Do you know anyone in the Cove who looks like me?" she asked Josie. "Same height, skin tone, hair, that kind of thing." Matilda hadn't been able to think of anyone Anahera hadn't already considered and warned. All probably fell outside the killer's preferred profile for one reason or another, but Anahera had thrown a wide net. Just in case.

This time, Josie sucked in a breath. "Oh, my God, I remember now. Those women, the way they looked . . . you grew up to look like them."

"You see why I'm asking. I've already called around to a few women." She listed the names.

"Okay," Josie said through shallow breaths, "let me think." A long pause before she said, "This isn't connected to Miriama, then, is it?" So much hope in the words. "I mean, she doesn't look anything like you."

It seemed a huge coincidence to Anahera that a beautiful young woman would go missing in the same small town that might've been a serial killer's hunting ground, and the two not to be connected, but none of it fit. All three hikers had vanished off the face of the earth. Miriama had been found. And no one could control the ocean.

"Hold on, I've got to serve a customer." Josie was gone for two minutes and when she came back, her voice shook. "It was Evelyn. She said there were police down by the beach, too, and she saw them load something on a stretcher into a big van."

Anahera knew this news wasn't hers to tell. And Matilda wasn't ready to handle an avalanche of sympathy. "He's still a cop, Josie," she said instead of answering the implied question. "He doesn't share everything."

"And here I thought you were going to be my new source of fresh gossip." Josie's voice continued to tremble.

"Take a breath," Anahera said gently. "Another. One more."

When Josie could finally speak again without breaking, she said, "The good news is, I can't think of anyone else in town who really fits . . . what do they call it? The victim profile, that's it. All those years of watching crime shows have finally come in handy."

Anahera tracked a fantail as the small bird with its showy tail hopped from branch to branch. "That's good."

"No," Josie cried, "it's not good! It means that you're the only possible target in Golden Cove."

# 54

Will walked through the familiar corridors that led to the forensic mortuary. It was always cold here, as if all the death that passed through had permanently stained the building.

He met no one on his journey; hardly surprising when the world outside was fading to darkness. But he knew Ankita would be waiting. Pushing through another set of doors, he clenched his gut, and went to enter the room where his friend and colleague probably had Miriama on a cold metal slab.

The door opened from the other side.

"Will." Ankita was still wearing her scrubs, though she'd removed her gloves and apron, and the smell that clung to her was of death gone to rot. "Perfect timing—I just finished the postmortem." The harsh fluorescent lighting caused an appearance of pallor even in the dark brown of her skin. "Come on, we'll talk in my office."

Will had no desire to see Miriama cut open. Not that laughing girl who'd brought him cake and told him she'd be back in a couple of days with another piece to tempt him.

He followed Ankita down the hall.

Once inside her office, she went to the coffee carafe on a side table, touched her hand to it. "I need to give a certain forensic tech a raise." She poured two mugs. "We can go outside if the smell's bothering you."

It coated the insides of Will's nose by now, the rot and the loss. "No, let's talk here." Miriama deserved the respect and Will had smelled death before, survived it. At least it wasn't the smell of burned flesh.

His stomach turned.

Placing one mug on his side of the desk, Ankita carried hers around and sank into the battered black leather of her chair. Will took off his jacket before he sat down in the visitor chair.

In front of him, Ankita's desk was as meticulously organized as always. Her compulsively neat nature was partly what made her such a good pathologist. Ankita never accepted anything at face value. With her, Will could be certain every suspicious bruise would be examined with a critical eye, every indication of a toxic substance analyzed.

She would do Miriama justice.

"How was the drive?"

Will shrugged. "Rain," he said. "You know what it does to otherwise sane drivers."

"Yes, I caught a bit of that on the way in, too." Putting down her coffee after taking a long drink, the pathologist leaned her forearms on the desk. "You know the problem with a body that's been submerged in water. Added to that, there was a significant delay before I had her on my table."

"Did you manage to find anything?"

"The water did so much damage to your girl that there wasn't a lot for me to find. The bruises, cuts, abrasions, the chunks missing from her flesh, it can all be explained by the waves crashing the body against rocks, and by animal predation."

Will would never forget Miriama's body lying on the beach, her beauty eradicated by the sea—and by the person who'd put her there. "Bones?"

"Badly shattered. Her face looks like a cracked eggshell." Ankita pushed across an X-ray that, when Will held it up to the light, told a violent story. "Impossible to determine if it happened peri- or postmortem." Putting down the pen she'd picked up, she leaned back in her chair. "But, I'm suspicious about a pattern of fractures and breaks along the left-hand side of her body."

"As if she fell or was thrown against a hard surface on that side?"

Ankita nodded. "If someone threw her from the cliffs and onto the rocks below, and she landed this way"—the pathologist used the flat of her hand to demonstrate the angle—"it could conceivably have caused the pattern."

She took a sip of her coffee. "I wish I could tell you more, but with the body being in the sea that long, it makes things difficult. I'm going to send the details through to one of my colleagues who has more experience with ocean damage, get a second opinion. The rest of what I'm about to tell you is pure conjecture based on over a decade of experience and my gut."

Will put the X-ray back on her desk, a sudden cold invading his blood. "She drowned," he said quietly, all the while hoping Ankita would tell him he was wrong.

But she nodded. "I'm going to do a diatom test, but even if it comes back positive, I won't officially be able to call it a drowning. Still, all the broken bones aside, that's how I think she died."

"Tell me you have something else." Because both a fall and a drowning could be explained away as accidental, but Miriama simply wouldn't have made that kind of a mistake.

"Your victim was pregnant. Three months, give or take."

Will sat motionless for a long minute before reaching forward to put his coffee on the desk between them. "You're sure?"

"The decomposition hadn't quite destroyed her uterus." Ankita picked up the pen again, clicking and unclicking it. "I'm certain."

"Do you have enough biological material to do a paternity test?"

"If you bring me a sample from the probable father or fathers, I can try to get the testing done for you. But, no guarantees."

Leaning back, Will did the math. *Three months.* That put Miriama's pregnancy right on the borderline. He'd check her journal, confirm the exact date she'd broken it off with Vincent, then line it up with when she and Dominic had first been intimate—not a conversation he was looking forward to having.

It was possible Miriama had had another lover in between the two men with whom she'd had a relationship, but Will had to start with the known potentials. As it stood, her pregnancy gave both men a powerful motive.

Vincent had vowed his love for Miriama, but when push came to shove, he'd chosen ambition. Miriama getting pregnant would've ruined the picture-perfect life he'd spent years creating, all of it aimed toward one goal. Especially if she'd refused to get rid of the baby.

If, on the other hand, it had been Dominic's baby, the young doctor would've had no reason to be angry at Miriama. A little shocked, yes, but in the end, the child would've tied him and Miriama even closer together. And, according to her journal, he'd already shown a willingness to be a father.

But what if it *hadn't* been Dominic's baby?

Will had no easy answers—because Miriama had written nothing about the baby in her journal. Not even in relation to how the pregnancy might affect her internship. Either she hadn't known . . . or that was the secret she'd obliquely mentioned at one point: *I've become so good at keeping secrets. Until I can't even write some things here, in a place no one else will ever look.*

He got to his feet. "Thank you. I need to talk to some people, get those samples for you." It was as he was putting his jacket back on that he felt the evidence bag inside. "I bagged her hairbrush for you." It didn't matter if everyone knew this was Miriama, they had to have official confirmation. Given the condition of the body, that meant DNA testing.

Ankita accepted the package, then walked him out to the car park.

As they stood in the dark lit by yellow lamps blurred by the now-misty rain, she looked up at him. "I can't officially make the accident or homicide call, but I trust your instincts. I hope you find the bastard who did this to her—all that potential, all that life just snuffed out. No one has the right to do that."

"I'll call you if anything breaks," he said, keeping a tight lid on his own anger. "Her aunt will be here soon." He knew that without having to check. "Will you make sure Miriama isn't alone until then?"

Ankita nodded. "I expected as much. She doesn't need to see the body, Will." Tired, empathic eyes. "I'll speak with her, find a less traumatic way she can say good-bye."

"Thanks, Ankita." Getting into his car after a final handshake, he watched Ankita return inside, then picked up his phone to call Anahera. "How are things?"

He could hear noises in the background, the sounds of people talking. It was no surprise when she said, "Town's gathered in the firehouse. Matilda wanted people to talk about Miriama, celebrate her life. She gave me permission to share the news and told me to ask that everyone get together." She took a breath. "Liaison officer got us clearance to do a *karakia* on the beach where I pulled her out of the water. Matilda left soon after."

Prayer, Will knew, was important to Matilda. Being able to offer one at the site would've given her a small outlet for her grief. "Who's with her?"

"A group of her closest friends. I'm handling the gathering—after, I'm going over to Josie's."

Will started up his engine. "I'm on my way back. If things break up before I get there, make sure you have an escort back to Josie's—Matthew, the Lees, the Duncans, none of their names have come up in the investigation." He hesitated before saying, "Don't get into Tom's van."

A sucked-in breath on the other end. "You can't just drop that bomb on me and not say anything else."

"I found out something in his past that worries me, but right now, he's not any higher on the list than anyone else. Avoid Peter Jacobs, too." The mechanic might have an alibi for Miriama's death, but the skeletal remains were another matter—and Will hadn't forgotten how Peter's name had come up in an American rape investigation.

"Is Josie in danger?" Anahera demanded. "Her son?"

"No." Anahera's best friend fell outside the profile. "I'm being cautious, Ana. If I'm wrong, Josie never has to know anything."

"Fine," Anahera said at last, her tone clipped. "I wonder if I'll trust anyone by the time this is over."

Staring out at the bleak scene outside, Will thought of broken bones and missing flesh and a woman who'd never smile again. "Don't go to the cabin."

"No need for orders, cop. I've got no intention of ending up another victim."

Though she didn't ask him about Miriama, he could feel the questions on her lips. And he knew he'd probably break confidentiality and share what he'd learned. He could tell himself it was for a practical purpose—because while he remained an outsider to many, Anahera was a local. People who wouldn't necessarily talk to him with total frankness would talk to her.

But the truth was that he talked to her because he wanted to talk to her, wanted to get her input. A dangerous thing to think for a man who'd so long preferred distance from life—especially about a woman so emotionally entwined with multiple suspects on his list. "We'll talk when I get home."

Her voice remained curt when she answered. "Drive safe."

Hanging up, Will headed out. As he drove, he put aside Tom Taufa and Peter Jacobs, and considered two other men. Men who'd loved the same woman.

And he considered the puppy whose head had been bashed in with a rock.

# 55

Anahera had stayed by Matilda's side until the *karakia*—at that point, she'd been shooed away by an older woman who'd traveled from some distance outside town. That woman, like the other friends who'd gone with Matilda, had seen Miriama grow up, had helped mother the child she'd been, and now they would mourn with Matilda.

Eyelids swollen and nose red, new lines etched permanently into her face, Matilda had said, "I see her every time I close my eyes." A hoarse whisper, her throat ragged from crying. "My pretty, kind Miriama with so much *aroha* in her heart."

Twenty minutes later, when Matilda's friend and her husband began to lead Matilda out to their car, which would follow the liaison officer's vehicle, Matilda had looked back at Anahera. "Will you be all right, Ana?"

Humbled by the generosity of this woman who had suffered the loss of a cherished child, Anahera had nodded and told Matilda her intention to overnight at Josie's.

Now, as the last of the gathered began to leave, she saw that Tom had already gone home. Relief was a weight off her shoulders. At least she didn't have to come up with some excuse to not go with him.

Her stomach ached with the ugliness of feeling any kind of suspicion toward Josie's husband. But there was no reason to believe she'd be in any danger in the family home—and she could get a firsthand look at Josie and Tom together.

"Do you need a ride, Ana, dear?" asked a subdued Evelyn Triskell, her hands on the handles of her husband's wheelchair.

"I'm okay, thank you," she said. "Nikau brought his truck—I'll catch a ride with him." She didn't have her Jeep because Raewyn had driven them to the beach, then to the fire station.

As the Triskells nodded and continued on to their car, Anahera decided she'd organize better security for the cabin tomorrow so that she could return home. She wasn't planning to be stupid, but neither did she intend to let fear drive her decisions. "Nik?" she said, walking over to him. "Can you run me over to Josie's?" Her best friend hadn't attended the gathering, too far along in her pregnancy to be around this much stress and pain. Anahera would've sent her home if she had turned up.

Nikau, still sporting a heavy five-o'clock shadow that was turning into a beard, nodded. It wasn't until they were in his truck that he said, "When's your cop getting back?"

Anahera shot him a hard look. "What the hell is up with you?" It wasn't the first edgy comment he'd made about her and Will tonight. "I know you're not jealous."

He didn't speak again the entire drive, finally bringing his truck to a stop in front of Tom and Josie's place. Sitting in the vehicle with him, his mood dark and turbulent, Anahera realized she might've made a stupid mistake after all. Because this Nikau wasn't the man she'd once known, was angry inside in a way that verged on frightening. It wasn't a stretch to imagine him taking out his anger on a vulnerable woman. Punishing her in place of—

*Oh, God.*

She, Josie, Matilda, they'd all made a mistake: Anahera *wasn't* the only person in town who fit the summer killer's preference. Keira had been dyeing her hair to a light brown shade with blonde streaks since she turned eighteen, and often wore gray or green contacts. Strip away the artifice, however, and she was brown eyed, black haired, with skin and bone structure like Anahera's.

Her mouth went dry.

"It's got nothing to do with you, or with Will," Nikau said suddenly. "I'm just being a bastard because Keira is pregnant." He spit out the last word. "She's going to have that asshole's baby."

"Who told you?"

She expected to hear that it had been a gloating Daniel.

"Keira." His pain was too big for the truck, a suffocating pressure. "She came to see me, told me she didn't want this kind of anger between us during her pregnancy. Asked me to chill it. Said we should be friends."

Focused on survival, Anahera didn't say what she thought. At least not until she'd undone her seat belt and pushed open the door. "Look," she said, "it's not good for you to be around her all the time." Stepping out, she shut the door, but leaned down to speak through the open window. "Get out of this town and move on, explore the world through your career. You're a great guy, Nik. So many women would be happy to be with you."

Nikau shot her a look of anger so cold that she moved away from the window. "I can get her to love me again."

Anahera decided to keep her mouth shut on any further comments. If Nikau was a monster under the skin, then she might inadvertently put Keira in the crosshairs. Saying a quick thanks for the ride instead, she began to walk up Josie's drive.

Nikau's truck didn't move.

*One second, two, three—*

Josie opened the door, her pregnant form silhouetted in the light behind her, and Anahera finally heard Nikau's truck revving off and away, taking with it a friend who'd turned into a stranger.

# 56

Darkness shrouded the road into Golden Cove, the trees seeming to lean in to embrace the night. The twin beams of Will's headlights were the only points of brightness in the pitch-black landscape. Take away the road markings, cut off access to the outside world, and the land would swallow you up until nothing remained.

Or until only bones remained.

Robert had called him an hour earlier to say he was attempting to get new copies of the dental and medical records of the missing hikers; the ones in the original case files were no longer in the best condition. "Speed things up for the forensic anthropologist," the other detective had said. "Everyone should have a name."

Yes. No one should be buried in a grave without a name.

Will's eyes skimmed the glowing digits of the dashboard clock. It was well past eleven at night. He should let Anahera rest. But, after all the death today, and even if she was angry with him for doubting Tom's family man persona, he had a craving inside him to see her alive and vibrant.

The supermarket's great big corporate symbol blazed against the night, but, as always at this time, the store was shut—along with nearly all the other businesses in Golden Cove. Only the pub remained open, patrons and staff moving beyond the street-facing windows.

He was about to bring the SUV to a halt by the police station so he could call Anahera, when he saw a hint of something on the horizon that captured his attention. It twisted like fog against the bluish black of the night sky, but that made no sense. There was no sign of fog anywhere in the vicinity and what he'd seen was rising too fast.

*Smoke.*

Will stepped out of his vehicle into the cold, the wet tarmac gleaming in the beams of his headlights, but the sky was clear of rain. He didn't smell any hint of fire on the air currents, but he had not a single doubt that was smoke on the horizon.

And it was drifting in from the beach end of town.

Normally, that would've made it less of a threat. Especially with the weather having been so damp. Things were too wet for the vegetation to catch fire. But not only was that smoke too strong, too high, it was coming from the direction of Anahera's cabin.

Getting back into his vehicle, he drove screamingly fast to the firehouse, then jumped out and used his emergency key to get into the building. Golden Cove had too small a population to have volunteer firefighters standing by, so the town had come up with another system.

A second after he entered the firehouse, he pushed the button that set off a piercing siren, then used his authorization to send an emergency message to the pagers worn by all the volunteers. He relocked the door to protect the gear inside, as the trained volunteers all had keys, and was back in his SUV before anyone responded.

He knew it wouldn't be long. The brigade's total response time was a matter of minutes—Will had been their timekeeper during the last test.

Activating his vehicle's hands-free system as he drove toward Anahera's cabin, he made a direct call to the leader of the volunteer firefighters. "It's Will," he said. "I'm pretty sure Anahera's cabin is on fire. I'm heading in that direction to confirm."

The other man didn't waste time on unimportant questions. "I've just reached the firehouse. You want us to wait or do you want us to head out straightaway?"

Will could see even more smoke now. It speared out through the darkness, thick columns of gray smudging the night. "Get your people to the location as fast as possible."

He screeched into Anahera's drive.

The red glow of flames crackled hot against the shadowy backdrop of trees, and a second after he braked to a shuddering stop off the gravel path so that the firefighters could come through, the roof collapsed in a shower of embers.

Stepping out, he braced himself. The heat pulsed against his face, the smoke coating his nostrils, his throat, sinking into his clothing. It was a nightmare come to life, one that threatened to suck him into the abyss, but Will wasn't fucking done yet. If Anahera was in that house, he'd damn well get her out.

No matter what the price.

Grabbing his phone, he called her.

It rang and rang and rang—"Will?"

He staggered against the driver's-side door of the SUV just as the fire appliance turned into the drive, its siren going full blast. "You're all right!" he yelled, barely able to hear himself. "Is there a reason anyone else would've been in your cabin today?"

"No, I locked up when I left," she said. "Are you at the fire? Tom left to—oh, my God, is it my cabin?"

"I'm sorry, Anahera."

But she'd already hung up, and he knew she was on her way. A number of others arrived before her, probably the folks who'd been in the pub, or who lived closest to the center of town. But they let Anahera pass to the front, their faces soft with pity and sorrow except for two drunks who stared at the flames, their eyes reflecting the greedy yellow-red tongues.

Anahera said nothing when she reached Will; the two of them stood a third of the way down the drive while the firefighters worked to control the blaze. Will caught the locked tension of her muscles, but he also saw the shimmer of water in her eyes. And he remembered that this had been her mother's home. It was the safe haven Anahera had come to, to lick her own wounds and attempt to heal.

He didn't have any words to comfort her, so he just put his arm around her and tugged her against his body. She resisted, her hands fisted and her jaw a brutal line. "There was no gas inside," she said. "My tank ran out last night just as I finished reheating the stew and I haven't had a chance to return the empty and pick up a new one. And you saw me turn the electricity off at the mains."

"Yes." She'd opened up the box mounted to one side of the porch right before they left for Matilda's what felt like a lifetime ago.

"My mother taught me to do that if I might be away overnight because the cabin was all the way out here by itself. She worried about shorts in the wiring."

Will heard the firefighters shout to each other, their faces glowing with sweat. "I don't think this was an accident," he said. "It's too much of a coincidence with everything else that's going on."

A massive crackle as a wall collapsed inward.

"Did you have a run-in with anyone tonight?"

A short pause before she shook her head. "No."

"You can't protect your friends now."

"Nikau was acting off, but that's because he just heard Keira is pregnant." She blew out a breath. "She looks like me. Under the dyed hair and the colored contacts."

Will thought of Nikau's alibi for the time of Miriama's disappearance, and then he thought about the three hikers and how Anahera's picture would fit right in. "I'll find out where he was earlier tonight." The fire could've been set an hour or more ago, a small flame left to slowly creep across the cabin.

"There's something else." Anahera glanced at him before returning her gaze to her cabin. "It's all over town that you spent the night here. And it's far easier to get to my place than it is to yours."

She was right. Will's home was in the middle of a neighborhood, complete with nosy Evelyn Triskell only three houses down. "You were attacked to send me a message." He'd been rattling cages, asking questions, while Anahera was a local come home and should've been safe. It made more sense than a serial killer suddenly changing the way he stalked and attacked his victims.

Anahera closed her hand over the forearm he had across her chest. "I was attacked because this person is a coward. Don't let them mess with your head, cop."

Will forced himself to unclench his jaw. "I know the cabin meant a lot to you," he said, "but did you lose anything else important?"

"Both my laptops and my passport," she told him. "But I can get the passport replaced, and my work's all backed up in the cloud so I'm fine there." Her hand rose to her throat, to the *pounamu* carving he'd never seen her without. "This is safe." Strong fingers curving around the greenstone, her body finally softening slightly into his. "I still have photos of my mother, all backed up in triplicate, including a set on Josie's computer. That's the most important thing."

"Good." Will wondered at his chances of getting a fire investigator out here. With no fatalities and the only casualty an old cabin with what would be considered suspect wiring, it was probably highly unlikely—but Will had been on the force a long time. He'd see if he could call in another favor.

"You were burned in a fire." Anahera's back stayed pressed against his chest, her eyes on the cabin. "This must remind you of it."

Will's instincts recoiled against the memories, but he shook his head. "No, because you weren't inside." He could've stopped at that, but he gave her the whole ugly truth. "The rapist husband killed his wife and child by setting their supposed safe house on fire."

"You tried to save them."

"The bastard had doused the entire place in kerosene. It went up like paper. Part of a wall fell on me." Breaking nothing, just searing his skin and trapping him in place until smoke inhalation took him under.

He'd survived because the firefighters he'd called before going into the house had hauled him out. "The pathologist later confirmed both bodies were found in their beds. I like to imagine they never woke, were never afraid, that the smoke got them before the flames." But he'd never know for sure.

Sometimes, he had nightmares where he imagined three-year-old Alfie screaming and screaming as his flesh melted off.

Anahera shifted to his side, then slipped her arm around his waist, hugging him tight. "Then," she said, "using fire to get at you isn't a coincidence, is it?"

Yes, it was cunning and vicious both. "I want to point the finger at Kyle. He's vindictive enough to do something like this—but he isn't the only person I've pissed off recently." Just because Kyle Baker was a psychopath didn't mean he was also a firestarter.

"What about Vincent?"

"He strikes me as too controlled." Everything and *everyone* in its place, including his wife and his mistress. Both marionettes Vincent had manipulated to get them to dance to his tune.

"I suppose you're right." Anahera didn't look away from the cabin, but her tone said she was thinking of something else. "It's just . . . I remember, when we were teenagers, it was always Vincent who started the bonfires. He was just so good at it. We used to joke that he must have a Boy Scout badge for starting fires."

The hairs prickled on the back of Will's neck. "Did he ever start fires outside of the bonfires?"

"Not that I know of," Anahera admitted. "We were all brought up to be very careful with fire, what with the risk of forest fires in summer. The only place we felt safe to have a bonfire was on the beach. And Nikau, Daniel, even me, we were all into it just as much as Vincent."

Her fingers clenched on the back of his jacket. "Truth is, I don't really have any reason to suspect Vincent. It's just that I don't like him much now that I've spoken to Jemima."

People began to rustle behind them as the flames started to stutter and die one by one.

The spectacle was over.

"I get the feeling he went shopping for a wife," Anahera added. "Jemima has the right pedigree, the right kind of beauty, even the right kind of personality—she's never going to leave Vincent, no matter what he does."

"Do you think she'd assist him if he decided to get rid of an inconvenient woman?" Because—and assuming the baby had been Vincent's—that was what Miriama would've become in his eyes the instant she fell pregnant.

"I don't know, but if he did it and Jemima knows, she won't tell. She loves him too much to ever turn him in."

"It could work the other way, too," Will said softly. "Jemima getting rid of the competition."

Sucking in a breath, Anahera said, "I get the feeling she's too passive . . . but Jemima also *loves* Vincent. Desperately."

Her words hung in a disturbing pocket of silence.

Up ahead, the firefighters were smothering the last embers. It helped that the cabin had been wet from the rain, and though it had blazed hotly for a short period, there hadn't been enough fuel for it to keep going once the place was drenched with firefighting foam. Now it sat there, a crumbled ruin frothing with white.

# 57

Anahera didn't sleep that night and, come dawn, she left Will's bed without waking him. It had taken painstaking care, but he needed his sleep after the long drive the previous day and the hours he'd spent at the site where the cabin had once stood—writing everything up and making calls that had woken more than one person.

One of those calls had led eventually to a fire investigator. The other man had agreed to come to Golden Cove today, see if he could confirm their suspicions of arson.

Anahera needed to say good-bye to her home first, needed to say good-bye to her mother.

Throat thick and body reclad in the same clothes she'd worn the day before, she pulled on her boots and walked out of the house. She made no attempt to take the police SUV—a walk would do her good. Fog rolled around her ankles and a cool morning wind whispered across her cheeks as she strode along the road heading to the beach.

The small stops she made left her hand wet and color in her grasp.

When she heard an engine behind her, she glanced back—and wished she hadn't.

Jason Rawiri brought his truck to a stop next to her. "Heard about the cabin," he said, his jaw grizzled gray but his hair black. "I'm driving out to see."

The invitation was unspoken.

Anahera wanted nothing from him, but neither could she allow him to go there alone, not after what he'd done. Ignoring the passenger-side door, she hauled herself up onto the bed of the truck and sat with her back to her father as he drove on through the fog.

Thankfully, it was a relatively short drive.

Jumping off the instant they arrived, Anahera walked to the ruins of the small home where her mother had been happiest. She didn't attempt to go into the debris—if there was anything for the arson investigator to find, she didn't want to contaminate the evidence. Anahera didn't need to enter to see that it was all gone.

Burned down right to the foundations.

Gone with it was the last place in this world where Anahera had felt the echo of her mother's footsteps. There was no grave; Haeata had told Anahera she wanted to be cremated when she died, her ashes scattered into the ocean.

Anahera had followed her mother's wishes.

She placed the wildflowers she'd picked beside one corner of the foundations. Then, filling her lungs, she sang a *waiata*—singing in the tongue of her people again for the first time since she'd found her mother's body . . . and cracking the hard, scarred shell that encased her soul. And because she knew her mother was in a better place, she sang it not as a lament but as full of piercing hope even as her eyes burned and her chest ached.

Only after the last echoes had faded from the air did she turn and meet the eyes of the man who had abused her mother until even Haeata's gentle and warm spirit couldn't take it. "I want nothing to do with you," she said calmly in Māori. "I have no forgiveness in my heart for you and I never will. Forget you ever had a daughter."

He was old now, her father. So many lines on his face, so many cracked veins from his drinking days, his bones pushing up against the sinewy brown of his skin. He'd been bigger before, with a thick neck and thicker arms, a physically strong man who'd yelled for his dinner, yelled for

Anahera to shut up, yelled for his wife to bring him a beer or he'd give her a busted lip. Now he was smaller, grayer, more pathetic, but Anahera would never forget what he'd been.

"Your mother wouldn't have wanted this," he said.

"No, you don't get to bring her up. You lost all rights to her the first time you beat her, the first time you kicked her, the first time you made her less than a person." She saw him flinch at her unvarnished words, but she wasn't about to hold back.

He'd never held back his fists or his kicks or his words. "You're the reason she was living alone in this cabin so far from town. Even if you didn't push her, you're the reason she lay at the bottom of the ladder for three long days before I found her."

Anahera had been studying then; she shouldn't even have been back in Golden Cove that day, but, homesick, she'd decided to surprise her mother. As always when she first stepped through the door, a part of her had been braced to discover that her father had finally beaten her mother to death.

What she'd found had been far worse.

Haeata crumpled at the bottom of a fallen ladder, the glass front of a framed picture of her and Anahera smashed on the ground beside her, and her dried blood a dark stain against the wood.

All those dreams of happiness gone. Just like that.

Later, the authorities had told her that her mother's heart had given out, but they hadn't been able to meet her eyes when she asked if it had been before the fall or after. They'd wanted her to believe Haeata had died quickly and without suffering, but it was equally possible that she'd lain there too hurt to summon help but conscious and in pain.

Her mother's heart hadn't always been weak. It had been destroyed by stress, by fear, by the constant anguish of living with a man who treated her worse than he would a stray *kurī*. "I'd like it if you got off my property." She didn't take her eyes off him. "And don't come back or I'll have you charged with trespassing."

A twisting flash on her father's face, his hand fisting by his side.

"Yes," she said softly in English, "leopards never do change their spots."

Angry red rising under the darkness of his skin, Jason jumped back behind the wheel of his truck and reversed out of the drive in a grinding screech of rubber against stone.

Only after she was certain he was gone did Anahera turn back to the ruins and allow her tears to fall. Those tears were for her mother, for all the dreams that Haeata hadn't been able to realize, for all the pain she'd suffered in her forty-one years of life. And for all the dazzling hopes she'd had for her daughter.

"*Auē, aroha mai, māmā, aroha mai,*" Anahera said, the words of apology a rasp and the smell of burned wood in her throat. "I'm so sorry I came so close to giving up on life. I promise you I won't do it again. I'll fly again, get out of this damn town." Rubbing away her tears, she went to the cliff edge and watched wave after wave crash onto the sand in a natural symphony as haunting as those she'd heard in the great performance chambers of Europe.

At the sound of footsteps on gravel, she turned expecting Will. He might've been out cold when she left, but she knew he wasn't a man who slept much. But it wasn't Will walking toward her. "Vincent," she said, trying not to think about those bonfires on the beach and how eagerly he'd crouched by the kindling. "What are you doing here?" At the same time, she realized she hadn't heard the sound of a vehicle.

"Decided to get in a run before a set of virtual meetings."

His clothes seemed to bear that out: running pants in black that hugged his legs and a fitted long-sleeved dark gray hoodie with black stripes down the sides, his hands gloved against the cold. Mud coated his shoes and splattered his running pants halfway up his calves.

"Took the bush track down from my place," he said, catching her glance. "I heard about the cabin, wanted to see how bad it was." He pushed back the hood to reveal the golden strands of his hair, his tawny eyes returning to her after a quick look at the ruins. "I'm sorry. I know how much it meant to you."

"I'm just glad I wasn't in it at the time." Using the excuse of turning to regard the damage, Anahera took several steps away from the edge of the cliff. Paranoia or not, she felt a hell of a lot safer now that she wasn't any-where near an edge over which she could be pushed. "Do you remember that summer when my mum and I moved in and we all had a picnic in the yard?"

Vincent angled his head slightly, his breath fogging the air. "I wasn't here, remember?"

Frowning, Anahera thought back, the past unraveling in a string of faded Polaroids. "No," she said slowly. "You weren't. I guess I'm so used to thinking of you as part of my childhood that I put you into memories where you weren't actually present." He'd been one of her closest friends for so many years, before life splintered them into shards going in different directions.

Before they all made choices.

Vincent's smile was that guileless, sweet one that made her heart ache. "It's funny," he said. "I do that, too. We had some good times, didn't we?"

Anahera nodded, far enough away from the edge that she felt comfort-able talking with him. "Too bad we couldn't stay children," she murmured. "But then, I never much liked being a child." Playing with her friends had been one thing, but the helplessness of her size had eaten away at her. All she'd wanted was to get bigger so she could physically fight her father when he began to beat on her mother.

"Neither did I." Vincent's smile faded. "Always had to listen to my parents telling me who I was supposed to become, the man I was supposed to be." He flexed and closed his hands by his sides. "Sometimes, I felt like a prize poodle, being trained and given pats on the head when I behaved properly."

It was odd, Anahera thought, how thoroughly he'd stifled his anger as a child and teenager; they'd felt sorry for Vincent but he'd seemed fine going along with his parents' demands. "Your parents took tiger parenting to the next level," she said aloud. "But you've found your own way, reached for your own dreams." That wasn't quite true, but she wasn't heartless enough to point out that he was still following the blueprint the senior Bakers had drawn up for his life.

"I loved her, you know." A soft confession by a handsome golden-haired man gilded in the morning light. "She was the first thing I loved in all my life that was mine. That no one had trained me to love, trained me to like."

Anahera stilled. "You're not talking about Jemima, are you?"

"Don't pretend, Anahera," he said, dropping his head. "You're sleeping with that cop. I'm pretty sure he's told you."

Anahera didn't say anything, waiting, watching.

# 58

"Miriama was the most beautiful woman I had ever seen," Vincent murmured, his eyes on the ocean in the distance. "Like a dancer even when she was standing still. I wanted to wrap her up and freeze her in time so that nothing would ever hurt or destroy or taint her. At the same time, I wanted to take her to every glorious corner of the earth and show the world that she was mine." A rough exhale. "I booked us a surprise trip to Venice. It was to be this month."

"I think she must've loved you, too." Anahera didn't have to lie to speak those words. "For her to break the rules by which she'd been raised. I remember how she and Matilda always went to church on a Sunday, rain or shine." Matilda in her best matching long skirt and top, Miriama in her white church dress with a ribbon in her hair.

Vincent held her eyes, his own welling with pain. "She resisted at first, but I kept on pursuing her, kept on courting her." A faint smile. "That's such an old-fashioned word, isn't it? But that's what I did with her. Because she was like that. Had to be treated with care."

Vincent, Anahera saw, had put Miriama on a pedestal. And she'd walked away from him. Had the rejection pushed him over the edge, caused him to seethe until he lashed out and destroyed the very thing he professed to love? Men did that. Anahera's knowledge was born of a thousand dark memories of screams, of the sound of a fist hitting flesh, of guttural, drunken swearing that turned a person into a thing.

"Did you hurt her?" she asked because the question was a ticking bomb between them.

Vincent's smile turned lopsided. "Thank God you asked—it's so stupid to just ignore it, isn't it? No, I didn't hurt my Miriama." He swallowed, his throat moving. "If I was going to murder anyone, it'd be Jemima."

The flatness of his tone had Anahera very grateful she'd put distance between them. "You don't mean that," she said, thinking of Jemima's recent joy and the Vincent the other woman must've seen in comparison to the one standing here now. "She's deeply in love with you."

"I didn't say I would." Another smile, as if they were talking about the weather or old memories. "I'm just saying it would make more sense. Jemima's the trap, while Miriama was my freedom. With her, I could be the man I would've been if my parents hadn't decided to mold me into their image of a perfect son. If only Miriama had been patient a little longer, I would've made it happen."

With every breath she took, she inhaled the memory of fire until it seemed to be in her hair, her skin, her mouth. And she remembered another fire. The one that had ended with two dead people and Vincent finally free of his parents. "Were you thinking of divorcing Jemima and marrying Miriama?" she asked, playing along with his delusion that he'd been willing to walk away from his perfect life for a girl with the wrong pedigree to fit that illusion.

"I already bought the ring," he said in a voice so soft it was nearly snatched away by the quiet wind. "I just wanted her to wait until my kids were a little more grown, but she couldn't. And now she's dead."

Anahera's heart began to thump, her skin burning from the inside out. Maybe it was grief causing the flat patches in Vincent's delivery—or maybe it was a cold kind of calculation. All the smiles, all the sadness, what was real and what wasn't? What kind of a man could talk so unemotionally about murdering his own wife?

"Jemima told me you came to see her," he said without warning. "She's very happy to have made a friend in town."

*Oh, Jemima.* Controlling men like Vincent didn't like for their wives to have friends. "I understand what it feels like coming into a tight-knit community," she said, trying to make light of the situation. "It was the same for me when I moved to London. All the people I met were friends with Edward. It was hard to make friendships of my own."

Vincent's intense expression gentled. "You two don't actually have that much in common."

"I know." She said what he wanted her to say, what he needed her to say—alone on a windswept cliff was not the time to antagonize a man who spoke with easy casualness about ending his wife's life. "I don't expect us to become best friends. But I'm still enough of the Golden Cove girl to not want a visitor to feel unwelcome."

He chuckled. "Jemima would've had an easier time of it in South Africa, but she didn't have the head to go into the family business. Being my wife, looking after my children with the nanny's help, looking good for photos, that's more her strength. She'd last about two minutes in the real world."

Anahera stared at his profile as he turned to look at the ocean; he wasn't even attempting to be subtle. Or was he so used to putting Jemima down that this was his normal, and Anahera had just never spoken to him long enough on this subject to see it?

There was another, more dangerous option: Vincent didn't care about showing her his true face because he didn't expect her to have a chance to tell anyone about it.

"Will you be happy together now, do you think?" She kept her tone friendly with furious effort of will. "Can you get past your feelings for Miriama?"

"Yes, I'm sure." Vincent's tone changed, became almost confessional. "Miriama made me happy inside from the instant I saw her as a woman, but I've always had something else that never fails to give me joy. I've decided to go back to that old hobby."

Anahera took a step backward, her body poised to run . . . But she was too late. The Taser was in Vincent's hand well before she was out of range. "It's so hard to get an unregistered gun in this country," he said. "Especially when you have a profile and people want to hold things over you. Even getting this was a bit of a mission—but it's worked out the better choice for my needs."

Anahera held up her hands. "What are you doing?" She thought of the phone she had tucked in her back pocket, knew there was no way she could make the call before being hit and disabled.

"Haven't you figured it out, sweet little Ana?" The same angelic smile he'd given her so many times across the years. "Slim, dark haired, dark eyed, vibrant with *life*—my father kept her in Auckland, introduced me to her on my thirteenth birthday, when it was time for me to become a man."

His face twisted. "Be a man, Vincent! Fuck her like you mean it! Slap and choke the bitch until she does what you want! Baker men aren't pussies!" The ugliness faded, the angelic smile back in place. "I got a taste for a certain kind of woman."

Anahera's gorge rose. "That's unforgivable. You were a child."

"You're a good person, Ana." The hand holding the weapon never wavered. "It *is* a little sad to be so predictable in my tastes, but oh well, it makes me happy." He chuckled, as if he'd made a joke. "And the bastard's bones are worm food, so it's not like he can crow over it."

Anahera's breath came in shallow pants. "The murders," she said. "The hikers."

"Clap, clap." His voice was smooth, warm. "I didn't feel the urge to indulge while I was with my Miriama. But with her gone, I need to find happiness in life again."

"What about all those years after the three hikers?" Anahera scrambled to keep him talking. "You and Miriama only got together after she turned eighteen."

"Yes, I differ from my father there—I don't like children." A shrug. "I travel a lot. New Zealand is an inconveniently small country for a man with my needs." He sighed. "People here *miss* women."

A knot formed in the pit of Anahera's stomach. If he was openly telling her of his murderous history, there was no way she'd be able to talk her way out of this. But the longer she kept him talking, the longer she gave herself to think.

Her one advantage was that he seemed to *want* to talk, want to boast about his exploits. "You killed Miriama because she walked away from you?"

Patches of red on his face, his eyes blazing. "I would've won her back! That pissant doctor has nothing on what I could've given her." Cold words that trembled. "I didn't put a finger on my Miriama. All I did was love her."

Anahera ran rapidly through her options. She could go right, toward the bush, or she could go left, toward the cliffs. She had no idea of a Taser's range, but she knew Vincent was a fast runner. He'd been a sprinter in high school. He was also dressed in running shoes while she wore her normal everyday boots.

Out in the open, he'd catch her in a heartbeat. Her only chance was to go into the bush and lose herself amid the dense dark green.

Sweat trickled down her back. "Since it's just the two of us," she said, slowly putting down her hands while making sure to keep them in open view, "can I ask you some questions before you kill me?"

He raised an eyebrow. "Are you hoping your washed-up cop will come rescue you?"

"I don't expect any man to rescue me."

Expression nearly tender, Vincent said, "Your father's a cowardly shit. If you want me to get rid of him, I'll do it as a special favor."

"No, I want him to stew in regret." She flexed her muscles as much as she could to prepare for her break toward the trees. "As for the questions, call it curiosity. It's not every day I find out my friend is a serial killer."

His laugh was golden sunshine. "I always loved the smart-aleck things you'd say." Such affection in his voice and yet he planned to brutalize then murder her. "It's all for the greater good, Ana. You should be proud to be one of my women."

"Strange, but pride's not my topmost emotion right now."

More laughter, utter delight in every inch of him. "All right, ask your questions," he said after wiping the tears from his eyes. "We've got plenty of time and I'll hear anyone coming down the drive. If the cop does get suspicious, the pathetic creature I married will say exactly what I tell her to say."

Anahera knew Vincent was feeding off her fear, but she couldn't stop her heart from beating faster, her blood from pumping harder and harder. "When did you find out you liked murder?"

"It was by accident," he said in a conversational tone. "I was walking in the bush one day, pissed off at my spineless excuse for a mother, when I ran into a dark-eyed Italian hiker who reminded me of my father's whore and how much fun I'd had slapping her around."

His smile reached his eyes. "All that repressed anger, you know? God, it was fun to have an outlet. Best gift the bastard ever gave me." Affection in his voice, so real she might've believed it if she hadn't already realized that Vincent put on emotions like other people put on clothes. "The hiker was really cute and she was all smiley and she said hello with that accent, and I had a rock in my hand and I just smashed her head in with it."

# 59

Anahera flinched.

But Vincent wasn't finished. "She didn't die, not straightaway. She kept on trying to talk even though I'd smashed one of her eyes almost out, and only half her mouth was moving. I sat beside her for a long time, stroking her hair, and telling her it would be all right. My mother used to stroke my hair and tell me it would be all right." A dreamy look to him. "After."

"After what?"

A sly smile. "After my father tucked me in at bedtime like a good dad. A picture-perfect dad."

Nauseated, Anahera said, "Did he—"

"Talking about them is boring." Plastic smile, unwavering aim. "My hobby's the interesting thing. After the hiker started gurgling blood, I picked up my rock and smashed her and smashed her and smashed her until her face was pulp." He shrugged. "I know, not very sophisticated, but in my defense, I was only fourteen."

"Why were you so angry at your mother that day?" Anahera whispered, realizing that though he chose victims who reminded him of his horrific first sexual experience with a woman, his rage came from a far different source. "What did she do?" Or *not* do.

"I don't remember. And I told you"—he looked straight down his arm at her with eyes that held nothing—"talking about the bastard and his bitch is boring."

Anahera changed tack. "What happened to the hiker's body?"

"I finally realized I'd been an idiot." Vincent made a face. "I hadn't taken any precautions or made any plans. Dumb teenage lack of impulse control." He smiled, asking her to smile with him. "Eventually, I dragged her off the path and covered her up with leaves. I figured she'd be found, but my pretty, smiley girl hadn't logged her hike with anyone, was still there the next day when I came back with a shovel and an axe and a tarp. Do you know how hard it is to chop up a body? Blood and viscera every-where."

"You didn't." It came out a rough whisper.

"Scout's honor." Vincent grinned. "I took off all my clothes before I started, put them in a plastic bag; and I brought water to wash in. It took me hours to carry the pieces out in my daypack."

"Where is she?"

"Buried in the bush behind the house. Cadaver dogs never came that far when they finally did a search."

"Is that why you decided to target more hikers? Because they were less likely to be missed at once?"

He nodded. "I met the second one on the trail and she came with me when I said I could show her a secret local waterfall. I managed to get her close enough to my burial ground to keep all of her—and I didn't use a rock that time. No broken bones."

And Anahera knew. "The skeleton Shane found."

"I dug her up after my dear departed parents weren't around to spy on me, then spent weeks cleaning up her bones. I kept her in my basement workroom that Jemima knows never to go into." Another one of those lopsided grins. "But that first summer, I was still a kid, took the third one too soon in the same area. After I saw how the cops swarmed, I decided I'd have to be clever, not hunt so close to my home ground."

Anahera frowned. "Did you put the bracelet in our cave on purpose?"

"Yes. Showing off to my friends." His smile faded. "I was sorry later, when none of you wanted to go back there to hang out." Voice quiet, poi-gnant with sadness. "I was happy in that cave."

"I don't understand one thing," Anahera said, wondering if she'd imagined the flash of movement in the trees behind Vincent's shoulder.

"What?"

"You must've had other victims between that summer and your first trip abroad on your own." After killing three times in a single summer, Vincent couldn't have gone dormant until he began traveling internationally. "And you pointed it out yourself—we live in a small country. Why did no one make the connection between all the victims?"

"I've never been stupid, Ana, you know that." It was a chiding statement. "I sat down and thought about what made me happy and realized I didn't have a racial preference. Māori, Tongan, Italian, Indian, I found pictures of women with the right look and imagined . . . playing with them. The joy, the release of tension I felt was the same."

Anahera curled her fingers into her palms, flexed her feet.

"I favor nicer girls and spend the most time with them"—Vincent's eyes skimmed her body with a chilling kind of warmth—"but the right whore will do to plug the gap, especially if she's young and relatively unspoiled." Roughness in his voice there, before it smoothed out to calm control again. "Age can vary from nineteen to a young-looking thirty-five or so. I did kill younger teenagers, but that was when I was a kid myself. You'd be surprised how many nice girls will meet a good-looking rich boy for a secret date."

He shrugged. "Once I understood all that, it was easy to vary things up so I was satisfied, but no one would see a pattern. Take a good churchgoing girl, follow it up with a cheating soccer mom in another town, throw in a hell-raising runaway—no pattern, nothing to see."

"Except you," Anahera pointed out. "*Someone* should've noticed a boy whose name kept turning up again and again."

"I told you I got clever," he replied. "I did my research before each kill, had a place to dispose of the body." Pride now, iridescent beneath the golden smile. "The churchgoing girl went into a fenced-off geothermal pool so hot she's probably sludge by now. I drove the soccer mom's SUV into a lake—it wasn't found for years. Runaway's buried in the woods on a friend's farm. We met in town and I convinced her we'd smoke dope to-gether if she snuck into the barn after lights-out."

Vincent *had* been smart, scarily so. No signature, no attempts to play with the police. For him, the hunt wasn't an act of blinding rage. Neither was the body dump. No, the rage came in between, *after* he had the women under his control.

A man like that could hide his crimes for decades.

But his intelligent choices had left him with no way to tell the world what he'd achieved. Anahera, however, was a captive audience he planned to silence.

Fuck him.

She'd use his arrogance to save herself. The arm with which he held the stun gun had to be getting tired. All she needed was a second's inattention as he readjusted position and she'd take her chances. It had to be harder to hit a moving target than a stationary one, especially if that moving target was weaving and dodging in an unpredictable way.

"How many?" she asked, not looking in the direction where she'd seen movement. If someone *was* out there, she wasn't going to give them away to Vincent.

"You know," he said after a long pause, "I've never counted, but I think it must be something like twenty-seven."

He was lying.

Whether it was the low number for a man who'd killed three times in a single blistering summer, or that he hadn't counted, there was a lie in there somewhere. But then again, Vincent was a psychopath who'd success-fully fooled people his entire lifetime. Lying was part of his oeuvre.

"Stop pulling my leg, Vincent." His arm had to start quivering soon. "You were the best of us at keeping track of things. That's why we always asked you to be the judge in any challenge."

He gave her that beatific smile with no hint of evil to it, and moved the Taser from one hand to the other so fast that she had no time to react.

*Keep him talking,* she told herself instead of panicking. *Give yourself time to think.* It wasn't hard to follow the instruction—because even though she was standing face-to-face with him while he threatened her, she still found it difficult to believe that the boy she'd once raced across the sands had turned into a monster.

Her questions were infinite.

"Busted," he said with a huge laugh. "But the number is my special secret. No one will ever know what I've done. Not the whole of it."

"Were you always like this?" The question came from deep inside her. "When we played as children, did you go home and torture animals?"

He tilted his head partially to the side. "Could be I was born this way," he said and his eyes were laughing again, his amusement inexplicable and slippery. "Or could be it was the third bedtime tuck-in or the thirtieth that did it." Another shrug. "Personally, I'm going for nurture over nature—my baby brother is definitely having a hard time hiding his crazy these days. I don't know what the hell is wrong with him. I dealt with the problem, didn't I?"

Cold fingers on Anahera's neck. "Where's Kyle, Vincent?"

# 60

"He burned down your cabin, Ana. I'm sorry." Streaks of red on his cheekbones, his tone abashed. "Such a petty, vindictive little shit—and he wasn't smart enough to change out of his kerosene-splattered jeans before he came home. I didn't make clever choices all these years to be brought down by a spoiled brat who thought he was the big bad in the family."

"Did you look him in the face when you killed him?"

"No." Several golden strands of Vincent's hair lifted in the slight breeze before settling back down. "Do you think I'm a monster? He was my baby brother. And if he'd kept on being a good little psychopath and hiding who he was from everyone, I'd have been a proud sibling. But no, he had to go and start playing asinine ego games."

No doubt Vincent would brush off Kyle's disappearance by saying his brother had gone traveling abroad. Nothing strange in that. Nothing strange in Kyle settling down in another country, either.

No, Vincent wasn't stupid.

Anahera had seen no more movement, accepted that she'd fooled herself in her desperation. "So," she said, "what do you plan to do to me?"

"My tastes have become far more sophisticated than with my first . . . lover." A softness to his gaze, memories of murder and pleasure. "There's no fun in just bashing in a woman's face. It's the difference between sculling a mug of cheap beer and savoring a fine wine. These days, I like to take my time."

"I'll be missed," Anahera warned. "Just like Miriama was missed."

"I *told* you, I had nothing to do with her death!" It was the first time he'd lost his temper, his voice rising and his hand shaking on the Taser.

A loud noise sounded in the trees at the same instant.

Vincent swung that way instinctively—and Anahera took the chance to run.

"Ana!" he shouted from behind her, but she kept on moving in an erratic weaving pattern, her feet pounding the earth and her lungs bursting.

"Drop it." The words were cool, calm—and accompanied by the sound of the safety being disengaged on a gun.

Skidding to a halt, Anahera looked back and saw Will standing less than seven feet behind Vincent, a rifle pointed to the back of Vincent's head. "You're too smart to risk it," he said when Vincent didn't drop the Taser.

"You're not authorized to have a gun." The words were bitten out. "I checked with my source. Your paperwork's still pending."

"And you're not authorized to have a Taser," Will replied in that mild tone that gave nothing away. "There's no way I'll miss at this range. In case you're hoping I'll blow out your brains so you can go down in a blaze of glory, you should know I intend to shoot out your spine. I'm sure the prison hospital staff will be gentle as they turn you over so you don't get bedsores, and when they reattach your catheter."

Anahera couldn't see Vincent's face, but she could imagine the expression on it. To a man who'd been a prince, then a king, the idea of being helpless in anyone's hands would be an enraging one. And, when it came down to it, Vincent Baker was a coward.

She wasn't the least surprised when he dropped the stun gun.

"Turn around," Will ordered. "Hands behind your head."

Vincent obeyed, his eyes meeting Anahera's across the clifftop clearing as Will closed in on him. "I guess our date will have to wait," he said, that perfect, innocent smile on his face. "We would've had so much fun."

# 61

Vincent's arrest pounded a shock wave through Golden Cove. Especially when it came out that there was a recording of him confessing to his heinous crimes. Will had turned on the recorder on his phone partially through the standoff, and the device had picked up both Anahera's and Vincent's voices. Not everything but enough.

"Thank God," Anahera said to Will four days later, when they finally had a chance to be together.

Will had been caught up in the logistics and legalities of making sure Vincent would never again walk free. The one thing he hadn't had to explain was illegal use of a firearm. Because the rifle he'd used to disarm Vincent was one of the decommissioned pair that hung in his rental; it wasn't capable of firing even a single shot.

As for why Will had brought it with him—he'd run into Evelyn Triskell just as he was leaving the house. She'd stopped her car while passing his place, and yelled out a "Yoohoo!"

It turned out she'd gone for an early morning coffee-and-croissants run to Josie's. But what she'd wanted to tell Will was that, on her way back, she'd glimpsed a hoodie-clad figure cross the road in the distance, moving from the hillside bush track to a track that Will knew led to the cliffs.

"The one he came from, it's no doubt a messy track to run at the moment," Evelyn had said. "Rain always turns it into a bog for at least a week, usually causes a rockfall or two along the way." Pursed lips. "It's probably one of the local boys wanting a challenge, but you really should do something about blocking off that track while it's unsafe."

Will's instincts had kicked in.

"I memorized the track routes during the search for Miriama," he'd said afterward, his eyes like chips of slate. "I knew the track Evelyn was complaining about started at the Baker property. I figured it had to be Kyle. I could see him setting the fire to get back at me—and I knew that's where you must've gone."

"I thought I'd be safe in bright daylight."

Will had nodded. "Evelyn's sighting was why I parked on the road and walked in through the trees. I didn't want my presence to provoke the asshole into doing something stupid if he'd just come to admire his handiwork."

He'd taken the gun because he knew both Vincent and Kyle had a firearms license and Evelyn hadn't been able to tell him if the jogger she'd seen had been holding anything.

Anahera owed her life, at least partially, to the town gossip.

Anahera, too, had been trapped in an endless loop of police interviews. She hadn't balked, not even when she was asked to repeat details for what felt like the ten billionth time. She'd do anything in her power to keep the world safe from Vincent.

Now, at long last, the two of them sat naked in Will's bed, having stripped off each other's clothes the instant after walking in the door. Anahera didn't need to be a psychologist to know it was the need to celebrate life that had driven them to the most primal sex she'd ever experienced.

Limbs heavy in the aftermath, she sat with the sheet tucked up over her breasts while she bit chunks off a family-size bar of chocolate she'd dug out from Will's pantry. It was apparently courtesy of an elderly townswoman who thought he was too thin. He, in turn, was halfway through a cup of coffee so dark she'd worry it'd keep him up all night except that they were both so exhausted that sleep would come whether they wanted it or not.

"I didn't delay helping you just to get more damning footage," Will said.

"I know." He wasn't built that way. "I'd still be thanking you even if you had. Vincent needs to be locked up forever."

Will rested his free hand on her sheet-covered thigh. "He was so calm. I needed him unbalanced enough that he'd fall for a noise in the bushes and you would have time to get out of range—then you said that about Miriama being missed."

"I think his calmness through it all is what I'm having the hardest time handling." Closing her own hand over his, she ran the pad of her thumb over his knuckle. "It's as if his actions had no real impact on him."

"I'm sure the prison shrinks will have a field day with him." Will absently stroked her thigh. "They found Kyle's body in the trunk of Kyle's own car—Vincent told us he intended to bury his brother far from Golden Cove, in another isolated section of bush."

"Is he still insisting he had nothing to do with Miriama's death?"

Nodding, Will said, "Shrinks are convinced he's lying to himself because he killed the woman he loved—as much as someone like Vincent can love."

"You don't agree?" Anahera put the unfinished chocolate bar on the side table.

"I don't know." Folding his arms behind his head, Will stared at the opposite wall. "He's open about his other crimes to the point of bragging. Didn't blink when walking me through how he pulled off his parents' murder—or how he slit Kyle's throat. But he becomes enraged if I so much as mention Miriama in connection with his other crimes. Hasn't once budged from saying he never hurt her."

Anahera blew out a breath. "Is there anything you can do to find out if he's lying or not?"

Will stared into the distance, but he was still there, just thinking. "Yes," he said slowly before turning to look at her. "You're going to have to trust me on what I'm about to ask you to do."

"What's the plan?"

## 62

Will took the first step while Anahera was in the bathroom throwing water onto her face to wake herself up for their planned excursion. He wanted to keep her out of this and out of possible danger until he had an answer for better or worse.

Picking up his phone, he input the call. "Evelyn," he said when she answered. "I'm sorry to call so late, but I'm finalizing Miriama's file and I didn't want to bother Matilda or Dominic." No lie there. "I was hoping you could help with some of the details."

"Oh, of course," the gossipy but ultimately kind woman said. "Mattie's in no state to talk to anyone and that poor young doctor's gone to pieces. What do you need?"

"It'd be useful if I could track down any X-rays Miriama might've had done recently. My guess would be that Dominic was no longer her doctor."

"Oh, that one's *easy*. I ran into her once when she was catching the bus to go get a prescription for hay fever, I think it was—I asked her why Dominic didn't just write her one and she said there were rules about doctors dating patients." A quick breath. "Anyway, she told me who she was off to see and I was happy for her. Dr. Symon is a lovely man, saw my cousin through a bad bout of shingles."

"Do you have a full name for him?"

"Roger, I think . . . No, wait, it's Richard. Dr. Richard Symon."

That took care of the chain of evidence—as long as Evelyn's information was correct. If it wasn't, he'd have to go to Matilda after all. And he'd have to break her heart again—because she'd want to know why he was asking the question when Vincent had already been arrested.

"Thank you," he said, and hung up before Evelyn could burst out with her own questions.

Now, to confirm the name without tipping his hand, or causing Matilda fresh suffering.

"Ready?" Anahera stepped out of the bathroom.

Will nodded. "Let's go."

They walked to their destination: the Golden Cove doctor's surgery.

Breaking into it at night wasn't exactly the Great Train Robbery. The only reason the place wasn't regularly vandalized was probably because Dominic kept his drug samples locked up in an ancient metal filing cabinet so heavy you'd need a crane to lift it. The lock on the cabinet was all but impossible to pick.

The same couldn't be said for the front door.

While Anahera stood as lookout, Will made short work of that lock and stepped inside.

He went straight to the less-than-new computer that held patient files.

This was where it could get tricky, but when he booted it up, it took him straight to the main page, no password required. That small-town mentality again. It was, however, to his advantage this time around.

Quickly bringing up the file he wanted, he saw the words he'd expected to see: *Patient file closed.*

Below that was an explanatory note:

*Miriama Hinewai Tutaia is switching to another general practitioner as she is in a personal relationship with me, the physician of record for Golden Cove. To be clear, she has never been my patient and I was not aware that she was on the practice's roll at the time that we met. It appears she was enrolled at this surgery as a child, but has had no need to visit it in the past three years.*

*To maintain ethical lines and give her access to a primary phy-
sician who can keep track of her overall health, I have referred her
to a fellow practitioner in the nearest town. Referral letter anno-
tated to file.*

That referral letter was to Dr. Richard Symon.

He shut down the computer and made sure everything was as it had
been, then exited the clinic, the door lock snicking quietly behind him.

"You have it?" The oval of Anahera's face looking at him from under the
black knit cap she'd pulled on.

He nodded. "Let's get out of here."

It wasn't until they were back home and making themselves a midnight
snack that Will said, "I'm going to have to go out of town tomorrow. I'll
leave before dawn so I can make the trip and be back by midmorning."

Anahera nodded. "If you don't mind, I'll use your computer to sort out
a new passport for myself." She finished stirring sugar into her hot cocoa.
"I might swing by the cabin, too."

To reclaim it, replace the memories of Vincent's violence with peace.
"I'd rather you wait until I'm back," Will said. "Or if you want to go alone,
give me another twenty-four hours."

Dark eyes locked with his. "You think Vincent is telling the truth."

"I'll know after my visit tomorrow morning." Hit by a sudden cold that
reached into his bones, he closed his hand over her wrist. "Come with me."

He knew she was a woman who valued her freedom, but after studying
his expression, she said, "I need to buy some more clothes and a new laptop
anyway. Will I be able to get those where you're going?"

Will exhaled silently. "I know a place."

They left the next morning in the misty gray time before true dawn.

Anahera said only, "Good luck," when he dropped her off at the small
mall that held both an electronics store and clothing shops.

The mall wasn't yet open, but the café out front was doing a brisk business.

Waiting until after she'd walked into the café, Will drove on to his destination. The visitor parking lot was empty at this early hour, but he spotted a couple of cars in the small staff lot.

He rang the bell.

The door was opened by a cheerful Indian woman with small daisy earrings in her lobes. "I'm afraid Dr. Symon isn't starting for another fifteen minutes," she said. "Do you have an early appointment? You're welcome to sit inside where it's warm."

Will showed her his identification. "I'd like to talk to Dr. Symon. It shouldn't take long."

The woman's eyes widened, but her tone remained professional. "Come inside. I'll go fetch him."

A slender man with graying brown hair appeared from a back room less than a minute later, crumbs of toast on his tie. "Detective," he said, holding out his hand. "How can I help you?"

"Perhaps we can talk in your office," Will said after they shook.

"Of course." The other man held up his mug of coffee. "Would you like one, too?"

"If it's not too much trouble."

They were soon seated in the doctor's office with the door shut behind them. "I'm going to ask you about a patient," Will began after taking a generous sip of the hot liquid.

"I'm sure you're quite aware of medical privilege," Dr. Symon began.

"The patient is dead. Murdered."

Richard Symon put down his coffee with a dull thud. His eyes skidded slightly up and to his right before landing on Will again.

Will went motionless; *this* was why he hadn't called ahead. "You know exactly who I'm talking about."

The other man made a game attempt to recover. "Hard to miss, what with her death being linked to a serial killer. It's been in the news nonstop."

Will put down his coffee on a clear spot on the doctor's desk. "You and I both know you were aware of her death long before then. Is Dominic de Souza a good friend?"

"A colleague." Dr. Symon pulled at the knot of his tie. "We—the doctors who work on the West Coast—try to keep in touch, help each other out when we can."

"He referred Miriama Tutaia to you."

"I suppose there's no harm in confirming that. I am, after all, her physician of record." A short pause. "Do you need medical data to verify her identity, is that it?" He smiled shakily. "I've never been in this position before, but I can't see any problem with such a request."

Will locked his eyes with Dr. Symon's. "What I'm about to ask you is tied directly to Miriama's murder. Think carefully before you answer."

# 63

Anahera asked Will to drop her off by her Jeep when they drove back into Golden Cove. It was still parked in front of Matilda's house. "At least this didn't go up in flames," she said as they transferred over her clothing purchases.

"You heading to the café?" asked the cop who'd somehow become more to her. "Passport application?"

"No, I managed to finish that at the mall." After setting up her laptop, she'd used her phone hot spot to start the process of obtaining new travel documents; it helped that she'd scanned and backed up all important documents in the cloud. "I'm planning to call Jemima, see if she'll see me."

The police had taped off the Baker estate as a crime scene. Jemima and her children were currently staying in the guesthouse on Daniel's estate, but neither Daniel nor Keira was in residence. They'd left the country the day after Vincent's arrest, after Keira's Canberra-based grandmother had a severe seizure and was placed in intensive care.

Jemima kept the gate locked and wasn't answering calls. The police had gone to her for interviews, rather than force her to come to the station—probably because they knew the circus that would follow should she leave the May estate.

You'd think Golden Cove's remote location would help protect Vincent's family from the impact of his notoriety, but the media were camped out at the gates. Some would no doubt have jumped them by now if the police hadn't stationed a patrol car there and made it clear that anyone who stepped onto private property without permission would be arrested.

While certain journalists might've shrugged off the possibility of a trespass conviction in their determination to get an exclusive, the bloodsuckers were smart enough not to take on the vicious dogs currently roaming the property. Matthew Teka had quietly offered Jemima the dogs when a reporter managed to reach her front door, and she'd accepted.

That was the only communication anyone had had from her since the arrest.

"Be careful." Will's gray eyes held her gaze. "Matthew's dogs took a chunk out of a cameraman's leg yesterday."

"He shouldn't have been trying to sneak up to the house." Anahera had no sympathy for those who preyed on the pain and heartbreak of a woman who'd had nothing to do with her husband's horrific crimes. "If she doesn't want me there, I won't go." Simple as that.

"You realize she might blame you for what happened to Vincent?"

"Yes." She touched her fingers to his jaw. "Go be a cop, Will. I'm going to be a friend if she wants one."

He left her with a hard kiss and a silent warning she heard as clear as day: *Don't let down your guard. Jemima might not be as innocent as she appears.*

That, of course, was what the media hounds were baying. They wanted to scream at Jemima, ask her if she'd known. If she said no, they'd ask her how she could've possibly *not* known.

Anahera wasn't naïve. She didn't think Jemima was innocent in everything. The other woman had known about Vincent's affair but helped him create the image of a perfect family man nonetheless. But Jemima wasn't involved in murder, of that she was certain. Vincent hadn't valued his wife enough to bring her into his psychopathic daydreams.

After placing her new laptop bag on the passenger seat of the Jeep, she brought up Jemima's number and made the call. She'd already tried once, but Jemima hadn't responded. Not wanting to put further pressure on a woman already trapped in a nightmare, she'd left it at that, sure that Jemima's wealthy family would swoop in and rescue her. But either they were total assholes, or Jemima had frozen them out, too, because no strangers had come through the Cove except for the reporters.

Once again, the phone rang and rang. She was just about to hang up when Jemima picked up. "Ana?"

"Yes, it's me," she said. "You want company? I can bring up coffees."

A pause before Jemima said, "Can you get hot chocolates for the kids, too? More milk than chocolate? They're going stir-crazy cooped up in the house."

"Consider it done. Should I push the buzzer at the gate when I arrive?"

"No, call me on your phone. The reporters kept pushing the buzzer so I disabled it on this end, and someone's smashed out the security camera so I can't see who's at the gate."

Probably an unscrupulous reporter hoping to sneak up without being spotted. "I'll be there in about twenty minutes."

Once in the café, Anahera placed the drinks order with the temporary barista Josie had hired—one of Shane Hennessey's groupies. It turned out the girl had been a barista in Wellington before she came to Golden Cove. And she was good. But it was unsettling to see another beautiful, lissome girl behind the counter.

"How's the job going?" Anahera forced herself to ask.

Dark eyes shone at her. "It's a little weird. People keep asking me about the girl who died, and I didn't know her. But mostly, it's nice. Super busy with all the out-of-towners—I'm glad I'm not having to manage alone."

"Tania's good company." Josie had hired Tania Meikle to wait tables at the same time that she'd hired the barista; Josie herself was now out of commission. Her ankles had been heavily swollen yesterday when Anahera dropped by to see her before heading to Will's place.

"Yeah, she is. She's just popped out to deliver an order to the B&B." Frothy steamed milk poured onto the reduced amount of chocolate.

"She got the sitter situation sorted?"

"Her husband's mother—lady's kinda prune-faced, but Tans says she's nice to the baby." She put the lids on the children's drinks, then began on the coffees. "You want some cake, too?"

Memory slammed into Anahera. Of another girl and another piece of cake.

"Yes," she said. "Box up six cupcakes." The kids would enjoy them and Jemima could probably do with a little sugar and comfort, too.

She managed to get everything to the Jeep in one trip, as the barista had put the drinks into a cardboard holder that proved stable, and the cakes were in a small carry box. Drinks balanced on the passenger seat and kept from falling by the cake box on one side and her laptop bag on the other, Anahera pulled out into the street.

She made sure all her windows were raised and her doors locked before she turned into the drive of the May estate. Halfway along and her upward momentum turned into a crawl; the sides of the drive were lined with TV vans from both national and international networks, large SUVs with radio station logos and satellite dishes on the top, even a small bus.

Vincent's arrest had made news headlines around the world. He'd visited a lot of towns and cities, and all those towns and cities were currently combing through their missing person files, looking for women and girls who fit the profile of Vincent's known victims. So far, the authorities had revealed five possible matches.

Every single face had sent a chill up Anahera's spine.

All those faces, all those women, they could've been her sisters. Different races, different cultures, but there was *something* eerily similar that tied them together.

Able to see the knot of reporters up above, she kept her eyes on her goal. The vultures swarmed around her the instant she got within reach. Honking her horn, she continued to move forward. The instant she stopped, the rabid mob would take it as a cue to keep her locked in place until she gave them something.

That's what they'd done after Edward's death. It hadn't been this bad, of course. There'd been no questions around the nature of his passing, but the media had still wanted a sound bite from the "grieving widow" of "a dramatic genius taken before his time."

Anahera had given them nothing then and she'd give them nothing now.

Lighting flashes through the windscreen, the photographers taking her image in the hope of somehow being able to use it. Someone would eventually identify her, but it mattered little in the grand scheme of things. This wasn't London, a city she'd first inhabited as Edward's "ingénue bride," the "unspoiled" young woman who'd stolen his heart right under the noses of society beauties.

Everyone had wanted to meet her.

Anahera had never been comfortable in that role, but the glamour and attention made Edward happy so she'd gone along with it. It was a small sacrifice, she'd thought, when he loved it so much. Then her music unexpectedly caught the attention of a record executive and her identity was reshaped again—from ingénue to "gifted pianist." Edward had gloried in that, too, in being part of one of London's "reigning creative couples."

He'd been proud of her skill, had spent hours lying on the couch on Sunday mornings listening to her play.

That had been no illusion.

Right then, as she fought the media, she was unexpectedly glad he'd had those moments in the sun, her flawed, talented, lying, loving husband.

Camera crew jostled for space, trying to get better shots of Anahera's face. She didn't attempt to hide it—she'd be in court sooner or later as a witness anyway.

Finally halting, with her bumper only an inch from the sliding gate, she waited until one of the patrol officers reached her, then lowered her window. "Mrs. Baker is expecting me," Anahera said. "She'll open the gate when I call."

The cop said something into the radio at his shoulder, listened as he received a message back. "Give us two minutes to clear the horde from the gate. And look out for the dogs—they'll come running the instant the gate begins to open."

As Anahera watched, the cops got on with the job. The reporters didn't resist much—probably because the memory of that dog-mauled cameraman was still fresh in their minds. Ana made the call after the officer gave her a nod. "Jemima, I'm at the gate."

It began to slide back almost at once.

Waiting only until it was open just far enough, Anahera slipped through, then told Jemima to close it.

Four huge black dogs boiled out of the trees at that moment, snarling and barking and heading straight for her Jeep.

# 64

"Jesus, Jemima."

"Drive," the other woman ordered. "They'll go for the people at the gate. Matthew assured me they know not to cross that barrier."

Anahera wasn't so certain of that, but she kept on driving as, behind her, the gate slid shut again. Barely in time. One of the dogs slammed into it, its jaws wide open. No wonder Jemima was keeping her kids indoors.

Parking her Jeep right by the front door of the glass and timber guesthouse, Anahera opened her own door with care. She couldn't hear the dogs, but she still moved as fast as humanly possible to grab the drinks and cakes. Jemima was waiting for her in the doorway, sea green eyes jaggedly brilliant in a face as pale as porcelain.

"Here, I'll take those," she said with a graciousness that seemed habitual.

"Those dogs, Jem." Anahera shut the door behind herself, then took the drinks from Jemima. "I can see they're doing a good job, but they're vicious."

"Matthew's going to pick them up tomorrow," Jemima told her, leading them into a large living area made warm and snug by the crackling fire in the hearth.

Her face changed as she entered, her expression brighter and happier. "Sweethearts, look what my friend Anahera's brought! Treats!"

The two children jumped up from where they were playing with Lego bricks on the floor. Fidgeting, their small faces aglow, they nonetheless remembered to say, "Thank you!" to Anahera before they reached out to pick a cupcake each from the box their mother held open.

"I'm going to put your drinks here," Jemima told the children, placing the hot chocolates on a coffee table by the play area. "You both know you have to sit at this table to eat and drink."

Two happy nods, faces already smooshed with pink and purple frosting.

Putting the extra cakes on the dining table to the far right of the open-plan space, Anahera following suit with their coffees, Jemima smiled at her children and it was incredible, the fierce power with which she held back her sadness and grief in their presence. "If I leave these cakes near them, they won't be able to resist, and their little tummies can only hold so much."

Anahera took off her anorak and hung it on the back of the chair before taking a seat across from Jemima. "They're sweet kids." Well raised rather than polite robots too scared to step a foot out of line. Currently, they were giggling as they painted mustaches onto each other's upper lips with the frosting from their cupcakes.

Jemima's face crumpled for a second before she slapped the cheerful mask back on. "I don't know what this will do to them," she said in a low tone that wouldn't reach Jasper and Chloe. "To grow up being known as the children of a serial killer?" Her anguish was a raw wound. "Daniel's coming back into the country tomorrow to deal with some urgent business matters. He said he'll fly us out of here. At least I can take my babies away from the center of it all."

"Good. You don't need to have that ugliness on your doorstep." Those vultures wouldn't be leaving anytime soon. "It's good of Daniel to offer to fly you out." The news choppers did the occasional flyover here, but they tended to concentrate on the activity at the Baker house and the crime scene in the bush behind it—Vincent's private burial plot. If Daniel timed it right, he could be in the air and away before anyone realized he wasn't alone in the chopper.

"Vincent never had a nice thing to say about Daniel, but he doesn't want anything from us. When the police came and said we couldn't stay in the house, I didn't know what to do, but Daniel and Keira were there minutes later."

Anahera figured Daniel must've been tipped off by a police contact—and she also figured she knew the name of that police contact. "Daniel's not a bad guy." Arrogant, yes, but when it mattered, he stepped up.

Jemima squeezed her takeout cup, denting it. "My family wanted to fly in the instant they heard, but I told them to stay away. They came anyway, are waiting in Christchurch." She swallowed. "I had to get things straight in my head first. I couldn't deal with my father telling me what to do while my sisters organized my life."

Anahera sat back and let Jemima talk, and she learned that Vincent had chosen the most soft-spoken and submissive of four sisters, the woman least likely to question his actions.

"I went along with everything," Jemima whispered. "The nights when he just disappeared, the days when he'd shut the door to his basement workroom and ignore me and the children, the way he'd be so cold to me when we were alone and so warm and affectionate when we were out in public—I pretended that was the real Vincent. Because that was the Vincent who courted me. Who married me."

Anahera nodded. "I understand."

The other woman's expression fractured, her lips quivering. "You're the only person who can say that and that I know actually does understand. Thank you for sharing your secret with me. I won't tell anyone."

It was such a stark thing to say, stripped of all pretense. "And whatever you tell me," Anahera replied, "it stays between us. No matter what."

"You're with that cop."

"I'm my own person." She also understood the ugly truth that long-term abuse had an insidious impact on the psyche; no one who hadn't walked in Jemima's shoes had the right to judge her. "My father beat my mother for most of their life together. And she stayed. She even stuck up for him against people who called him a bully. She told them he was a wonderful husband and father."

Jemima stared at Anahera. "Did she ever get away?"

"Five years before she died. The first time he punched me." Anahera could still feel her head snapping back with violent force, her body flying back. "I got into the middle of a fight between them and he went for me. I never knew before that day why he'd never once touched me even in the worst of his rages. Because that was my mother's bright line." The one thing Haeata would not forgive.

Jemima frantically wiped away the tears rolling down her face, shooting a quick look toward the children to make sure they hadn't seen. "I was getting to that point," she whispered. "He'd started to ignore the children more and more except when he needed to bring them out for a photo op.

"They'd run to him for hugs and . . ." She stared at nothing for long minutes. "Vincent never yelled, but he'd be so cold, like our babies were stray animals who had nothing to do with him." Her fingers clenched again around the takeout cup. "At night, in the darkness, I lie awake and I wonder if I would have left him if he'd carried on that way. Or if I would've stayed while my children suffered."

Glancing at the two frosting-smudged kids currently sitting with their elbows braced on top of the coffee table while they drank their hot chocolates, Anahera said, "As far as I can see, they're happy and well-adjusted. Whatever Vincent withheld, you gave them in spades."

A tremulous smile. "You think so?"

"I've never lied to you."

The smile brightened then disappeared. "I didn't know," the other woman said, her voice hollow. "Those nights when he disappeared, I thought he was going out and sleeping with other women. Maybe prostitutes. It was the worst thing I could imagine."

"I don't think murder is the default assumption for any wife when her husband goes missing overnight." Anahera leaned forward. "The media are going to hound you. If you decide to do an interview, control it."

"I won't be talking to reporters," Jemima murmured. "My oldest sister, Catherine, is a lawyer. She's always been the strongest and mostly, I try to keep out of her way, but I called her and I asked her if the children and I can disappear."

A long exhale, traces of her South African accent slipping back into her words as she continued. "Catherine said it'll be next to impossible in a small country where every news channel and outlet is going to be carrying this story for months, maybe years, along with photos of Vincent and me. At least they've been decent enough to spare the children."

She took a gulp of the tepid coffee. "It's also a huge story in South Africa because of my family's standing there." More whispers of the accent, more cracks in the veneer of perfection demanded by Vincent and produced by this woman who'd loved him. "My face is apparently everywhere."

"You need to go somewhere you can start afresh." Some people might call that running away, but fuck those sanctimonious pricks. They weren't living this horror. "Europe?"

"Yes, that's what I was thinking. Vincent's known in London, and in a few cities like Paris and Milan, but most of his business interests are in the US and China. Catherine says the story hasn't gained much traction in Europe beyond London."

Jemima turned her lips inward to wet them before continuing. "I was an exchange student in Germany during high school. I speak the language and I know how things work there. It has a population of tens of millions. We could vanish in all those people, just three more blond heads in the crowd."

Anahera reached out a hand, closed it over Jemima's wrist. "Go," she whispered. "Take care of yourself and your children. Be selfish."

"The police haven't told me I can't go, but they've strongly suggested I stay in the country. They want me to give evidence of the nights Vincent was gone over the years." A haunted look in her eyes. "I kept diaries." Pressing her lips together desperately, she squeezed her eyes shut for long seconds.

"Did you hand them over?" Anahera asked when she was sure Jemima could speak without breaking.

"During the second interview," was the husky reply. "After I couldn't lie to myself any longer, after they played me a tape of Vincent confessing to the most horrible, awful things."

"Then you've done more than enough. Vincent's happily talking—he's never again going to walk free, whether or not you testify." Anahera knew that if Jemima didn't get out now, she'd be caught in the endless loop of trials and appeals and game-playing by Vincent.

"He called me." Jemima's fingers trembled around the coffee cup. "From the prison. And he was my Vincent. Oh, God, Ana, if I stay here, I'm so scared I'll never break free." A harsh whisper. "He'll always have me."

"I'll help you in any way I can." No way was Anahera allowing Vincent to claim another victim. "If the police have frozen your assets, I'll give you my bank card for my London account." There was plenty of money in it, more than enough to help a woman who needed to get on her feet. "You can access it all over Europe and no one will ever trace it to you."

Jemima glanced over at her children, then back at Anahera. "What if . . . what if I knew something? What if I suspected in the darkest part of night? What if I saw a speck of blood on one of Vincent's polo shirts one night after he came home?"

Holding those eyes of sea green, Jemima's pupils hugely dilated, Anahera kept her voice quiet as she said, "What did he do to you after he came home those nights?"

Jemima's hand flew to her mouth, muffling a cry. "How did you know?" she whispered through white-knuckled fingers.

Because she'd looked into a friend's face and seen a monster hot with sexual arousal. Death, fear, it had been erotic to Vincent. "He wears masks, Jemima. Husband, friend, reliable member of the town. But beneath it all, he's fundamentally twisted."

Tears shimmered in Jemima's eyes. Dropping her hand, she said, "Do you think it was because of what his father did?"

"I don't know." The elder Bakers weren't here to defend themselves against the accusations. "But to have two sons turn out . . . wrong. It's tough to believe that's coincidence."

"I know it's a horrible thing to say, but I want the abuse story to be true." Jemima threw a desperate glance toward where Jasper and Chloe were involved in an animated discussion about building a castle. "Then my babies can be free. They'll never have to worry about being born with evil inside them."

"I remember playing with Vincent on the beach when we were maybe six. He used to make disgusting noises with his armpit, laugh at how the seagulls fought, make me crazy by putting sand down my back then running like hell when I chased him, all normal little-boy things." Anahera had nearly forgotten that distant childhood summer.

It hurt to remember it now, to remember that bright-eyed boy who might not have been born a monster. "He got quieter slowly. I never really thought about it, it was so gradual, but he changed in a deep way from the wild little boy who collected shells for our sandcastle and who only watched the hermit crabs but didn't catch them."

"Thank you," Jemima whispered, her hand clutching at Anahera's. *"Thank you."*

They watched the children for several long minutes.

"It wasn't rape," Jemima said so low it was barely audible. "It couldn't be rape. I loved him."

But in Jemima's face, Anahera saw that she didn't believe her own words. "Promise me one thing," she said. "You'll talk to someone about all of this once you're safe. A therapist, a priest, someone."

"Will you . . . will you stay in touch?" A hunted, flinched look.

"Try to get rid of me." She made eye contact, held it. *"Kia kaha*, Jemima. You've survived evil that sought to crush you. You will endure."

# 65

Will went straight to Dominic de Souza's surgery after separating from Anahera. The Closed sign was on the door, but when he walked over to Dominic's place, no one responded to his knock.

"He left a while ago," a neighbor yelled out to Will. "Poor fella. Just walking, shoulders all hunched in."

"Did you see which direction he went?"

It was inevitable that she'd point toward the ocean.

That was where this had begun. And that was where it would end.

Making the drive to the cliffs, Will headed down to the part of the beach where Anahera had dragged up Miriama's body. It was now marked by flowers put there by her friends and family. The crime scene tape had been blown away that first night, but—and though both Pastor Mark and the local *kaumātua* had come and said a blessing over the area—nothing could erase what had taken place there.

Dominic knelt beside the flowers, his shoulders shaking as he sobbed. Will made no attempt to hide his footsteps. The sand absorbed all sound regardless. So he did a wide circle that would bring him within Dominic's peripheral vision, but the doctor didn't show any awareness of his presence.

He didn't react even when Will sat down on the sand next to him, having already mentally patted him down—Dominic was wearing only a thin white shirt and a pair of dark brown pants that looked like they might go with a suit jacket. The wind pasted the clothing against his body with every small gust. It was obvious he had nothing hidden on him, and all he held in his hands was a bracelet.

It sparkled silver and gold and bronze in the sunlight.

"Is that Miriama's?" Will had seen the shine of it on her wrist more than once.

Dominic gave a jerky nod before lifting the bracelet to his mouth and pressing a kiss to it while tears ravaged his face. "Her favorite," he said. "She left it at my place the last time she stayed over."

Dropping his hands to his thighs, the bracelet still clutched in the fingers of one hand, the young doctor stared out at the water. "I still can't believe she's gone. She was so alive, so vibrant. My sunshine."

Will had situated himself so he could see Dominic's face. Now he saw that the grief was real. "I just came from talking to Dr. Richard Symon."

It seemed as if it was relief that swept across Dominic's face. "Oh," he said, staring down at the bracelet again. "I knew someone would, eventually."

"We all just assumed you were Miriama's doctor," Will said. "Small town and all that."

"I could've had my registration yanked if someone had wanted to make trouble and say that I'd seduced a patient." Dominic swallowed hard. "She never had reason to come to the clinic after I took over from Dr. Wong. Once we got together and I figured out she was on the clinic roll, I referred her to Dr. Symon. Keep all the ethical lines clear, you know."

Will nodded. "It was a good thing you did," he said. "You should've left it at that."

Another burst of sobs, Dominic's face breaking apart in front of Will. Falling back to sit on the sand with his knees raised, he banged his head against the bracelet. "I just got so worried," he said after a long time, his voice raw. "She was going to see the doctor more times than she should. When I asked her, she'd say, '*Kāore he raru*. Don't worry, lover.' She was just feeling a little off, and wanted to check her iron levels since she used to have low iron as a girl."

Raising his head, the other man stared out at the water again. "I didn't quite believe her, but I let it go. I thought it might be something a woman would consider embarrassing—it's funny how people can be, even with a doctor. I never wanted her to feel that way with me."

"When did you find out?" Will asked.

"We'd been dating a couple of days shy of three months when she came to me all nervous and said, she was sorry, but that her birth control looked like it had failed. She was pregnant, and did I mind very much?"

His laugh was wet with tears. "Mind? I was ecstatic. I thought that meant she belonged to me now. I promised her we'd marry before she began to show, so none of the gossips would have a go at her. I said I'd give her a proper proposal, not cheat her out of anything. I already had the ring, knew how I wanted to ask." The echo of happiness weaving through his voice.

Will didn't interrupt. Sometimes, the best way to interrogate someone was to just let them talk. And it looked like Dominic de Souza had been waiting to talk for a long time. Unlike with Vincent, it wasn't bragging. It was a desperate catharsis.

"I was so excited that we had this secret between us. I felt as if I'd burst if I didn't tell someone, but the only other person I could talk to about it was Dr. Symon." He played compulsively with the bracelet. "I resisted for a week, then finally picked up the phone. He congratulated me after I told him that Miriama had shared the news. I didn't want to put him in a tough situation, wanted him to know I already knew."

Will nodded, though the two men had been skirting ethical lines at best at that point. Still, if it had ended there, everything would've been fine and Miriama would still be alive.

"I was joking about how I was acting like all the silly expectant fathers we heard stories about in medical school. How I had the same fears and the same worries even though I knew Miriama was young and fit and probably in the best condition possible for a woman to give birth."

"You were happy."

Dominic's smile was twisted. "I was. That's why it took a little while for it to sink in when Dr. Symon said I must've gotten Miriama pregnant the first time we were together, for her to be three months along." He stared at the bracelet with a fixed gaze. "He was doing that nudge-nudge wink-wink thing between guys, congratulating me on my prowess. And he was so involved in it that he didn't notice I'd gone silent."

Dropping his head, he said nothing for long, wind-lashed minutes. When he looked back up, tears—silent and hot—ravaged his cheeks. "I hung up soon afterward, then I went through all our photos together just to be sure I wasn't wrong. I knew I wasn't wrong. But I had to be sure, you see, I had to be absolutely sure."

His breathing was uneven now. "I always took photos on our dates. And I took a photo the night Miriama and I first . . . when we were first together that way. It was of the two of us sitting on the beach, her hair blowing back in the wind while I wore this goofy look on my face. Just after that photo was taken, she put her arms around my neck and kissed me and said, 'Let's go to your place.'"

One hand dug into the sand by his side, clenched hard. "I'd been hoping, but I'd never pushed because I knew how much her faith meant to her. But that day, the same day she got back from an appointment with Dr. Symon, she said yes. And I didn't know how brainless I was then, didn't know how she was using me. I was happy."

"Why?" Will asked, so that Dominic de Souza could no longer lie to himself about ending the sunshine.

"Because she already knew she was pregnant," he said. "Before we ever slept together. I wonder how she planned to explain the baby to me when it arrived two months early. Did she think I'd buy a premature birth story? I'm a fucking doctor."

"According to her journal," Will said, "she thought you were a good man, a man she could have a future with, a man she was starting to love. I think she would've told you the truth if you'd given her a chance."

Dominic turned eyes mad with grief toward him. "Please don't say that. Please *don't say that*."

"Tell me what you did, Dominic." It was time. "Miriama deserves that. She trusted you not just with herself, but with her child."

Dominic's entire self just crumpled. "After I spoke to Dr. Symon, I didn't know what to do. I thought about breaking it off with her, but how could I let Miriama go? She was mine. The most beautiful woman I'd ever seen and she was mine."

Perhaps he had loved Miriama, Will thought, but it had been about possession as well. Just like Vincent, Dominic had wanted to capture a beautiful, precious creature and brand her as his.

"She kept asking me what was wrong and I kept saying nothing. I tried to make things like they were before I knew. More than a week passed and it was okay. The day—" Gulps of air. "I made her a picnic lunch that final day and we laughed together and I thought it would be all right."

He exhaled. "But as soon as I left her, all I could think was that she was lying to me each and every minute we were together. The scream kept building inside me until I couldn't stand it anymore. I came to the cliffs planning to call and ask her to meet me there . . . and then there she was, running toward me." A sick smile. "It was like our meeting was meant to be. She smiled when she saw me."

"You had an alibi." Though it wasn't a perfect one; the timeline was difficult, but not impossible.

"She must've sprinted that last part to the cliffs. She did that sometimes. She was out of breath when she arrived . . . And my car was right there."

An extra two, three minutes. The cost of a life.

"Did you go directly to the whirlpool?" That black maw of water and rocks was the only possible scene of death, given the time frame.

"No. We took a short forest track that runs parallel to the cliffs and there's this bit where it kind of opens up and you're right by the whirlpool. Not near the edge," Dominic whispered. "Safe, by the trees."

Will had looked under the trees, but the wind-tossed leaf fall there had made it impossible to spot a disturbance.

"Miriama stopped smiling when I accused her of tricking me." Dominic dashed away tears with the back of his hand. "She begged me to listen, said she'd never wanted to use me. Said I was the best man who'd ever come into her life. I couldn't hear her, I was *so* angry. I told her she had to choose—the baby or me. I told her she had to get an abortion, that I wasn't going to raise another man's bastard. She was *mine*."

Will could see the scene in his mind's eye, wildly alive Miriama on the edge of the cliff, arguing fiercely with this man who thought he'd captured a star in his hands and wanted to own it body and soul. "What happened?"

"The way she looked at me when I said that," Dominic whispered, "the way she crossed her arms around her middle and just looked at me. Like I was a monster. And I got this red haze across my vision and I don't remember what happened next. What I remember is that when the haze passed, Miriama was dead in my arms. There were marks around her neck, one side of her face crushed in like I'd punched her, the rest of her face all puffed up, and her eyes bloody."

Will wasn't buying the idea of rage-induced memory loss. Oh, there had been rage, of that he was sure. Dominic hadn't gone out with a plan to kill Miriama. He'd done so in a fit of anger. Paradoxically, his lack of planning was why he'd almost gotten away with it—he'd made no call that could be traced back, altered no plans, bought no weapons.

And he'd been genuinely devastated in the aftermath.

But, it took a lot to strangle a woman to near death with your bare hands; it wasn't a thing of seconds but minutes. Dominic remembered what he'd done, even if he was too cowardly to look into the past and into his own horror.

But the punch . . . that explained why Dominic had no scratches on his face or arms, why there'd been no signs of a struggle. Will would never know for certain, but he had the strong feeling Dominic's punch had knocked Miriama out cold. Easy prey for a man determined to strangle her to death. "Was there blood?"

"I don't know." Dominic swallowed hard. "But I always have a change in the car in case a patient throws up on me or something when I'm out at the farms. I dressed in my car on a lonely part of the road, threw the used clothes in a bin the council sets out for campers."

No one, Will realized, had noticed because Dominic consistently wore white or light-colored business shirts and dark pants as his work uniform.

"I picked her up and threw her into the whirlpool," Dominic whispered. "I threw my beautiful Miriama into the whirlpool before sprinting back to my car. I just had to carry her a few feet. She was tall, but she wasn't heavy. I threw my Miriama into the black water."

"She drowned."

Dominic screamed and screamed and screamed. "I'm a doctor! I checked her pulse!"

And yet Will trusted Ankita's call. Miriama had drowned. Maybe Dominic had made a mistake in his shock . . . and maybe he'd made a cold-blooded decision that he would have to live with for the rest of his life.

The screams went on and on until Dominic's throat turned raw, and then there was only a wind-stirred silence for a half hour.

"Can I say good-bye to her before you take me in?" Dominic's voice, so hoarse it was a croak.

When Will nodded, the young doctor rose and picked up a large bouquet he must've brought with him. Taking the flowers and the bracelet, he walked to the edge of the waves. Will was up on his feet a second later, even as Dominic de Souza tried to run into the ravenous ocean.

Dragging the other man back from the water that tried to suck them both in and under, Will slammed Dominic down on safe ground. "You don't get to take the easy out," he said. "You'll answer in court for your crime, and you'll look Matilda in the face while you tell her what you did to Miriama."

Dominic de Souza sobbed into the sand, the bracelet still clutched to his chest and his mouth shaping a single word. "Sunshine."

# EPILOGUE

Two months and a lifetime after they'd laid Miriama to rest, Anahera stood on the cliffs, staring out at the water crashing onto shore below as the wind rippled through her hair. "I can't stay here," she said to the man who stood beside her. "I came to hide, but that was never what my mother wanted for me."

"Where do you want to go?" Will closed his hand over her chilled fingers.

Anahera shook her head. "I don't know."

"How about San Diego, for starters?"

Turning to face him, Anahera said, "What aren't you telling me?"

"I've had requests to consult with police departments all over the world. Apparently, since he keeps asking to talk to me, they consider me the Vincent Baker expert—and they have a lot of cold cases to close."

"What about your job here?"

"I think I've had enough of hiding, too." Gray eyes that let her in, let her see the man within. "There'll be a lot of travel back and forth—I have to keep talking to Vincent, see if I can help find the bodies of his other victims."

"Is he giving you anything?"

"He wants credit." A whisper of rain in the air, hitting the side of Will's face. "He'll play games, drip feed us information, but he knows the only way to stay in the spotlight is to remain relevant. One by one, I'll locate the bones of his victims."

Relentless, like water on rock, that was Will.

"I can work with San Diego." Her wings unfolded inside her as the rain hit her own face, and with the cold droplets came a surge of music, pure and rising in a crescendo.

Her art had never been a creature of sunlight.

# ACKNOWLEDGMENTS

When I began to write this book, I realized there was so much I didn't know.

My first port of call was the New Zealand Police media team and they were very helpful in answering my general questions about sole charge stations and related matters. At the same time, I reached out online to the staff who run the Christchurch City Libraries/Ngā Kete Wānanga-o-Ōtautahi Twitter account for a piece of local knowledge, and got a cheerful and helpful response from Donna.

Life then brought someone into my sphere who was able to answer my forensics and postmortem questions, and who was extremely giving of their time.

I also needed help with Te Reo Māori. My friend Mihiteria King started me off by generously answering a long list of questions, then Fern Whitau helped me go deeper, most specifically into the Ngāi Tahu/Kāi Tahu dialect, with kindness and patience. Another friend, E. V. Lind, stepped in to help me find the right person to get a piece of information I needed.

I have to give a special shout-out to Alison Shucksmith, who read a pre-edited copy of this book and picked up an error I would've regretted very much had it gone to print.

Thank you to each and every one of you. I very much appreciate your time and willingness to share your knowledge. If there are any mistakes in this book, they are mine. The same with any artistic license taken.

To Cindy, Nephele, Erin, Elaine, Bridget, Rita, and Jessica, as well as all the incredible people behind the scenes at both Berkley and The Knight Agency, you're amazing and I'm so lucky to work with you.

To my writing friends. Thank you for being so excited about this project from the very start.

And to my family—thank you. For so much.

Last but not least, thank *you* for picking up this book set in a remote part of what will be, for most of you, a distant country. Come visit. It's lovely and dangerous and beautiful.

—Nalini